CASTLE GATE

Book 1 in the Maxwell Curse Trilogy

also by Lisa Bonnice

Shape Shifting – the Body/Mind/Spirit Weight Solution

The Shape Shifter's Daily Diary

Fear of Our Father
(co-authored with Stacey M. Kananen)

The Poppet Master

The Fairy Falls

in the works …

Books 2 & 3 of
The Maxwell Curse Trilogy

Lisa Bonnice is truly an amazing writer. Her dedication and passion in researching and writing *Castle Gate* (Book 1 in the Maxwell Curse Trilogy) exploring ancestral trauma and healing, is brilliant and so needed in today's times where we must understand our families' histories to help us heal our past. The story's depth, spanning centuries and continents, offers a powerful illustration of how historical events can impact generations. In this time of great challenges where we are being forced to wake up and evolve, this brilliant story shares with us how we can heal our ancestral traumas so we can be free to live the life we are destined to and will help to create a better future for humankind.

—Sandra Ingerman, MA, world-renowned teacher of shamanism and award-winning author of 13 books including *The Book of Ceremony*

Stunning, Unique and Exceptional! *Castle Gate* by Lisa Bonnice entices you into the gripping true-life story of an actual curse that began at a striking moment in the history of her own ancestors. After years of extensive historical research, and using her mediumship ability, Bonnice brings into life the moment the curse was invoked on her family. She continues by beautifully articulating the true human stories of these historical people, their relationships, and the hardships they constantly endured from that moment forward. The author artfully describes and humanizes the power of human thought and emotions to unleash a curse of tragedy across time and space. This is essential reading for anyone who has ever wondered if curses are real.

—Tina Zion, award-winning author and internationally acclaimed expert in medical intuition and mediumship

Lisa Bonnice has taken the nuts and bolts of her family history research and turned it into a compelling novel with lively prose and descriptive details. Based on a thorough examination of the historical documents about her family, as well as blending it with social history about the events, *Castle Gate* tells the story of her coal-mining, immigrant Maxwell ancestors who came from Scotland and settled in Utah. This is the first book in a planned trilogy that delves into generational trauma, something common to most families, making her novels engaging reads for anyone interested in family history and how the hardships of one generation, and even an ancient family curse, can impact future generations.

—Sharon DeBartolo Carmack, Certified Genealogist®
and author of *You Can Write Your Family History*

Castle Gate by Lisa Bonnice, the gripping true-life adventure of descendants of Scotland's Maxwell Clan interwoven with witches, curses, spirits, and karma is impossible to resist. Bonnice's engaging writing style transforms the reader into a first-hand observer of the hardships, drama, and love experienced by the Garroch family during their sojourn from the squalor of Scottish coal mining towns to the wild west of 1920s Utah. Bonnice, an Ancestral Healing expert, has spent years researching the facts and history of this family as well as the spiritual and scientific basis of multi-generational trauma. *Castle Gate* demonstrates the chains of karma cast long shadows that span generations and the search for the key to unlock those chains may take you from this world into the one beyond...

—Mark Anthony, JD Psychic Explorer®, fourth-generation psychic
medium and award-winning author of *The Afterlife Frequency*

In *Castle Gate*, Lisa Bonnice seamlessly weaves history and spirituality into a deeply personal and profoundly moving narrative. Her use of the *Beloved Dead Oracle* adds a unique and spiritual layer to the story, channeling the voices and wisdom of her ancestors. Lisa's commitment to historical accuracy, combined with her intuitive storytelling, creates an authentic and emotionally resonant narrative. *Castle Gate* is a heartfelt tribute to the past, a spiritual journey, and a testament to the sacred act of storytelling. I wholeheartedly endorse Lisa Bonnice's work, as it beautifully honors the beloved dead within her family's legacy in a truly unique and profound manner. This is a book that will linger in your heart long after the final page.

—Carrie Paris, creator of *The Relative Tarot* and *Beloved Dead Oracle*

This riveting historical adventure is a potent reminder that our ancestral stories are alive within us. Gorgeously written, this is a must-read novel for anyone interested in how the past creates our present realities.

—Perdita Finn, author of *Take Back the Magic:
Conversations with the Unseen World*

... what you now hold in your hands truly is a rare "LITERARY UNICORN." It is an amazing, well researched and creative historical telling of the story ... what you hold is a piece of art, square-bound in a canvas of papers. It is a love-letter to Lisa's ancestors celebrating their contributions in a now almost forgotten time, in a mostly forgotten place, called Castle Gate.

—Darrin "Bobcat" Teply
Surviving Co-Director of the Eastern Utah Tourism & History Association

CASTLE GATE

Book 1 in the Maxwell Curse Trilogy

by Lisa Bonnice

This book contains a story based on genealogy research.
It is as true as the author could make it.

Please do not judge any of the characters,
as they were only human ... at the time.

CASTLE GATE

Copyright © 2023 by Lisa Bonnice

Cover by Jessica Bell Design

ISBN: 978-0-9799999-9-4

For Helen, Buchan, Will,
Geordie and Robert Burns
who pushed through the hardest.

In honor of the men killed in
Castle Gate Mine #2 on March 8, 1924,
their families, and all who did what they could
in the aftermath to make things right.

CASTLE GATE

Table of Contents

PROLOGUE

October 12, 1916
The Somme and the Great Beyond

What's it like to die, you ask? I can answer that. Lance Corporal Buchan Littlejohn, Second Battalion, Royal Scots Fusiliers, at your service. I just took a bullet to the face at Le Transloy, almost four months into the Somme Offensive. Our battalion advanced on the German line at Bayonet Trench, drawing heavy machine gun fire. That's when I was shot in the left cheek, just next to my nose and above my lip.

I didn't die immediately; it took a few minutes. Death was almost a relief, after months in the trenches with the rats and lice, covered in mud and blood, in a state of constant dread. I say "almost" because I was plenty angry that some pampered officer got to decide my time to go.

We'd been ordered—by men safe from harm—to run, bayonets fixed, straight into a wall of flaming lead. We were nothing but bullet fodder, sent in to drain the enemy's ammunition. Time slowed and I saw bursts of fire popping out of the barrels of their machine guns. The madness brought to mind the song my mates and I sang while marching, to the tune of Auld Lang Syne, "We're here because we're here because we're here because we're here ..."

I heard the bullet when it hit, a wet *thwok*, and I felt the impact, sure, but it didn't hurt. My head snapped back and the force knocked me off my pins, into a deep puddle. My left cheek went numb … felt like it had been blown clean away. No pain, only the calm realization that my family would soon receive a telegram.

The pain came, though, as time began moving again. I thought I was choking on puddle water, but it was my blood I was drowning in. I gasped for air and felt that same burning, stinging inside my nose as when I almost drowned swimming in the river when I was a wee lad.

For a moment I thought that, if I breathed only through my right nostril, I could keep the blood from rushing down my throat. That thought didn't last long.

I heard myself choking and gurgling, and that scared me more than anything else. Many took a bullet and lived, but men who made these sounds rarely survived. If they did, they wished they hadn't because their shot-up faces guaranteed they'd never win a pretty wife.

I panicked for what felt like forever but was probably only a minute, until an impossibly large hand pulled me up by the collar of my muddy uniform, up out of the liquid burning the inside of my head and filling my air passages.

It took a few seconds to realize I didn't need to fight for air anymore because I wasn't in that body anymore—I was floating above it, watching it twitch and choke. My mates were retreating to the trench, chased by Germans. I saw now they weren't all the filthy Boche. Most were terrified lads fighting for their King and Country, like us.

I looked down at my shuddering body and saw its face was intact, not half blown off like I thought. There was a hole above the lip, sure, and plenty of blood, but the cheek was still there.

The damage looked worse last summer when I was wounded at the Battle of Hooge, facing German flamethrowers. I hoped to be discharged permanently after that but they ordered me back four months ago, after nine months on the mend, and I've been fighting for my life ever since.

The further I rose the less interesting my body was, along with the battle those lads were still fighting. I looked up and saw on the horizon a timeline view of my life from start to finish, like one of them moving picture shows I saw once on leave. All I had to do was focus on a point on that line and I was pulled into it.

It started with my birth in May 1894 in a coalminers' row house in Dreghorn, a wee two-room but'n'ben with eight wee'uns already living there, including my ten-year-old sister Helen. She was touching the tip of my nose with her wee finger, saying, "Aw, Mam, he's so tiny! Can I hold him?" Helen became my second mam after our mother died when I was only four.

That thought shot me further ahead in time to me at age five with our brother Geordie. Geordie was sixteen, a year older than Helen. He was goading me into untying her apron when she was too busy to see me sneaking up behind. She chased us out of the house, hollering and swinging the broom, but it was all in good fun and she mostly pretended to be angry.

The memory of Helen's annoyance pulled me forward in time to when she was truly angry, years later, when I enlisted to fight in this "Great War." I was bunking with her and her family after our da died and I was the only one left at home. She wanted me to work in the mine with Will, her husband, there in the wee village of Coalburn. "Miners are just as patriotic as soldiers," she scolded. "Without coal, the whole country'll go dark and cold, and here yeh'll be safe from the dirty Boche."

I argued, "It's not safe in the mine, either. I'm tired of being tucked away, so far from the big cities. Coalburn isn't what I'd call a hopping good time."

Och, I yearned for excitement! I was young, full of piss and vinegar, and I wanted adventure! Only I didn't know that recruiters lie about soldiering being glamorous. I see that now, sure, from this great height ... just as I see how Helen's heart is gonna break when she receives the telegram informing her of my so-called glorious death.

As I considered this, my view changed from a moving picture show to a vast panorama filling the horizon, with my family's history as coal miners spread out over hundreds of years. It's what most of us men did, like ants digging tunnels. It was a wonder the earth above didn't collapse with so many holes dug by just my kin alone ... fathers, grandas, brothers, uncles, cousins ... the name Littlejohn seemed to mean coal, either digging it or running the mines.

But way far back, generations down the family line, a bright spark caught my eye. A Littlejohn granda married a woman sprung off from the Maxwell family. It was her spark I saw, but it wasn't from her particular shine, it was from the fires that dotted her lineage, fires that brung to mind the wall of flames I was running toward when I was first wounded and just now when I was killed.

All I had to do was wonder and I was pulled through Granny Maxwell —I don't know how else to describe it … there are no words—down a tunnel, back another hundred years to her distant kin, Sir George Maxwell. He was a Covenanter who secretly preached the Presbyterian gospel despite fines and imprisonment by the Catholic king.

When Sir George fell awful sick, five people were accused and found guilty of witchcraft and burned at the stake. One of them, in a rage, blasted the Maxwell family and their descendants with a curse to suffer as they suffered, families ripped apart, to burn as they burned.

The furious force of that curse blasted me, arse over tea kettle, back to floating above my body, watching the panoramic story unfold on the horizon. I saw the curse staining the life stories of people around the world who don't even know they're related to the Maxwells. I surely didn't know about it and I just died by fire, and my family has been ripped apart in many ways over the years.

I wondered how to fix it and the answer came quickly: the curse could be broken, the stain could be lifted, but only by the living and none of them knew about it!

I saw ahead into the years that Helen would flit to America and her kin would be killed by fire in the mine our brothers oversaw. Their wee'uns lives would be distorted by the curse, too, unless someone discovered and ended it.

Next I was lifted higher by a light pulling me upward but I fought to go back to my body. I had to warn someone! I struggled downward, swimming against a strong current. I slipped back into my skin, but the body was choking on blood. I couldn't override the lack of air in the lungs. There was no going back.

As I let go, I bobbed buoyantly upward into the light and saw my parents waiting, smiling, offering a warm embrace. I hadn't seen Mam since I was only four. Da looked so young, beaming to be with her again. Soon, I was surrounded by grannies and grandas who died before I was born, but I knew their names when I looked at their faces.

One made her way forward, the one with the spark, Granny Maxwell. She said, "No worries lad, yer work isn't done, even if yer body is."

"What d'yeh mean?" I asked.

She said, "Yeh can help from here, and finish what needs to be done."

4

Granny passed her hand over the scene below and the blood and mud vanished, replaced by a scene of a woman a hundred years hence. I 'knew' she was Helen's great-granddaughter, my great-grandniece.

She was sitting at a desk tapping away at a keyboard, in front of some sort of newfangled electrical device. The device magically told her our family history, and she had just discovered the curse. She stared in disbelief at the information in front of her as if, surely, this story cannot be true. She was as stunned to see that as I was to see that such a device can even exist.

A memorial plaque with my name on it, which Helen will receive as my next of kin, hung on this woman's wall. She didn't know she discovered the curse because I had been nudging her from over here to watch for clues. I was just learning that I would be doing that, as well.

At the thought, I stood near her and tapped her shoulder, to see if she could feel it. She didn't notice my touch consciously but her shoulder did twitch a little as if she felt a twinge.

Granny Maxwell said, "Wee man, yer time's run out in that body. It's dead." She pointed downward and I saw my corpse, now bereft of life. Granny continued, "If yeh want to play a role, you can help Helen's grandwee'un end it."

This was the work ahead of me. I now saw the 'coincidental' breadcrumbs I'll be dropping to lead to this discovery which affects everyone stained by the Maxwell curse, thousands by now, all over the Earth.

"Come with me, laddie," Granny said, taking my hand. I followed her through a velvety black tunnel toward a light so pure and brilliant and ecstatic that I no longer wanted to go back.

I could wait, knowing I wouldn't be forgotten and that I had a job to do, far in the future. But now, it's time to rest for a while. I've been at war for so long …

CHAPTER 1

September 3, 1920
Coalburn, Scotland

Helen Cochrane Littlejohn Garroch was not a tall woman—only five foot three—so when she hoisted the bucket of water, she had to lift it to shoulder height to pour its contents into the huge kettle atop the cast-iron stove. Years of practice allowed her perfect aim—she rarely slopped water into the pots and pans on the range top, in which the evening meal was simmering, or down through the slots around the hotplate into the coal fire below.

Although the muscles in her upper back were used to this kind of labor, today they protested, and she thanked God for the indoor water supply here at her home in the miners' row on Railway Terrace. At least she didn't have to go outdoors to fill the bucket at the pump. Not everyone in the mining town of Coalburn had such a luxury.

Jessie—her sister-in-law who lived down the hill at Tinto View—had to go to the communal pipe to fill her buckets. Helen's sister Lizzie—who lived across the field at Ivy Cottage—had to use a well-pump across the road. Railway Terrace was downright modern, especially compared to the conditions at Springhill Six Rows in Dreghorn where the Garroch family had their humble beginnings, before coming to Coalburn ten years ago.

Helen yearned to sit down. It had been a long day and she was tired. Her recently discovered pregnancy was a factor, but it was no excuse to shirk her duties—after all, she'd probably lose the baby anyway.

It's the way all her pregnancies ended these past five years, with the poor wee lambs sliding out too soon, so to allow herself to feel either joy or sorrow was to invite needless misery. At least a miscarriage wasn't as heart-wrenching as a live-born premature baby dying in her arms, as had happened with the previous five pregnancies before God chose to take them early and spare her that extra agony.

"Och," she sighed, wiping her brow and pushing a wayward strand of dark hair out of her face, "keep goin' Helen, it'll be time to rest soon enough." It was late afternoon and she had plenty more to do. Her husband and fifteen-year-old son, Will and Willie Jr., would be home from the mine soon, filthy with coal dust and needing a good scrubbing. That meant—in addition to cooking the evening meal—she had to heat enough water to fill the round, zinc tub that otherwise hung from a peg on the wall of the main room of the Garroch family's two-room home. She was on her final kettle, and the quitting-time whistle at the mine had blown. They should be home soon, their bath ready in time.

Only the working men got a daily bath. Family bath night was Saturday, timed so everyone would be clean for church Sunday morning. Bath-time pecking order went from oldest to youngest—Will, Helen, Jeanie, Willie and finally Helen Jr., nicknamed Nellie, but that took place in the larger metal tub which was stored under Willie's set-in bed on the far wall of the kitchen. Jeanie and Nellie shared the other wide bunk that was set into the wall and, also, the storage space beneath it.

While the water heated, Helen got busy with the meal. Peeled potatoes were on the boil and sausages in the skillet to fry. Onion gravy simmered in another pan, and the loaf of bread was ready to come out of the oven. She scooted the loaf pan back onto the warming burner to keep it from cooling too much. Will liked his bread that way.

"There," she said aloud, pouring the last of the hot water into the zinc tub. "Youse can come home anytime now, yer bath is ready." A warm bath in front of the hearth—along with the delicious smells of the evening meal —made for a jolly 'welcome home', indeed, on a chilly late summer evening.

As she restoked the oven with coal from the scuttle, the kitchen door opened from the outside and the brisk evening air that rushed in made her grateful for even the dwindling fire. Summer in Scotland always ended far too soon.

Jeanie—Helen and Will's sixteen-year-old daughter—knocked the mud off her shoes on the stoop before entering. She hung her shawl on the hook by the door and fixed her dark blond hair, which had been knocked askew by the garment, back into a tight bun.

"Evenin', Mam," Jeanie said, as she grabbed the broom to sweep out any dirt and leaves she may have tracked in, keeping ahead of the endless cleaning that came with being a woman.

"Hello, hen," Helen replied, wiping her coal-dusted hands onto her apron, "Yeh're just in time. Put the kettle on for tea and turn the sausages, would yeh? My hands are black. Nice day at work?"

"Fair enough," Jeanie said, hurrying to the stove where the skillet of bangers sizzled on the crowded range top. "How that family makes such a mess is beyond me, but they keep me in wages, don't they?" she mused, skillfully flipping each sausage with a fork without piercing their skins, one by one, to brown the other side. While she was at it, she used the fork to test the potatoes. "Tatties are almost done," Jeanie said, placing the fork on the ceramic utensil holder on the range top. "Where's Nell?"

"Up the row, helping Mrs. McAllister with her new wee bairn, just born last night," Helen said. "Yeh know, she'll do 'most anything to keep from lifting a finger in her own home, even if it means changing shitey nappies for the neighbors." She cocked her head at the sounds of a man's hacking cough over the din of children playing outside, and said, "Is that your father, up the road? Sounds like his cough."

"I reckon," Jeanie said. She poked her head out the door to peek. "Aye, it's them, and Wullie looks gutted. Something's wrong."

A thrill of terror shot through Helen's body. Rarely a day went by without a mine accident, many of them fatal or dismembering. The mining company didn't always blow the alarm siren—sometimes it was better to keep quiet, so rescue workers weren't hindered by crowds of wives asking after their men.

"Is it both of 'em?" Helen asked, rushing to the door, nudging Jeanie out of the way.

"Aye, I said so!" Jeanie harrumphed, "I said it's *them*, din't I?"

"Sorry, hen," Helen said, "you gave me the fear, is all." She stepped outside and peered up the road into the twilight. The usual group of miners were trudging home from Number Four Pit, lugging their tools and empty lunch pails, their shoulders perpetually hunched from working stooped over underground. Barely a one could stand up straight, even on a Sunday when their backs had a day of rest.

A few of the children out front playing Kick the Can ran happily to greet the men. Those who reached them first and saw their demeanor quieted themselves and shushed the late comers.

Although all the men in their scruffy work clothes were black with coal dust, Helen recognized her husband and son's silhouettes. Sturdy Will was not as tall as some other men, but five inches taller than her was enough for her taste. His graying brown hair was blackened after a long day underground, as was slender, lanky Willie's brown hair. Slightly shorter than his da, there they were—her boys—plodding home.

Normally, the bawdy bunch would be joking and jostling, done with another workday, looking forward to a hot meal. Not today, though. Helen was too far away to see Willie's facial expression, but his sagging posture gave it away that he was bothered. All the miners were bothered.

She allowed herself a flood of relief that death hadn't visited her family. She was spared this time, but someone else had just become a widow or lost a son. She didn't hear a wailing woman nearby, so it wasn't a neighbor. Surely it wasn't Will's brother Pete, his nephew Tam, or her sister Lizzie's husband, John—elsewise, she'd have heard the news by now. In fact, there was John walking past, on his way home. He nodded a somber greeting to Helen and slogged on down the road. And there was wee Pete, with his prematurely grey hair black with coal dust, and even handsome Tam, who both waved a minimal greeting but kept walking.

Neighbor or no, some poor family had just been devastated. While the death of a beloved husband was heart-breaking, at least a widow could remarry. Otherwise, a wife could have a seriously injured, possibly forever-crippled husband to nurse back to health, not to mention the loss of his income and sunny disposition, especially if his injuries led him to drink. And, living in tied-housing, without employment at the mine the family would be expected to vacate immediately. Helen offered a brief prayer for the poor wife, whoever she was.

"Wull!" she called from the stoop, not caring if she was shouting like a fishwife. "Who was it?" Will lifted his hand to wave, gesturing that she should be patient. He would tell her when he got there.

He was less than a quarter mile away, but he wasn't moving fast enough for her. Helen didn't bother to grab her shawl before hurrying up the road. As she neared them, she saw in her son Willie's blank eyes that he was in shock. The other miners were respectfully quiet, greeting their wee'uns in muted tones, but whatever had happened was weighing on her lad a lot heavier, and in a different way, than it was the other men.

She stopped them in the road and demanded, "Wull, who was it? Does his wife know yet?" Already, in her head, she was springing to action. When disaster struck, the wives banded together to offer emotional support, child-tending and hot meals, and she needed to know who to help.

"It was Walt Baxter," Will said, barely loud enough for her to hear, "crushed dead. A huge stone fell from the ceiling. He didn't stand a chance."

Helen darted another glance at her son's face. Willie's peaked cap was pulled down low on his forehead to hide his eyes—after all, he was a grown man of fifteen and grown men don't cry—but his eyes were red and the coal dust on his face was streaked where he had been wiping away escaped tears. The Garrochs didn't know the Baxter family as well as others. For Willie to be impacted like this, there was something more.

"What's wrong, love?" she asked.

"Leave it, Helen," Will barked and she jerked her head in angry surprise to glare at him. It wasn't like Will to speak to her in such a tone: he knew Helen didn't take kindly to being spoken to severely.

About to snipe back, she read his eyes and saw a pleading warning that this really wasn't the time. She swallowed her annoyance and said, "Aye then, let's get youse two home. It's awfully cold out here," she said, squeezing between them for warmth and taking their arms. "There's a hot bath waiting for youse, and I've got bangers and mash for yer tea."

Jeanie stood in the open doorway, waiting. Helen scolded, "Lass, yeh're letting the cold air in. We'll all catch our death! Is the kettle on the boil? It ought to be, been on long enough."

"I'll check," Jeanie said, going back inside, followed by her family. The kitchen was lit by oil lanterns, and the warm light made it feel cozy, instead of cramped. "What happened? Who was it?" she asked, testing the kettle. "Aye, it's boiling."

"Thanks, hen," Helen said. "I'll let yer da tell yeh. Mind, turn the sausages again and start a pot of tea. Oh, and give the gravy a stir."

Will and Willie dropped heavily onto kitchen chairs and pried off their boots as Helen said, "There yeh go, get outta them filthy clothes and into the tub. Then youse can tell us what happened."

"Wait 'til Nell gets in. I don't want to tell it twice," Will said to Jeanie's dismay. He stood to peel off his grimy shirt and threw it over the back of his chair. Naked from the waist up, he gingerly dropped to his knees, groaning from pain, and ducked his arms and head into the wash tub. He stayed under as long as he could, relishing the soothing, hot water. He finally came up for air and gasped, "Aye, that's good." The water turned black as Helen lathered and scrubbed his hard-to-reach places with strong lye soap and a scrap of an old towel. She handed him the soap and cloth once she was done, and he took care of the spots he could reach himself.

After he washed off the day's sweat and coal dust, Will leaned out across the tub and Helen poured a jug of water over him to rinse, then handed him a drying cloth. He took his clean clothes into the other room to change.

Next, Willie took off his filthy shirt and bathed in the same water. "Want me to get your back, love?" Helen asked.

"No," he muttered. He ducked his head under the water and came up dripping. He scrubbed everywhere he could reach, missing a large patch of black between his shoulder blades.

Will came from the other room and said, "Yeh missed a spot, there, wee man," he said, pressing his finger into the back of the boy's neck. He stood by and supervised until his son was finished. As Willie scurried into the other room to change into his clean shirt and trousers, Will dragged the heavy tub out front and dumped it.

Brown-haired, blue-eyed, eleven-year-old Nellie returned home then, ducking past her father, and burst into the room. "Mammy, you have to see Mrs. McAllister's new bairn!" she gushed. "He held onto my finger with his wee, plump hand and wouldn't let go. I cannot wait to have a wee'un of my own!"

"Enough of that blether, yeh have years to wait for that," Helen admonished, "now set yerself down to supper."

"Bangers and mash?" Nellie whined. "We had that last week!"

"Aye, and we're having it again this week, cheeky lass! Yeh're lucky to have a father who puts meat on the table," Helen scolded, with an eye peeled toward her husband's mood. This was not the night for one of Nell's adolescent snits. "Now hush, you. Set yerself down and get it in yeh."

Finally noticing that everyone else was somber, Nellie sat and waited while Will led the family in the Selkirk Grace in the old Scots language:

Some hae meat and cannae eat;
and some wad eat but want it.
We hae meat and we can eat,
and sae the Lord be thankit.

Once they began tucking in, Nellie couldn't wait any longer. "What's wrong?" she asked.

Jeanie replied, glad her sister had asked, "They wouldn't tell us until you got in. I think someone down the mine was killed."

Will pounded his fist on the table and bellowed, "Good God! A man's death isn't idle gossip!"

Helen laid her hand over his clenched fingers and said to their daughters, "It was Walt Baxter."

"Och, aye!" Jeanie cried. "They live up the row a ways. I went to school with his lad. He'll be right gutted."

"Aye, more than gutted," Willie finally spoke up, fighting a break in his voice. "He was there, next to his da, when it happened. He saw … everything."

"That's enough!" Will barked. "Gory details aren't suitable supper talk. Your mam worked hard to put a good, hot meal on the table, and I'll not have it ruined."

Nellie, ignoring her father, demanded, "But we don't know the Baxters very well. How's everyone this upset? We've had better friends killed, and we didn't see this kind of blubbing," she said, gesturing brattily at her older brother.

Willie, eyes blazing, opened his mouth to blast her, but their father beat him to it.

"Enough, I say," Will said through gritted teeth, shooting his younger daughter such a withering look that she instantly shut up and focused instead on her food. "Yer brother's not blubbing," he said, "and we'll have no more talk about it."

"One thing, Wull," Helen dared to venture, "what about his family? We ought to call on 'em, y'know, see what we can do to help."

Will said, "Walt's wife is dead, so his wee'uns are orphaned."

"Orphans?" Nellie asked, wide-eyed. "Och, that's the worst thing ever!" She fought back tears of her own and said to Helen, "I don't know what I'd do if youse two died!"

"We'll be around a long, long while, nae worries," Helen said absently, distracted by her thoughts of Walt's children. "Och, the poor wee things, I'll put together a basket for 'em ..."

Will said, "His sister lives in town, so I reckon she'll be taking them in. Perhaps yeh can call on her, see what she needs."

"Aye, we'll do that," Helen replied. "Girls, we'll do that the morrow."

The family ate in silence and, after every scrap had been consumed, Helen said, "Nellie, hen, help me clear the plates. Jean, tend the fire, would yeh?"

The womenfolk set to work while Willie stood and said, "I'm goin' for a walk." He grabbed his coat and wandered outside.

Will stayed at the table long enough to roll a cigarette. He finally stood and said to Helen, "Come out front, will yeh?"

"Of course," she said. "Girls, see to the dishes." She bundled up in her heavy, crocheted shawl and followed him out the door. Jeanie and Nellie, eyes wide with curiosity, watched their parents leave.

He led Helen toward the dirt path across the grassy field that lay between their home and the mine, out of earshot of their daughters. Willie Jr. was nowhere in sight, off in the other direction into town in search of friends or the comfort of his latest girlfriend.

Will lit his cigarette and took a long pull. Finally, he said, "It was horrible, hen. Walt's lad was right there, nearby, when the rock fell on his da. He didn't see it fall, but he heard the thud ... must have felt it, too, shaking the ground. The stone was somewhere near six or seven hundredweight."

"Och, there's no surviving that," Helen commiserated. "But Wullie said Walt's lad saw everything."

"Naw, he didn't see the rock fall, but he saw the insides of his da's head. That's what Wullie meant by ... 'everything.'" Will paused and gazed off into the distance before he finally spoke again, "The lad could have been killed, right alongside his father. He found him, skull crushed, blood and brains and ... eyeballs ... right there, on the ground."

Helen's stomach turned and her gorge rose, but she swallowed it back. "Stop," she said, "you'll give me the boak." It wasn't like her to vomit at stories like this. This was life in a coal town. Men died all the time, in grisly ways. It was the pregnancy, making her react so.

"Aye, that was bad enough, but his lad, he ..." Will paused, searching for the right words, "... he broke down, Helen. He was pure bawling, like a

13

bairn. That's to be expected, I suppose. It was his father, after all, and it's for none of us to judge how a man reacts to something so heavy. But he couldn't stop … they had to call the doctor to sedate him."

Will took a moment to compose himself. Finally, he said, "It pure broke my heart, seeing the wee man so upset. All I could think was, what if our Wullie saw me like that … head all smashed on the ground? That's what's bothering him, hen. The poor lad has the fear it's gonna happen to me, that he's gonna see his own da, lying in a pool of blood beneath a giant slab of rock, dead. A lad ought never see his da's brains."

"Hush," Helen warned, laying a finger over his lips. "Don't talk that way. It's bad luck." He nodded in agreement, and she went on, "The poor wee lad. Nae wonder Wullie was fighting tears."

"Aye," said Will, taking a drag off his cigarette, "and it's got me thinking." He exhaled a cloud of smoke and finally said, "I've been thinking about this for a long while and, after what happened today, I'm gonna take your brother Bill up on his offer of jobs for me and Junior. We're going to America, where work conditions are safer."

Helen's eyes grew wide. "What? Wull, no!" she begged. "My family's here and I'll never see them again!"

"D'yeh think I want to leave my family behind? Besides, Lizzie's the only one of yer kin livin' here in Coalburn," Will demanded, "The rest are miles away in Dreghorn and yeh haven't seen them in years. Your parents are dead, and three of yer brothers … including Geordie, yer pal … are over there, across the pond in Utah." He stopped, waiting for Helen to confirm that he was right, but her silence was all he needed.

"Besides," he went on, "I cannot name a single miner in Coalburn … hell, in all of Scotland … who would pass up a chance like this. I'm a fool to not take advantage of having a brother-in-law who runs one of the safest, most advanced mines in America."

"D'yeh think Lizzie and her man might go with us?" Helen asked. "I'd hate to go alone, with no close family. Aye, John and Geordie are in America with Bill, but I don't know them anymore ..." Other than Geordie —who was 37, unmarried and able to visit Scotland occasionally—Helen hadn't seen her older brothers in over ten years, they had sailed for America so long ago.

Will interrupted, "The offer'll surely be open to John, being married to your sister and all, but we're going, either way." Helen's lip started to quiver, so he rushed on, "The working conditions here are shite, especially those open lifts, dropping at speed! How many men have lost an arm in one of them? How long before it's my turn to have my brains dashed out, or my arm cut off, or to suffocate from black damp? Or Wullie? How long before he's killed?"

"Sake, stop talking like that!" Helen cried, angry this time. "Are yeh tryin' to curse us?"

Will had a point, though. Much of her family lived more than twenty miles west, mostly in Galston and Dreghorn, but Will's younger brother Pete and his wife Jessie and Will's dashing nephew Tam—a war hero—and his lovely, fragile English bride Bertha, lived here in town. They felt more like family than her Americanized brothers and it was this family she didn't want to leave behind.

Helen reached into the maelstrom of her whirling thoughts and grabbed the first that flew by. "We cannot go," she said, "what about Jeanie? She's got her mind set on going to Glasgow for nursing school. It would pure break her heart to give that up."

"Aye," Will argued, "but d'yeh think there's no nursing schools in America? It's the land of opportunity!"

Will flicked his cigarette hard at the dirt road and ground it out with his toe. "I've made up my mind. We're going. That's that. I'll not have my lad watch me die like that, if I can help it. Your brother's been bragging about that mine of his long enough. The wages are better, the mine's safer—hell, it's got electric lighting! The houses are better than this shitehole ..." he gestured at the row of miners' housing. "Christ, I can smell the shite with every breath."

Helen took his hand and led him back toward their dwelling, saying, "Och, away with yer blether ... we're standing near the privy. Yeh cannot smell it when yeh're inside our house, and you know it. And, this is the nicest place we've lived since we were wed. Isn't our home here sturdier? Less crowded?"

Will insisted, "Bill says it's even better there, in Castle Gate." He walked her past their door, not ready to go back inside. "We'll have our own free-standing house, with our own privy out back. There'll be no sharing it with four other families."

"Och, aye, that would be luxurious," she admitted. A privy of their own ... even better ... a *house* of their own, with no shared walls. No more hearing their neighbors fighting or making babies, no more worrying about their neighbors hearing them do the same.

15

Will watched her face soften and plunged forward with renewed enthusiasm, "Aye, and there's a bathhouse for the workers, too. Yeh won't have to boil me up a bath each night. We'll get a hot shower and come home in clean clothes."

"Is that right?" Helen asked.

"Aye," Will said, "d'yeh not remember? Bill bragged about the showers in one of his first letters after he got the job in Utah."

"Yeh'd think I'd recall a detail like that, out of pure envy if nothing else." Helen chewed a loose hangnail and thought about what her husband was proposing.

Will was silent as he watched her face. She was on the verge of okaying the move. Not that it mattered—he had made up his mind—but the process would be more pleasant if she agreed. It broke his heart to leave, too, but he never wanted to see that look on his lad's face again, much less be the cause of it. Miners knew it was dangerous work and, although they keenly felt the loss of a fellow miner, they knew how to mourn and move on quickly, else there'd be no stew in the pot at the end of the day. Losing a family member was another story.

Lost in his own thoughts, Will hadn't noticed that Helen's demeanor had changed. Coming out of his reverie, he saw that his wife was silently weeping. "What? Don't cry, hen," he said, startled, and pulled her into his arms. "It'll work out. Bill says there's plenty of work. Shall we ask Pete and Tam to bring their families with us, too?" He pulled back to look at her and said, grinning, "We'll be a hoard of invading Scots. Mebbe we'll show up in kilts, blowing bagpipes, just to show them Yanks what's what!"

Helen allowed a small smile and wiped her tears on his clean shirt. She rested her face on his chest and said, "Aye, it would be nice to invite them along, but that's not why I'm crying. I haven't told you yet, but I'm pregnant again. This would be a bad time to flit."

Helen couldn't see Will's face go white, but she felt his arms tighten a little. "Are yeh sure?" he asked.

"Aye, I just found out," she said, pulling back and peering into his eyes there in the twilight, trying to decipher his reaction. "I've missed my monthly twice now, and I've waited to see if I'll miscarry again. I wasn't gonna say anything until I had to, but with you wanting to flit to America, we've gotta think whether it's wise for me to go on such a long journey, while I'm big as a house and probably sick and all. You know how hard it goes for me. I've had nothing but miscarriages for five years and before that …"

"Aye," he nodded, interrupting before she could remind him of the five babies who had died shortly after birth. "When would yeh be due? Are yeh sure?" Will asked.

"Near as I can reckon, it would be February or March, and aye, I'm sure enough to bring it up," Helen stepped back out of his embrace, so she could fully see him, and replied. "I'd have kept it to myself, 'til I was certain, otherwise."

"Well," he sighed, "we can wait and go in the spring. We need to save the money anyway, for ship's passage and the train to Utah from New York."

"Och, but Will," she protested, "I wouldn't want to travel so far with a new bairn, not after burying poor wee Annie at five months. The others died so soon after birth, I didn't get to know 'em. Losing them was a wrench, sure, but Annie lived long enough to take her place in my heart. I couldn't take losing another wee'un like that."

"Aye," Will said, "but Annie didn't die from travel, she died of whooping cough, the others were born too soon and we have no way of knowing what'll happen with this'un."

He took her by the shoulders and said, "Helen, love, I've made up my mind. We're going. Might as well make the best of it. And if we have to do it with a new bairn, then that's what we'll do." He got in one last dig, saying, "Just pray that nothing happens to me or Wullie in the meantime."

With mixed feelings that didn't matter anyway, Helen gave in. They were moving to America.

CHAPTER 2

September 28, 1920
Coalburn, Scotland

"Jeanie, hen, pour Bertha and yer Aunt Jessie some more tea," Helen said.

Today was Helen's birthday and she was now 36. Her sister-in-law Jessie, her niece-by-marriage Bertha, her younger sister Lizzie and daughter Jeanie took a break from their workdays for a wee mid-day celebration without the men around, complete with gifts and the reading of tea leaves later.

Jessie gave her a hand stitched "Home Sweet Home" sampler, which Helen hung over the mantle. Lizzie brought a tin of store-bought shortbreads to enjoy with their blether and cuppa. Jeanie offered to cook and clean up after the evening meal so Helen could have the night off. Bertha brought a jar of her strawberry preserves, tied with a decorative bow, and the women sampled a bit of the jam on the shortbread.

Lizzie's teacup was full—she was too busy chasing two-year-old Johnny away from Auntie Helen's breakables, with her nine-month-old baby—also named Jean, after Helen and Lizzie's mother—hoisted on her hip. As Jeanie lifted the brown glazed-clay pot to pour a refill for her aunt, Jessie covered her teacup with her hand. "Thank yeh, no, hen, that's plenty," Jessie said, "but what I do want is for yer mam to stop changing the subject!" Her oldest child, seven-year-old Peggy, was at school so Jessie sat enjoying afternoon tea with her lady friends with four-year-old Annie on her knee.

Jeanie turned to Bertha, the pretty, mild-mannered English lass her cousin Tam had married during the Great War, who sat rocking her sleeping two-year-old Margie. Bertha said, quietly as to not wake the child, "Ta, I'll have a top-up."

Jeanie filled Bertha's cup, took a shortbread and sat with the older women, keeping an eye peeled toward her young cousins, ready to jump up and stop them from breaking something. The house hadn't been baby-proofed in years, and Aunt Lizzie had her hands too full to contain rowdy, wee Johnny.

Jessie, the smallest yet fiercest of the four women, with dark hair and flashing blue eyes, insisted, "Helen, out with it! We all know yeh're gonna tell us, so get it told."

"Aye, I will," Helen laughed ruefully. She turned to her daughter and said, "Jeanie, hen, I've not told anyone but your father, so I'm trusting you, as a grown woman, to keep my secret."

Jeanie's eyes widened. Her mother had only recently begun treating her as an adult, now that she was contributing to the household kitty. She worked as a housekeeper for a neighbor family whose mistress was overwhelmed with her family of ten. The woman's older sons worked in the mine, so she paid for Jeanie's help with their extra income.

"I promise," Jeanie said.

"It isn't a good secret. I'm pregnant," Helen blurted out.

"Are yeh certain?" Jessie asked, "It could be yeh're going through the change."

"No, I'm pregnant, sure," Helen said. "I saw the doctor. And with Wull insisting …" She stopped and shot Jessie a look.

"Yeh may as well tell her, hen," Jessie said, reaching across the table to pat Helen's hand, "she'll know soon enough."

Helen sighed and said, "Jean, yer father wants us to go to America. Yer Uncle Bill, my oldest brother, is the superintendent of a mine in a place called Utah, and he's offered yer da a job."

Jean was silent as she pondered. "When?" the girl finally asked.

"We're to go soon as we can save up the money, but with this new bairn on the way …" Helen began.

"Mam," Jeanie cried, "you cannot travel! It's not safe! Never mind if the baby even lives, what about you?"

"Give yerself peace, lass," Aunt Jessie interrupted, "nobody's going anywhere before any baby comes. Yer mam'll put her foot down with your da, I'll see to that. We're not going before then, sure."

"Yeh're going, too? You and Uncle Pete, and the girls?" Jeanie asked, somewhat mollified.

"Aye, and Tam and Bertha, and wee Margie, sure," Jessie said.

"What about Aunt Lizzie and Uncle John?" she asked, turning toward her other aunt.

"No," Lizzie said, shaking her head, "John's family would ne'er forgive us if we left Scotland."

Jeanie turned again to Bertha, who nodded and whispered in her Yorkshire accent over Margie's sleeping head, "Aye, we're going, too."

Jessie said, "Aye, we're all going! We'll just have to wait a wee bit, is all. Your Uncle Bill has been bletherin' on about jobs since he took over that mine years ago."

"Aye," Helen said, "he's been recruiting family and friends for years. Jean, your uncles John and Geordie have been working with him since before the Great War. Uncle Buchan would be there, too, no doubt, if he hadn't been killed in France. He was always one for adventure. That's why he enlisted. He would have loved the idea of travelin' the world. Aye, as long as Bill's in charge, there'll be jobs."

"There, you see?" Jessie said, "No hurry. We'll have more time to save up and say our farewells."

"Och," sighed Helen. "I cannot help feeling something bad's gonna happen, though. I keep dreaming of Buchan telling me not to go, but Wull swears his second sight is right and mine's wrong. He says he sees disaster in our future. He's got his knickers in a knot, in an all-fired hurry to go."

"Oh aye," laughed Jessie, "he shoulda kept his knickers on or tied his tadger in a knot so yeh wouldn't be in this state!"

They guffawed at Jessie's bawdy talk, even Bertha who blushed as she giggled quietly, trying to not wake Margie. Jeanie pointed out, "You and Uncle Pete don't have to wait, nor Tam and Bertha."

Jessie said, "Yer Uncle Bill is yer mam's brother, a Littlejohn. He's no relation to us Garrochs. Pete is yer da's brother and Tam is yer da's sister's son. Without yer father married to Bill's sister as a go-between, it'll be awkward. Besides, I'm in no hurry to say goodbye to my kith and kin. Yer da's the only one in a rush."

Jeanie chewed her lip, considering how her life had changed in the past few minutes. "But Mam," she finally said, "what about nursing school? Polly and me were going to Glasgow together. Can I not stay here and go to school? Yeh said yerself I'm a grown woman."

Helen shook her head, no. "Yeh're only sixteen. If yeh were married, that'd be a different story, but yeh don't even have any prospects for marriage."

"But Mam, it's all I ever wanted!" Jeanie cried, "Yeh know that. Ever since I was a wee girl, I've wanted to be a nurse!"

"I'm sure there'll be nursing schools in America, hen," said Aunt Jessie.

Jeanie argued, "But it won't be the same. Polly and me, we've been scheming for years to go together."

"Are yeh sure yeh want that, hen?" Helen asked. "Nursing's hard work. Remember when Uncle Buchan was here with us after he was wounded?"

"Aye, it was grisly," Jeanie said, "but I'm not afraid, I've proved that. Uncle Buchan was all busted up, but that didn't scare me off from helping, did it?"

"That's not what I mean," said her mother, "and you were only twelve, so yeh were shielded from the worst of it. I meant it's hard on yer heart, watching someone suffer, crying in pain and not being able to help." Helen paused before continuing. "It's different, helping someone die. I've done it, with my own mam, and it was the hardest thing ever, watching her suffer."

Jeanie asked a question she had long wondered about, but never wanted to bring up a painful subject, "What was Granny like, Mam?"

"Well," Helen began, "yeh know that you and yer wee cousin there," she said, indicating Lizzie's baby, "were both named Jeanie after our mam. Aw, she was sweet, wasn't she Lizzie? Such a soft heart."

"Aye, from what I remember," said Lizzie, "I was just a wee'un when she died, but when I think back on her, they're kind memories."

Helen continued, "I must have been fourteen when Mam had her stroke. Our older sisters, Maggie and Tina, were off and married, so it was me who cared for her, moaning in pain like she was and half out of her head. It was a nightmare, wondering if she'd die or what to do with her if she lived. Lizzie was only eight and our da and older brothers were all in the mine, so it was up to me to take care of the whole house while also nursing our poor, sick mam. And our house was just as full as the one yeh're workin' in."

"Och!" Jeanie gasped. The woman she worked for had almost died trying to keep up—having not fully recovered from her most recent childbirth—she wore herself to a nub, chasing after her passel of wee'uns, with their mountains of dirty nappies. Finally, the doctor gave her husband a choice: hire some help or dig an early grave.

Helen continued, "Auntie Jean was in school. She was just nine, so she and Lizzie couldn't do much but take care of themselves and stay out of my way. Poor wee Buchan was only four."

She paused and silently offered a prayer for her dead brother before she continued. "I'm not telling yeh this to bemoan my lot. Plenty of people have it hard, sure, but the hardest part was watching Mam die, slow like, and in pain. Nursing is … not what yeh think. It's not romantic, like yer schoolgirl visions of bandaging handsome soldiers. It's ugly and painful, all blood and shite."

Helen abruptly stopped talking and took a shortbread from the tin. She dunked it halfway into her hot tea and bit into the soggy cookie.

"Mam, I didn't know that about Granny," Jeanie said, "but remember how I helped nurse Uncle Buchan when he was here?"

"Aye," Helen said, "he came here before he was sent back to France, but he was already on the mend when he arrived. Imagine seeing a man freshly tore up, ate up with the shell shock."

Pete and Jessie were still living in Kilmaurs then, so Jessie didn't witness his time with his family before being ordered back to the front. She listened with rapt attention, letting her tea get cold. Bertha listened, too, her hand over her heart, uttering little moans of compassion. After all, Tam could have been killed in combat, too. Lizzie silently wiped tears from her eyes as Helen spoke.

Helen continued, "Och, Buchan was a bloody mess, at first. Hurt so bad they let him stay home for eight months, before they sent him back just to be shot dead. It lays heavy on your heart to see someone you love suffer."

"Of course," Jeanie replied. She remembered Uncle Buchan well. She wasn't much older than Nellie was now, when he died five years ago at age 22. When he lived with them, before the war, he was friendly and boisterous and, to him, she was a pesky kid with braids to be pulled. When he returned for his convalescence he was pale and quiet, tortured by nightmares, and didn't say much.

Jeanie said to Helen, "Even so, I want to go to nursing school. It's a respectable occupation for a girl, and I don't want to just be some miner's wife, cranking out wee'uns and waging a constant battle against their filth."

"Yeh cannot fault her logic, hen," Jessie said, "the lass is right."

"Well," Helen sighed, "that may be so, but you'll not do it here in Scotland. You'll have to be an American nurse and land yerself a well-to-do American man if yeh want to escape a life of drudgery."

Will wasn't home to hear them talk like this, so Helen took this opportunity to enlighten her daughter. She said, "My father raised his children to be proud and he wasn't happy when I married an ordinary, uneducated miner. Da's cousin was the coalmaster and a church elder in Galston. My brothers got educated—that's how Bill could become a mine supervisor and offer good jobs to his family."

"Och," Jessie interrupted, "life as a miner's wife doesn't bother me. I'm happy. The Garrochs are an affable bunch and Pete and I are well suited." Jessie's adoration of Pete shone in her eyes, as she spoke. While the Garroch brothers were both good-humored, with quick smiles and twinkling eyes, Pete was a favorite with the ladies. Although he was prematurely grey, and not a very tall man—only 5'6"—mirth bubbled up from him and attracted folks to him like moths to a flame. That he had chosen Jessie, out of all the girls who had set their caps at him, made her content with her lot.

"Aye, I'm happy with Wull, too," Helen replied. "He may not be as irresistible as Pete, but he's solid and makes me feel safe. We're a good match."

Helen sipped her tea and continued educating Jeanie, "I never expected life to be easy—schooling was never in my future. I was the oldest unmarried girl at home, and Da depended on me to keep house until my wee sisters were old enough to take over. By then, I was old enough to marry and saw no need to wait for someone wealthier than yer father to come along. The only men I met were coal miners."

And now the man she had married was about to whisk her away across the world, to live in a strange land among brothers she hadn't seen in years —away from the only land she'd ever known, away from her sisters, away from the graves of her parents and her wee infant babies, which she'd never be able to visit again.

She dipped the rest of her shortbread into her tea, soaking it thoroughly, and stuffed the whole thing into her mouth. It was the only thing she could think of to stop herself from sobbing. It was, after all, supposed to be a happy day—her birthday.

CHAPTER 3

February 1921
Coalburn, Scotland

As expected, Helen had a difficult pregnancy. She was no spring chicken, and she didn't have the luxury of pampering herself throughout the ordeal, the kind during which a wealthier woman might have been ordered to stay in bed. Although Jeanie and Nellie did what they could, there were only so many hours in the day, and they had their own responsibilities. There was little rest to be had by anyone in the household under ordinary circumstances, and Helen's lessened strength and endurance meant hardship for everyone. No one expected the baby to survive. Their concern was that Helen might not make it, either.

Both girls took on added responsibilities, lugging Will and Willie's coal-stained clothes to the washhouse and scrubbing them by hand, wringing them out and bringing them home to dry in front of the fire. Jeanie cut back on the number of hours she worked outside of the home so she could gather water and heat the daily bath.

Willie helped by taking the chamber pots, in the mornings, to the privy to empty them so Helen wouldn't be sickened by the stench. Will rose before Helen to stoke the fire, so she could wake up in a warm house. Both men made a point of demanding as little of Helen as they could.

Even young Nellie could see that Helen wasn't strong enough to do any more than she did. The girl often silently cried herself to sleep at night with worry over losing her mam for some damned baby who wasn't going to live anyway, hating her da for putting Helen in this position, a concept she was only beginning to understand.

"What a lovely family I'm blessed with," Helen said to them one night at tea—an exceptionally fine meal of beef and kidney pies—turned out with pride by Jeanie and Nellie. "I feel wretched seeing youse doing my chores, when I could be doing more."

In reality, however, she could not. Her body ached with soreness and fatigue and, with every day that her belly grew larger and her skin stretched further, her ordinary household tasks posed a greater challenge.

"Aye," said Will, "you wee'uns have done me proud, taking care of your mother and all." The kids, unused to effusive praise, ducked their heads to hide their blushes. To earn it wasn't the reason they helped so willingly.

When Helen went into labor in the wee, small hours of that blistering cold Monday in late February, Will was shooed out of the room and seventeen-year-old Jeanie was called in to assist the midwife. He sat helplessly at the kitchen table until it was finally time for Willie to set off to the mine. He said to his son, "Let them know I'll not be in today. With yer mam's history, I need to be home."

After a nervous Nellie left for school Will tried to catch a few winks in Willie's bunk, when he wasn't pacing the floor and smoking, but with all the caterwauling in the next room he was unable to nod off. So, he lay there awake, staring at the cracks in the ceiling and worrying.

In addition to Helen's survival, he worried that coal prices had plummeted and layoffs were looming. Control of mine operations were set next month to be returned to the owners, after government wartime subsidies of miners' pay expired. Wage cuts were certain and would probably result in a bitter strike. This was a bad time to delay their flit to America, and these concerns allowed him to think of something other than his wife in the other room with his eldest daughter by her side.

Jeanie hadn't been in the room when her previous brothers and sisters were born. She was only eleven the last time a baby was born alive—wee Isabella, who only lived an hour. This time, watching Helen strain, scream and bleed while a slimy wee creature fought its way out of her bloated frame was almost Jean's undoing.

More than once she wanted to flee but she was an adult now, who wanted to be a nurse, so she stayed by Helen's side holding her hand and gritting her teeth as Helen squeezed her knuckles almost to the point of breaking. She concentrated on blotting Helen's forehead with a cool cloth, jabbering about mindless nothings to distract her, while the midwife took care of the bloody business.

In the end, as Helen cradled her new daughter—almost delirious with exhaustion—she held Jeanie's bruised hand more gently and said, "Thank yeh, hen, I couldn't have done it without yeh here."

The midwife had kind words, too. "Good job, aye," she said as she cleaned up the bloody linens and spilled water. "It's not easy work, birthing a babe. Some find it too gory for their likin'. Well done, lass. Sit with yer mother and wee sister and rest a bit."

Jeanie sat on the edge of the bed, her mind reeling, and poked her finger into the baby's clenched fist to feel its tiny grip. "What'll yeh name her?" she asked Helen.

Helen smiled weakly and said, "We'll give Isabella another try."

"But why, Mam?" Jeanie asked. "This'll be the third wee'un you've given that name, and the first two didn't make it. Isn't that bad luck?"

"Och," said Helen, "if it was bad luck I wouldn't be here. I had a sister with the same name as me who died years before I was born, and when I came along, the next girl in line, I got the same name, after my granny. Uncle Buchan was the second one with that name, named after our granda. The first Buchan only lived a few weeks, then when the Buchan you knew came along, he got the name as well."

"It's so confusing," said Jeanie, "how d'yeh keep track of everyone with the same names in all the families?"

Helen laughed weakly, "It's tradition. First daughter, like you, gets named after the mother's mother, that's how yeh're Jeanie Cochrane Garroch and why you have so many cousins named Jeanie Cochrane, all named after my mam. Poor wee Annie was my second daughter, so she was named after your da's mother, Annie McConnachie Garroch, just like Uncle Pete's second daughter, yer wee cousin Annie. After our Annie passed, yer da broke the tradition. He didn't want to use the name again on another bairn. The third gets named after its mother, so Nellie has my name, Helen Littlejohn Garroch, Jr., and Wullie was named after your granda. And this wee thing," Helen lightly jostled the sleeping, swaddled infant, "will be Isabella, after your da's sister, yer cousin Tam's mother."

"Doesn't she get a middle name?" Jeanie asked.

"No," Helen explained, "Auntie Isabella's last name was Garroch, so that would give your wee sister the name 'Isabella Garroch Garroch'."

They chuckled, grateful for the levity, and Jeanie asked, "What if she'd been a boy?"

Helen said, her fading voice a sign of her weariness, "I suppose we'd have tried for James again, because he's my next brother in line."

The midwife patted Jeanie on the shoulder and said, "Let yer mam rest, dearie, she's pure knackered. I'll go inform the nervous father. He'll be curious whether he has a new wee lad or lassie."

"Will she be okay?" Jeanie asked.

The woman said, "No worries, hen, yer mammy'll be right as rain, soon enough." Her final words to Helen, though, before leaving the room with a bundle of bloody linens, were sternly delivered. "I know yeh're planning to flit to the States but that bairn is far too wee. She's got strong lungs and may live, God willing, but if yeh don't take care, this'un will go down the same path as all them others to God's glory."

"Och," Helen said, weakly, "tell that to her da, would yeh? He's in a fool's rush to get to America."

"I'll have a word," said the midwife, "but one look at this poor, wee babe ought to be enough. Now get some rest." She and Jeanie exited the room and Helen heard her say, as she pulled the door shut behind her, "Wull, yeh've a fine wee girl, but …"

Helen dozed lightly until she heard the door open. "Aw, hen," Will said, as he entered, "look at youse two." He sat on the edge of the bed and kissed Helen's forehead. "I'm that relieved … the midwife says yeh'll be fine." He scooped up tiny Isabella and rocked her slowly as Helen drifted off to sleep.

It wouldn't take much convincing on the midwife's part. It was plain to Will that Isabella had the same gaunt look as her siblings who didn't survive. Unlike Jeanie, Willie, and Nellie—who were born robust—this one was too quiet, as gawky as a freshly hatched bird, all skin and bones.

A twang of conscience hit his gut … he was responsible for Helen and Isabella's conditions. The females in his life had been casting baleful glares at him as Helen grew larger and weaker, silently blaming him. Only Willie seemed to understand—a man has needs and taking care of them was a wife's duty, if she didn't want him wandering elsewhere.

Now he just had to pray that the delay didn't mean strike poverty or, worse, death in the mine. His second sight was showing him visions of horrific explosions, and he couldn't wait to get to the safety of the modern American mine.

27

Meantime, he had a new wee baby girl and a wife he loved, both of whom needed his attention. "Baby Isabella," he crooned, lightly touching the tip of her nose, "my new wee lassie. I hope yeh live to grow up in America. See that yeh do."

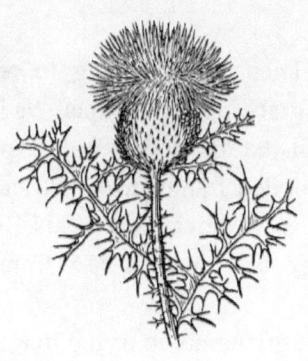

CHAPTER 4

November 1921
Coalburn to the TSS Cameronia: Glasgow

Baby Isabella, nicknamed Ella, was now three months older than Annie had been when she died at five months. She was thriving, beyond the danger point. It was time for the Garrochs' journey to America, at least the menfolk. The females would stay behind while the men earned enough in Utah for their passage. They wouldn't easily raise the full amount needed here in Scotland after the Britain-wide strike in the spring of 1921.

After the mines were deregulated and returned to the control of their owners in late March, wages were lowered beyond pre-war, pre-subsidy levels. Miners who wouldn't accept the extreme wage cuts were locked out of the mines, free to go elsewhere to find work.

After a three-month lockout—during which communities supported the strikers with soup kitchens and other welfare events—miners who had no options were making twenty percent less than before the war began in 1914. Even Jeanie was affected, as her employer could no longer afford her wages. She had to find work at a local fruit farm but, now that harvest season had passed, pickings were slim.

Will's decision to leave Scotland was finalized when he received new correspondence from Bill. "Look," Will said, handing the letter to Helen—written on Utah Fuel Company letterhead—as they sat at the table after evening tea, "yer brother's offering to train me as brattice man. I'd still earn wages by weight but have added responsibility and extra wages. But I have to get there soon."

"What's brattice?" Helen asked, trying to read the letter with Ella squirming on her lap and grabbing at the paper. "Is it safe?"

"It's how yeh control the air flow," Will explained. "A brattice man builds canvas-covered wooden frames to block and direct the air currents. It's the kind of job a man of advancing years, like me," he said wryly, "aspires to. It'll give my old bones a rest from all the crouching and crawling."

"Aw, Wull," she said, giving up on trying to read while the baby was so intent on snagging the paper from her hand, "that's good of him. We all look forward to our workloads easing a bit." Bill's previous letters had promised they would have their own free-standing house near the company store, school, and library. Being the superintendent's family had its benefits.

The next day, Will sent a telegram to Bill confirming that he would be joined by Willie, Pete and Tam, with their families to follow along later. That night after supper, Willie went off with his friends, Jeanie sat on her bunk reading and Nellie played with Ella on the other bunk. Will sat with Helen at the table—he with a dram of whisky and she with a cup of tea— and said, "Well, hen, I've written to Bill that I'll be on my way soon."

A ripple of dread raced through her gut, the sharp pain making her wonder if she should hurry to the privy. As long as the idea was just gab, she could enjoy the fantasy of a better life and ignore her concerns. Now, they came rushing in and she blurted out the first fear that came to mind, "But Wull, it's winter! What if yeh hit an iceberg? Mind the Titanic?"

Will laughed, "Aye, but they've learned from their mistakes. Give yerself peace. Yeh may as well be afraid we'll be blown up like the Lusitania."

Nellie, who couldn't help overhearing, turned to her father with eyes big as saucers. Helen dismissed the child's fears with a wave. "Don't laugh at me, Wull Garroch," Helen scolded, "or I'll not wait for yeh to be killed at sea. I'll make myself a widow."

"Alright, pet," he said, grinning, "but we'll be safer aboard that ship than we ever were in the mine. For a whole two weeks, yeh'll not have to fret about us like yeh would if we were here, working. I've saved up enough to keep youse afloat until I can send money home," he said, "and between me and Wullie, that shouldn't take long. Youse can visit yer relatives before you come to America."

The details were soon settled. Jessie would stay in Coalburn, where she would find a job while the girls were in school. Tam's wife Bertha made plans to visit her mother in England before moving in with Tam's parents in Strandhead. Jim Littlejohn and his wife Agnes would squeeze Helen and the girls into their already cramped miners' cottage in Dreghorn, with ten children of their own.

Helen wrote in advance to Agnes, "It's an imposition, sure, but we'll make our stay as short as we can and I'll tell the girls to keep their footprints light and their voices down." Not that Jeanie needed reminding, but Nell still needed the threat of a skelped ear from time to time.

The men booked second class passage aboard the ocean liner TSS Cameronia for Friday, November 4, leaving out of Glasgow. Second class was several steps above dormitory-style steerage—they would share cabins, two men apiece, and their passage included the costs of meals, so they wouldn't have to bring their own food. It would be comfortable enough for a two-week trip.

They worked until the last possible day, putting in as many hours as they could before selling their tools and packing their belongings. Bill had advised them to travel light and replace anything left behind once they arrived in Castle Gate so their wives packed the bare minimum in their duffle bags—three clean shirts and two pairs of trousers. They would bring their good, church clothes as well and try their damnedest to keep them all clean.

Finally, the day of departure arrived. They boarded the train north for Glasgow, and Pete dropped into the seat next to Will for the first leg of their long trip. Will paid no attention to his brother, who was muttering to himself and scowling for reasons unknown. Will allowed himself to get lost in his thoughts—life had been moving quickly, and this was the first time he could just sit and think. He stared out the window as Willie and Tam chatted to while away the time and Pete sat brooding.

Will missed Helen already but, if he was honest, he looked forward to some time alone. This move was a massive undertaking, better done without the constant nattering of the females in his family. This wasn't the same as when the family relocated from Dreghorn to Coalburn. If Coalburn hadn't worked out, they could have always gone back to Dreghorn. Not so with going to America. The chances of coming back to Scotland, without the kind of wages and safety net that Bill Littlejohn was offering, were practically nonexistent.

Not that Helen nattered—that was Jeanie and Nellie's department—but he had the big picture to think of, an entire ocean and then a continent to cross. First, they had to get on the ship. Then, he had to find a ticket agent for their train from New York to Utah and find the train station in a big, unknown city. And once they arrived in Castle Gate, what then?

Bill's last letter arrived in Coalburn after Helen left for her brother Jim's house with the girls. It said that if their arrival was delayed, Bill may not be there to greet them. A widower, he was marrying his second wife on Friday, November 25, the day after an American holiday called Thanksgiving, so he might be off on his honeymoon if there were unexpected delays. Helen's other brothers—John and Geordie—were on standby, just in case.

Will reckoned their itinerary in his head: the Cameronia was supposed to steam into New York by Saturday, November 19 and the train took three days—they should leave for Utah immediately to ensure their arrival before Thanksgiving and the wedding.

Bill also wrote that Helen needn't be concerned about flitting with her pots, pans, dishes and such, as Elsie—his wife-to-be—was a widow with a well-established and comfortable home of her own. Elsie looked forward to passing on any duplicated household items once she moved into Bill's home. Helen would be happy to hear this. She fretted greatly, not knowing what she should bother packing and toting.

Will allowed his mind to drift as the Lanarkshire countryside whizzed by, thinking about Bill getting remarried. Bill had been a widower long enough, with Mary being dead of ladies' cancer these two years, and his poor wee'uns in need of a mother. Will hadn't known Mary well, beyond her reputation within the family as the 'perfect wife'—hadn't seen her since they all lived in Dreghorn, before Mary joined Bill in America in 1911.

Bill's new wife would have large shoes to fill—Mary was someone who people turned to for guidance and support, from young girls who wanted advice on their love lives, to widows and orphans who needed an open heart and a strong shoulder to cry on.

Will leaned his forehead against the cold window, his warm breath forming clouds of frost, and watched his homeland pass into history. This might be the last time he ever saw Scotland. The excitement about their new future was now overshadowed by a melancholic nostalgia for the land where he'd spent his first thirty-nine years.

His thoughts drifted into sleep, and he was shaken awake by Pete jostling his shoulder and Willie's voice, saying, "Da! We're here, in Glasgow."

Will opened his eyes to see Pete grinning, ready to jostle him again, "Get up, big man!"

"Yeh seem to have recovered from yer mope," Will said, stretching and kneading his eyes with his fists.

"Aye," Pete said and moved into the aisle so Will could stand. "Just worried about Jess and the girls. Jessie'll be fine, sure. I pity anyone who says otherwise. Mind, I'll miss her and the wee'uns, but innit nice to be away from the clucking hens for a while?"

"Aye," said Will, "I was having a bit of a brood about that, myself. What about you, Tam?" he asked his nephew, "D'yeh miss Bertha yet?"

"Och, aye, I do miss her," said Tam, "Bertha's a sweet girl, and she takes good care of me and our Margie. What's not to miss?"

"I'll tell yeh one thing I will miss," Pete muttered to Will, under his breath, as he gathered his bag, "when these two aren't in earshot. I hope we'll find a place where a man can buy some of that."

"Enough of that talk," Will chuckled and said, after making sure his son wouldn't hear, "we'll see our wives soon enough. No need to resort to whores, yeh know."

"Aye, I know," sighed Pete, "I was joking, anyhow. Yeh know I wouldn't step out on my Jessie. Besides, she'd cut off my clackers and feed 'em to me if she found out."

They stepped out of the train car—which had become stuffy with the windows closed—into the brisk, sea-scented air. "Listen," said Tam, "it's sea gulls."

The men were quiet for a moment and listened to the birds as they took in the rare sights of a big city, a hustling, bustling port town. Only Tam—who fought with the Royal Scots Fusiliers in Africa during the Great War—had traveled much.

"Now what, Da?" Willie asked his father.

"Now we find our way to the ship," Will said. He made his way through the throng of passengers and flagged down a porter. He asked, "How do we get to the shipyard?"

"Follow the crowd," the porter said, pointing at what was now obvious. Several of the people piling off the train, carrying luggage, were following the signs leading them to where they, too, were about to board the Cameronia.

It wasn't a long walk, a few blocks. The crowd was so thick and the men were so rushed that they were barely able to take in the sights, not that there was much to see beyond portside pubs and cargo being offloaded from horse-drawn carts and the occasional motor vehicle. "If we had more time," Pete said wistfully, as they passed by a pub where they heard raucous laughter and the strains of someone badly playing the bagpipes, "I'd say we stop for a pint. Sounds like a good time in there."

"Aye," said Will, "We'll have a wee dram when we're on board. I'll buy."

"Me and all?" Willie asked.

"Yeh're a working man," Will said. "As long as they'll serve yeh, yeh can have a pint with yer evening meal."

They arrived at the terminal with little time to lose, according to the large clock mounted over the entry door. Willie's heart leapt in his chest as they approached the boarding agents. "We're really doing this!" he said, "We're going to America!"

"Aye, I cannot believe it myself," said Tam. "Here, this is the queue for Second Class." The men stood in line for several long minutes, fidgeting as they listened to the agents grilling each passenger ahead of them for their personal information. By the time they reached the front of the line, they knew what would be expected of them.

Tam was first and the bored agent barely looked up when he asked his first question, "Name?"

"Thomas Trow," said Tam. The agent flipped through the pages of a large ledger book until he found Tam's name already written, in pencil, at the top of one of the pages.

"Last address in the United Kingdom?"

"Bellfield Office House, Coalburn, Scotland," Tam replied. "That's just a mailing address now, the best I can offer yeh."

The agent glanced up at Tam for a moment and went back to the book, ready to tick off Tam's answers as they were delivered.

"Occupation? Age?"

"Miner, thirty," said Tam.

"Country of intended future permanent residence?"

"America," Tam grinned.

"Ticket, please," the agent said. Tam handed over his ticket and the agent pierced it with a paper puncher. He handed it back to Tam and said, "Next!"

Tam moved to the side and Will and Willie stepped forward. The agent began his questioning again. "Name?"

"Garroch," Will said, "Wulliam and Wulliam Jr."

The agent flipped through the book again until he found the list of names that began with G. "Last address in the United Kingdom?"

"17 Railway Terrace, Coalburn, Scotland, but Bellfield Office House is our mailing address, just like Tam before us," said Will.

"Occupation? Age?"

"We're both coal miners," said Will. "I'm thirty-nine and my lad's sixteen."

The agent scrawled Will's answers on the page and asked his final question, "Country of intended future permanent residence?"

"America," said Will. He had their tickets already in hand and passed them to the agent. who punched a hole in each, handed them back and said, "Next!"

It was Pete's turn with the agent, who asked, "Name?"

"Peter Garroch," he said.

"Address?"

Pete replied, "Tintoview, Coalburn, Scotland.

"Occupation? Age?"

"Coal miner," said Pete "and I'm 38."

"Country of intended future permanent residence?" he asked.

"United States of America," said Pete. Seeing on the ledger page that the agent had reached the end of the line of questions, Pete turned to go, but the agent stopped him.

"Not so fast, laddie, give us yer ticket," he said.

"Oh, right," said Pete. He dug into his coat pocket and pulled out his ticket, entangled with a wad of cash. He handed the ticket to the agent, who scolded, "Put that away, yeh numpty! Are yeh asking for a clubbing?"

Pete tucked the cash back into his pocket and muttered, as the agent punched a hole in his ticket, "Don't worry about me, old-timer. Worry about yerself."

The men made their way through the bustling concourse to the massive ship, their eyes agog at its pristine beauty—the Cameronia was less than a year old—over five hundred feet long, sleek and black, with a massive smokestack pushing up through the center of the decks.

Will spied the gangway and ushered his kin forward. "Here we go!" he said. They leaned their way up the incline, the gangway bouncing beneath their feet. Willie grabbed the railing to steady himself, and a man behind him taunted, "Get used to it, laddie! It'll be worse once we're out there at sea. Hope yeh don't get seasick, or yeh'll be boaking over the rails for the next two weeks!"

"I'm fine," Willie said to the man. He let go of the rail and made it the rest of the way without incident.

They stepped on deck at the top of the ramp and were greeted by a ship steward. "Welcome aboard the Cameronia," the Englishman said, "May I see your tickets? I can then direct you to your cabin."

Will handed their tickets over and said, "My lad and me, we're sharing a cabin. And these two," he gestured over his shoulder at Tam and Pete, "are sharing as well."

"Here's mine," said Tam, offering his ticket to the steward. "And mine," said Pete, doing the same.

"I see," the steward said. He glanced at their tickets and said, "Your cabins are side by side. Follow the signs here," he said, pointing at the sign attached to a nearby stairwell, "and those people ahead of you. They're going the same direction. Have a safe crossing." He dismissed them and turned to the next passenger coming aboard, "Welcome aboard the Cameronia. May I see your ticket? I can then direct you to your cabin."

They hoisted their bags and followed the signs and their fellow passengers down a set of stairs and into a long, brightly lit, carpeted hallway, where they joined several people who were chattering excitedly and looking for their cabin numbers, their neighbors for the next two weeks.

Finally, Willie said, "Here it is." He pointed to a number plaque on their cabin door, which opened into a spotless room with two bunks on one wall, a built-in padded bench on the other, a small dresser, and a sink. "This is nice!" he said, tucking his duffel bag under the bench.

"Aye, lad, finest digs I've ever seen. Yeh know yeh're getting the top bunk, don't yeh?" Will said, dropping his heavy bag into a corner, out of the way.

Willie laughed, "Yer old bones couldn't climb up there, anyhow."

"As long as we understand each other."

Pete came to their door and said, "Our room looks like this, too. Who knew they'd be so bonnie? I may sign on as a stoker and never go home! I can shovel coal just as well here as anywhere else."

Tam joined the conversation, "Aye, and d'yeh think stokers get rooms like this? Naw, they're stuffed below decks, like pork into sausage casings. Now, come on. We have two weeks to spend in these rooms, and we'll get mighty tired of them before long. Let's go up top and say our farewells to bonnie Scotland."

They left their belongings and went back upstairs to join the second-class passengers on their deck. First class passengers on the upper deck were allowed a loftier view of the passengers still boarding and luggage being loaded, but the class delineation barely registered with the men. Their fellow passengers were in high spirits, many beyond excited to be going to America to begin their lives anew. They waved at the folks below, some with tears of joy streaming down their faces, some with tears of sorrow at saying goodbye, possibly forever, to loved ones who had come to see them off.

After what felt like an eternity, the Cameronia finally set sail, first stop Moville, then Malin Head—both at the northern tip of Ireland—to pick up the last passengers from the United Kingdom before steaming across the Atlantic to New York. The engines, fully stoked, grew louder as the ship slid into the River Clyde, which would empty into the Firth of Clyde, taking the ship past Ayrshire where they were all born. It picked up speed as the tugboats led it into the open waters.

Will was somber as he gazed back at the dock and said, "If yeh'll permit, this would be a fine time for some Rabbie Burns." He stood erect as he recited, "O Scotia! my dear, my native soil! For whom my warmest wish to heaven is sent …"

Other voices joined him—his brother, his son, his nephew—and even a few other passengers, "… long may thy hardy sons of rustic toil be blest with health, and peace, and sweet content."

"No turning back, now," said Tam. He glanced toward his uncles and cousin and saw that all three, like himself, were tearing up. No more words were spoken as they watched Glasgow slipping away from their view. Indeed, there was no turning back.

CHAPTER 5

November 4-17, 1921
The TSS Cameronia:
Atlantic Ocean to New York City

Willie looked up from his reading as the steward delivered drinks to the table for his father, uncle and cousin. They sat in the smokeroom, where the men could play cards. It was one of the fancier places any of them had ever seen, more ornate than any pubs in Coalburn, with its polished wood paneling, upholstered chairs and carpeted floor. He couldn't imagine how First Class could be nicer. The whole ship was that way, with its electric lights and hot and cold running water, one awe-inspiring luxury after another. It made him feel like a bumpkin.

He sipped his tea while Will, Pete and Tam toasted and clinked their glasses. It wore on him that he was only allowed a pint or two with his evening meals. Sure, he may be only sixteen, but didn't he risk his life down in the mine just as they did? Wasn't he a man, down there, where it counted?

He asked the steward for more tea and went back to reading the twelve-page booklet supplied by the Cameronia to each passenger. In it, they could find instructions on how to get along for the two-week crossing—for example, breakfast was served from 8:00 to 10:00 AM, lunch at 1:00 PM and dinner at 7:30 PM. It also told where to find library books and railway timetables, and how to send letters and telegrams.

It was after Willie looked through the brochure on the first day that the men checked in most of their cash to the ship's safe, after he read that the ship's Purser would do that, free of charge. Will also sent a telegram to Helen before the ship left Ireland, and the UK, for good, letting her know what Bill said about Elsie supplying them with her duplicated items, saying: GIVE AWAY UNSENTIMENTAL THINGS STOP BILL HAS HOUSEHOLD ITEMS STOP

Willie's pamphlet included a list of passengers who bought advanced tickets, their names in alphabetical order. He, Pete and his da were on the same page, and Tam was on the last page. Willie was now perusing the passenger list to suss out the last name of a girl he fancied, called Agnes. There were several Agneses on the list, and it was his chosen task to figure out which one she was. She traveled with a brother and sister, and two parents, so his plan was to find an Agnes who fit those criteria, as long as her father had purchased their tickets in advance.

He couldn't concentrate, though. The men were having a raucous good time, reveling in their rare vacation from responsibility and back-breaking work. He rolled his eyes, wishing they'd quiet down. They had been embarrassing him the entire voyage with their constant ribbing and enjoyment of their temporary bachelorhood.

Of the three, Uncle Pete was relentless. "Get yer nose outta that bloody book," Pete demanded. "Play cards with us."

"I don't want to," Willie replied, darting a glance around the room.

"Come on, wee man," Pete said, kicking him under the table, "d'yeh not ken how? I'll teach yeh."

"Da," the boy said to Will, "is it fair that I can't drink with youse? It's no fun sitting around with a bunch of drunks if I can't join in."

"Drunks!" Pete declared, "I'll have yeh know, lad, I'm just gettin' started."

"Aye," added Tam, who shared a cabin with Pete, "and no doubt yeh'll be boakin' in the sink again all night, too."

"I know, lad," said Will, who was not too inebriated yet, "but we're minding that we can only drink until we get to twelve miles out from New York. Prohibition's the law there, and we'll not be able to drink ever again, at least unless we find a bootlegger in Utah."

"All the more reason to let me drink, now!" Willie said.

"Aye, the lad's right," said Pete. He glanced around to make sure no one was watching, then slid his glass across the table to his nephew. "Get it down yeh, quick."

Willie looked around, too, and—without hesitation and before his father could object—slammed back the whisky that his uncle had given to him. "Cheers," he said.

"Aye, that'll warm yer bones," said Pete, "and maybe now yeh'll stop bawlin' like a wee fanny."

Willie shook his head, exasperated, and stood. "I've had enough of youse. I'm going for a walk." He loved his uncle and normally they got along, but when Pete had a snootful, he could be a real wanker. As Willie strode toward the door, he heard his father chuckle and say, "Yeh ought to leave him alone. He's as tall as you now and might kick your arse …" and then Tam laughed and said, "My wee Margie's almost as tall as Pete."

Willie opened the door and stepped outside into the brisk ocean air. The contrast between that and the warm, smoky room hit him like a bracing slap in the face. While the ship's smokeroom smelled nothing like the pub at home with its beer-soaked floorboards and faded scents of puke and piss— the Cameronia was just six months old and had only been briefly seasoned with the sweet, manly aromas of whisky and cigars—it was stuffy and close in there.

For mid-November, the weather was surprisingly warm but when the wind gusted, it brought with it a frosty bite and the scent of snow. Willie leaned on the rail and gazed out over the ocean. He was finally used to not seeing any land, anywhere, no matter which direction he looked.

The water was almost still as glass, a welcome change—he had spent the first few days heaving and boaking as the ship pitched and rolled. The sun was above the western horizon, about an hour from setting, its reflection stretched across the Pond. He took in a deep, salt-scented breath and grinned. The whisky was kicking in and he felt great.

He'd noticed that Agnes often went to the library at this time of day, so he went below decks to get the book he had borrowed, *Tarzan the Terrible*. He had begun to read it but once he discovered it was the eighth book in the series, he decided to ask if the library had the first book so he could read them in their proper order.

Before going back up to the B deck, he took a minute in his cabin to wash his face and hands. This was a luxury he could get used to—hot and cold running water, whenever he wanted it—not only indoors, but in his own bedroom, which held the most comfortable bed he'd ever lain upon. And, the privies were sanitary water-closets that were cleaned every day, not smelly latrine-style holes like he had grown up using.

Willie thought he had died and gone to heaven when he discovered he could book a private, twenty-minute bath without sharing it with anyone. This was the kind of life he could get used to. He dreaded going back to a hard life and vowed to follow in Uncle Bill's footsteps to get an education so he could rise in the ranks.

His da and Uncle Pete were harder to impress. Although they took advantage of every comfort, they said things like, "Don't get used to it," and "Must be nice for the minted bastards who get to live like this." Tam, who spent the War in muddy trenches, took these things with an 'easy come, easy go' attitude.

Willie grabbed the book from his bunk and headed to the library, arriving before Agnes. He was saying to the steward, "D'yeh have the first book in the Tarzan series?" when Agnes entered with her siblings. Distracted, he barely heard the steward say that the first book was only available in the more fully stocked First Class library.

He tried to appear casual as he wandered toward the framed map of the world hanging on the wall, on which he located the British Isles. He reckoned they were more than halfway across the Atlantic, so he guessed that they might be south of Newfoundland by now.

Moving his attention to North America, he looked for Utah. All he knew was that it was in the western half of the country. To his dismay he saw that America was almost as wide as the Atlantic Ocean. It didn't look like they'd ever get there.

He grabbed a random book from a nearby shelf and sat in one of the upholstered chairs pretending to read, surreptitiously watching Agnes across the room where her younger sister whispered in her ear. Both girls turned and looked pointedly at Willie and giggled. He ducked his head back toward the book in his hands and finally noticed that he was holding a copy of *Little Women*. His ears burned red as a deep blush overtook him.

Agnes's mother entered the library and, as the door was open, Willie heard from outside the raucous voices of his father and uncle. "There he is, in the library, with his nose in another book! What's wrong wi' the lad?" Pete said, and Will replied, "At least he *can* read."

Willie sighed with resignation. Throughout his life, Helen had admonished her husband and brother-in-law to behave whenever any of her snooty Littlejohn kin were around. Willie had always taken the Garroch's side but today, for the first time, he understood his mother's perspective. They were embarrassing.

He got up and left the book on the chair to beat a hasty retreat before Will and Pete came in. He shot one last glance in Agnes's direction but saw, instead, her mother standing between them, glaring at him. Agnes poked her head around her mother's ample form and smiled at him, her dimples deepening and eyes twinkling. From one teenager to another, she conveyed her understanding: parents can certainly get in the way.

His heart skipped and he blushed again but, before darting out the door, he grinned shyly and bobbed his head in greeting. He stepped outside just in time to block the two men from entering.

"Here, let's get back to the cabin," Pete said. "We've a surprise for yeh." Willie led them away from the library and Pete opened his coat just enough to show Willie that he had a bottle of whisky stashed inside. "If yeh cannot drink in public, at least give yerself a snootful in private."

Willie looked to Will for confirmation and his father said, "Aye, lad, yeh made your point. This may be your last chance to enjoy some good Scottish whisky, so we're moving the celebration below decks."

"Cheers, Da," Willie said. "Where's Tam?"

"Och, aye," Pete said, "he's down in our cabin, writing another letter to Bertha. We'll go back to yers and let him be, for now."

Willie was about to complain about Uncle Pete's willingness to leave Tam alone yet continue to harass him, the younger nephew, but he was too grateful that Uncle Pete was including him. If it came at the price of too much ribbing, so be it.

∞

Announcements were made on November 15 to the passengers that the Cameronia would arrive in New York in two days, barring any unexpected weather conditions. It was then that the Garroch men decided to curtail their celebratory whisky intake until the evening hours because they had business to attend to.

Will said to his son, on the second-to-last morning as he shaved over their cabin's washbasin, not yet dressed for the day, "Did yeh read in yer wee book where we're to purchase our train tickets?"

Still in bed, luxuriating while he could, Willie reached to the top of his bunk where he had a stash of reading material and pulled out the ship's brochure. He flipped through until he found the information and read aloud,

"Railway timetables may be consulted on application to the Music-Room Steward."

Will dried his face and got dressed. "Wouf," he said as he pulled on his drawers, "these trousers are pure ripe. I wonder if I have time to get them back from the laundry before we get to New York."

"Yeh shoulda taken more baths, like I did," said Willie, "My clothes aren't half so boggin'."

"Better things to do, lad, better things to do," his father replied and then banged on the wall between the cabins. "Hey! Get out of bed!"

Tam's voice could be heard, faintly, through the wall, "Aye, we're up, give us a minute."

Willie muttered, "It'll take longer than that." Then he said, aloud, "Da, why do the Littlejohns think they're better than us? They're family and all."

Will sat on the cushioned bench to put on his shoes and said, "Near as I can reckon, it's because a lot of them could get educated and we couldn't, so some of them lift their noses at us. But yer Uncle Bill, he's a good sort. They're all good folk, just a wee bit snooty."

Willie said, "Uncle Buchan once told me their family's descended from gentry. That means I am too, even if you aren't. They oughta treat me better, any road."

"Och, don't talk pish," scoffed Will. "Mebbe, lifetimes ago, they may have been gentry but that's no matter now. We all work underground, like the common folk we are. Except your Uncle Bill, with his fancy desk job. But don't forget, lad, he started out helping his da pick out clinkers, just like you."

"How come you didn't get an education?" Willie asked.

"I couldn't," Will explained. "Yer mam has more brothers so their house had more earners than mine. Da died when me and Uncle Pete were still wee'uns, so Mam worked as a washerwoman and didn't have anyone but my older sister to bring in a wage. Auntie Maggie did what she could, but as soon as Uncle Pete and me were old enough, we went straight into the mines and haven't looked back. The Littlejohns had too many men to fit under one roof, so your granda sent Bill, the oldest son, out when he was your age to finish his schooling. He went to college in Edinburgh. Did yeh know that?"

"No, I didn't," said Willie. "All I know is he's a high mucky muck now." He was silent for a moment and then asked, "Da, d'yeh think I can go to college when we get to Utah? Can Jean go to nursing school?"

"I hope so, lad. It's the land of opportunity, right?" Will said. He stood and mussed Willie's hair, and said, "Come on, let's see about getting our train tickets. Then we'll be that much closer to finding out."

Tickets purchased, they spent their final night celebrating with the other passengers. While a string quartet played upstairs for First Class, the Second-Class passengers met in their lounge for a Scottish shindig. Various musicians, who met during the passage, banded together and offered up a lively concert.

There was much whoop-de-doo as the passengers danced to the strains of the fiddle, accordion, drums and bagpipes. Willie, after sneaking a couple wee drams for courage, asked Agnes, "Would yeh like to dance?" Her parents were busy with their own celebrating, so she hopped up from her seat and danced the night away with him.

Finally, too early, Will pulled him aside with Pete and Tam and said, "Och, lads, we shouldn't stay any later. They'll be giving us a doctor's exam before letting us off the boat and, if we don't pass, they'll ship us back to Scotland. I dunno about you, but I've come too far to turn back, now."

"Aye," said Pete, "I can't drink any more. I cannot believe I'm about to say this, but I've had my fill of whisky."

"Well, I didn't say *that*," Will chuckled, "but it's time to take our leave and get some sleep. It's a busy day tomorrow."

"I'll be right there," Willie said, "I want to say goodbye to Agnes. I'll meet up with youse."

"Be sure to give her a big smooch," Uncle Pete teased, "but don't keep your da awake, wanking all night. He needs his sleep."

Willie rolled his eyes and watched Will, Pete and Tam say their own cheery-byes to friends they had made during the journey. He rejoined Agnes and pulled her to the side, away from the crowd, where they could hear one another speak. He said, "I dunno if we'll ever see each other again. Where are youse ending up?"

Agnes said, glancing in her mother's direction to ensure they weren't being watched, "We're going to Detroit, where my older sister lives with her husband. Da's going to work at Henry Ford's factory with my brother-in-law."

"Och," said Willie, "nowhere near Utah. My uncle is the mine superintendent and he's given jobs to me and my kin. But I'm not gonna work in the mines forever. I'm goin' to college as soon as I can."

Agnes said, "I wish you and me were going to the same place. I don't have my sister's address, so you can't write to me."

"I don't have my new address yet, either," said Willie. "We'll just have to hope that someday our paths cross again."

Agnes glanced around to make sure the coast was clear and planted a kiss on Willie's cheek. He turned bright red and grinned. Then he, too, looked around before kissing her full on the mouth. Suddenly shy, though, he said, "I gotta go. Hope to see yeh again." He darted out of the room to join his father in their cabin where he would have great difficulty not keeping Will awake all night.

⚘

Willie lay awake most of the night, tossing and turning, listening to his father's snoring over the now familiar sounds of the droning engines and ocean waves slapping against the skin of the ship. The ship's bells, marking off the time in half hour increments, made the night crawl by. Willie fretted about whether he'd see Agnes again. Maybe he'd see her on deck in the morning to tell her to write to him in care of William Littlejohn at the Utah Fuel Company in Castle Gate until he had an address of his own.

His thoughts were a blend of excitement and anxiety. Departing from Scotland felt similarly anxious, but not quite as frightening. At least there the harbor agents were mostly Scottish, with a smattering of Englishman, and most of the passengers and crew on board were British. But the idea of New York and a new country ... the bigness of it filled his mind. Would the Statue of Liberty look like he expected? Would all go well at Ellis Island? Would they be turned away, like Da feared they might?

He had overheard other passengers talking about the medical exam for all passengers—if they didn't pass, they would either be sent back on the next ship home or quarantined at Ellis Island, possibly for months. This was why Will insisted they curtail heavy drinking and go to bed early. Rumors said the inspectors could diagnose a man in six seconds. All it took was watery, red eyes, with dark circles under them and pale skin, to be pulled out of line and sent to the infirmary or back home.

Even if they did pass the inspection, Willie fretted, how would they find the train station? What if they were late and missed it? They had same-day tickets because the men agreed they would rather not stay overnight and spend money on a hotel. The Cameronia was arriving ahead of schedule,

45

and they wanted to get to Utah as fast as possible so they could start earning money right away. The whole plan felt very rushed.

Finally, the ship's bells rang 7:00 AM and Willie could lie in bed no longer. The sun was coming up and he wanted to watch it rise for the last time on board the ship, where the sunrises and sunsets were usually spectacular.

Up on deck, he headed east to the stern and watched the sun cresting the horizon, glittering on the choppy waves. He couldn't gaze too long, though, because the reflection on the water was blinding. He headed toward the bow of the ship to see what lay on the western horizon. There he saw land to the north. After almost two weeks there it was … America.

Tears filled his eyes, obscuring his vision, and he blinked them away. He leaned on the ship's rail and inhaled the ocean air, which still held the night's chill. His body felt so alive, so … on the edge of something unnamable … he couldn't put it into words. He wanted to burst with laughter and excitement and feel like this forever.

Willie had the ship's brochure folded in his pocket so he flipped through the pages looking for its list of landmarks. He perused the list and surmised that he might be looking at either Nantucket or Fire Island. He had no way of knowing which, but at least this meant the Cameronia was close to New York City.

His reverie was disrupted by a group of people further up the bow bursting into cheers and applause. He hurried forward to learn the cause and saw that the western horizon was now showing land, as well. "It's New York!" one of the passengers cried and tears again flooded Willie's eyes.

"Oh my God," gasped another passenger and a few began openly weeping.

"Where's the Statue of Liberty?" asked a girl of about twelve years of age.

"We'll not see it until we turn into the harbor, and we're still a ways out," replied a gruff old man. "I've made this trip before, so I know what I'm talkin' about."

Willie had enough time to run below decks and gather his family. They wouldn't want to miss this. He hurried to the cabin and was glad to see Will was dressed and putting on his boots. Willie pounded on the wall between the cabins and called to Pete and Tam, "Come up top. We're gonna see the Statue soon!"

Will banged on the wall as well, and shouted, "Lads, get yer britches on! Let's go …"

Pete was at the door before Will could finish, Tam behind him. "Alright," he said, "this is what we've been waitin' for …"

They hurried up the stairs and Willie led them to the bow where he had been standing with the small group of people, but the crowd was thicker now. They had to jostle to get to the railing for a good view.

"Aw, there's no statue …" said Pete, leaning both elbows on the rail and getting ready to taunt his young nephew, when the same old man who spoke earlier said, "Give yerself peace, lad. It's up ahead, between those two land masses. See 'em? We'll go between them and turn up into the harbor, and that's where yeh'll see yer statue."

More people gathered and pushed closer together until the deck was packed with passengers, all waiting to catch a glimpse of the famous landmark. Everyone wanted to see it with their own eyes, after the trials and tribulations, the scrimping and saving, and the long journey they had undergone just to get to this very moment.

So much more slowly than Willie could have imagined possible, the ship finally entered the harbor, with a hard swing to the north toward Manhattan Island. A middle-aged woman, bundled in a plaid woolen scarf, shrieked and pointed, "Jings! Is that it? Up ahead?"

Too small to be sure, up ahead to the left, there did appear to be a bright green blip on the horizon. Until he could be sure it was the Statue, Willie focused on their other surroundings; New York City to the right and New Jersey to the left, and the tugboats in the water below, guiding them forward. Glasgow may have been an impressive city—the biggest he'd ever seen—but it had nothing on New York.

He saw now that the green blip was, indeed, the Statue of Liberty. "There it is," a nearby woman cried, "that's the Statue, there!" She pointed frantically and, as others caught sight of it, raucous cheers broke out. Willie grinned so hard his eyes teared up.

He quickly wiped the tears away and was gratified to see that his kin were in the same condition. Everyone on deck, he saw as he glanced around, was beaming and bawling as the ship moved forward and soon passed the iconic landmark.

"There's Ellis Island," he heard someone say as the ship passed a stately brick building on an island of its own, just north of the statue. "Isn't that where we're going?"

"No," said someone else, "we'll be docking up ahead ..."

He turned, as they passed, to watch the Statue as long as he could to burn the memory into his brain. The ship docked at the pier and most of the nearby passengers broke off into a scurrying mass, heading back to their cabins to prepare to disembark.

"Don't we go to Ellis Island?" Willie asked Will, or anyone else who might be listening.

The same know-it-all Scotsman was still nearby, in no rush to fight the crowds. He said, "No, lad, that's for Third Class, down in steerage. They'll take them by barge back to Ellis Island and interview First and Second-Class passengers here on the ship. They figger, if we can afford to pay this much for passage, we'll not be a burden on American society and that's what they're lookin' for."

Willie sighed with relief and said, "Thank yeh, sir, yeh've been most helpful," He turned to follow his family, who were heading back to their cabins.

"Happy to be of service, lad," the man called out, behind him, "Best of luck to yeh in America!"

Willie bumped into his father entering the cabin and Will said, "Hold on, what's yer rush? It'll be a while before they let us off."

"Why? We're that close..." Willie sputtered.

"Lad, we still have to wait in line to be interviewed," Will said. "Gather yer things and we'll go up, but no hurry."

Willie checked the cabin to make sure he didn't leave anything behind. He hadn't brought much but what he did bring was necessary. Once they gathered their belongings, father and son left their cabin for the last time, along with Pete and Tam.

They stood in line on deck and gossiped and marveled with other passengers over being in New York City at last. Finally, it was Will's turn and a kindly older officer jotted down Will's answers in a large ledger book, asking questions like those posed in Scotland, with a few more thrown in. Will answered for both him and Willie.

"Do you have tickets to your final destination?" the officer asked, in a flat, nasal voice. Willie grinned, marveling at his American accent.

"Aye, we both do." Will replied.

"Are you in possession of fifty dollars, and if less, how much?"

"Aye, in British pounds," Will said.

The agent looked up from his ledger and said, "You'll want to exchange them for American dollars. There's an agent down on the pier who'll give you a fair rate. Be careful about flashing your money around. There's pickpockets all over the docks, looking to skin someone fresh off the boat."

"Aye, thank yeh," said Will. "I'll do that."

"Are you going to join a relative or friend, and if so, what is their complete address?" he asked, his hand poised ready to jot down Will's answers.

"My brother-in-law, his uncle," Will said, gesturing at Willie, "His name's William Littlejohn, and I don't have an address, but he's in Castle Gate, Utah."

"Ah, coal miners, I'll bet," the agent said, writing Will's response. "We get a lot of miners coming through on their way west to Utah. How long are you planning to stay in the United States?"

"For good, if all goes well," said Will.

"Well, good luck to you." The agent moved on to the next question, "Are you a polygamist?"

Will, startled by the unexpected query, shook his head and said, "No."

"Anarchist?"

"No."

"Ever in prison," the agent continued, "or alms house, or institution for care and treatment of the insane, or supported by charity? If so, which?"

Will was again taken aback and said, "No, neither of us, for any of those things."

"No offense, mister," the agent looked up at Will and said, "I've got to ask everyone these questions. You're not the only one coming through the golden gates of opportunity, you know." He looked Will and Willie up and down and said, "you both look healthy enough, not crippled," and jotted down his findings. "Height?"

"I'm five foot eight, and the lad here is five foot six," Will said.

The agent peered at Will's face and said, as he wrote, "Fresh complexion, fair hair, grey eyes." He then looked at Willie and said, "Same," as he scribbled. "Any identifying marks?"

"None," said Will.

"Alright, thank you, that's it. Next!" The agent waved them aside and moved on to Pete, asking him the same questions, and then Tam as well.

Willie grabbed his dad's arm and whispered, "That's it? I thought it would be harder."

"Aye," said Will, "it is harder if you don't give the right answers or if yeh're sick. We gave him nothing to pause over."

They waited until Pete and Tam were finished processing and the four of them disembarked down the gangplank. Willie had heard of people kissing the ground when they arrived and he considered doing so, just for laughs, but opted out when he saw the weather-beaten boards of the pier, splattered with seagull crap and tobacco spit. Instead, he simply stopped for a moment and took it all in.

At the ripe old age of sixteen, Willie Garroch's feet were touching America.

CHAPTER 6

November 17-20, 1921
New York City to Castle Gate, Utah

It was a one mile walk to Pennsylvania Station and the roads were icy, the sidewalks deep with fresh snow that shopkeepers were shoveling out. Horse-drawn carriages and automobiles struggled to move forward, and pedestrians had to take great care to not slip and fall. Even so, the men had been cooped up almost two weeks with another three days confinement on the train in their near future. Harsh weather was a way of life in Scotland and their duffel bags were light compared to their mining tools, so they chose to walk to the train station instead of waiting their turn to catch one of the limited cabs.

"I'll be glad to finally get to Utah," said Willie, with a wistful sigh. "I feel like I've been traveling my whole life."

"Just a few more days, lad," said Will. "As long as the train runs on time, we'll be there by Sunday. I'm hoping Bill puts us to work on Monday."

Tam pointed toward a book shop/newsstand a few doors up and said, "I'm gonna get something to read for the trip."

"Aye," said Pete, "me and all."

They stomped the snow off their pants and boots at the door and squeezed into the crowded shop, which was crammed from floor to ceiling with shelves laden with books. Will picked up the *New York Times* from the display up front, his first American newspaper, while Willie asked the clerk, "D'yeh have the first book in the Tarzan series?"

The clerk said, in what Willie was beginning to recognize as an American accent, "I suppose I do, young man, somewhere. It's a few years old, but let's see what we can find." He led Willie to the fiction section and found it, saying "Here you are, son, Tarzan of the Apes." He handed over a 400-page, hard-bound book with a maroon cover, the title embossed in gold print.

It looked expensive. Willie hadn't expected it to be quite so thick. "How much?" he asked.

"That's a dollar thirty," said the clerk.

Willie didn't know what that meant in British sterling, but it was probably a lot. When Will exchanged their combined pounds for dollars at the pier, he handed Willie two dollars spending cash to last the rest of the trip. This book would cost more than half that.

"I only have two dollars to live on for a few days," Willie said.

"Let's see if I have a used copy," the clerk said. He went back to the shelf and found a slightly more tattered edition. "Sixty-five cents, half price."

Three days on a train, with people whose company was wearing on him, loomed in his future so he bought the book. Will paid two cents for his newspaper and Pete paid fifteen cents for a copy of *Western Story Magazine*.

Tam was still browsing, mentally debating whether to purchase the *Saturday Evening Post*, when the clerk said, "I have next week's Thanksgiving issue, if you'd prefer. It's too soon to put them out, but they're here if you want." He reached behind the counter and lifted a packet of magazines still tied in a bundle. "Same price," he said, using a sharp knife to cut the string. "Only five cents."

"Cannot say no to that," said Tam, paying the man.

"Say, where are you gentlemen from?" the clerk asked. "Is that a Scottish accent I hear?"

"Aye," said Pete, grinning, waving his copy of *Western Story Magazine*, "we're heading out west to make our fortune."

"Well, good luck to you," said the clerk. "Welcome to America."

Willie bobbed his head in a nod. "Thank yeh, sir," he said.

"Enjoy your book, son," the clerk said as they left the shop to trudge through the snow toward the depot.

Inside Penn Station, they goggled at the vastness of the soaring arched ceilings and glittering skylight windows. "Holy God," Will said, "it's like a cathedral in here!"

"Aye," Tam said. "Perfect place to ask the Lord to help us find our way to the train."

Now seasoned travelers, they didn't need divine assistance. They knew to look for the signs for departure timetables and track numbers that matched their tickets. In no time they were where they needed to be, waiting to board.

They shared a wooden bench while they waited and Pete said, showing his magazine to the others, "Look, there's a cowboy on the cover. D'yeh think they'll really look like that, out west?"

Tam glanced at Pete's magazine and said, "Bertha and me saw Buffalo Bill's Wild West show back home. That's how they were dressed."

Willie saw now, with fresh eyes, how they looked in their faded black trousers, peaked caps and well-worn black wool coats, compared to Americans in their clean, more fashionable garb. "We look like immigrants," he said.

"Naw, we look like workingmen," said Will. "We're miners, going to a mining town. They'll not judge our clothes there. Besides, we *are* immigrants. No shame in that. Immigrants built this country. Mind the Statue of Liberty? Gimme yer tired, yer poor ..."

"... yer filthy miners ..." Willie said.

Tam held up his *Saturday Evening Post* and said to Pete, "Yeh think yer magazine has a strange cover, look at this'n!" He showed them the darkly cartoonish cover drawing of a baby boy wearing an apron, a chef's hat and an executioner's mask, with a butcher's cleaver in his hand, standing over the word *Thanksgiving*.

"I keep hearing that word, 'Thanksgiving,'" said Pete. "What d'yeh s'pose that is?"

An American, overhearing their conversation, answered, "It's a national holiday next week, where everyone eats too much and thanks God for their good fortune."

"What's that got to do with a spooky wee'un waving a butcher's knife?" Pete asked him, pointing at Tam's magazine.

The man glanced at the cover and said, "It's the Saturday Evening Post. What do you expect?"

The subject closed, Will consulted his pocket watch. Right on time, the conductor called, "All aboard!" They had plenty of time to settle into their Pullman sleeper car which, during the day, was set up to accommodate seated passengers with the sleeper berths folded up and out of the way.

All four were travel-weary so they retreated into their reading materials as the train rolled out of New York, only glancing up occasionally to watch the scenery. It was dark by Philadelphia and the porters set up the car for the night, folding the seats down into single beds and pulling upper bunks down from where they were stowed in the wall above. The men slept hard as the train rocked them with its steady rhythm of rolling wheels cachunking their way across Pennsylvania. When Willie awoke, they were in Pittsburgh.

While they were in the dining car for breakfast, the porters folded up their sleeping berths and they spent the day the same way, not talking much, reading and staring out the window. Eventually too tired to read, Willie gazed out the window and watched as the Pennsylvania mountains, streaked black with coal, lessened to flatland as they headed toward Ohio. The wheels' clackity-clacking hypnotized him into a stupor and, before he knew it, they were at Cleveland's Union Depot just off the shore of Lake Erie. Because they had half an hour before the train left the station, many passengers got off to stretch their legs. Willie and his kin joined them.

While Will sent a telegram updating Bill Littlejohn on their expected arrival, Willie wandered the cavernous terminal and found a train-route map on the wall. The states were labeled and the map was sprinkled with names of cities he'd never heard of. An arrow with the words "You are Here" pointed to the southern coast of Lake Erie. He followed their route west, with his finger, until he found Utah almost all the way across the map.

His heart fell. If they had only traveled as far as Cleveland—and Utah was still that much further—the distance on the map looked interminable. The longer they traveled, the grumpier Will got, the quieter Tam got, and the more annoying Uncle Pete's wisecracks got. Willie was bored with them and they were bored with him. He was even bored with himself.

Willie decided then to sleep as much of the trip away as possible. It was easy to doze, with the train's rocking. '*That's how wee Ella must feel in Mam's arms*,' he mused. With that thought, pain jabbed his chest with homesickness that even the excitement of his American adventure couldn't cut through.

The conductor called the passengers to board and Willie grabbed a printed timetable to help him track their progress. Just like on the Cameronia with the ship's pamphlet, knowing where he was along the way helped pass the time.

All four men spent the trip snoozing and snoring, only waking when it was time to eat or when they just couldn't sleep any longer. Unlike onboard ship, there wasn't the luxury of space to walk about, and their rear ends were sore from sitting. Although the train moved at a fair clip, it seemed to crawl across the country: South Bend, Chicago, the Quad Cities, Des Moines, Omaha—the land was flat and brown, the skies gray and dull with winter. Willie could barely take the monotony and trepidation grew: is this what America's like?

Finally, after the train pulled out of Denver on Saturday afternoon, the clouds broke and the sun-dazzled scenery became more interesting. Willie watched out the window as the Rocky Mountains whizzed by, their snow-capped peaks towering overhead. The ground was dusted with sparkling snow, as were the tall pine trees that dotted the landscape. Night fell too soon, now that there was something to look at.

When they woke Sunday morning, the train was almost to Green River, Utah. The soaring Rockies had been replaced by equally beautiful scenery of another kind. On either side of the train, they saw high sandstone bluffs and craggy rock formations, so Pete pulled out his magazine to find photos he had seen of the Grand Canyon. "Is this where we are?" he asked one of the porters.

"Naw sir," the porter said, "that's further south, in Arizona. It's bigger and deeper than what you see here. Utah's got some beautiful scenery, too, you'll see."

They got off the westbound train in Green River to transfer to another, shorter train taking them north. Willie found another printed timetable for the remainder of the trip, and Will said, "Come on lads," as he hoisted his bag onto the train, "we're almost there."

"Gads," huffed Pete, "Not a moment too soon. I'm ready to drop."

"Me an' all," said Tam. "I'm half dead."

Willie's head buzzed with weariness and the sky grew cloudier. Onward and northward, the train chugged along, the landscape becoming more rugged with brown and yellow sandstone bluffs to the east and a snow-covered mountain range off in the distance to the west.

A woman passenger said to her child, "We're only an hour from Helper. We'll be home soon, so please stop fidgeting."

According to Willie's timetable, Helper was the last town before Castle Gate. His heart leapt with excitement and, at that moment, the sun burst through the clouds to cast glorious fingers of celestial light onto the tall eastern bluffs, highlighting and shadowing their beige and golden craggy folds. '*This*,' he thought, divinely grateful to be almost there, '*must be what Americans mean when they talk about Thanksgiving.*'

During a brief stop in Price, the seat of Carbon County, a few passengers got on dressed in their Sunday best. Shortly after, the train made its next stop in Helper, a sturdy little town—the main street running parallel to the train tracks—which looked remarkably like one of the Old West settlements from Uncle Pete's cowboy magazine, with the western-style wooden buildings, many of them saloons, among squat, brick hotels and shops.

In Helper, families of various nationalities and skin tones boarded the train. Pete nudged Tam and said, "D'yeh hear that? There's just as many languages here as in New York City."

Willie nodded, agreeing. After days of only hearing the American accent and seeing mostly Caucasians—except the brown-skinned people in the big cities and the Pullman porters, who were the first Negroes Willie had ever interacted with—he was shocked to see so many Greeks and Italians, and even a few Orientals.

Even though they looked and sounded different, Willie recognized them as mining families by the men's black-stained hands and fingernails. His own hands, as clean as he'd seem them in years—after three weeks out of the mine—would soon look like that again.

It was just a handful of miles before they arrived in Castle Gate, within a canyon that was tightly surrounded on both sides by majestic, reddish-brown sandstone cliffs and tree-studded hills. The businesses and stores of the town center were crammed in together, there being little space to fit them into the narrow canyon. The train chugged to a halt at the tiny Castle Gate station, the smallest they had seen since they left Coalburn. They were finally here.

Will pointed out the window and said, "I think that's Bill, there." On the platform stood a dignified man in his late forties, dressed in an expensive topcoat and fedora. Although Willie hadn't seen his uncle since he was a toddler, he recognized a family resemblance. This man looked like a taller version of Uncle Geordie. In fact, this man looked like Willie himself might at that age.

They grabbed their bags and got off the train, their legs wobbly from sitting so long. Will led them toward the man in the hat and greeted him with a hearty hello, "Bill! We made it!"

Bill Littlejohn smiled genially and stepped forward, taking Will's hand and shaking it between both of his own. Bill said, "It's good to see you, Will. I'm glad you're here." His Scottish brogue had been tempered by his many years in America. He asked, "And who have you got with you?"

Willie stood with Pete and Tam silently as Will made the introductions, starting with Tam, who was closest. "This here's my nephew, Tam," he said.

Tam shook Bill's hand and said, "Pleasure t'meet yeh. Thomas Trow's the name. Uncle Wull here is my mam's brother."

"Nice to meet you, Tam," Bill said, "and is this Pete? Lord, I haven't seen you since you were picking clinkers!"

"Aye," Pete said, giving Bill's hand a firm and friendly shake, "it's been many a year. I was chums with yer wee brothers, John and Geordie. Are they still here?"

"Yes, they are, for now," Bill said. "Geordie's planning a trip home soon to visit the relatives. You're crisscrossing paths." Bill finally turned to Willie and said, clapping him on the shoulders, "Is this my sister's boy? Lad, you've grown! You were just a wee'un when I last saw you!"

"Aye," said Willie, "Mam told me I was just two when you came to America."

"That's right, it was 1907. So that makes you what, sixteen?" Bill asked.

"Sixteen, aye," said Willie.

Bill stopped short and said, "Where are my manners? You lads must be done in. Come on, let's get you checked in at the boarding house. I'll drive you to my house after we get your bags dropped off."

Uncle Bill had an automobile—Willie caught Tam's eye and raised his eyebrows as if to say, "Isn't that something?" Tam gave him a similar look, right back.

Bill continued, "Elsie, my future wife, is preparing a fine meal. I told her not to go to such a fuss, being so busy planning the wedding and all, on top of Thanksgiving, but she wouldn't hear of it. She's excited to meet her new relatives from the old country."

They followed Bill past the nearby tipple, a structure any coal miner would recognize anywhere in the world, no matter the local construction style. Every coal mine needed to load their product into railway hopper cars to ship the coal elsewhere. Mine cars filled with coal were taken, by tramrail, above the railroad track into the tipple where the coal was tipped into the hopper cars, below.

The Castle Gate tipple was a long, narrow wooden building far above their heads with openings on either end, a tramrail going in one side and out the other, with the words CASTLE GATE COAL painted in letters large enough to cover the entire face of the building. One side of the tramrail ran overhead toward a cement-structured entrance in the side of the sandstone bluff on the west side of the tight canyon. The other side of the rail crossed the canyon and snaked around one of the eastern hills, disappearing around the curve to the south.

Bill pointed at the opening in the western bluff and said, "That's the entrance to Mine Number One, where you'll be working." He pointed toward a large bluff at the south end of the canyon they had just entered and said, "Mine Number Three is inside that hill and Mine Number Two is in the next canyon over, about a mile or so from here. See where the tramrail rounds that bend? It ends at Number Two."

"Can we start tomorrow?" Will asked.

"Certainly," said Bill, "if you have tools. I didn't see you carrying any off the train."

"Naw, we didn't bring them with us," said Pete, "we wanted to travel light, so we sold them off, but we have the money to replace them, sure."

"Tomorrow morning," Bill said, pointing to a nearby, two-story brick building with a stairway to the second floor built onto the side of the structure, "go to the mining office, up those stairs, to check in and then downstairs to the company store and get what you need. One of the boys'll make sure you get started. They know you're coming."

They approached the bathhouse near the tipple and Bill brought them inside a long room lined on both sides with wooden benches. He pointed toward the ceiling and said, "See those hooks? Lower them by rope, here," he showed them which ropes to pull to lower the hooks and continued, "Before your shift, you'll hang your everyday clothes on them and change into your work clothes, and switch back into them after your shift and shower. The showers are right through there," he said, pointing to a doorway to the shower room on the other side of one of the bench-lined walls.

Bill then took them to the boarding house in the town center where they rented two rooms, each with two beds. Their landlady, Mrs. Mueller, was a German miner's widow who took in boarders to survive since her husband was killed years ago in a mining accident.

When Bill asked if she could recommend a washerwoman, she said "I do ze vashing, ja. Give zem to me, and you'll have fresh britches in ze morning."

The foursome was so tired that they longed to crawl into their new beds, but there was a home-cooked meal waiting at Bill's house. They stowed their gear in their rooms and, before heading to Bill's car, Will pulled them aside and whispered, "Don't tell Helen we're staying in a Boche home. It'll tear her heart out to know we're under the same roof as Germans, after what they done to wee Buchan."

"But Da," Willie protested, "Mrs. Mueller didn't do it …"

Will interrupted, "I know, lad, but yeh know yer mam. Buchan was like her own wee'un, and she holds a grudge, don't she?"

They piled into Bill's shiny new Buick sedan, roomy enough to hold five passengers. Even though Willie and the others were wearing their Sunday best, he couldn't help noticing the contrast between the expensive vehicle's upholstery and the shabby clothes they wore.

Bill wove his way through town, indicating points of interest. "Over there is the hospital and the amusement hall, the post office, the meat market … you'll learn where everything is, soon enough." He drove north past a grouping of a couple dozen small, brown saltbox houses and said, "Your families will probably end up living in one of these, as houses become available." He pointed up the road ahead of them and said, "See that? That's what the town is named after."

His passengers looked out the front window. About a mile to the north, previously blocked from view by a curve in the road and a bluff jutting out from the western wall of the canyon, stood a pair of massive sandstone spires that looked like castle abutments—one on each side of the road—which seemed to guard the entrance into the valley. "That's the mouth of Price Canyon," Bill said, "and when you're driving into or out of the canyon, as you follow the curve of the road it looks like a castle gate that opens and closes."

Willie's mouth hung open with awe. Finally, he said, "It's beautiful!"

"Aye, it's bonnie, indeed," said Tam.

"It is stunning, isn't it?" said Bill. "Between the scenery, the community, and the exceptional quality of Castle Gate coal, it's a fine place to live and work."

He turned onto a side road that took them across the railroad tracks and a bridge over a small creek into a small grouping of larger houses built on the slope of the western sandstone bluff. He pulled into the driveway of the largest one and said, "Here we are. And that's my Elsie, at the door."

Bill's fiancée Elsie Tanner—at least twenty years younger than Bill's forty-six—stood at the front door, waving cheerfully. Her brown hair was neatly coiffed, and she wore a tidy Sunday dress protected by a spotless apron. "Hello, boys," she called out in a Midwestern twang, "Y'all are just in time. Dinner's about ready. I hope y'all like pot roast." She stepped back and held the door open for the men to enter.

"Sunday roast, aye!" said Will, "Thank yeh kindly, Elsie, that'll do just fine."

They stepped into a small foyer which led into a tastefully decorated dining room to the right and a posh parlor to the left, the soft glow of electric lamps illuminating the rooms. In the parlor sat two men, a woman and a passel of children, varying in ages between two and sixteen. The adults were seated on the sofa and cushioned chairs, near the front windows, while the kids played board games on the floor at the back of the room.

The house was warm and cozy, filled with heavenly aromas from the kitchen. The newcomers' stomachs growled in unison, but the sounds were drowned out by one of the men calling out, "There they are!" He stood and Willie saw that the man—handsome with piercing eyes, thick, unruly brown hair and a bushy moustache—was slightly shorter than he was. In fact, he was wee Uncle Pete's height.

Pete said, in disbelief, "John? Is that you?"

"It is, laddie. And you remember wee Geordie, don't you?" John Littlejohn gestured toward his younger brother George, who also stood.

Geordie was closer to Helen's height, only a few inches over five feet tall. His square jaw was cleanshaven and his dark hair was thinner and shorter than John's, receded like Bill's. Willie saw in his two balding uncles his own future, recognizing their hairlines as similar to his own. Most Garrochs generally had thick hair—in fact, Pete had an outrageous cowlick shooting upward out of his forehead—but Willie saw now that he inherited the Littlejohn forehead.

"Aye! Lads, it's great to see youse," said Pete.

The men took turns embracing until Bill cleared his throat for attention, and John and Geordie turned to the others at the door. Bill said, "You all remember Will, Helen's husband. This is their son, Willie, and nephew, Tam."

"Of course," Geordie said, embracing Will and his nephew. His eyes sparkled with mirth, which matched his impish stature. "I haven't seen youse in far too long. And wee Wullie, yeh're taller than yer Uncle Geordie, lad! How do, Tam?" He shook Tam's hand, turned back to Will and asked, "How's life in Coalburn?"

"Well, with the strike and all, times are tough," said Will, "Helen and the girls send their love."

"Aw, I miss them," said Geordie, "and you've got a new wee lassie now! I'll be heading home to visit soon …"

"Come in, sit, sit, sit," interrupted Bill. "What can I get everyone to drink? We've got beer, wine, whisky …"

Pete and Will looked at one another with wide eyes. "But," said Pete, "Prohibition …"

"Pfft," Bill said, waving his hand dismissively. "This is coal country. The authorities know that many won't stay if they can't have their hooch. As long as no one makes any trouble, they look the other way."

"I'll have a pint," said Will, "maybe a wee dram after supper." Pete and Tam requested the same and Willie looked at Will for permission. "Aye, and give the lad a pint as well."

Bill went to the kitchen to bartend, and Elsie directed them to sit in the cozy parlor. It was a tight squeeze, but everyone found a seat. Willie ended up on an ottoman at the back edge of the room near his young cousins.

"Kids, come meet your relatives from Scotland," said John. The children, who had been ignoring the goings on, gathered around. "First," John said to the newcomers, indicating the slender, brown-haired woman seated next to him, "this is my wife, Bethia. And these are our kids: Claude, twins Laurence and Clarence, Betty, Mary and wee Max."

Everyone nodded 'hello' and John continued, "These are Bill's kids: Alex, twins Jimmy and Jeanie, and wee Rob. And these are Elsie's children, Naida and Malcolm."

"Och," said Will, "looks like twins run in the Littlejohn line!"

"Aye, they do," said John.

Elsie interrupted and said, "Bethia, would you help me in the kitchen please? We're ready to serve and, Jeanie, I need you to set the table." John's wife and Bill's daughter joined Elsie as Bill returned to the parlor with the beverages.

Bill's oldest son Alex tapped his cousin's shoulder and whispered to Willie, so none of the adults would hear, "Your dad lets you drink beer?"

"Aye," said Willie, puzzled, "yeh cannot have a pint with yer meals?"

"No, of course not. I'm only sixteen, and you look to be the same." said Alex.

"Sixteen, aye. Not even after yeh come home from the mine?" Willie asked.

"I don't work in the mine," Alex scoffed. "I'm still in high school."

Willie didn't know how to respond to his American cousin. Alex's clothes were clean and pressed while Willie's Sunday duds, the cleanest he had available, exuded a whiff of stale body odor every time he moved. Alex's hair was neatly trimmed and combed, and Willie's looked like he'd been traveling for three weeks.

For the first time since arriving at his uncle's house, Willie paid attention to his surroundings. Uncle Bill's furniture was as nice as the furnishings on the Cameronia. The dining table was polished wood, with two leaves added to make it longer to fit extra guests. Most of the flooring was covered with manufactured rugs, unlike the braided rugs at home. The electric bulbs were decoratively shaded, and the fireplace had a delicately woven metal mesh in front of the fire, to prevent sparks from flying onto the nearby rug and ashes from dirtying the marble hearth. From what he could see of the tiled kitchen, it was furnished with modern appliances like an icebox and an enameled stove. He wouldn't be surprised to learn that the house had an indoor water closet.

"Come and eat, everyone," said Elsie, from the dining room, "You young'uns will eat in the kitchen, and Max and Malcolm can sit on our laps, Bethia. You big kids grab a plate and balance it on your knees in the parlor, if you promise to be careful. All you grownups, please join us in the dining room."

She retreated to the kitchen where a hired woman dished out the plates. Elsie and Bethia delivered dishes stacked high with food to the men, who seated themselves at the dining room table. To Willie's dismay, he saw that all eight chairs were taken—in this household he wasn't one of the adults.

Bill's older kids—Alex and the twins, Jimmy and Jeanie—each took a loaded dish and silverware into the parlor. Willie stood at the kitchen doorway and watched, awkward and unsure. The hired woman handed him cutlery and a plate piled with food, and said, "Go on now. You enjoy your supper."

He took his plate to join his cousins and sat again on the ottoman, careful not to spill a drop. He put his beer glass on the nearby coffee table and twelve-year-old Jeanie cried, "Use a coaster!"

Willie flushed red with embarrassment. "What's a coaster?" he asked.

Jeanie giggled and said, "One of these, silly." She picked up a square tile from a stack in the center of the table and slid it under his glass. "It protects the wood from water rings. How come you get to drink beer?"

Alex answered for him, "He works in the mine so he gets to drink beer."

Willie was unsure but he had a suspicion that he was being made fun of.

"What's your name again?" asked Jimmy.

"Wullie," he said. "My da's named Wull, we're both Wulliam, so they call me Wullie to tell us apart."

Jimmy said, "Your 'da'?"

Jeanie burst into laughter and asked, "Your name's Wooly? Like a sheep?"

Willie looked longingly toward the adults and wondered if there was another chair somewhere that he could pull up to their table. The kitchen table was overflowing with little kids and there didn't seem to be another chair available.

"That isn't what I said. I said," he enunciated very clearly, "my name's Wullie."

"You said it again!" giggled Jeanie, "Wooly!"

"Leave him alone, Jeanie," said Alex, "he's from the old country and that's how they talk."

"Well," argued Jeanie, "our 'da' is named William, too, and he's from the old country, too, but no one calls him Wooly."

"Dad's been here a long time …" Alex began but Willie stopped listening. He ignored his cousins and choked down his Sunday roast, wondering why there was no Yorkshire pudding served on the side. Unable to enjoy the feast, he listened to the adults chatting. Uncle Geordie was talking about his upcoming trip back to Scotland and Willie wished, with all his heart, that he could go with him.

His uncles had lost a bit of their Scottish brogues, Uncle Bill sounding the most American, although he still rolled his Rs a bit. Uncle Geordie sounded like home, but not as strongly as the newcomers fresh off the boat. Uncle John's brogue was somewhere in the middle. All of them, the more booze they took in, became more Scottish by the minute. Geordie's accent became even more pronounced when he was storytelling and now he was regaling Pete, Will and Tam with the tale of how the company store was once robbed by the famous outlaw Butch Cassidy, who got away with thousands of dollars in the miners' payroll.

Finished with his meal, Willie slammed down the last of his beer and took his plate into the kitchen. He handed it to the hired woman, thanked her and moved into Will's line of sight in the dining room. "Da," he said, "I'm going for a walk. I need to stretch my legs."

"Don't go far," teased Uncle Geordie, "we can't have yeh getting eaten by a bobcat your first night here!"

The adults laughed and, blushing again, Willie took his leave. He strolled down the driveway and up the road toward town, paying careful attention to where he had come from so he'd know where to run in case Uncle Geordie wasn't kidding about bobcats. He didn't know his way to the boarding house so he couldn't walk there, as much as he wanted to.

From here, up on the side of the hill, he saw the town below. It was just past dark and many of the windows were illuminated by hearth fires and oil lanterns. Even surrounded by alien landscape, he was reminded of home and he felt a jab of longing, which he quickly suppressed—it hurt too badly. This was his home now and he had better get used to it.

As he walked further toward town, the sandstone bluff to his left was no longer an obstacle to a view of the Castle Gate rocks. The moon was almost full, the air brisk and the sky crystal clear, the way that only a crisp, wintery night can be. The beauty of the moment took his breath away. He might just like it here in Utah.

If only he didn't miss Scotland—and his family left behind—so much.

CHAPTER 7

January, 1922
Overtoun, Scotland to
Southampton, England and beyond

Jeanie dipped her finger into the small cup of whisky before rubbing eleven-month-old Ella's gums to ease the pain of a cutting tooth. Ella had been fussy all day and refused to nap, no matter how Jeanie tried to soothe her. It didn't help that the house was packed to the rafters with wee cousins. Even with four of Uncle Jim and Aunt Agnes' ten children not yet returned from school, and the two oldest at work, that left four home in the two-room miners' row house, with three of them under the age of four. Despite the older girls' efforts to get the babies to sleep, they couldn't keep wee Billy and Janet quiet enough.

With a mixture of relief and dismay, Jeanie heard Uncle Geordie outside shouting hello to a neighbor, arriving with the clip-clop of a horse-drawn wagon. Although Geordie's room-filling presence would ensure Ella wouldn't nap, it also meant Helen was home from their trip into town and Jeanie could pass the baby to her.

"I've got it hen, don't worry yerself," Geordie teased his sister, his voice carrying inside amid muffled sounds of wood banging on wood.

Helen replied, annoyed, "Och, yeh're no bigger than me. Yeh cannot get it down yerself!"

At the sound of her mother's voice Ella perked up, eyes wide. "Who's 'at?" Jeanie asked, matching the baby's excitement, "Is that Mammy? Let's go see!"

Jeanie joined her curious cousins at the window to see what her mother and uncle were arguing about. They were a comical sight, a tiny twosome, as they tried to not slip on the ice while wrestling a huge steamer trunk down from the hired wagon. They each grabbed a handle on either side and trudged through the snow into the house.

Nellie, who had been pretending to be busy in the other room to avoid helping Jeanie with the baby, came out now that Helen was home. "Who's that for?" she asked, eyeing the trunk.

"It's for you, my wee lassie," said Uncle Geordie, "we're gonna stuff yeh inside and stow yeh away to save money on yer ticket." He wandered to the hearth to warm his hands at the fire, keeping a tight poker face, so Nellie looked to Helen for confirmation that he was pulling her leg.

"Don't listen to him, hen," Helen said, sweeping out the snow they tracked in, "we wouldn't have room for yeh in it anyways, with everything we need to pack."

Ella cried out and reached for her mam, who was taking too long. "Aw, poor wee babe," Helen said, as she took off her coat, "are yeh having a rough time of it?" She took Ella from Jeanie and said, "Give us the whisky, hen."

"Is she teething or was big sissy pinching the baby?" Geordie teased.

Jeanie handed her the cup and Helen, too, wet her finger and rubbed Ella's gums. "My finger's like ice. That ought to feel good on wee missie's toofers. Where's Auntie Agnes?" she asked.

"Down the shop," replied Jeanie.

"Hey, give us some of that whisky," said Geordie, "I don't have a toothache, but I could use a wee dram before I head back to town, sure, after trottin' yer mam all over."

"Och, hush yerself," said Helen, bouncing Ella who was chewing vigorously on Helen's finger. "Chasin' after that trunk was yer idea."

"Aye, and a good yin, too," said Geordie. "Yeh'll thank me later, hen. This trunk'll fit under yer berth and won't take up any room in yer cabin. I'm not moanin' about the trunk, it's everything else yeh bought today. Och," he moaned to Jeanie and Nellie, "yer mam had me running every which way!"

Helen ignored him and said to Nellie, "Open it, hen."

"Here," said Uncle Geordie, "turn it up on its side. Go ahead, look inside."

Nellie turned the trunk upright and, when she opened it, saw it was lined with powder blue fabric and had, installed into one side, a set of drawers. On the other side was space to hang clothing from the built-in wooden hangers. She opened the top drawer first and found a quart-sized glass jar labeled *Mellin's Food*, alongside two glass baby bottles with rubber nipples fitted onto their narrow necks. Stuffed between the glass items, to prevent them from knocking together, were several soft, new cloth diapers.

"Och," Helen said, "I spent more than I liked, but these will make the trip easier. Look in the next drawer down, pet," she told Nellie, "I treated our wee lass to some of those newfangled rubber pants, though I daresay they're a bigger treat for us. Our clothes will stay dry, and we'll not smell like pish around the other passengers."

Jeanie pushed past Nellie to get to the rubber pants. These were a luxury she had to see! She loved Ella, but she was fed up with her clothing getting wet when she held the baby. The oiled-wool nappy covers Ella wore only worked so well.

"Let's put these to use. She's due for a change, anyhow," Jeanie said, grabbing the protesting baby from Helen, along with a new diaper and a pair of rubber pants. She laid a hollering Ella down on the set-in bed that she shared with Nellie and two younger cousins, at least until Thursday when they would leave by train to meet their ship in the south of England, departing for America on Friday.

"What's this, Mam?" Nellie asked, holding up the jar of Mellin's Food.

"It's like powdered milk, made specially for babies. Yeh add it to water," Helen said, "so yer wee sister can have a bottle while we're traveling."

"How clever!" said Nellie. "Did yeh buy anything for me?"

"Aye," said Helen, "look in the next drawer down. I got youse each a book that yeh can swap when yeh're done." Nellie tore into the drawer to discover a copy each of *Alice in Wonderland* and *Oliver Twist*.

"Thank yeh, Mam," said Jeanie, still battling the squirming baby, "I'll take *Oliver Twist*, if it's all the same to you, Nell. I've been wanting to read that."

"Fine with me," said Nellie, "I'd rather read *Alice in Wonderland* anyway. Who wants to read about a passel of wretched orphans?"

"You will," taunted Jean, "once yeh're in the middle of the Atlantic with naught else to do ..."

"Well, that works out lovely for everyone, don't it?" interrupted Geordie. "Besides, there's a library on the ship where youse can borrow more books. Now about that whisky …"

"Och, away with yeh," said Helen, slapping her brother's arm as she brushed past him in the crowded room. "I'll get yeh a wee dram, sure, if yeh'll get out the way while I start supper. Jeanie, hen, did Aunt Agnes say what we're making for tea tonight?"

"Naw, she didn't," Jeanie replied.

"I'll peel some tatties. We'll be sure to have them," said Helen. "And it's time for youse two to get packing. Yer suitcases are under the bed. Leave out enough clothes until Thursday. We've only one more full day here."

"When are Bertha and Aunt Jessie coming, Mam?" asked Nellie.

"I've told yeh," Helen sighed, weary of repeating herself. She poured whisky into a glass and handed it to Geordie, after taking a wee sip for herself and ignoring him as he spluttered, "Hey! Get yer own!"

Helen explained, "Jessie and Bertha have to wait until Pete and Tam save up enough. We're only going so soon because I have generous brothers and two earners in America."

"Aye," said Geordie, "and they all make lousy bachelors. They need some women to do their cooking and cleaning, and that's where youse come in."

"I'm glad we're finally going," Nellie said, fingering the pages of her new book. "It's awfully crowded in this house and," she whispered, pretending she didn't want her cousins to hear, "I don't think they like us bein' here."

"I don't like yeh here," piped up fifteen-year-old Maggie, who had been arguing with Nellie all afternoon. She stuck out her tongue and Nellie returned the favor.

"Hush, the both of youse," Helen said, "They like us fine, it's just too many folks under one roof. We'll be just as glad to go as they'll be glad to see us leave."

"I cannot wait to see our new house," sighed Nellie. "Thanks for helping us, Uncle Geordie."

"Yeh're welcome, lassie," said Geordie, sipping his whisky. "It's not just me, it's yer uncles John and Bill, who pitched in, and yer Uncle Jim, lettin' youse stop here. Yer da and brother put in the lion's share, we just helped it happen faster. And just you wait 'til you see Castle Gate! It doesn't look like Scotland, but a mining town's a mining town, with everything yeh need. There's an amusement hall, a library, a good school ..."

"How about moving pictures?" Nellie interrupted.

"Aye, they show films in the Amusement Hall on Mondays," said Geordie.

"Girls," Helen interrupted, lifting a cast-iron skillet she was packing into the trunk, "get cracking or I'll brain youse with this. Whatever isn't packed when it's time to go is getting left behind."

"Fine!" Nellie huffed and fetched her suitcase from under the bed. Jeanie finished changing Ella and put her down to stand on the floor with her hands on the mattress. The baby wobbled for a moment and sat down, hard, on the cold floor.

"No more whisky for wee Ella," Geordie laughed. "She's steamin'! And what about you, hen?" Geordie said to Helen, "How are you on packing? Mind, Bill's wife is setting youse up with everything yeh'll need, so yeh'll not need to take that skillet."

"Aye, Wull said, but just a few words in a telegram," said Helen "How do I know she'll have a good, seasoned pan like this'un?"

"She's a dentist's widow, sure. He died during the great influenza epidemic," said Geordie. "He didn't pinch his pennies so, when she married Bill, she had a double household and even her old stuff is better than anything you've got here, so save yerself room and leave that behind."

"New linens!" gushed Jeanie. "She wasn't married to a miner, so they'll not be stained grey like ours. I cannot wait."

Helen put the skillet down and picked up her Brown Betty teapot. "I'll leave the pan with Agnes, but I'm taking my teapot," she said. "It was a wedding gift, and yeh'll not talk me out of it."

"Aye," agreed Geordie. "They don't sell those Brown Betties in the States. I brought one back with me last time I was here."

"Yeh'll not talk me out of this, either" she said, retrieving a small object wrapped in muslin from her bunk. Helen opened the folds of fabric to reveal a round bronze plaque, almost five inches across. Embossed on the front was the image of Britannia, the female warrior icon, and in small, raised block letters, the name *Buchan Littlejohn*. After running her fingers gently over Buchan's name, she handed the plaque to Geordie.

"Aw, that's beautiful, hen. Poor wee Buchan." He bowed his head for a moment and also ran his fingers over his dead brother's name. "Where'd yeh get it?" Geordie asked.

"They were commissioned by King George to commemorate soldiers who died in the War," Helen said. "Buchan was living with us when he enlisted, so he put me down as next of kin." She tucked the plaque into the trunk and passed Geordie the bottle of whisky after pouring a wee dram for herself. It was going to be a long night, and she could use a little cheer as she packed up their life and left so much behind.

ᛒᛪ

The train to southern England took all day. They boarded before the sun rose at 8:30 and arrived in Southampton hours after the 4:30 sunset—a slow and miserable journey, filled with starts and stops and passengers getting on and off. As the locomotive trundled south from snowy Scotland, a combination of cold air from the continent and moist air from the Atlantic covered southern England in a thick cloak of fog, so they didn't even have changing scenery to distract them.

They took turns entertaining cranky Ella for the sake of other passengers, some of whom glared at Helen whenever the baby fussed too much. One older English woman, across the aisle, even tsked and said to her husband loudly enough to be overheard, "Our children were better behaved than that!"

The tension was thick and Nellie continually moaned that they wouldn't be stopping in London to sightsee. Jeanie finally snapped, "Shut yer geggie! Yeh're not the only one who doesn't get what they want. Da says we're to go, so we're goin'."

Nellie was about to snipe back when she noticed that Helen—who was turned toward the window with Ella curled up, finally sleeping, in her lap—was quietly sobbing. Mam had been telling her how wonderful it would be, moving to America. What did Helen know that she wasn't telling?

It was too much to consider, so Nellie pushed it out of her head. She had always wanted to see the famous clock tower in London so she whined, "I'll never be back in England again, so I'll never get to see Big Ben!"

"Never say never, hen," said Geordie, preempting Jeanie who was opening her mouth to tear into Nellie, "yeh're still young. I've come back from the States, time and time again, and you can, too. Besides, it's too foggy today to see anything."

Nellie harrumphed and opened her book, trying to ignore that her mother was surreptitiously wiping tears away as she stared out the window into the pea soup cloud that enveloped the train.

They changed trains at Waterloo Station in London and had about an hour before boarding the boat train to Southampton. Geordie nudged Nellie and said, "Let's see if we're close enough to spot Big Ben from here."

Judging by the map on the wall near the ticket counter, the famous clock was only a half a mile away. They stepped outside into the cold damp and Geordie said, "Och, it's too foggy to see from here." He checked his pocket watch and said, "We have time, if we walk fast."

Jeanie's face brightened and she stepped forward to join them before Helen cried, "Yeh're mad! I'm not missing the train because youse are out larking about."

"It's just around the corner and we'll run," said Geordie. "Besides, we can't lose track of time starin' at a giant clock, can we? Jeanie, are yeh comin'?"

Jeanie sighed and said, "I reckon not. I don't want to miss the train."

"Your loss," he said, and took Nellie's hand. "Come on, hen, let's go see yer Big Ben."

"Button yer coat and tighten yer scarf, missie," Helen called as they took off, "If yeh're not back in time, we're leaving without youse. I mean it! We'll leave without youse!"

"Wheesht," he shouted back. "We'll not miss the train!"

Uncle and niece darted into the mist, holding hands. Geordie said, "Keep yer eyes peeled for Westminster Bridge Road. We'll turn right there and Big Ben is just across the river."

"Thank you, Uncle Geordie!" Nellie gushed, breathless and exhilarated, "Mam would never let me go if you weren't with me." She peered into the fog as they reached the intersection of a busy thoroughfare. "I've never seen so many motorcars!" she marveled. "There," she said, pointing, "Westminster Bridge. Let's go!"

They hurried west across the massive bridge—the largest she'd ever seen—and over the River Thames. "Look!" said Geordie, pointing ahead at the misty silhouette of towers and spires, "That building is the Palace of Westminster, and that's Big Ben to the right."

Nellie squealed, "I see it! Hurry!" She darted forward, dragging him with her.

At the far end of the bridge they crossed the road and stood across the street from the enormous clock tower, now directly in front of them. The locals hurried past, going about their business, ignoring the gaping tourists. "Take it in quick, lassie," said Geordie. "Look at the time. It's five 'til the hour. We better hurry back before yer mam goes into conniptions."

Glancing over her shoulder to get in a last few glimpses, burning the sight into her memory, Nellie followed her uncle back toward Waterloo Station. As they turned the corner, the bells of the giant clock began tolling the Westminster Melody and chiming out the hour, loudly enough to be heard blocks away.

Helen stood right where they left her, impatiently tapping her foot, with a miserable Jeanie holding wailing Ella at her side. "Are yeh done larkin' about?" Helen demanded. "Our train leaves in ten minutes!"

"Calm yerself, hen," Geordie said, taking on the tone of an older brother. "I wouldn't do anything to endanger our trip. Yeh'll have to cheer up if we're goin' to enjoy it at all."

"Och, yeh wouldn't understand," Helen said. "I'll say no more. No one wants to hear what I have to say anyway."

Geordie sighed. Helen was in one of her moods. "Well, I guess it's up to me to keep everyone happy, eh, girls?" He chucked Jeanie under the chin until she smiled. "Here," he said, taking sobbing Ella off her hands, "I'll carry this'un for a while. Isn't that right, wee Ella? Come to yer favorite uncle."

With ruffled feathers smoothed, they boarded the train with plenty of time and continued south through London, and a few hours later disembarked at Southampton. They stopped for their evening tea at a nearby chippy and took a cab to the port. Although the ship wouldn't leave port until morning, the captain was allowing early passengers to board and check in to their cabins.

The SS Lapland was almost fifteen years old. It had been called into commission as a troop ship during the Great War and in 1917 was damaged by a mine. It was a sturdy ship, but its luxury had faded and it smelled of musty, stale cigar and cigarette smoke, which had been absorbed into the wood paneling and carpets over years. "Don't worry, hen," Geordie said, noticing Helen's wrinkled nose, "yeh'll get used to it and not even notice it before long."

Nellie remarked, as they found their way to their cabins, "Da wrote that his ship was brand new. How are we stuck on such an old one?"

"Try to be grateful, hen, and see it as an adventure," Helen groaned, lugging Ella who was whimpering and chewing her fingers. The baby had ceased trying to hold on and was now limp, dead-weight. They trudged down the narrow hallway crowded with other passengers looking for their cabins, passing restroom doors marked *Ladies* and *Gentlemen*. Helen said, "Just think … we'll have electricity and indoor plumbing and won't have to heat our water to bathe."

"Aye," agreed Jeanie, "nor will we have to cook or clean."

"Aye," sighed Helen. "Nor will we have to cook or clean."

"Here's my cabin," said Geordie. He looked at Helen's ticket for her cabin number and peered down the hall. He pointed and said, "Yeh're a few doors down, on the other side."

Helen said, "Thanks, Geordie, I'm done in. Come on, girls, let's get this'un into a dry nappy."

Jeanie opened the door to their cabin which held a bunk for each of them—two on each side of the room—with a sink and mirror built into the far wall, between them.

"I want one of the top bunks," Nellie said.

"Yeh'll get no argument from me, lass," Helen replied.

"Och, I cannot wait to get into my goonie," Jeanie sighed, dropping her suitcase and changing into her flannel nightgown. "I'll take the other top bunk, Mam, so's you don't have to share with Ella."

Helen said, "I reckon she'll curl up with me tonight, so choose whichever yeh like."

"Well," Jeanie replied, "if it's all the same to you, I'll sleep down here. But if yeh want me to go up top, I will."

"Thank yeh, hen," Helen smiled wearily, "yeh're a comfort." She laid Ella down to change her diaper and the cranky baby began howling. Helen said, "Jeanie, pop down the hall to ask Uncle Geordie for the whisky. I forgot."

"I'm already undressed for bed," Jeanie protested.

"Put yer coat on over yer goonie. Nobody'll see," said Helen and, while Jeanie went across the hall, Helen changed Ella and mixed a bottle of formula. She then washed the day's nappies in the sink and hung them over the edge of the bowl to dry.

Jeanie came back with a half-empty bottle and said, "Uncle Geordie said to keep this one, he's got another. He said, 'Enjoy it while yeh can, there'll be none on the train ride to Utah.'"

73

Helen's face fell and she moaned, "Och, I forgot. We cannot have it even for medicinal purposes. What are we to do for the rest of the trip?"

"I guess we ought to enjoy it while we can," said Jeanie, ever practical, climbing into her bunk.

Helen soaked the baby's gums in whisky, adding a bit more than was needed for teething pain to help the wee girl sleep after such a stressful day. She gave Ella the bottle, rocking her back and forth, and recited an old nursery rhyme as the baby drifted off, "Deedle deedle dumpling, my son John, went to bed with his stockings on. One shoe off and one shoe on, deedle deedle dumpling, my son John." She lay Ella down on the inside of the bunk and curled up next to her, not yet changed out of her traveling clothes, and fell instantly to sleep.

ᔥᔦ

In the morning the rest of the passengers boarded, causing a logjam of people in the hallways. Helen, Geordie and the girls pushed their way upstream to get to the dining hall for breakfast, which was light fare— porridge, toast and tea—as full breakfast service was not offered until they were out to sea. Helen and Jeanie relished being waited on but Geordie, a man who was used to being served by womenfolk, didn't give it much notice. He did, however, dandle Ella on his knee so Helen could eat in peace.

Nellie was more interested in people watching and looking for cute boys than in appreciating her circumstances. One large group, sitting in the dining hall, caught her eye. "Listen, Mam, Uncle Geordie …" she pointed toward the boisterous cluster of twenty or so young adults, chattering in languages she had never heard before. "Where d'yeh think they're from?" Nellie asked.

Geordie listened and said, "I dunno for certain, but it sounds like Russian and French to me."

The group laughed and gossiped among themselves, clearly aware that all eyes were on them and enjoying the attention. "Who d'yeh think they are?" Nellie asked.

"Mind yer own business," Helen said, "and eat yer breakfast."

"I'll see what I can find out," Geordie whispered and winked.

Just before noon the Lapland steamed out of port, beginning its trek across the icy Atlantic. "Did yeh know, hens," Geordie said to Jeanie and

Helen, as they took in the brisk air at the rail, watching England disappear on the horizon, "that this ship brought the survivors of the Titanic's crew back to England?"

"Och!" cried Helen, "How d'yeh bring that up now? Don't let's talk about the Titanic until we're all the way across. Good job Nell's in the loo and didn't hear that!"

Geordie laughed and agreed, "Aye, yeh're right. I wasn't thinking."

Nellie returned then, bubbling with excitement. "I found out who they are!" she gushed, "that group of Russians, they're actors and dancers on their way to New York to perform on Broadway!"

"How d'yeh know that?" Jeanie demanded.

"I asked the steward," said Nellie, "and he told me they just finished performing in London."

"Well," said Helen, "stay away from them. Theater people cannot be trusted."

Geordie raised an eyebrow and said, "Now hen, they looked like perfectly fine folk t'me."

"Aye, they would," Helen snorted, "to you, who's ne'er been married and are free to trot about the globe. But to plain folk like us, we'll just stay away, thank yeh very much."

"But Mam," Nellie protested, "did yeh feel that way when I was in the school play?"

"Course not," said Helen, "I'm talkin' about traveling vagabonds, those gypsy sorts. What kind of woman would travel in a pack like that, and what sort of man would want a woman who did?"

Geordie kept silent, which didn't escape her notice. Helen huffed, "Tell me, George Littlejohn, what's yer esteemed opinion?"

"Now hen," Geordie said, "It takes all sorts to make the world go 'round, and theater people make it a wee bit less dull. And those folks are on their way to Broadway from the London stage, so I wouldn't call them vagabonds. They're as close to respectable as yeh can get in the theater. Besides," he winked, "the sort of man who might be part of a theater troupe might just leave the women alone."

"I don't want to know how you know that!" Helen said, raising her hands in exasperation, "I've much bigger things to worry about."

"Aye, that's right," said Geordie, "you go on about yer worrying, while I take these lassies on a tour around this great big ship."

"Och, that would be lovely," said Helen. "I'm sorry for being such a pain. I just need a wee rest. I'm that worn out."

"Calm yerself," soothed her brother, "yeh've had a hard time, taking care of these wee'uns on yer own." Jeanie frowned at her uncle, who lumped her in as a 'wee'un'. Geordie continued, "Go on back to yer cabin. I'll take care of the girls."

Helen watched Geordie lead her daughters away, holding on to one of Ella's hands while Jeanie took the other, encouraging the baby to walk. Nellie bounced alongside them, saying, "Let's find the actors again. I want to see them up close."

Geordie replied in a loud stage whisper, "Hush now, yeh don't want Missus Grumblebritches to hear yeh." He turned back to Helen and winked then spoke to Nell in a normal voice, "Did yeh know that Douglas Fairbanks and Mary Pickford took their honeymoon on this here ship?"

Helen headed back to her cabin where she rinsed her face in the glorious stream of warm tap water. She unpinned her hair and lay down on her bunk. The silence of no children was deafening, until she noticed the sounds of the ship's engines churning and the ocean waves slapping the side of the ship. Between the slight rocking and the white noise, Helen drifted in and out of a light doze where thoughts tumbled through her mind unfettered.

Geordie was right, she thought, it had been hard these past months without Will and Willie, but their absence was also a relief. While she looked forward to hugging their necks, she felt a tightness in her chest thinking about returning to the hard work that came with their presence.

She chuckled as she recalled Geordie teasing her with that old nickname from years ago, Missus Grumblebritches. She hadn't heard that since they all lived together in their father's house. Back then, that name would send her into a fury, which was—of course—her older brothers' intention (the younger siblings didn't dare or she'd skelp them). But today, she wasn't a fourteen-year-old girl forced by tragic circumstances into a life of servitude. No wonder she grumbled! Wouldn't anyone in her britches?

Thinking about those days made her stomach hurt, so she tried to think of Utah … what would it be like? Her gut cramped again, so she changed her thoughts, again. No more worrying. It wasn't helping. This would be a lovely time for a wee nap, so she focused on the sounds of the engines, the waves, and the occasional muffled conversation out in the hallway as fellow passengers walked past her cabin door. Before she knew it, she was sound asleep.

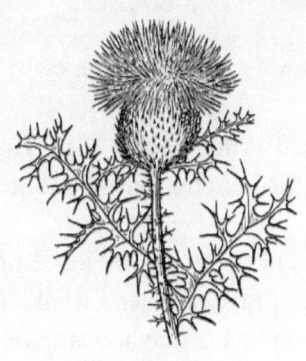

CHAPTER 8

January, 1922
Castle Gate, Utah

"That'll be the last of it," said Will, easing his end of the davenport onto the wooden floor of the front room in their new, four-room home. He and Pete pushed the finely upholstered sofa up against the longest wall. "This house will have the missus speechless," said Will, "something yeh'll not often see."

"I'd buy a ticket," said Pete.

"And that view!" Will said, gesturing out front to the Castle Gate rock formation, which could barely be seen from the center of town due to the curving of the road, but was framed perfectly by their parlor window. "Wait'll she sees that, right out her front window."

Willie set a box of dishes on the dining table in the adjoining kitchen and added, "Aye, Mam's not often dumbstruck, but she'll not know what to say about all this."

"She'll no doubt start with 'We cannot accept this, it's charity!'" Will said, looking around the parlor with its furnishings, gifted to the family by Bill Littlejohn's new wife, Elsie. "I've ne'er hit yer mam, son, but I might give 'er a clout if she tries to give this back."

Tam came in along with a young man named Tommy Hilton, both carrying small boxes of the men's personal belongings. They planned to stay at the boarding house until Helen's arrival, so they left behind their shaving kits and clothes for the week. Today, they were filling the house with its new furnishings on their only day off between now and then.

Tam retrieved a Mason jar of moonshine out of a box and said, "Who's for a wee dram?"

"I wouldn't pass up a drink," said Will. The men adjourned to the kitchen where Will unpacked enough glasses to go around and poured one for each.

"Just a quick'un," said Tommy, in his Yorkshire accent, "Lois is expectin' me, and she doesn't like it when I drink on a Sunday."

"Aye," said Willie, "but this is fine hooch. Even a kiss from Lois cannot warm yeh like a sip of this."

Tommy laughed, "Can it, heck! You've obviously never kissed Lois. Besides, I didn't say I'm not havin' a belt, but too many and I won't be collecting any kisses."

"Cheers, Tommy," said Will, raising his glass and looking around their new home with appreciation, "thanks for yer help today. Let's drink, shall we, to our new digs? May we have many happy years here."

The men raised their glasses in toast and slammed back the clear liquid that burned smoothly down their gullets before jolting them all a-shudder as the booze hit their systems.

"Hoo," Pete exhaled with a dragon's breath, "that's good."

"Aye," said Will, "let's have another."

"Ta, but I have to go," said Tommy. "Lois awaits. See you tomorrow, Willie."

"Aye, tomorrow," Willie said to his friend, a young man who had come with his parents to Castle Gate from Manchester, England just a month before the Garroch men. Tommy Hilton, at 19, was only a few years older than Willie and the boys started work at Mine #1 within weeks of one another.

All the men were in proper awe of Mine #1, with its 25-foot-thick coal seam and ceilings so high they could barely be seen in the dim light of the carbide lanterns attached to the miners' caps. They were used to the deep shaft mines in England and Scotland, where it wasn't unheard of for a man to lose a hand or an arm, if he got too close to the edge of the lift on the way down to the low-ceilinged, wet tunnels, to pick their way forward either crouching or on their knees. Mine #1 was spacious and decked out with modern equipment, including electric lights along the main track. The Castle Gate mines were of the highest industry safety standards.

From the boarding house in the center of town, Willie and his kin only had to walk to the nearby tipple and cross the rail bridge across the narrow canyon to the mine entrance. Their new home was further north than the boarding house, yet still close enough that they couldn't complain.

Will plopped down on the davenport with a satisfied sigh. He sipped his whisky, taking his time instead of slamming it like the first glass, and said, "Aye, life is good. The women will be here soon, I like brattice work, we have a fine home … we are blessed."

"Aye," said Pete, seating himself in the wooden rocking chair, "Those tall ceilings are a treat. Just give me freedom to move unencumbered, taking a full swing with my pick, and I'm a happy man."

Tam joined Will at the other end of the sofa and said, "Och, how'd we ever work in them tunnels only a few feet high, down on all fours? If God's will for us is back-breaking work, at least He relieved some of the pain."

Willie brought a chair in from the dining table and sat on it reversed, his legs straddling its back. He sipped his whisky, relishing the slow burn.

"Sometimes," Will said, gazing upwards, thoughtful, "I snuff out my lantern and stand alone in that inky blackness, listening to the mine's creaks and pops. It's pitch black and, far away, I can hear the chatter of the fellas in the tunnels, with the sound of pickaxes chipping away at the rock face. I just stand there in the dark, feeling the pulse of the mine and the flow of the air currents. It's like we're inside a living, breathing creature down there."

"Aye," said Willie, "I've done the same."

"Every miner has," said Tam, "but I don't know that they'd agree we're inside a creature. Surrounded by Tommyknockers, mebbe ..."

"I miss going to Helper," sighed Pete, out of the blue. "What d'yeh say we head down for one more night on the town before yer women arrive? It may be our last chance."

After they first arrived from Scotland, they spent many an evening hopping the short-ride train to Helper and carousing in the saloons there, once they learned that Prohibition was mostly ignored in Carbon County. The main street of Helper—a modern-day version of the Wild West—was lined with saloons and brothels, and law enforcement turned a blind eye, as long as everyone behaved.

Will grinned and said, "I have to be mindful, now that folks know I'm related to the big boss. I don't need any stories gettin' back to Helen."

"Aw" Pete argued, "there's no shame in enjoying drinks and poker. And can we help it the best whisky in town is served in a saloon where the prettiest painted ladies socialize?"

"Not another word," said Will, holding up his hand to silence his brother. "What I don't know, I don't have to lie to yer wives about."

Pete and Tam were adults and the upstairs girls had been friendly to them, between Tam's good looks and Pete's boisterous humor, but Will minded his own business. There was nothing wrong with making sociable conversation with a pretty girl. If anything beyond that occurred, he didn't know so he couldn't tell. He kept a careful watch on Willie, for Helen's sake, but he wouldn't begrudge the boy a cuddle with a friendly lass. He earned the money to pay for it by the sweat of his brow, like a grown man.

They hadn't been to Helper since they made friends in Castle Gate. As they learned where to buy homemade whisky, and that convivial poker was played at the Knights of Pythias Hall with others from the UK, there was no need. It quickly felt like home, with cheery old-country banter in familiar accents. They were included in Christmas and New Year's Eve celebrations and, after the holidays, to parties and potluck dinners with other families from the British Isles who couldn't wait to welcome the Garroch and Trow wives and children. The Scottish transplants even celebrated Burns Night, the annual January feast to commemorate the birth of their national bard, Robert Burns.

"Aye," sighed Will, taking another sip, "Helper was a good time, but I'm homesick for Helen's cooking. Mrs. Mueller's German food may provide fuel to burn, but it isn't like home."

"Are yeh sure Aunt Helen won't mind us staying here with youse?" Tam asked.

Will scoffed, "What, d'yeh think she'd make yeh pay for a boarding house when youse can save up faster for yer wives by staying here? We have four rooms, twice as many as any of us had back home."

Pete said, "Aye, but still, it's an imposition ..."

"It's settled," Will said, "the wee'uns will have the second bedroom, and youse two can put down a pallet here in the parlor. Yeh'll be closer to the fire than any of us, which'll make up for the hard floor. I daresay, she'd be put out if yeh didn't stay with us, in all this space."

Helen would be elated, Will knew, when she saw their new digs. They had spent their marriage crammed into two-room 'but 'n' ben' miners row housing, sharing a privy with their neighbors. Here, they had two bedrooms and their own outhouse, in their own backyard. Elsie had given them a wooden-cabinet chamber pot, so they could sit to do their business indoors at night instead of squatting and aiming at a bowl on the floor.

Will got up and wandered to the back door in the kitchen. He looked out the window into his new yard, which had a garden set up by the previous tenants, so the work of plotting and fencing it from rabbits was already done.

He turned toward the others and laughed, "I cannot wait to see Helen's face when she sees the things Elsie's given over. Look at this!" he said, gesturing at the upholstered parlor furniture, polished dining table with matching chairs and sideboard, dishes and pots and pans, linens, and more. "There's everything Helen would ever want, and more."

He gazed out the window again, letting the voices of the others fade, and wondered where in their travels Helen and the girls would be. Probably still a day out from New York. He hadn't received any telegrams from Geordie and he told himself, '*No news is good news.*'

He knocked back the rest of his whisky and took one last look around his new house before saying, "That's that, lads. Let's go get some supper. I'm about starved, even if it is knockwurst and sauerkraut on the menu."

CHAPTER 9

January, 1922
Somewhere in the Atlantic

"Aw, Mammy, I wish I had something nicer to wear," sighed Nellie. She gazed at her reflection in the window of the doorway into the salon, turning this way and that, trying to see a full view of herself in her best dress.

Helen rolled her eyes at Geordie. Nellie had been moaning all afternoon about what she was going to wear and had liked the dress just fine while they were in the cabin.

"Yeh look fine, hen," Uncle Geordie assured her. He threw his arm around her shoulders and pulled her in close for a kiss on the top of her head. "I'd say yeh're my favorite wee lassie, but the others'd get jealous. Besides, we're not here to look at you, we're here to watch a show, aren't we?"

Nellie brightened up and gushed, "Aye! How lucky are we? Let's get in and get good seats!" She opened the door and rushed her family inside, hurrying ahead to find four seats together, as close to the makeshift stage area as possible.

The crew of the SS Lapland had done a fine job rearranging the seating in the salon, a cavernous room usually used for socializing, into a performance place where the mysterious French and Russian theater performers—the cast of the Broadway revue *La Chauve-Souris,* or *The Bat,* as one of them had translated—had agreed to present a couple of numbers from their upcoming show, including a complex dance sequence called *Parade of The Wooden Soldiers.*

Their original sailing to the United States from Liverpool had been cancelled, and the delay and extra travel to reach Southampton for their departure was wearing on them. Many demonstrated that, in the absence of their esteemed director, Nikita Balieff—who did not accompany them on this journey—while "The Bat" was away, the mice would play, and the ship's captain had suggested that either they offer a performance, or risk reprimand for their rather free-wheeling behavior in the ship's drinking establishment.

It hadn't taken much persuading to get them to agree. Stage folk thrive best in front of an audience and, although the cast had enjoyed some down time for the first week of the journey across the ocean, most had become bored and restless and craved the adulation of an adoring crowd.

They happily arranged to put together a makeshift performance, albeit without their costumes which were packed away in numerous trunks below deck. The cast members—men and women alike—donned their flashiest clothing and waited in a "backstage" area where the ship's salon crew stored the table linens and serving-ware, while the passengers took their seats.

Nellie gestured wildly at her family to hurry to where she was standing at the middle aisle of the third row of seats, where she had found four chairs together. She was having a difficult time remembering her manners while trying to keep others who were just as interested in finding close seats from taking them. "Nae danger, lass," said the elderly gentleman sitting on the aisle with his wife, "we'll not let anyone in here but you and yer family."

"Thank yeh, sir," Nellie said, relieved, yet still waving Helen and the others to hurry because empty seats were becoming scarce. It would soon become standing room only. After they finally pushed their way through the crowd and squeezed past the older couple to their seats, Nellie squealed with delight. This was the most exciting thing that had ever happened to her, a live performance by actual singers and dancers who were bound for Broadway!

Nellie craned her neck to look around the room, to see what she could see. Her fellow passengers were all dressed in their finest clothes just like her own family but, even so, none were so overdressed that she should feel embarrassed by her own clothing. Helen had been correct that her dress was fine for the occasion, although Nellie would never admit that aloud.

She nudged Uncle Geordie, who sat between her and Helen, and asked, "Why d'yeh think they left so much room up there?" gesturing toward the front of the salon where the performance area was seemingly much larger than necessary, "They could've fit more chairs so we wouldn't be so crowded."

"I don't know, do I, hen?" Geordie said. "We'll find out, soon enough."

Finally, one of the performers entered the salon and seated himself at the piano. He turned toward the crowd and said, in broken English, "We're without our orchestra so I, your humble pianist, will be the star of the show." This brought about jeers from a grouping of other male performers, six of them, who now spilled into the room, one of them shouting comically, "We'll see about that!"

The six men stood before their audience for a moment, waiting for the laughter to die down and finally one of them began to speak, in an accent far too Russian to be understood by the mostly English and Scottish audience, but Geordie was able to pick up a few words and whisper them to those nearby, "He just said something about the Russian revolution and the Black Hussars ... those are soldiers ... and just now, he said something about lobsters."

Nellie gave him a wild-eyed look and began to ask, "What ..." but Geordie cut her off. "I don't know, do I, lass? I'm just telling yeh what I heard. Now listen ..."

The performers then launched into a rendition of a folksong with Russian lyrics that no one understood. The basso profundo lead was beautifully accompanied by the piano and the male chorus and, while Nellie appreciated the men's talent and the grace with which they sang, she was mildly disappointed as this style of music just didn't appeal to her adolescent sensibilities. Around her, however, most of the adults in the audience watched with rapt attention so she did the same, in an effort to appear grown.

Once the men were finally finished singing, they left the stage area to great applause and a grouping of several women replaced them, all dressed in their finest clothes made of satin fabrics in colors brighter than Nellie—or any of her family, for that matter—had ever seen.

After the applause for the men had died down, one of the women stepped forward and said, in a French accent which was slightly easier to understand, "And now, we will share a number which many of you will enjoy, *O sing to me the auld Scotch sangs*."

The pianist started them off with a glissando, after which they sang in soprano tones:

"O sing to me the auld Scotch sangs,
I' the braid Scottish tongue.
The sangs my faither loved to hear,
The sangs my mither sung,
When she sat beside my cradle,
Or croon'd me on her knee.
And I wadna sleep, she sang sae sweet,
The auld Scotch sangs to me.
I'll bless the Scottish tongue that sings
The auld Scotch sangs to me..."

The singers continued through all its verses and, after it was over, it was easy to tell which of the passengers were Scottish, as they applauded the loudest and many wiped tears from their eyes as homesickness overcame them. The reality of never seeing home again weighed on many a heart, including Helen's. She bounced Ella on her knee especially vigorously to distract anyone from seeing the pain, which she felt would be obvious, on her face.

Jeanie leaned over to Uncle Geordie and said, "I've never heard that song before, have you?"

"Aye, but not for a long while," Geordie replied. "Now hold yer wheesht, they're about to start up again." He gestured toward the stage where a group of about twenty cast members were gathering in formation. It was now apparent why so much space had been allowed for the staging: the cast needed every inch of it to stand in one long line, from side to side, across the room.

"You'll have to imagine … you can use your imaginations, no?" teased another French cast member, a man this time, "…that we're all in costume, dressed as wooden toy soldiers, with bright red uniforms and tall, fluffy white hats … and that we're all in a beautiful, grand Broadway theater, with room for the entire cast, instead of just a handful of us, and a full orchestra instead of just … him …" he gestured toward the piano player, who responded by plunking his hands discordantly across the keys.

The audience laughed and the pianist launched into a sprightly song, a marching tune. To the delight of the watching crowd, the cast performed a seemingly impossible series of in-line marches of incredible precision, this way and that, creating two lines, then four, then forming a star which rotated with exact movements, as soldiers would after drilling for months under a strict commanding officer.

Finally, after several minutes of dazzling the audience with their complicated maneuvers, the cast formed one long line again, across the stage the way they began, all but one turned to face stage left. At the front of the line stood one lone 'soldier' who pantomimed holding up a gun and shooting the soldier in front of him square in the chest, with no reaction from the soldier who was shot. The shooter stepped forward and mimed taking a deep breath, blowing a huge gust toward that first soldier.

Slowly, oh so slowly, the first soldier fell backward into the waiting arms of the soldier behind him, who fell oh so slowly into the arms of the soldier behind him, impossibly slowly, on and on, as the pianist played a slow, declining glissando. It seemed to take forever for the line of soldiers to collapse, one into the next, until finally momentum carried them backward into a full crash onto the floor, where a large cushion had been placed to break the fall of the final soldier.

The crowd broke into applause, and the 'soldiers' sat up and turned in unison to the audience to salute as the pianist played several notes of a triumphant finale. All in the audience leapt to their feet, offering a standing ovation, with hoots and whistles, much to the enjoyment of the cast members. They took numerous bows as the piano player continued to tickle the ivories and finally, once the applause began to die down, the cast bowed one last time and hustled back into the staff area where they had all crowded prior to the evening's performance.

Amid the buoyant conversation of their fellow passengers, Nellie gushed, "Aw Mammy, Uncle Geordie, I want to do that someday! I want to be a dancer on Broadway!"

"Och! Don't talk rubbish," scolded Helen, "yeh'll not be joining any theater troupe while I've got breath in my body."

Nellie's face fell and she turned to Jeanie to commiserate. After all, Jeanie's dreams of nursing school had been dashed as well. Geordie pulled Helen aside and said, "How'd yeh have to say things like that? She'll not really do it, it's just a young lassie's pipe dreams. Let her have them, will yeh?"

"Yeh're right, she'll not have any chance away off in Utah, will she?" Helen said. "I'm just in a foul mood, is all. But she'll have to learn someday that we don't get to do what we want, we do what we're told."

Geordie shook his head in disbelief at his sister's statement and said, "Why don't yeh order yersel' a nice wee Pimms and pretend yeh're in Blackpool?" He turned and said to Nellie, "D'yeh think yeh could keep up with those marches? I bet yeh couldn't."

Nellie smiled a bit, slightly mollified yet still upset by her mother's rebuff. "Aye, I could do it. But I can't, can I?"

He pulled Nellie aside and said quietly, "Give yer mam peace, would yeh lass? Her life's been turned upside down, and she's not herself. You can be a great dancer if that's what yeh want to do. Yeh can join the school plays in Castle Gate and get to be on stage."

"They put on plays there?" Nellie asked, eyes wide.

"Aye! There's all sorts of performances there, and in Helper. There's the moving pictures, and the local brass bands play at social events. Yeh'll fit right in."

Helen watched with a mixture of gratitude and dismay as her brother comforted her middle daughter. She didn't like snapping at her children, but better their heads weren't filled with unrealistic hopes and dreams when their lives were plainly laid out before them. A woman either married and settled down, or risked God only knows what. And in a coal mining town, the pickings for a husband who wasn't a miner were slim.

She sighed with resignation as she felt the familiar sensation down there that meant she had better hurry back to her cabin and take care of business before her clothing was ruined. But at least this explained why she was feeling so grouchy.

"Here, Jean, take the baby. I'll be back soon," Helen said, handing Ella to Jeanie, "I've got to run downstairs and take care of … something." She gave Jeanie a knowing look, saying without words that her lady's time was upon her. Jeanie took the baby and went back to her conversation with her uncle and sister, and her fellow passengers.

Geordie watched Helen leave in a hurry and asked Jeanie, "Where's she rushing off to?"

"She has to … it's private," Jeanie stammered, unsure how to tell a man what was going on with her mother.

He now understood Helen's moodiness and changed the subject quickly, "Well, give me that wee'un. I haven't smooched that wee, pudgy face in too long!" He took Ella from Jeanie and kissed her loudly on her rounded cheeks until the baby giggled and squealed.

Helen hurried belowdecks to her cabin to dig out one of the several flannel rags she had brought with her. She'd prayed that her lady's time would wait until after they arrived in Utah but she wasn't entirely surprised that it hadn't. It came on a few days earlier than she had anticipated, however, so she had left the cabin unprepared.

She found one of the rags, stuffed it into her bag and toddled down the hall to the public lavatory, thighs clamped together, to clean herself up. The doors were all locked, in use, so she waited impatiently for one of them to open, hiding her bag behind her, embarrassed to think anyone would guess why she was waiting for the loo.

Finally, one of the doors opened and out came a woman with whom Helen had chatted over the past several days. "Oh, hullo, hen," the woman said, "fancy meeting you here. Are yeh not watching the show upstairs?"

"I was, but I had a bit of an … erm … emergency …" said Helen, "if yeh know what I mean …"

"Och! Don't I know it! It's the curse of every woman alive, intit?" the woman commiserated. She dropped her voice to a whisper and asked, "Have yeh tried those new Kotex? Just ask one of the stewardesses, or the nurse, to get some for yeh. They make it so much easier to travel, worth every penny!"

"No, I haven't heard of them," said Helen. "Can we talk about this later? I'm in a bit of a rush."

"Och, of course, hen, I'm sorry for gabbing on," said the woman, "I'll go get yeh one. I just finished and I have one or two left. Yeh have to try them."

Helen hurried into the unoccupied lavatory and took care of the messy business of being a woman, grumbling about her luck, "Yeh couldn't wait until I get into my new home, could yeh? Had to come early and ruin my trip, din't yeh?" The thought of washing bloody rags by hand and hanging them to dry in the ship's cabin—or, worse, on the train—was enough to make her dread the rest of the long trip, as if she didn't have enough other reasons. Men don't have to even think about these things: no wonder they love to travel!

She cleaned herself up as best she could, taking advantage of the luxury of as much toilet paper as she needed, and laid the rag in place. She was just about to go back into the hallway when she heard the woman outside the door, lightly tapping. "Are yeh still in there, hen?" she asked.

"Aye," said Helen, cracking the door. The woman pushed her way in, much to Helen's chagrin. She wasn't raised to be so forward and didn't know quite how to react to the woman's familiarity, especially squeezed so tightly into the small room.

"Here yeh go," the woman said, handing her a blue box with the word Kotex, in white letters, on the side. "Yeh'll wonder how we ever did without them. There's two left here, but yeh can get yer own box, right here on the ship. They were invented by nurses during the Great War, as bandages to soak up blood off those poor lads. Now that's over, they have another use entirely."

Helen's mind reeled—too much information, too much going on, for one evening. "Thank you," she said, opening the door again, nonverbally suggesting the woman exit. She ducked the box modestly behind her back and hurried back to her cabin. "I'll talk to yeh back upstairs, in a bit."

"No rush, take yer time," the woman said, waving and turning to go back upstairs to rejoin the frivolity of the evening of rare entertainment.

Helen hid the box under her pillow—to be examined later—and hurried back upstairs. No time to waste down here in the cabin when there was life going on overhead, despite her funk. Wavering between dreading the rest of the long trip and enjoying the new experiences on the ship, she would be sad for the journey to end.

For the first time ever, she'd been able to enjoy a Burns Supper, a raucous Scottish holiday every January 25 to celebrate Rabbie Burns, knowing she wouldn't have to clean up after all the revelers. And now, up yonder, another great event that she didn't have to lift a finger for was still hooplahing the night away. She wasn't going to let her lady's time ruin a good thing.

"Okay then, lassie," she said to herself, as she climbed the stairs to the deck above, "get yersel' back up the stairs and be nicer to yer wee daughter. She can't help it she's a flibbertigibbet."

With a resigned chuckle, Helen did just that.

🐍🐍

"See that building, hen, the tallest one?" Geordie asked Nellie, pointing at the Manhattan skyline up ahead, leaning on the ship's rail as it entered the harbor. A light snow was falling and Nellie was only halfway listening, unable to tear her gaze from the Statue of Liberty, her eyes filled with tears.

89

"That's the Woolworth Building, tallest in the world, sixty stories high!" Geordie continued, nudging Nellie to get her attention, "Twice as high as yer Big Ben. That's a sight to see, intit?" Nellie impatiently nodded that it was, indeed, an impressive sight, and turned her eyes back toward the iconic statue.

Helen gazed at the skyline, excited for the first time in days. She dreaded leaving behind the electric power, indoor plumbing, and prepared meals, but this was a thrilling moment. They were, all but Geordie, about to step on American soil for the first time.

She could already feel the difference between Great Britain and America, and she wasn't even off the ship yet. Maybe it was the beehive of activity she was witnessing as the ship slid into its landing dock—the motorcars zipping down the city streets, the newness of the skyscrapers, the dock workers hollering to one another—or the strangeness of the accents she was hearing. Perhaps it was the squeeze of the crowd pushing their way through customs; some folks fearful of being turned away, others simply excited to start their new lives. Whatever the case, she was no longer surrounded by the sheep-dotted, green hills of Lanarkshire where people took their time getting from here to there.

Helen swallowed hard to keep a sudden wave of homesickness from spilling out of her throat in the form of a moan. Her girls were giddy with excitement, and she didn't want to ruin it with one of her moods.

Geordie, who knew her better than most, took one look at her face and gave her shoulder a squeeze. He offered a chipper grin and said, "Come on, hen, whaddya say? Shall we go see the big city?"

"Aye, let's do that," Helen replied. "What first?"

"Just follow me," Geordie said. "I know all the shortcuts."

Helen sighed with relief and said, "Thank goodness you traveled with us. I couldn't have done it on my own, with none of us ever traveling before!"

He led them through the Customs line and when she responded to the intake official's query over how much cash she had with her, the agent said, "I'm pleased you have a man with you—one hundred and fifty pounds is a lot of money, especially for a woman traveling alone." Geordie's presence meant the official needn't refer her to the Traveler's Aid agent, as was required for unaccompanied women. She was released to her brother's charge.

Geordie maneuvered them through Customs and down onto the dock, where he took Helen to exchange her British pounds for American dollars. He put the bulk of her cash in his money belt for safekeeping, leaving Helen with some spending money tucked away safely in her handbag. He then arranged for a cab and ensured that their luggage was accounted for.

He directed the cabbie to a hotel near the train station, and checked them into two rooms, paying for everything with his own cash, despite Helen's objections. "Now, hen, let me do this for youse. I have money to burn, and I want youse to have a day to plant yer feet on solid ground before we get on the train. Besides, yeh may never pass this way again, so youse oughta see some of New York City."

"I'll pay fer yer dinner, tonight," Helen insisted, "and I'm not taking 'no' for an answer. Now, first things first, I need to find a shop to restock Ella's Mellin supply before we get on the train." The formula Helen purchased for the trip had been a godsend, and it was almost gone.

"Aye, there's a chemist up the street. We can stop after some sightseeing," said Geordie.

While the sights were fun and fascinating, the girls were more interested in browsing the shops for souvenirs. Both wanted a Statue of Liberty memento, but didn't want the same one, so Jeanie chose a statuette figurine while Nellie picked out a snow globe. "This way," she said, shaking it and showing it to Helen, "I'll remember it just the way I saw it, with snow falling on it."

At the pharmacy, Helen bought two jars of Mellin's Food for Ella, even though one would last them all the way to Utah. She had no way of knowing what the stores out there carried. She also purchased—at the pharmacist's recommendation—some of Mrs. Winslow's Soothing Syrup for Ella's sore, teething gums now that whisky was no longer available. "This will do the job," the kindly pharmacist assured her, "it's a mixture of morphine and alcohol, and will soothe Baby in no time."

Geordie raised his eyebrows and said, "Give us a bottle of that, too, would yeh son? That sounds better than hooch!"

"Now, now," scolded the pharmacist with a wink, "that's medicinal."

The men shared a chuckle and Geordie led his charges out the door. "I meant to ask yeh," Helen said to Geordie, as they bustled down the street toward their hotel, "yeh said on the ship there'd be no whisky on the train to Utah, which implies we can get some there. Is it legal?"

Geordie laughed, "It's not legal in any of the States, but that doesn't mean yeh can't find any. The Greeks make some of the best whisky yeh've ever tasted and the Italians make some lovely wine. We just have to get from here to there without drinking all of Miss Ella's magic elixir." He winked and pinched the baby's cheek.

Before stopping for the evening, Geordie steered them into a family-owned Italian restaurant for dinner. "I ate here last time I was in town," said Geordie, "and their tomato gravy is first rate. Try the spaghetti and meatballs," he told the girls, pointing to the selection on the menu.

Finally, back at the hotel, Helen got the girls settled into their room after saying goodnight to Geordie, who went off to his room with a newspaper under his arm. The early-morning train departure was on her mind as she lay in bed, unable to sleep, with a rumbling pain in her gut. Nerves, probably. At least, that's what the doctor back in Coalburn had told her, that her nervous stomach was the cause of her occasional digestive upset.

This felt different, though. Helen wondered, as she darted down the hallway to the water closet, if there was something in the New York food that didn't agree with her. Maybe it was the tomato gravy at that Italian restaurant.

The hotel offered the luxury of toilet paper and Helen inwardly kicked herself for not buying some at the pharmacy before heading across America to cowboy country, where they would be back to using newspaper and pages torn out of a catalog in an outdoor loo.

Another gut cramp reminded her to steer her thoughts away from going back to a life of hard physical work. She tried to think of a distracting song and hummed a tune she'd heard on the radio earlier that day, about innocent young boys who saw the world as soldiers but then had to go back home, *How ya gonna keep 'em down on the farm after they've seen Paree?*

Not for the last time Helen wished that she'd never been given a glimpse of what life could have been. If she'd never gotten spoiled using flush toilets, or having someone else do her laundry and cook the meals, clean the dishes …

A knock on the lavatory door shook Helen from her thoughts. "Occupied," she called out. After the cramping passed Helen pulled herself together, prepared to apologize for the delay, but the person who knocked was gone. It was cold in the hallway, so she hurried to their warm and cozy room, where she lay awake for hours, fretting over making it to the train on time.

CHAPTER 10

February 3, 1922
Castle Gate, Utah

It was a cold and sunny Friday afternoon, with the temperature just below freezing when the train finally arrived in Castle Gate. Scrubby, prickly brown bushes poked up through the thick dusting of snow. Otherwise, the entire valley's landscape—from the enclosing walls of the surrounding cliffs to the high-desert ground underfoot—was a rusty beige. Some of the canyon walls displayed veins of coal running through them and the drab colors blended to create a rather dreary scene—even the uptown buildings were plain and dull. The only colors that stood out were the clear, blue sky above, and a bit of green poking through the snow that covered the pine trees on the hill above town.

The drabness matched the mood of the new arrivals—the final days of the trip had been long and silent, spent huddling against the blasts of winter air as passengers boarded or disembarked during one of the never-ending stops along the way. Everyone was tired, even Ella, who was usually full of energy when she wasn't in pain from teething and under the influence of Mrs. Winslow's Soothing Syrup. She drowsed on Helen's lap, sucking her thumb as the train rocked and rocked and endlessly rocked.

Geordie, in his aisle seat, kept busy reading the newspaper, with front page stories about the new Pope and the second murder trial of film star Fatty Arbuckle. Jeanie buried her nose in a book she had purchased at Union Station in Chicago, having finished both novels they brought with them on the ship. Nellie sat next to Geordie, staring out the window, dazed by the

93

strange, brown landscape. Utah looked nothing like Scotland, and she wasn't sure she liked it.

Helen dozed fitfully, drifting in and out of sleep, trying not to obsess over her anxious thoughts. It had been over two months since she had seen Will. Since he left in November, she had time to wonder whether her life would have been happier with a more business-minded man. Surely there must be more to life than being a miner's wife.

Even so, Helen reminded herself, Will was a good man. Sure, he may be rough around the edges and he made some of her family uncomfortable with his lack of couth. But he was a good husband, a steady provider, and he made her laugh. He would make sure everything was okay.

She adjusted Ella, careful not to rouse the child, to prevent her dress from becoming too wrinkled. She had kept her favorite frock set aside for today, carefully packed, so she would look her best when she saw Will again. She needn't have worried about waking the baby, as Ella curled back up and whined a little for Helen to hold her more tightly.

Again, she got lost in her thoughts. This was the longest Helen and Will had ever been apart. What would she say to him after all this time? What would he say to her? Then came a thought that made her blush: as much as she resented the messy inconvenience at the time, she was now grateful that her lady's time had come and gone while they were traveling, so their personal reunion wouldn't be postponed.

"Here, hen," Geordie said, nudging Nellie and tapping his newspaper, "See that Fatty Arbuckle murder trial, ended in mistrial, and here's a story about an actress from his pictures, Mabel Normand, involved in another murder, some movie director shot and killed!" Even Hollywood gossip couldn't rouse Nellie from her mood, so Geordie sighed and went back to his paper, resolved to finish the trip in silence.

After several minutes Nellie spoke, half to herself, "It's bad luck to move into a new home on a Friday."

"Pish," Geordie said, "that's only if youse have a choice. Yeh didn't choose to flit on a Friday, so it doesn't count."

Nellie turned to her uncle and asked, "Is that true?"

"I dunno, do I lass?" Geordie winked and said, "I don't make up the superstitions. I reckon it's as true as yeh want it to be."

"I guess," she shrugged and went back to staring out the window.

Finally, after stops in Price and Helper, the train entered Price Canyon and the conductor announced, "Castle Gate, next stop." Although it wasn't yet evening, the landscape was in shadow due to the sun's rays being blocked by the high sandstone bluff on the west side of the valley. Helen looked out the window at the small crowd gathered at the station, either waiting to depart to destinations north, or to greet incoming passengers.

There, among them, was the first familiar sight she'd laid eyes on for far too long. Dressed in his Sunday suit and tie Will stood out from the others, the fob chain of his pocket watch stretched across his vest, his battered fedora atop his head, reminding Helen that she had meant to get that old hat replaced once they had the extra money.

She hadn't expected him to meet them at the train. She assumed it would be Bill or Elsie because Friday was a workday and Will never missed a shift. Yet there he was, dressed in his best, anxiously peering into the train's windows, trying to spot his womenfolk. Helen grinned as she leaned up to the window and knocked, waving to get his attention. "Look!" she said to the girls. "It's yer da!"

"Where?" Nellie asked, and then saw him and waved vigorously, "There he is! We're here! Och, thank God, we're finally here!"

Jeanie tucked her book away and waved as well, and Will finally saw them. He burst into a grin and took a few steps forward in anticipation. The train ground to a squealing halt and, once the conductor opened the door, the entire family spilled out, glad not just to see Will, but to set foot on solid ground. While Will hugged his family and they him, Geordie collected the luggage, also relieved to be home.

"Wull, I'm that glad to see yeh," Helen gushed as she threw herself into his arms in a rare public display of affection.

"Aw, hen," Will said, hugging her tightly, "I thought yeh'd never get here. We've all missed yeh, me and Wullie, and the boys. Wait'll yeh see the house. We've got it all fixed up for youse."

Will released Helen and hugged his daughters, one at a time, saving baby Ella for last. This one he bounced in his arms and chucked her chin, saying, "Remember me? D'yeh mind yer ol' da? I remember you!" Ella stared at him, eyebrows furrowed, leery of this man she hadn't seen in so long before finally bursting into a toothy grin and giving him a kiss on the cheek.

"Aw, that's my wee lassie," he beamed. "I've got Bill's motorcar," Will said, handing the baby back to Helen. He picked up the steamer trunk, leading the way toward Bill's Buick sedan. "Don't tell me there's no advantages to bein' the supervisor's kin. They let me off early, which I don't think they'd let many men do."

"Och," laughed Geordie, "they may let 'em off, but they wouldn't get to use Bill's car."

"Right you are," said Will. "Get in the car, youse," he said to his womenfolk as he loaded their luggage. "Geordie, yeh want me to drop you at yer house, or d'yeh want to come see our new digs?"

"I live just up the block here, so I'll walk home." Geordie said, "I'll see yer house another day. I'm sure these ladies have seen enough of old Uncle Geordie."

"Wheesht, you," teased Helen, as she climbed into the car with the girls, who were marveling at its shiny newness, "what yeh mean is, yeh've seen enough of us!"

"Can't pull the wool over this one's eyes," said Geordie. "Aye, I've had enough of this hen party. I'll get myself home where a man can drink his brandy and smoke a cigar without a passel of nattering females."

Crammed into Bill's sedan with all their bags, Will maneuvered his family through town, grinding the gears in his inexperience. The three older newcomers peered about trying to take in the shops and business they were passing.

"Look, hen," Will said, pointing out the front window of the car at the massive stone structure that was now visible up ahead. "That's how the town is called Castle Gate."

"Och," gasped Helen, "it's beautiful!"

Jeanie and Nellie scooted forward from the back seat to look out the front windshield as the stately Castle Gate rock formation came fully into view. "Oh, it's pure lovely," gushed Nellie, and Jeanie gasped and said, "It surely is."

"Well, you just wait," said Will, "yeh can see it from our front window." He turned the car onto a smaller dirt road into a grouping of twenty-five saltbox houses in neat rows of five, every house identical and painted reddish brown. The houses were, compared to the miners' rows in Scotland, quite new and much bigger, each with their own patch of land for a garden and a single-seat wooden privy in the back of the yard, far enough from the house to keep the smell to a minimum.

"Here we are," said Will, pulling the car to a stop in front of one of the houses, "number nineteen. Mind the number. There's no street names here, and the houses all look alike."

Jeanie and Nellie were bursting to be released from the back seat of the car to explore their new home. "Hurry, Mam, let us out!" cried Nellie.

Helen laughed and took her time getting Ella out of the car. "Don't tell me how fast to move, lassie," she teased. "These old bones'll not rush for you."

"Come out my side," said Will, opening his door and helping his daughters climb out. "Mind, grab yer bags. Door's unlocked. G'wan in." The girls gathered their luggage and ran up the porch steps, into the house, in such a rush that they didn't close the door behind them.

Will said, "Och, I got the fire going before I picked youse up so it'd be warm, and they're letting it all out." Helen heard their exclamations of joy as she waited for Will to untie her trunk from the roof of the car, heave it onto his shoulder and lead her into their new home.

Inside they went and Helen's eyes widened as she viewed her new digs —a front parlor filled with fine upholstered furniture and, at the far end of the long room, a well-appointed kitchen including a sturdy coal-burning stove and a sideboard stacked with dishes and utensils. She drew in a deep breath and tried to take it all in but was distracted by her daughters' squeals of delight.

"Mammy! We have our own bedroom!" Nellie cried from elsewhere in the house.

"Aye," said Jeanie, as excited as her younger sister, "with beds for us all. There's even a crib in here for Ella!"

"Oh my!" said Helen, joining them at their bedroom doorway, admiring the beds and crib already made up for all four children. Elsie must have done this, because the beds were too neatly made for one of her men to have done it. She turned toward the parlor to ask Will, "What about Pete and Tam? Where'll they sleep?"

"Where are they, come to mention 'em?" asked Jeanie.

Will said, "They'll be along shortly. The workday's just about done. They'll make a pallet here on the floor near the fire, to stay warm. We've been staying at the boarding house, 'til the last, so's we didn't have to cook our own meals."

Helen looked around the lovely parlor, paying more attention now to the fine quality of the furniture. Upon further inspection, it showed minor signs of wear, as Elsie had used it in her own houseful of wee'uns up until recently, but its original purchase price was higher than anything Helen had left behind in Scotland. If these were Elsie's cast-offs, Helen could only imagine what finery Bill was supplying his new bride. This furniture wouldn't stay good for long, with four miners in the house.

Just as Helen was resigning herself that there would be no keeping the davenport, chairs and rugs looking as new as they did now, she heard men approaching outside. One of the voices she recognized was Willie's. "Go see yer da," she said to Ella, and handed the baby to Will. "I hear yer brother!"

Helen rushed to the door, threw it open and cried, "It's my boys! Come here, youse!"

The three men came up the walk, lugging their duffel bags from the boarding house. "Aye, there she is," hailed Pete, "it's our Helen! Hen, yeh're a sight for sore eyes!"

Willie grinned and bounded up the porch steps into his mother's arms. Helen hugged him tight and wiped away a tear on her sleeve. She stepped back to usher Pete and Tam inside where it was warmer. Once all were inside, she looked up at Willie and said, "Och, I have to bend my neck to look up at my lad, even taller than yeh were before yeh left." She pulled his face down and covered it in kisses. Once she was finally done smooching him, Willie went inside to greet his sisters.

Helen hugged and kissed Pete, genuinely glad to see him, before Pete sought out his nieces to say hello. She turned to embrace Tam, who gave her a one-armed hug because he was holding a large casserole dish, which he then handed to Helen. "This is from Mrs. Mueller. She knew yeh wouldn't want to cook yer first night, so she sent this over."

"Aw, isn't that kind?" Helen said, taking the casserole to the kitchen table. She lifted the lid and sniffed the lumpy green substance. "What is it?"

Tam said, "That's her cabbage rolls. Took us a while to get used to German food, but we learned to like it."

Helen turned on Tam and demanded, "German food? I'm not eatin' Boche cookin'."

Will saw Tam's pained expression which said, *I forgot it was a secret*, so he winced and quickly stepped over to say, "Aye, hen, I guess I forgot to tell yeh, our landlady is a sweet little German widow. She's not like the dirty Boche yeh're thinking of."

Tam used Will's interruption as an exit point and joined Pete and Willie in the parlor to say hello to the girls. Helen was dubious, so Will continued, "She and her late husband left Germany years ago, long before the War.

She's more American than some of the native-born Yanks 'round here. Give her a chance."

Subject closed, he pulled her into his arms, his face close to hers. "Now, forget about her, and everyone else. Yeh haven't seen our room yet," Will spoke more quietly, his voice a little huskier. "Shall I show yeh where it is?" he asked, wiggling his eyebrows suggestively. Even through her heavy traveling clothes, Helen could feel how glad he was to see her.

She blushed and lightly slapped his chest. "You let go of me, Wull Garroch. The wee'uns are just over there."

Will released her and grinned, "Aye, but I'll not be put off so easily once they're asleep."

"I may not put you off," Helen smiled, "if you ask pretty enough."

"Alright, youse two," called Pete, from across the parlor. "Yeh'll be alone soon enough. The sun's still out, for God's sake. We haven't yet had our evening tea!" He turned toward the others and said, "Can youse believe that pair? It's like they haven't seen each other in three months."

"Enough of yer blether, Peter Garroch," Helen teased. "Now girls, help me get to know this kitchen and get some supper on the table. I'm starved, even if it is German cabbage."

CHAPTER 11

October, 1922
Castle Gate, Utah

Once again, a mining strike influenced the family's travel plans, but this time the strike was in Utah, and it got violent. Not wanting to bring their wives into such an unstable environment, Pete and Tam postponed buying their tickets until autumn—better safe than sorry.

A nationwide strike for unionization began early in the year but, in Carbon County, the Greek miners added their own grievance: they demanded equal pay with the white miners, claiming they were being shortchanged for their full day's work. The Greeks were joined by the Italians and the Slavs, and other swarthy, "non-white" men who dared to speak up. Their demands were shrugged off, and the standoff eventually led to bloodshed, with one miner shot and killed.

In June, the governor sent National Guard units to Carbon County. That same day, a sheriff's deputy was shot and killed, and the general manager of the Standard Coal Company was wounded. In Helper, the National Guard enforced martial law, and strikers—who had been thrown out of their company housing and had moved into tent cities—were removed. The strike eventually ended with no satisfaction on the part of the Greeks, and many were convicted of assault, murder and a range of other crimes.

The Garroch men and other white miners worked short-staffed shifts with strikebreakers shipped in via train from other cities. Although their Scottish, socialistic leanings were in sympathy with other working men, there was no contending with the nationalistic complaint that the "oily Bohunks" couldn't be bothered to learn to speak English and assimilate to the American way of life, when they were immigrants themselves, but lucky enough to speak mostly understandable English.

Once the strike was over and settled enough to bring their wives, Pete and Tam sent for Jessie and Bertha. When Helen met them at the train station with their husbands, their wide-eyed reaction to their surroundings that Friday afternoon in early October reminded Helen how far she had come in the nine months since she arrived. She and the girls must have looked the same to Will, dazed and dazzled. Even though their greetings were loud and boisterous, Jessie and Bertha were worn ragged, and wee Margie, Annie and Peggy looked like frightened kittens, their eyes darting about taking in their new surroundings.

The next day, after a good night's sleep in their new homes, Helen walked with Jessie and Bertha into town, passing on bits of gossip about people they didn't yet know … gossip like "The Morrisons live down the street, there, in the third house. They're related to our Bill by marriage. His name's Bill too … a widower, his poor Maggie died in 1918 during that awful influenza epidemic that killed Elsie's husband. He lives there with his mostly grown wee'uns, and he and two of his sons work in the mine with our boys."

In the town center, Helen led a tour of the businesses, beginning with the company store to stock their kitchens with everyday staples. Before going inside, she paused to share a few helpful hints like, "Don't ask for porridge. It's called oatmeal here. And, don't be surprised that bacon is nothing like back home. They call what we eat Canadian bacon, their bacon is shriveled and burnt to a crisp. Don't get me started on the lack of square sausage and, och! What they call tea here!"

"Yeh're not making it sound too pleasant, hen," Jessie said.

Helen chuckled and said, "At least youse two have me to show yeh the ropes. I had to find my own way, sure. Bill's wee Elsie helped when she could, but her time's taken up bein' the superintendent's wife, with her posh luncheons and bridge parties with the upper crust wives. The neighbor ladies were a bigger help … yeh'll see, they're a fine bunch."

"See there?" Helen asked, pointing across the canyon toward Elsie's home on the side of the western bluff, "She and Bill live up the hill over there. The locals call it 'Silk Row' … those fancy houses across the railroad tracks. Elsie's a sweet girl, but she's not a miner's wife. She lives too far away to see every day and she doesn't have time to gab over the washtub."

Helen paused and continued, "Come to think of it, Elsie has a hired woman who uses one of them newfangled wringer washers, so we," she said, gesturing at Bertha and Jessie, "who scrub our clothes by hand over a washboard with lye soap—we don't have much in common with my sister-in-law."

Jessie and Bertha tsked in commiseration and Helen went on. "No worries, though," she said, opening the door and ushering them inside the general store, a long, narrow shop with wooden floors, lined with wooden shelves and glass display cases, where a smattering of other customers milled about. The shelves and display cases were filled with packaged foods and household items for purchase using company scrip. "Yeh'll not stay strangers for long," Helen continued. "Our houses are in with some the American families and others from Great Britain. We speak the same language and have similar customs. It may not look like home, but it feels close enough."

"Why do you say they speak the same language?" Bertha asked. "What other language would they speak?"

"There's folks from all over the world," Helen said. "Wull told me that, down in Helper, yeh can hear almost thirty different languages. Most of the wives are nice as pie, just hard to understand sometimes. Yeh'll see. They live on the other end of the valley," she told them. "I'll show yeh when we get outside."

They completed their shopping and stepped outdoors. Helen gestured south and said, "The Greeks and the Italians live down that way. So do the Negroes and Spanish speaking families. Around the bend there," she said, pointing southwest, "in Willow Creek Canyon, that's where Mine Number Two is. That's where the Japanese families live. There's more nationalities here than I can shake a stick at! They keep to themselves—not out of hatred so much, although that strike didn't help matters. It's more about languages and customs. Och! And the food! Who knew there's so many ways to prepare a meal!"

Some of the Greek wives, she informed them, sold excellent homebrewed whisky, and several Italian wives sold delicious breads and wine. "We swap recipes, the ones who speak English, that is," Helen went on. "I always say 'no' to tomato gravy recipes. Something about it gives me the cramps."

"It really doesn't look much like home, does it?" said Bertha, gazing at the varying skin tones as they walked among the other weekend shoppers. Her eyes fixed on a Negro man in his fifties, walking down the road carrying a parcel, greeting his neighbors.

He and Helen nodded hello and Helen said, as he wandered out of earshot, "That man's named Prince Alexander, can yeh believe that? Here we thought we left royalty behind and his name's Prince! He's a lovely man, a former preacher. He works down the mine, too."

As they walked past the two-story Amusement Hall, with its windowed front and railed porch on the second floor, Helen said, "Inside there, there's a soda fountain where the wee'uns can buy penny candy. We had an ice cream social with the brass band at the town gazebo last week. They did events like that all summer with plenty of sports for the men and boys in yon park, even with all that strike brouhaha. Willie's on the Scottish football team and his friend Tommy plays for the English. Yeh'll like Tommy," Helen said to Bertha. "He's from Yorkshire, like you. Manchester, I think. He's at our house quite often."

The sun was just past the western bluff by the time they got home, with afternoon shadows growing across the valley bringing a chill after a warm and sunny noontime. Helen said, "Yeh'll get used to the difference in climate. Warm weather starts in April and ends in September and there's not as much rain here. I think that's why, aside from the pine trees up in the hills, the plants here aren't so green."

Helen said as they got close to their houses, "Drop yer packages off away home and come over to mine for a nice cuppa and a wee gab."

Jessie and Bertha took their purchases inside their nearby houses and Helen headed home to prepare for her long-awaited family to begin a new tradition of tea and blether in their new country.

Jeanie greeted her as she entered, "Mam, can we take the wee'uns into town?" She and Nellie had been minding their young cousins as their mothers shopped. "Ella's asleep and they're itching to do something. I thought mebbe we could pester Uncle Geordie into buying us an ice cream soda."

"Their mams will be here in a minute, so ask them," said Helen, "but I reckon they'll agree if youse go now and not spoil their appetites for supper." She put away her groceries, stoked the coal stove and put the kettle on to boil for a pot of tea. The little girls hopped excitedly, waiting for their mothers to okay their trip into town, and watched out the window for their arrival.

"There they are!" squealed wee Margie, pointing out the parlor window.

Peggy opened the front door and all three younger girls spilled outside, clamoring for permission. "Mammy, Mammy! Can we go into town with Jeanie and get ice cream?"

Bertha smiled and said to Margie, "Of course, flower, as long as it's okay for Peggy and Annie, too."

"Aye," said Jessie, "g'wan with youse. Mind Jeanie. Behave."

"Aw, we always behave," said Peggy. "Come on Jeanie! Come on Nellie! Let's go!" The girls headed into town, giggling and exuberant.

Jessie said, looking around Helen's home. "Och, I'll never get over the nice things you have here! Elsie was generous. This makes our own homes look shabby, compared. I'd have been happy to see how they're furnished, otherwise."

The mining company supplied basic starter furniture, paid for in installments from the men's weekly wages, to be upgraded as their income allowed. Unlike Elsie's 'old' things that Helen had in her home, Tam and Pete's furnishings were bare bones.

While Helen and their husbands collected the newcomers at the depot on Friday, Jeanie and Nellie had stayed behind to put the final touches on their assigned houses, not far from #19, with hand-stitched samplers and vases of freshly picked Joe Pye flowers. Housewarming gifts, with plenty of welcome baskets during get-to-know-you visits from the neighbors, would arrive once their needs were better known—some immigrants arrived with their entire households in tow, and others with only the barest essentials. These two were somewhere in the middle.

Helen invited Bertha and Jessie to her kitchen to sit down. "Look at this table!" Bertha said, running her hand along its polished surface. "Have you ever seen anything so fine in a miner's house?"

"Aye," Helen said, "I'm pure grateful."

After settling into their chairs, Jessie said, "We didn't forget your birthday, did we Bertha?" She handed a small rectangular package to Helen, wrapped in a beautifully embroidered handkerchief.

"Did we, heck! We brought your favorites from home," said Bertha. She reached into a cloth bag she had brought with her to retrieve a decorative tea tin and gave it to Helen.

"Och, that's lovely, Bertha!" cried Helen, "If only yeh knew how much I miss Scottish tea. American tea is second rate. I hope yeh brought plenty, you'll miss it that much. I'll make some now."

"Open yer other gift, first," scolded Jessie.

Helen untied the handkerchief and found within—wrapped in parchment paper—a block of tablet candy. "Made by yer sister, Lizzie," said Jessie. "Yeh know she makes the best tablet in town. She asked me to bring this, special for yer birthday. She sends it with her love. The handkerchief is from me. I hand-stitched some roses and your initials."

"Och, they're lovely gifts," Helen said, using the new handkerchief to wipe away tears. "Thank you. It feels just like home, doesn't it? I only wish Lizzie had come with youse. I miss her so." She stumbled a bit as she rose and said, "Help yerself to some tablet while I make some good, Scottish tea."

"Are yeh well, hen?" Jessie asked, her brows furrowed with concern. "Only yeh look that pale."

"Oh, aye," Helen said, dismissing the question with a wave. "Just homesick. And I'm still recovering from another miscarriage a few weeks ago. I don't bounce back like I once did."

"Aw, Helen," Bertha said, her hand upon her heart, "we didn't know. Did it go the same as always?"

"Aye," Helen replied, "Only I think this time it might have been the heat. It gets awful hot here in the summer, not like back home. I reckon the pregnancy must have took hold shortly after my arrival, when me and Wull couldn't keep our hands off each other and I wasn't paying as much attention to my cycle."

"I wish we could have been here for yeh," Jessie said.

"Och, it's fine," Helen said. "You know me, fertile as can be, got pregnant on my wedding night and haven't stopped since, even if I cannot carry 'em full term anymore. And the neighbor women were such a help. I'm fine. Just a little weak, after a long day running errands. I'm not a spring chicken anymore."

Helen set up a brew as she talked and brought it to the table, passing out teacups and saucers. "Besides," she said, "neither are youse two! Yeh both looked worn ragged yesterday when youse got off the train. I recognized the bleary looks in yer eyes because I felt that way myself the day we landed. Yeh'd just survived three weeks of chasing restless wee'uns halfway around the world."

Jessie said, as Helen poured tea for each, "Yeh've got that right. My girls were like wee monkeys on that train. They couldn't sit still no matter how I scolded. And asking, 'are we there yet?' Och!"

"Oh, aye," said Bertha, "and Margie spent her time pouting because we weren't moving fast enough to get to her daddy."

Helen said, as she sat, "I warned Tam and Pete to not expect youse two to be bright and chipper after such a long journey, and I was right, wasn't I? And they didn't listen, neither, did they?"

"Och!" Jessie cried, "I could barely keep Pete offa me!" She added, winking, "Not that I wanted him off."

Bertha blushed and said, "Well, Tam's a gentleman, but I don't think I could have put him off if I tried."

Tea made, candy served, Helen began the hen party with a little more background on some of the locals she knew best. "I told yeh earlier," Helen said, "about the Morrisons, they're related to my brother Bill by marriage to his first wife, poor Mary who died of the cancer back in 1919. She was a Lindsay, yeh know, and she left behind six wee'uns when she died. Elsie has her hands full, sure, as their stepmammy. Bill's wee'uns are very Americanized, and yeh cannot hardly tell their parents are Scots."

Bertha and Jessie tsked into their tea and Helen continued. "Bill Morrison's daughter Isabella married Clyde Hasemyer and took in her poor sister's orphaned daughter Ina, after Janet died of the TB. Janet's husband Jim, who was my brother Bill's wife Mary's brother, died in a mine explosion down in New Mexico about ten year ago, and then poor Janet died of tuberculosis when Ina was only two."

"Goodness, hen!" cried Jessie, "It's like one of those serial films. I cannot keep track of who's who!"

Helen laughed and said, "I don't expect youse to keep track. I'm that glad to see the botha youse, I couldn't stop bletherin'!"

Bertha smiled and said, "We're that glad to see you, too."

"Good," Helen said, "because there's more. D'yeh remember Bill and Janet Glover? They're from Galston, so I don't know if yeh ever met, but they come over about a year ago, on the Cameronia, just like youse two, so yeh'll have something in common to talk about."

"Oh no! Don't talk about that bloody ship!" cried Bertha, dramatically clutching at her heart. Both Helen and Jessie's jaws dropped to hear Bertha swear.

"I'm sorry for my language," Bertha said, "but I still get ill just thinking about that endless rocking. My heart felt like it was about to jump out of my chest, and I must have vomited every day, the whole way across."

"Aye," Jessie added, "she was pure miserable. And I can't hear no more about people I've not yet met. Try again once I have faces to go with the names."

"Aye, sure," said Helen, "It's a lot to take in."

"Good," said Jessie, "my head's about done in. Now, finish your tea and I'll read the leaves for youse. So close to All Hallows' Eve, the spirits are restless and ready to speak!"

"Och, I don't want to finish it, it's that good," Helen sighed, savoring her Scottish tea.

Jessie said, "Well, hen, yeh can always have another cup, after. I'll do Bertha first, though, so yeh don't have to hurry."

Bertha, who laid no claims as an oracle and gladly allowed Tam's aunties to lead the game, drank the last of her tea, leaving just enough behind to swirl the tea leaves that remained in the bottom of her cup and turn it upside down on the saucer.

Jessie picked up Bertha's cup and peered into the dregs for a few minutes, tilting her head this way and that, before she finally said, "I'm seeing Tam in his soldierin' uniform, bein' honored for his service in the Great War." She tilted the cup toward Bertha and showed her, as if the tea leaves were delivering a plainly visible message. Bertha shook her head, not seeing a thing.

"See there?" Jessie said, pointing into the cup, "I'm seein' him in his kilt, tall and proud and handsome … Handsome Tam …" she looked again, "… and I cannot tell what this means. I see you shakin' yer fist at God."

Bertha's eyes widened and she asked, "What for?"

Jessie put the cup back onto its saucer and said, "I can't see, hen. It's too dark and cloudy. Mebbe yeh didn't drink enough of yer tea. Perhaps yeh left too much behind for me to see properly."

To break the tension, Helen picked up Jessie's cup and said, "My turn. Let's see what the leaves say about you." She peered into the cup and finally said, "Well, I don't know if this is because of how yer Pete's been behavin' in yer absence," she teased, "but it looks like yeh'll be lowerin' the boom on him before long."

"What does that mean?" Jessie demanded. "What's my Pete been up to?"

Helen laughed and said, "Aw, nothing bad, hen, but our Pete does love to bend his elbow, don't he?"

"Aye," Jessie agreed, nodding her head, "I was hoping some of that Prohibition would rub off on him ... not entirely, mind, yeh know I enjoy a wee sherry myself, but aye, even last night, on my first day here when yeh'd think he'd stay sober enough to give his wife a proper welcome, he was steamin' drunk. Too drunk to ..." Jessie winked and said, "... finish the job, let's say, and I'll say no more."

"Aye," said Helen, "It seems that the boys, in our absences, found comfort in the Helper saloons a bit more than they want us to know about. Janet Glover told me all about 'em. The tea leaves here say yeh may have to use yer feminine wiles to convince him to change his wicked ways." Helen teased, "Cut 'im off, don't touch his wee tadger when he's had too much of the drink!"

The ladies laughed and continued to trade course comments, including Jessie's confession that Pete's tadger wasn't so wee, if she's telling the truth. Finally, Jessie picked up Helen's teacup and gazed for a while at the leaves before finally putting the cup down and saying, "I'm not seeing anything."

Alarmed, Helen demanded, "Jessie Garroch, I know when yeh're lying, and yeh're lying now. What d'yeh see?"

"Now, hen," Jessie stammered, "it's just like with Bertha's cup. I think yeh've left too much tea in the bottom. It's hard to see anything."

"There's no more tea in that cup than in yours," Helen insisted. "Now get it told."

"Alright, I will, but don't hold me to it. I'm sure I'm wrong," Jessie insisted before finally saying, "It looks like hard times coming your way, hen, like someone's gonna get sick. I see your Jeanie nursing someone ..."

Helen interrupted, "Well, Jeanie wanted to go to nursing college back in Glasgow but she hasn't raised the subject since we arrived, so maybe that's what yer seeing. Is she goin' to school?"

Jessie looked into the cup and said, "Oh, she'll bring it up again, sure, but that's not what I'm talking about. I'm seeing her takin' care of someone, and I'm seein' Wull workin' extra hard in the mine, him and Wullie both ..."

"Och, that's enough," said Helen, her first thoughts going to wee Ella getting sick and dying, like so many other babies in the past, after surviving for this long.

"Aye, that's plenty," said Bertha. "I don't like the sound of any of this, especially after Nellie was so quick to tell us it's bad luck to move into a house on a Friday. How can we help what day we arrived?"

"No worries, hen," said Helen. "She went on about that when we arrived, too, and I said the same. We got here on a Friday, and everything's been right as rain. But, aye, that's enough fortune telling for today." She stood and said, "I've got to get the evening meal started soon and so do youse, in yer new kitchens. Don't forget, yeh're all invited here to supper tomorrow. I'll be putting on a Sunday roast, just like back home."

"Och," Jessie said, "a homemade meal that I don't have to cook. Sounds like heaven. Thanks, hen." She rose and gave Helen a kiss on the cheek. "I'm that glad to see yeh. I've missed yeh so."

"Me too," said Bertha, rising and giving Helen a warm hug. "I'm so happy our families are back together."

Just then, Jeanie and Nellie arrived with the little girls in tow, sticky with ice cream on their cheeks, each clutching a small brown paper bag. "Mammy," nine-year-old Peggy said to Jessie, "Uncle Geordie took us for ice cream and bought us penny candy!"

"Me too!" boasted six-year-old Annie. Jessie's younger daughter held up her own bag of candy.

Bertha crouched before four-year-old Margie and peeked into her little brown bag. She asked, "And what about you, my wee chicken, did Uncle Geordie spoil you rotten as well?"

"Aye!" laughed Margie, pulling a peppermint stick out of her bag, "I like Uncle Geordie!"

"Everyone likes Uncle Geordie," said Helen. "He's a wee rascal, that one. Youse watch out for him," she warned the other women, "he's famous for spoiling the wee'uns appetites with treats before supper."

"Aw, that's sweet," said Bertha, licking her thumb and using it to clean the sticky mess off Margie's cheeks.

"Aye, it is sweet," said Helen, her heart swelling. Her family was together again, with her best mates finally here from Scotland. Pete and Tam had moved into their own homes and were no longer underfoot, and all was well.

It was sweet.

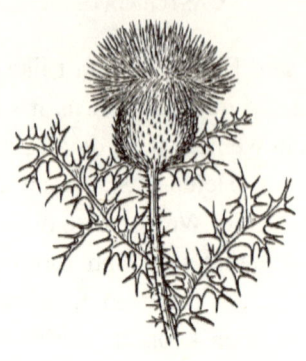

CHAPTER 12

November, 1922
Castle Gate, Utah

Helen woke with a sore head one mid-November Sunday morning, the consequence of too much elbow bending at Saturday's Armistice Day celebrations. It was a festive yet somber day, with parades and parties in remembrance of those who served recently in the Great War—an excuse for the men to argue and lament global politics, with England's Prime Minister David Lloyd George's resignation and Mussolini's Blackshirts marching on Rome, while the women fussed over tables full of food at the various gathering places around town.

Veterans were encouraged to dress in uniform. Geordie wore his American gear—he had enlisted in the US Army and served in the medical corps in Colorado, caring for wounded soldiers—while Tam wore his Royal Scots Fusiliers kilt, which Bertha brought from Scotland in her keepsake chest.

Toasts were toasted and songs were sung, the exact memories of which Helen now struggled to piece together. She vaguely remembered polishing Buchan's brass memorial plaque after arriving home last night and hanging it back in its place of honor in the parlor, running her fingers over the raised letters of her poor wee brother's name.

"Och, my head," she moaned to Will, who shuffled to the kitchen table in a similar condition. "Are yeh gonna eat this mornin' or will yeh be goin' back to bed?"

"Mmm ..." he replied, his tongue too thick to talk. He gestured for tea and Helen delivered it to him.

"I'll ask again later," she said, relieved. She joined him with her own cuppa, blowing to cool the steaming brew. They sipped in silence until Jeanie bounded into the kitchen, so excited she neglected to read the room.

"Yeh're finally up," she declared. "I've been waiting forever!"

Helen gave Jeanie the steely eye and said, "This isn't a good time, hen." She held her abdomen to suppress the urge to boak. "I'll not drink like that again, ever."

"Och, yeh'll forget and do it again," said Will, trying to chuckle. "That's the beauty and the curse of strong drink. Mebbe yeh need to sign a contract, like Babe Ruth did yesterday, to stay away from it."

Helen poked out her tongue at him and Jeanie demanded, "Listen, would youse? I just had my nineteenth birthday and I want to start planning my future. One of the girls told me last night about two nearby nursing schools, Holy Cross up in Salt Lake City and another in Provo."

"Yeh're not going to a Catholic school in Salt Lake," snapped Will, "over a hundred mile away!"

It finally sunk in for Jeanie that this was a bad time, seeing her father's snarly mood, but she had rehearsed her pitch and couldn't back down now. She knew they'd say no to Holy Cross—bringing it up first was intentional —so she was ready with her preferred school. "Provo's only sixty miles," she plowed on, "and I could come home on the train, on weekends. That's not a Catholic school. It's at Provo General Hospital."

"Not now," Helen scolded. "Can yeh not see yer father's in no condition? Nor am I," said Helen. She leapt from her chair, darting out the back door to vomit in the snow. Her head swam with the dizziness.

"Yeh want to be a nurse?" Will asked Jeanie. "Go take care of yer mother."

Jeanie stepped outside into the frosty air and briskly rubbed Helen's arms to keep her warm. "Are y'alright, Mam? Yeh're looking a bit peely wally," she said.

"Och, no," moaned Helen. She straightened and shook her head to clear it and reeled with vertigo. "Oof, that was a mistake," she said and grabbed onto Jeanie to steady herself. She picked up a clump of snow off the porch rail, rubbed it across her forehead and asked, "Would yeh mind making sure your brother and sisters get fed? I'm goin' back to bed and I think yer da will not be far behind me."

Jeanie sighed and helped her wobbly mother into the warm kitchen. She recognized what was going on, even if Helen didn't see it yet. It wasn't the drink—Helen could keep up with the others well enough, and she never drank enough to puke it back up. But another pregnancy would do it.

The girl was old enough to understand the ruckus she frequently heard coming through the walls from her parents' room. Even silly, wee Nellie had an adolescent idea of what they were up to in there. No matter how firmly Jeanie pressed her pillow over her ears to drown out their sounds and Nellie's giggling, there was no escaping the fact that Helen would soon have yet another bun in the oven.

Whether the pregnancy made it to full term or not, Helen would weaken and need extra help, which meant more work for Jeanie. Every outcome of another pregnancy meant no nursing school. It would be a hardship on her mother for Jeanie to go off to school. She would never be free to live her own life.

She led Helen to bed and pulled the quilt they brought from Scotland up under her chin. It was the same quilt that Jeanie had known her whole life, the same one that was always set aside every time Helen gave birth to keep it from staining. Tucking her mam in with it now made her homesick, missing even the hard times back in Scotland.

Jeanie shook her head to chase away these useless thoughts. No point in thinking about that now; there was work to do. Since Aunt Elsie had included her old cabinet commode as part of her generous housewarming furnishings, the ceramic chamber pot under the bed was rarely used so Jeanie didn't have to rinse it before setting it on the floor next to the bed where Helen could easily vomit into it, if necessary.

Helen was asleep by the time Jeanie finished setting up the familiar scene of taking care of her pregnant mother. It wouldn't do any good to resent that her dreams were again thwarted by circumstances beyond her control. One angry thought persisted, however, no matter how hard she tried to push it away: although Jeanie had never lain with a man, she had a head start on resenting that their need to rut overruled the needs of women, even those who weren't their wives.

ɸᴓ

Soon, there came another holiday, Thanksgiving. As Jessie and Bertha yammered on about how it was to be celebrated—whose house? how would they seat everyone? what foods would be served and who would prepare what?—only Helen knew that Bill and Elsie had invited just her household to Thanksgiving. Both Will and Helen preferred to stay home and have a good old-fashioned Scottish tuck in—putting the American turkey tradition aside—but they felt obligated to go to Bill and Elsie's.

It was an honor they shouldn't pass up, with Bill being the superintendent and no other miners invited, but that honor caused discord. Will said to Helen, "It isn't just deciding between a posh dinner and our own homey folks. Bill invites his highfalutin friends and, while they may be friendly enough to our faces, yeh know as well as I that they look down their noses at us working-class stiffs."

"I can't argue," Helen said, "yeh're right." Although her brother never overtly lorded it over Will, Bill's upper crust peers in Castle Gate knew Will was just an uneducated miner. She always noticed a touch of condescension in their tones, the way they smiled at him in his best suit with just-this-side-of-pity.

Helen and Jeanie made the trek up the hill the Saturday before the holiday to inform Elsie of their decision to stay home. Elsie invited them inside for a cup of tea and Helen explained, as they sat at the kitchen table, "We're the only family Pete and Tam have and they depend on us for family gatherings. Jessie and Bertha and their wee'uns have only been here a month."

"Well, we'll miss you," Elsie said. "It's our one-year wedding anniversary party next Saturday and you'll have to come for that. I won't take 'no' for an answer!"

"How d'yeh find the time to entertain so often?" Jeanie asked.

"I have hired help," Elsie winked. "Surely you don't think I could do this by myself. Heavens, no. Being the superintendent's wife is a full-time job, on top of day-to-day housework and raising a passel of young'uns." Elsie opened the newspaper and pointed to an ad on page five, "Since you're hosting your own, look here … Wilson's, down in Price, has Thanksgiving specials. I don't see their price for turkey, but they have pot roast for only ten cents a pound …"

"Och!" Helen cried, grabbing the paper, excited enough to fall back into her full Scots brogue, "Mutton's ainly seventeen cents a poond! Jeanie, hen, we'll take the train doon and stock up on messages. Lookit aw they canned goods on sale."

"Heavens, Helen," laughed Elsie, "your brogue is so thick sometimes I can barely understand you."

Mildly taken aback, Helen put the paper down and resisted mentioning Elsie's midwestern twang, but Jeanie jumped right in, saying, "Aunt Elsie, I cannot understand a word you say half the time. And Uncle Bill, he sounds more American than anyone."

"Yes, he surely does," laughed Elsie, "Bill's been here so long, he's lost much of his brogue, at least it must sound that way to you. When he's in his cups and quoting Robert Burns, though, you'd never know he's lived here over a decade."

"Aye," added Helen, "our Wullie has taken to sounding more American. He tries so hard to not sound Scottish."

"It's like he's ashamed," said Jeanie, reaching for a cookie to dunk in her tea.

"Well, no," said Elsie, "Bill has shared with me that Willie is trying to fit in with others his age. They tease him for his accent. He's rather a sensitive boy, isn't he?"

"Sensitive? Our Wullie?" asked Jeanie.

"He's not a boy," Helen laughed, "Don't let him hear yeh call him that." She thought and said, "Aye, yeh're right, though. He does feel things deeper than he lets on."

"Aye," said Jeanie, "now that yeh mention it, it's his fault we had to flit here, the way he broke down over Walt Baxter's death."

"Now, hen," Helen admonished, "we'll not blame Wullie. There's many reasons we came, like my brother offering yer da a fine job. Isn't that right, Elsie?"

Elsie smiled, relieved by the change of subject, and said brightly, "Yes, and we're so glad you're here. It's such a shame you won't be with us on Thanksgiving, though. Oh well," she said, "next year!"

Helen shuddered and held up her arm to show Elsie and Jeanie, "Och, look at the goosebumps on my arm when yeh mention next year! It's like a goose walked over my grave."

"Is everything okay?" Elsie asked.

Helen was silent for a moment and finally replied, "Aye, I think so. But we should go. Thank yeh for the tea, hen."

"You're always welcome," said Elsie, "and don't forget next Saturday, our anniversary party. It'll be a small get together with family and friends."

Jeanie and Helen said their farewells and walked home with arms linked to not slip on the icy road. Jeanie asked, along the way, "What was that about? Are you okay?"

"Aye, just a pain in my gut is all," said Helen, "it's my lady's time and I'm not feeling up to snuff. But … that shudder I felt when Aunt Elsie talked about next year …" she paused, and then said, "It's nothing."

"Well, that's a relief," sighed Jeanie. "I thought yeh were pregnant again!"

"What?" Helen asked, "How'd yeh think that?"

"Well," Jeanie said, "yeh've been boaking lately, and I've heard you and Da going at it like rabbits. The walls are thin, yeh know."

Helen blushed and said, "Hold yer wheesht, lassie, yeh're not too big to skelp. I just had a bit of the flu bug, is all. I'm not pregnant, thank the Lord."

Jeanie replied, "Thank the Lord, indeed. I know it's harder on you than me, but I thought I'd have to put off nursing school another year. I don't want to sound selfish, but I cannot wait to start my own life as a grownup. I'll not be getting married and pushing out wee'uns any time soon."

"Och, famous last words," sighed Helen. She bundled her coat and scarf a little tighter against the wintry air and said, "Let's walk a wee bit faster, mind that ice, though. I cannot wait to get home where it's warm." She glanced to her left at the soaring Castle Gate rocks. It certainly wasn't anything like Scotland here in brown and rocky Utah, but it was finally feeling like it was, indeed, home.

CHAPTER 13

December, 1922
Castle Gate, Utah

Their first Christmas in America, Helen, Jessie and Bertha were surprised by the celebrations and Santa Claus brouhaha. For Scottish Presbyterians, Christmas was just another workday. Celebrating it as a holiday was banned by the Scottish Parliament, centuries ago. Although the ban was later repealed, Christmas was not a day of celebration.

That was not the case in the United States. Newspaper ads and day-to-day conversations were filled with talk of parties, Santa and gift giving. Friends and neighbors erected and festooned pine trees in their parlors. Children rehearsed for their Christmas pageant, where they would sing carols with a gusto driven by the anticipation of gifts and goodies.

Nellie came home from school with yards of stringed popcorn and cranberries to use as garland, hoping her parents could be persuaded to have a tree. She was relentlessly persuasive, as were Pete and Tam's girls, so the families agreed to low-key celebrations. Hogmanay—called New Year's Eve here—was when the real celebrating happened. Will arranged for some higher quality whisky than usual and some lovely port for the ladies.

Helen told Will, the day he, Pete and Tam took the train into Helper to pick up their holiday booze, "I'll not be drinking much. I cannot hold my liquor like I used to, so don't buy too much."

"Och, yeh're gettin' old," Will teased, "mebbe it's time to trade you in for a newer model."

Helen raised an eyebrow, daring him to say more. He grinned and said, "Must be the American hooch. Maybe the more expensive stuff will suit yeh."

"I hope so," said Helen, with a pained chuckle, "I'm still not recovered from November and the nonstop parties."

There was something different about the American hooch, or the food— or the air—or something. Whatever it was, it wasn't agreeing with Helen and she couldn't overindulge occasionally like she normally would. More of the foods here were sending her rushing to the loo and she had to watch what she ate or drank. Her lady's time cycle seemed off, too. Even when she wasn't in the throes of the monthly curse, she was seeing blood in the commode. Her energy was sapped and she got tired earlier, even with the longer winter daylight here in Utah.

Bertha came to visit while the men were away on their booze run and the conversation turned to lighter subjects, like squeezing Geordie's birthday celebration into the mix, and how much to spend on Christmas gifts, an idea a frugal Presbyterian Scot like Helen was having difficulty accepting.

Their blether was interrupted when Will and Tam burst through the front door, stomping snow off their boots. Helen hopped up and grabbed the broom to sweep it back outside. "Do that out on the porch, yeh dafty," she scolded. "Och, yeh reek of cigars and whisky."

"Hold yer wheesht, woman," Will replied, staggering a bit, "Don't tell me what to do."

"Yeh're steamin', aren't yeh?" Helen demanded, and Will waved her off, leading Tam through the house into the kitchen.

"Look who's here," Will said, "it's our Bertha. Tam, look, it's yer lovely bride."

"So much for Prohibition," said Bertha. "How did they let you on the train in this condition?"

Tam, not quite so drunk, explained, "He wasn't so bad when we boarded. He's been sipping at his stash all the way home."

"So?" demanded Will, "I'm just havin' a good time. Youse all need to loosen up."

Bertha stood to put on her coat and said to Helen, "I'll take this one home. You've got enough on your hands. Come on, you," she said, hustling Tam out the door before he could sit down and make himself comfortable.

Helen did have enough on her hands. At least the town was hosting a community Christmas party, with Santa for the children, and a New Year's celebration at the Amusement Hall. Helen was off the hook for extra entertaining beyond a big family dinner on Christmas Day and making sure there were plenty of gifts to go around.

She'd already purchased Will's present, a new fedora to replace his old, battered hat. Nellie had made no secret that she wanted a new dress and some pretty hair trinkets she saw at J.C. Penney's. Jeanie and Willie, who were older and more aware how extravagant and silly this holiday was, were reluctant to offer ideas for a special gift. Everyone got excited, though, once Will began dropping hints.

"I'm buying something special for yer mam and I need yeh to help me keep it a secret," he teased as the family sat down to tea the Saturday before Christmas.

"Hush, Wull Garroch," Helen said, "if it's a secret then don't talk about it. Otherwise, get it told!"

"Oh aye, that's half the fun of a secret," Will said, "keeping it from someone!"

"Och, hold yer wheesht," she said, "or you'll not get a gift yerself." Helen continued, "I saw a bonnie Teddy Bear, almost as big as our wee lassie, this morning in the newspaper," she said, chucking the toddler under the chin. "Would yeh like a wee bear for yer Christmas?"

Ella didn't understand a word, but recognized a happy question, so she nodded and said, "Aye, peez."

Willie cut in as Helen flipped through the paper to find the ad, "It's 'yes, please,' Ella. Say 'yes'."

Ella grinned at her big brother, nodded her head and said, "Essss."

"Good girl," Willie said.

"Och, don't talk pish," said Will. "She's a wee Scottish lassie, and she'll learn to talk like an American soon enough."

Nellie asked, "Can we get a radio, Da?"

Will said, "We haven't any electricity. How're yeh gonna power a radio?"

"Can we get electricity?" Nellie moaned. "We don't have a piano either, like everyone else, so we can't play any music at all."

"'Everyone' doesn't have a piano, and there's no electric wires in this part of town," Willie said. "Only rich folks like Uncle Bill, or Uncle Geordie who lives uptown, have it in their house."

"Tommy Hilton has a radio, he plays it for the neighbors," Nellie replied, folding her arms across her chest. "How's he do that?"

"He powers it off a car battery. Now, give us peace, lass," scolded Will. "If it's music yeh're wanting, whistle a wee tune. Dance a wee jig for us."

"Nobody ever listens to me!" cried Nellie, and she stomped away into the bedroom.

Her fit of pique was needless because, on Christmas Day, Will surprised Helen with a wind-up Victrola. He enlisted the two older children, along with Jessie and Bertha, to gift Helen with phonograph records, knowing they could keep the secret. The kids danced the Fox Trot and the Charleston to tunes like Eddie Cantor's song *Oh, Is She Dumb!* and *Toot Toot Tootsie* by Al Jolson, while the women toiled in the kitchen and the men quaffed whisky, keeping the new machine cranked and egging the kids on.

When Hogmanay rolled around, Jeanie and Willie went off with friends, and Nellie babysat her wee sister and young cousins, bribed with cash in exchange for staying home. That was one good thing about America. The men made better money here. Back home, she'd never get paid for a family obligation.

Plenty of British transplants gathered at the KP Hall to ring in 1923 with the Robert Burns standard, *Auld Lang Syne*. The Scots who fought in the Great War, and who were sloshing in their cups by the time midnight came, linked their arms and laughingly sang the tune of the Burns song with words they'd sung in the battlefields in France: "We're here because we're here, because we're here, because we're here ..."

"Och," Helen declared to Jessie, wiping away tears, "poor wee Buchan told me they used to sing this while they marched. He told me, 'Yeh get so bored out there, waiting for something to happen and dreading it at the same time, all for no good reason. We're here because we're here, and nobody can give us a better explanation.' Och, I miss him so."

"I know, hen," Jessie said, embracing her sister-in-law. "We all miss him."

There wasn't a dry eye at the KP Hall, between those who were homesick and those who mourned friends and family that were killed. With the midnight hour passed, the Scots all took this opportunity to celebrate the tradition of stepping the first foot into their American homes with a fresh, new start. All in all, it was a beautiful and nostalgic end to an eventful year. With continued good luck, 1923 would be even better.

CHAPTER 14

January 8, 1923
Castle Gate, Utah

While a sense of relief was felt by all to get back to everyday life after the holiday hoopla, the letdown was palpable. Helen had nothing to distract her from the worsening pain in her gut and the blood she was seeing more frequently in the commode. She could no longer fool herself that it was related to her lady's time. It was coming from another place entirely. She needed to see a doctor.

Dr. Claude McDermid was an affable young man, well-loved in Castle Gate for his bedside manner and sense of humor. Dr. McDermid was about Helen's age—slender and tall, with brown hair and eyes—and he put her at ease by gabbing as he helped her lie back on the examination table and pressed her belly. "We've had a nice mild winter, haven't we, Mrs. Garroch?" Even with a Scottish name like McDermid, he pronounced her name as all Americans did, *Gay-rock*, without rolling the Rs or stressing the H. "Are you feeling any pain," he asked, "when I press here? How about here?"

"I wouldn't call it pain, more of a discomfort," Helen replied. "The pain has naught to do with pressing anything. It comes from the inside and feels like burning, like cramping up after a meal that doesn't agree with yeh." He continued pressing and finally Helen said, "Aye, that does hurt, right there."

"Let's get you an x-ray," he said.

While waiting for the results, Helen tried to keep from wandering into fearful thoughts but it was difficult. She'd never needed an x-ray before. Maybe this was the kind of thing American doctors always performed for their patients. After all, the mine here was much more modern than back home, why not the medical care, too?

What Doctor McDermid finally told her wasn't good news. "I'm afraid it's cancer and it's inoperable," he said. "It's already spread too far."

Helen asked, not comprehending what the doctor was telling her, "What can I do? Is there some medicine I can take?"

"There are no approved medications and I want you to stay away from snake oil remedies," Dr. McDermid said. "They do more harm than good." He continued, choosing his words carefully, "This is hard to say, and even harder to hear I'm sure, but you've probably got about six months. Use this time to say your goodbyes and get right with God."

"What?" Helen blinked, "I'm gonna die? In six months? How did that happen so quick? I haven't been sick very long."

"You've probably been experiencing symptoms for a while but didn't pay attention, or chalked them up to other things," Dr. McDermid said. "How long since you've felt entirely well?"

Helen thought for a moment. "Well, now that yeh put it that way," she said, "it's been a long time, but I ... chalked it up, as you say ... to being worn down. Life's full of weary-making work, intit, doctor? And there's no rest for the weary." She was silent and then said, "It doesn't help that I've always got a bun in the oven or just gave birth. There's always pain and blood, and yeh get used to it. I don't know how long ... *that* ... bleeding has been goin' on."

Before sending her home, Dr. McDermid patted her hand and said, "If you need anything, let me know. I'll do everything I can to help get you through what's to come."

His final words gave Helen a chill, like a goose walked over her grave. She was going to die, sooner rather than later, and it was going to be difficult.

The walk home from town felt longer than usual but it gave Helen time alone. She gazed at the Castle Gate rocks, capped with a layer of snow, as she strode north. It was a sight she'd grown to love.

Ella was with Bertha for the afternoon, so Helen was unhurried. She stopped when she reached her porch to take in her high-walled surroundings here in Price Canyon, a world away from bonnie Scotland.

This is where she would die. She would never see her family back home again. She would be buried in the town cemetery, around the bend in Willow Creek Canyon, the land under which miners burrowed in Mine #2.

Feeling the cold, finally, Helen went inside. She hung up her coat and stoked the fire, and decided to take advantage of the time alone to sit in her kitchen and have a nice, quiet cup of tea. She couldn't remember the last time she'd had the luxury of just sitting—not cooking, or cleaning, or sewing, or listening for a baby's cry, or …

She was only 38. That's not old enough to die, and she'd survived so much.

Just then she felt a familiar cramp in her gut. There it was. That's what was going to kill her.

This was the pain she'd been ignoring—there it had been, growing inside her, slowly taking over as she was busy scrubbing floors and wiping the baby's bum. Now that pain was tinged with a special kind of fear: it would keep getting worse until she died from the inability to bear it any longer.

"Mammy, Daddy," she cried aloud "I don't want to die!"

What would happen to her family? Who would raise Ella? Would Jessie and Bertha look in on her from time to time to make sure Will and Jeanie were taking good care of her poor wee lass?

And what about Nellie—Helen Jr.—named after herself? Nellie would be the same age as Helen when her own mother passed. Nellie would watch her die, just as she had watched her own mother, only this would be long and drawn out, lingering over the course of months instead of days.

What about Jeanie? Helen laughed ruefully as she said aloud in the empty kitchen, "Shoulda let her go to nursin' school." She knew Jeanie would be there for her—it was in the girl's nature—but Helen dreaded putting her through that. Nursing was bloody, dirty work. Poor Jeanie, the untrained nurse, would be tasked with tending her mother to her death.

Willie would take it hard. She had an unspoken understanding with her son, the only male child to make it past infancy. He kept to himself and his new American friends, but he could confide in Helen if he needed to. They could communicate with just a glance. It was always that way. It would be difficult to leave the Earth plane, knowing how hard he would take her death. A lad needs his mam.

Would Will remarry? Of course, he would. He'd have wee'uns who need a mother, and a man has carnal needs. There was no shortage of widows in a mining town and, God love 'em, they'd jockey for position to land a catch like her Will. Good thing he'd have Jeanie to help with Ella, or he'd have to rush into it with the first woman who set her cap at him. He was a good and sturdy man, a dependable provider and loving father, for all his gruff exterior. And if his new wife was the sort who enjoyed a man in her bed, she'd find he was always up for a good rogering.

"How soon before he'll resort to whores?" she tried not to wonder. Helen wanted to believe that he hadn't fallen into that, down in Helper, before she arrived in Utah. She hoped that knowing she wasn't long after him would help him keep it to himself, but he was only a man and none of them were worth a damn at keeping their peckers in their pants. She'd overheard men talking at various parties, when they didn't know there was a woman about, saying it doesn't count as infidelity if they pay for it. In that case, it was considered medicinal.

These thoughts of sex and death were taking her nowhere, though. She was torturing herself with nonsense. It was time to bring Ella home. Surely, she was awake from her nap by now and, even if she wasn't, Helen's mood had shifted and she now craved company.

She threw on her coat and crunched across the packed snow, taking a shortcut through the yards to Bertha and Tam's house. She wasn't halfway across Bertha's yard when she heard Jessie's raucous laughter coming from inside and her heart lifted. There was merriment in there and she couldn't wait to join in, leaving her morbid thoughts outdoors.

CHAPTER 15

January 27, 1923
Castle Gate, Utah

Helen's first Burns Supper in America should have been joyous, surrounded by her Scottish family and friends. The birthday of Scotland's national bard was an important holiday. She and Will had been looking forward to eating traditional Scots foods, singing songs by Rabbie Burns and imbibing the best locally brewed whisky in their new community.

The event was hosted by John and Bethia Littlejohn at their lovely home on Castle Gate's "Silk Row" where they had moved when John was promoted to inspector of the Utah Fuel Company properties. Now, they could afford this electrically-powered and well-appointed home near Bill's even grander house.

Geordie, who so loved planning parties, arranged a list of Burns' songs with solos pre-assigned to the best singers in the group. He even included a group sing-along or two, so no one was left out.

Sinking into Bethia's comfy sofa, enjoying the warm coziness of her brother's home, Helen felt a pang of guilt for spending the festive event with the posh folk instead of at Pete and Jessie's, where keeping warm meant sitting close to the fire. She needed an evening away from cooking and cleaning and playing the hostess. And, for once, Helen was able to spend time with Bill and Elsie as just another guest at someone else's party.

"It's that nice to see you and Bill," Helen said to Elsie, "without youse two being so busy hosting."

"Isn't it grand?" Elsie gushed. "I hardly know what to do with myself. I feel like I should be passing around a tray of nibbles."

Traditionally, it was the task of the host to "address the haggis" before slicing it open and serving the crumbly sausage with mashed turnips and potatoes, but John had asked their elder brother to do the honor, as he recited poetry so beautifully. When Bill raised his glass in toast and recited the traditional Burns poem *Address to a Haggis*, he deliberately spoke in his full Scottish brogue and thrilled them all with his perfect delivery:

> *Fair fa' your honest, sonsie face,*
> *Great chieftain o the puddin'-race!*
> *Aboon them a' yeh tak your place,*
> *Painch, tripe, or thairm:*
> *Weel are yeh wordy o' a grace*
> *As lang's my arm ...*

On the complex poem went and Bill recited it perfectly from memory, reminding Helen that her Americanized eldest brother—who had moved on to get his education when she was only six and then got married and flitted to the States—really was a Scot at heart.

This realization brought on a rush of sentimentality. Last year she was crossing the Atlantic on Burns Night and her worries were trivial in comparison. This year, Helen was wondering when to tell anyone about the cancer that was eating her up inside.

On one hand, if she shared the news she wouldn't have to bear the fear alone. On the other hand, it would change the way everyone looked at her. She would become diseased in their eyes, seen as weak and sick, an object of pity, which she couldn't abide. Once she told, there was no turning back.

She pushed the thoughts away and focused on her final Burns Supper. Never had haggis, neeps and tatties tasted so delicious. Never had the wee dram gone down so smoothly. And, never had she appreciated so much her brothers' combined presentation of Scottish conviviality. They worked together to pull off a fine celebration, making everyone—even the non-Scots in attendance—feel welcomed. So impressed by their display, and so wanting to savor the special occasion, she determined to put her own troubles aside for the evening.

After the meal, Bethia invited everyone to the parlor and Geordie and John rose to sing together, accompanied by Bethia on the piano. The scene stirred up for Helen memories of Burns nights and family singalongs during their childhoods in Galston and Dreghorn—their humble beginnings in the miners' rows, working hard to keep a roof over their heads.

These were her dear kin, with whom she had grown up and from whom she had grown apart, even though they were neighbors again. John there, belting out a tune with Geordie, was almost a stranger, he was so busy. He had little time to see his younger sister. Although he and Helen shared a cordial relationship, they were by no means as close as they were growing up despite the three-year age difference.

Geordie, who clearly loved singing and had a beautiful voice, was her dearest brother now that Buchan had passed. He was closest to her in age (and size)—fun-loving, annoying, teasing wee Geordie—and he was the one she would miss most. Or would she? *'Can we miss loved ones after we die,'* she wondered, *'or is missing the dead a one-way street?'*

Then Geordie sang his solo, *Ye Banks and Braes*, Burns' soulful song about heartache and betrayal along the banks of the beautiful River Doon in his hometown of Alloway. It was one of Helen's favorites and Geordie sang in such warm and mournful tenor tones, it was all Helen could do to keep from weeping.

Elsie placed her hand gently on Helen's arm, and asked, "Are you alright?"

"Aye, just homesick," Helen replied.

Next, Bill rose to perform, first delivering a speech in his Americanized accent, "As the Scots here tonight know, Robert Burns was the Ploughman Poet, a farmer's son who spoke for the common man even though he rose to a level of wealth and prominence. My favorite Burns song is a perfect expression of everything he stands for." Then Bill launched whole-heartedly into an a cappella version of *A Man's a Man for A' That,* rolling his Rs like a true Scot:

> *Is there for honest Poverty*
> *That hings his head, an' a' that;*
> *The coward slave-we pass him by,*
> *We dare be poor for a' that!*
> *For a' that, an' a' that.*
> *Our toils obscure an' a' that,*
> *The rank is but the guinea's stamp,*
> *The Man's the gowd for a' that.*

He sang the following three verses on his own, but invited everyone to sing along with him on the final verse and they did so with gusto, their hearts welling with Scottish pride:

Then let us pray that come it may,
As come it will for a' that,
That Sense and Worth, o'er a' the earth,
Shall bear the gree, an' a' that.
For a' that, an' a' that,
It's coming yet for a' that,
That Man to Man, the world o'er,
Shall brothers be for a' that.

Finally, Geordie invited everyone to a sing-along of the sprightly tune *There Was a Lad Was Born In Kyle*. Those from the old country jumped to their feet and sang while they danced and clapped, while the American guests simply danced and clapped along, unable to follow along with the lyrics:

There was a lad was born in Kyle,
But whatna day o' whatna style,
I doubt it's hardly worth the while
To be sae nice wi' Robin.

After singing and clapping along to the song with its many verses and rolled Rs over "rantin' rovin' Robin," Helen fell laughing into Will's arms and he kissed the top of her head, enjoying her happiness. It had been a while since Helen had lightened up and her giddiness was a relief.

After a dessert of cranachan—a parfait with layers of whipped cream, raspberries, and whisky-soaked toasted oats—the guests sang *Auld Lang Syne*, the traditional close to a Burns Supper.

Should auld acquaintance be forgot
And never brought to mind?
Should auld acquaintance be forgot
And days of auld lang syne?

As they joined voices in the many verses of a sentimental remembrance of old times past, Helen was struck by the raw fact that she'd never do this again. By this time next year, she'd be dead, and they'd be singing in remembrance of her, an "auld acquaintance." She envisioned her own ghost standing amongst them, waving in their faces, trying in vain to get them to see she was there.

She wondered whether Buchan was doing that right now and whether he was singing the proper words or the soldiers' words, "We're here because we're here…".

Whether through will or whimsy, Helen felt a brief flash of Buchan's presence—uninjured Buchan, like before he went off to war—waving in her face, taunting her, daring her to see him before he vanished just as quickly as he appeared.

Helen choked on the sadly nostalgic lyrics, her voice cramping in her throat, and she whispered to Will, "I need some fresh air." She ducked out the front door without her coat as surreptitiously as possible, but not without Geordie's notice.

He looked at Will with raised eyebrows and Will responded with a shrug of confusion. As the revelers continued singing, the two men followed and found her around the corner, off to the side of the house. She was up to her knees in a snowdrift, wretchedly bawling.

"What? Hen …" Will sputtered, alarmed, "what is it?" He waded through the snow and put his arm around her shoulders. He tried to pull her close but she sobbed and jerked away, unable just now to be held. Powerless to help otherwise, he took off his suit jacket and draped it around her shoulders for warmth.

Geordie pushed through the snowbank to stand on her other side. "Helen," he said, in his most soothing voice, "tell us what's wrong, hen."

Still crying hard, she could only make guttural sounds as she tried to talk. Knowing she must look like a wild woman, eyes frantic, nose running, she fell to her knees and let out another heart-wrenching sob.

Will fought her weight to pull her up, back to her feet, scolding, "Hen, get up out of the snow. You'll catch your death!"

At this, Helen burst into hysterical laughter. The dam broke and she was able to speak. "It's too late!" she cried. "I've caught my death!" Finally, she allowed Will to hold her with a comforting arm as she sobbed into his chest.

Geordie took her hand and said, "Helen, get it told. What's this all about?"

"I didn't want to tell youse, not yet," Helen began, sniffling, "I've got the cancer. I'll not be here next year … for all this … for auld lang syne. I'll be a ghost, waving my hand in yer faces trying to get yer attention!"

Will's face remained passive as he asked, "Are yeh sure? Have yeh seen the doctor?"

"Of course, I have, Wull Garroch!" Helen cried, jerking herself away from his protective arm and pulling her hand from Geordie's. "D'yeh think I'd invent dire pronouncements like that?"

"Now, calm down," said Geordie, "no need to bark at anyone. It's … a lot to take in. Was it Dr. McDermid? What did he say?"

"Aye, Dr. McDermid," she said, allowing a cautious Will to put his arm around her again. She buried her face in his chest and he tightened his grip. She finally said, her voice muffled by Will's shirt, "He told me it was inoperable. I have about six months to live."

Geordie clapped a hand over his mouth to stifle a gasp, recalling when Bill's late wife Mary was diagnosed with lady's cancer just four years ago, and her surgery didn't go well. She lasted only a few months and it was a horrible, lingering death.

"Wait. Yeh said yeh didn't want to tell us," Will reminded her. "How long have yeh known?"

"Almost a month," said Helen.

"So, does that mean yeh only have five months?" Will asked, his voice almost a whisper.

Helen laughed again, a humorless snort, "I don't know, do I? Alls I know is I'm dying and there isn't anything to do about it."

Around the front of the house, John and Bethia's guests were departing so they ducked further around the corner, out of sight, huddled together for warmth until everyone cleared away.

Finally, Will said, "Let's get you inside. I'll not have yeh catching pneumonia and leaving me sooner than yeh have to."

"Aye, let's talk about this indoors, just us family," said Geordie. He led her back to the house through the deep footprints they had punched into the snowbank.

The house was empty of everyone but Littlejohns. Bill and Elsie sat at the dining table with John and Bethia, sipping port out of elegant, crystal cordial glasses, reminiscing about what a delightful evening was had by all. The warm contentment didn't last long once they saw Geordie, Helen and Will coming in the front door, stomping and brushing snow from their clothing. Helen's eyes and nose were red from crying and the two men were somber.

"What's all this?" cried Bill, leaping to his feet. "We were wondering where you three disappeared to!" He hurried to lead Helen to the chair nearest the fireplace to dry her dress at the hearth. "Elsie, sweetheart, get Helen a drink, please."

"Certainly," Elsie said and brought Helen a delicate, stemmed cordial glass filled with port. "Here you are, dear. What on Earth are you three doing outside without your coats?"

"I'm having a whisky," said Geordie, pouring himself a dram. "Wull?"

"Aye, whisky," said Will. He sat in the chair next to Helen and reached to lay his hand over hers. He nodded his thanks to Geordie, as he was handed his drink, and the others seated themselves nearby.

Bill offered Helen his handkerchief to wipe her eyes and nose. "I'll wash this and get it back to yeh," she said to Elsie.

"You keep that," said Elsie, "Bill's got plenty. He won't miss it."

"Indeed, I won't," said Bill. "Now, what's this all about?"

Helen tucked the handkerchief into her sleeve, took a breath and blurted, "I've got the cancer. Dr. McDermid says I have six months to live … well, five now."

John and Bethia both gasped and Bill's face turned white. Elsie displayed no emotion other than a flicker of disturbance in her eyes. Bill pursed his lips and considered his next words. Finally, he asked, "What else did he say? Does he suggest any treatment?"

"No," said Helen, "it's too far gone, and he said surgery wouldn't help."

"Oh my," said Bill. "No, it didn't help Mary and we paid for the best medical treatment money can buy."

None of Helen's brothers wanted to tell her what Mary had gone through back in 1919, but they couldn't help recalling it now. After surgery, she wasted away over the next four months. She was wracked with pain but refused the morphine unless necessary, as she wanted to stay clear-headed. Geordie had just been discharged from serving at an Army medical base in Colorado and, after Mary's surgery, he helped care for her as he had for countless wounded soldiers. It was harder, he found, when it was family, especially someone so well loved.

And now, Geordie had to fight to remain expressionless. He was about to lose his beloved Helen to a similarly wretched death. Just as Helen had doted on their wee Buchan, Geordie had watched over her. They had finally become neighbors again and now God was going to take her away from him.

"Hen," said Will, "yeh've known this for weeks. How d'yeh not tell anyone, especially me?"

"I wanted everything to stay the same for a while," explained Helen. "I didn't want to become the object of pity, like I am now. I don't feel sick yet, at least, not enough to make a fuss."

"Well," Will replied, "we can talk about that when we get home. Meantime, what are we to do? Surely there must be something the doctor can come up with."

"Dr. McDermid is very good," said Bill. "If he knew of any form of treatment, he'd recommend it. For now, we carry on while Helen's health is strong and don't tell the children yet. In fact, we should keep it between us … maybe you can confide in your trusted lady friends, so you have support in your neighborhood."

She nodded and said, "Aye, I'll tell Jessie and Bertha, and swear them to secrecy."

Will shot him a look, disturbed that Bill—as head of the Littlejohn family—was trampling over his role as Helen's husband and advisor, but Bill didn't see it and continued, a faraway look in his eyes, "I can't help thinking, your Nellie is about the same age as you were when our mam died, isn't she?"

"Aye," Helen confirmed, "she's thirteen now, but she'll be fourteen by the time … by the time I go. At least our Jeanie is still at home so's it won't be all on Nell. Poor wee Ella will never know her own mam …" Helen stopped abruptly, as another word would bring forth a new batch of sobs.

"Here, have another wee sip of port," said Will.

"I will, cheers," said Helen, taking more than a wee sip. She put the empty cordial glass down on the side table and said, "Wull, I want to go home. I've made a scene and that wasn't what I wanted to do."

"I'll drive yeh, hen," said Geordie, "even though we didn't make it 'til the wee sma' hours o' the mornin' like good Scots should on Burns Night."

"Wheesht," scoffed Helen, "yeh've seen plenty of 'wee sma hours' for the both of us."

"Aye, that I have," chuckled Geordie. "Now let's get youse two home."

Bethia rose to retrieve their coats from the master bedroom, where they had been stowed on the bed. Bill said to her, "Get ours, too, would you please? I don't know about anyone else, but I don't feel much like celebrating anymore."

Helen said, with an edge in her voice, "I'm sorry to spoil everyone's good time. That's why I kept it to myself."

"That's not what I meant, dear Helen," said Bill, "but if anything does spoil a good time, it's knowing that you've been carrying this heavy burden on your own. You don't have to be alone in this, you know."

Bethia returned with the coats and Elsie affirmed Bill's sentiment, "Yes, Helen dear, please don't hesitate to let us know what you need."

John and Bethia also offered pledges of support as everyone said their goodnights. Bundled up against the cold January night, Bill and Geordie walked their passengers to their cars.

Geordie drove Will and Helen across the railroad tracks to what seemed, when they first moved in, to be a luxurious big house compared to what they left in Scotland. Now, in contrast to John's spacious home—with its electric lamps and velvet drapes—the four-room saltbox house seemed small and shabby with the light of a single oil-lantern glowing through the homemade, cotton-fabric curtains.

"That'll be Jeanie, burning the midnight oil," said Will.

"Give the wee'uns my love," said Geordie, as Will and Helen climbed out of his car and into the snow.

"Thanks for the ride," said Will, and he led Helen into the house as Geordie pulled away.

The parlor was chilly and Jeanie sat huddled on the davenport in her flannel nightgown covered by a crocheted afghan, nose buried in a book. She looked up and said, "How was yer evening with the uncles?"

"It was lovely. Yeh let the fire die. Are yeh not freezing?" asked Helen.

"Och! Sorry," said Jeanie, and she jumped to her feet to stoke the coals. "I was that engrossed, I didn't even notice."

"That must be some book," said Will, hanging up their coats. "Yer Uncle Geordie put together a fine evening of entertainment, sure, and the food was first rate."

Helen said, "Aye, Bethia puts on a nice spread. Did youse have a good time at Aunt Jessie's?"

Jeanie grinned in remembrance and said, "Aye, Uncle Pete's a hoot. Aunt Jessie sent home a plate for youse to share, in case yeh didn't like the food at Uncle John's."

Helen laughed and said, "That's our Jessie, always looking out fer us."

"Always gettin' her digs in, is more like it," said Will, heading to the kitchen to investigate the plate that Jessie sent over.

"Aye, that too," Helen agreed. "Are the wee lassies in bed? And Wullie? Still out with Tommy?"

"Aye, and I finally got Ella down a half hour ago," said Jeanie. "Nell's been asleep for a while. I think she was sneaking wee sips of Bertha's wine. She'll have a big head the morrow."

"Och, me and all," said Will, from the kitchen where he was digging into the leftovers. "You off to bed, hen?"

"Aye," said Jeanie, "I'll see youse in the morning."

"G'night, darlin'," said Helen. Jeanie went off to her room and Helen joined Will in the kitchen. "Anything good?" she asked.

"Jessie's cranachan is good but Bethia used better whisky," said Will.

"Those who can afford it …," said Helen. "I'm off to bed. Yeh comin'?"

"Right behind yeh," said Will. He turned down the lantern and the house was dark and cold, only lit by the glow of the fire. "Let's get under them covers."

They changed quickly into their nightclothes and nestled together beneath the quilts. As was their custom, Helen lay on her side with her back turned to Will and he lay close to her, belly to back, with his arm around her. While they usually huddled this way for warmth, tonight Will's arm held Helen a little more tightly.

It was their silent understanding that they would talk no more tonight. There were no words. Finally, Will heard Helen's breathing pattern changing to a soft snore. Then, he spoke his final words for that day, whispering into her hair, "Don't die, hen. Please. I couldn't bear it."

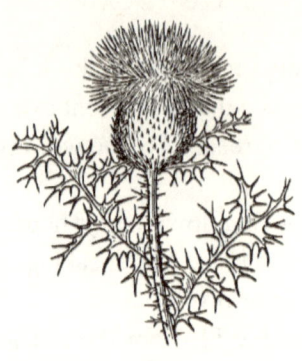

CHAPTER 16

Spring, 1923
Castle Gate, Utah

Life went on in Castle Gate. Snow melted, gardens were planted, scrub grass grew in patches and children ran barefoot again despite the spiky vegetation. And while the days grew longer and nights grew shorter, Helen grew incrementally weaker. She would be unable to keep her secret for long as it would soon become obvious that her strength was beginning to wane. Her knees sometimes buckled, causing sudden falls. Fortunately, she hadn't been badly hurt … yet … and it hadn't happened when anyone was home. There was no telling, though, how long before she'd get a black eye or knock out her front teeth, and what if she badly hurt herself or wee Ella when no one was home?

She kept her fear of being alone to herself because it wasn't yet as great as the legitimate fear of becoming a burden. To inflict her care on someone else would be hard enough on the family, but to add to the workload of others meant you must be suffering badly enough to ask it of them.

And it wasn't that bad … yet. Jessie and Bertha checked on her daily and helped in any way Helen needed. Their daughters were in school and their workloads were lighter than Helen's, who had a toddler and two men to clean up after.

Helen's goal was to keep the secret from her children until after Nellie's fourteenth birthday, in mid-March. She and Jeanie put together a little party for Nellie, inviting her girlfriends to come over for cake and to listen to records on the Victrola. Their record collection was growing, with the three teenagers buying new records regularly. The birthday girl's favorite was *Chicago, That Toddlin' Town,* followed by *That Old Gang of Mine,* but the crowd favorite was *Yes, We Have No Bananas,* a jaunty tune that poked playful fun at the accent of a Greek fruit merchant. Back in Scotland, none of the Garrochs would have been in on the joke, but now that they had Greek friends and neighbors, they understood the gentle humor.

In the weeks following, as Helen and Will discussed ways to break the news to their children, Jeanie's perceptive eye helped solve the problem.

One evening as Nellie was reading Ella a bedtime story and Willie was out with Tommy, Jeanie joined her parents at the kitchen table and asked, point blank, "Mam, what's wrong? Yeh're always tired and yer color's off. Usually when yeh're this peely wally it means yeh're pregnant, but that's not it, is it?"

Will and Helen glanced at one another, neither wanting to be the one to speak. After a long moment, Will finally said, "Lass, yer mother has the cancer."

Jeanie blanched and exhaled a deep breath. She fanned her face with her hand and said, "That's me then, all peely wally." She paused and asked, "When d'yeh go in for surgery? Will yeh be in hospital long?"

"There'll be no surgery," Helen said. "Dr. McDermid said it's gone too far."

Jeanie asked, "So … what'll yeh do? Take some kind of medicine?"

"No, lass," Will said, "yeh're not hearing us. Yer mam is gonna die." His heart broke a little watching his daughter bite her lip to fight back tears and he continued, "It's a wrench, I know, but I cannot put it more gently than that."

Jeanie nodded but then cried out, "Oh, Mam! What are we to do without yeh? Yeh cannot leave us!"

Helen wiped away her own tears and replied, "I don't want to go, hen, yeh must know that. But there's naught I can do. The doctor says so." Helen laughed ruefully and continued, "Believe me, I asked. Yer father and I have been trying to find a way to break the news to all of youse and yeh're the first one to know."

"I wish I didn't," said Jeanie. "I wish I could turn back the clock."

"Aye, me and all," Will said and Helen nodded in agreement. "How will we tell yer wee sister? She'll take the news the hardest."

Jeanie considered whether to argue that point … she had always been seen as the stoic, sensible one, which led her family to believe she didn't have feelings … but that was a battle for another day. Nellie, the dramatic one, may not take it the hardest but she would take it the loudest.

"Are youse talking about me?" Nellie asked, entering the kitchen. "What news?"

Will and Helen shared a glance and he said, under his breath so only Helen could hear, "I guess it's happening now." He said to Nellie, "Aye, hen, yer mam and me, we have some bad news. Sit down."

Nellie's eyes widened and she cried out, panicked, "What is it? What's wrong?"

"Sit here, hen," Jeanie said, pulling out a chair so her sister could sit beside her. Once Nellie was seated, Will said, "Mam's got the cancer. There's nothing the doctor can do. She's gonna die." He cut straight to the point to circumvent the question everyone, including him, kept asking about the nonexistent plan of treatment.

Nellie's face crumpled and she burst into sobs. Helen came around the table to her and Nellie folded herself into her mother's embrace and bawled, "No, Mammy, yeh cannot die."

Jeanie barked a gloomy laugh and said, "I said the same thing." She and Will met one another's eyes across the table and were silent as Nellie got it out of her system and Helen tried to soothe her.

Just then, Willie came home earlier than expected to find a surprising scene, his entire family looking as if their worlds had caved in. He hurriedly hung up his coat and joined them in the kitchen, asking, "What's wrong?"

Will sighed, "Jings, I have to say it again. It doesn't get any easier with practice."

"It's Mam, isn't it?" the boy intuited. When no one immediately responded, he said, "I knew it! I knew you weren't well, Mam. Is it your heart? Like your own mam?"

"No, wee man," said Will, "it's not her heart."

"I have the cancer," said Helen, not bothering to correct her son that it was a stroke that killed her mam. "It's inoperable and I only have a few months to make my peace with God."

"Oh," said Willie, dumbfounded. He dropped heavily into his usual chair at the dining table, the one where he sat during meals. "I knew something was off," he said quietly, "but I didn't expect that."

Nellie's sobs began to subside, so Helen released her and sat down next to Will, relieved to not have to stand any longer. It wouldn't do for her legs to give out now, when everyone was so raw.

"So," Helen said, "everyone who needs to know, knows now."

"Do Bertha and Aunt Jessie know? And Uncle Pete and Tam?" asked Jeanie.

"Aye," said Will, "we've told all the grownups. We waited until we couldn't wait any longer to tell all of youse ..."

Helen interrupted Will when she saw Jeanie purse her lips, offended at being left out, "Aye, we didn't want youse to worry. No point in making all of youse miserable."

"Why did yeh tell us then?" sniffed Nellie. "I wish I didn't know."

"It's time, hen," said Will, as gently as he could. "Yer mam is getting weaker and she's gonna need yer help."

"Oh, God," Nellie said, clapping her hands over her mouth, horrified as his meaning sunk in, "Mammy, no ..."

Helen, struggling not to cry, said, "Now don't start or yeh'll get me bawlin', too. We'll be a blubbering mess," she said, trying to laugh.

"Aye," said Will, "there's a hard road ahead. It's time to muck in together and help yer mam ... make her remaining days as easy as possible."

"Of course," insisted Jeanie, as her siblings nodded in agreement. "D'yeh want me to quit my job and be here with yeh?"

Helen said, "Maybe just give yer notice. Don't leave Mrs. McCormick in a lurch. Give her time to find someone else but then, yes, I think I'll need yeh home with me."

"I can help make dinner, after school," offered Nellie, who never volunteered for extra chores.

"Aw, hen," said Helen, "that's sweet. Thank you."

Willie asked, "What can I do, Mam?"

Will said, "You and me, wee man, we can pick up after ourselves a bit more. Maybe pack our own lunches. Lighten the load a bit." He looked around the table at his children and added, "And youse can all hug yer mam more often. Don't let her go without letting her know she'll be missed."

All three siblings nodded in agreement, all hanging their heads a bit in shame. Will made a valid, yet stinging, point. Assuming their mam would live to a ripe old age, they took her for granted. Now, though, every hug would be a reminder of pending death instead of just a warm cuddle.

"I don't know about anyone else," said Helen, "but I'm tired of talking about it. Anyone want to play cards?"

Although no one really felt like a game the topic needed to be changed, so the Garrochs spent the evening playing gin rummy. They played until the wee small hours, simply enjoying one another's company in the too-brief time they had left together.

$$\wp \cdot \wp$$

The social season in Castle Gate kicked into high gear along with the milder weather and later sunsets. Elsie had proclaimed last summer that this year Ella would be old enough to be left with a sitter so Helen could join clubs and make friends with the socially active women, but that was not to be, now.

Instead, Elsie visited Helen weekly to catch her up on what the ladies were doing. She timed her visits to coincide with Jeanie's trips to the shops to stock up for the week, so Helen wouldn't be alone.

"I brought you a book," said Elsie, handing over a copy of *If Winter Comes* by A. S. M. Hutchinson. "It's a little scandalous," she continued, blushing a bit, "but such a good story!"

"Thank you," said Helen, glancing at the book's cover. She tucked it aside away from her teacup so it wouldn't get spilled on and asked, "What's it about?"

"Oh, it's got a little bit of everything," said Elsie, "love, war, death, sex … all sorts of scandal. I'd tell you more, but I don't want to spoil it."

Helen smiled wanly and took a sip of hot brew. "That'll be nice," she said. "I've never had time to read. There's always something that needs doing. But I find myself needing a lie down in the afternoons when Ella's napping, and maybe reading a book'll help me feel like I'm accomplishing something and not just lazing about."

It wasn't just that which made Helen grateful for the distraction of a juicy novel. If she was busy, she could ignore what was happening to her innards. When she was too tired to keep pushing herself she had nothing to divert her attention from the sensations in her gut. So far the pain wasn't unbearable, as she expected, but there were twinges and burning, pinching sensations. Yes, they hurt, but before the diagnosis they would have been shrugged off. It was knowing that the twinges and pinches were the cancer that brought on the fear. A book would be a good distraction.

"Oh, you need more help!" said Elsie. "You shouldn't be worried about 'accomplishing' anything when you should have your feet up."

"Yeh're kind," Helen said, "but I have plenty of help. Jeanie's home with me now, and Jessie and Bertha are here all the time. Between them and our wee'uns, I'm not short of helpers."

"That's lovely," said Elsie, meaning it. "What would we do without our families?"

"Och, I don't want to think about it," said Helen.

Elsie changed the subject. "You should have seen Bill at the banquet last week. Mrs. Ruff got up to speak about 'Club Husbands' so you know Bill had to get up and reply with a speech about 'Club Wives'. Oh, did we laugh!"

"I wish I could have been there," said Helen, dully.

At Helen's lackluster response, Elsie replied, "You're tired, aren't you dear? I'll leave you alone so you can put your feet up while the baby's asleep." She rose and gathered her purse and coat. "You get some rest now, you hear?"

Helen walked Elsie to the door, grateful for her sister-in-law's empathy. She was tired but didn't want to be rude and ask Elsie to leave. She waved goodbye, shut the door and leaned against it, eyes closed. She stood and thought for a minute … she did have time for a nap, but there was plenty of time to sleep when she was dead.

The house was tidy enough, and it was still early afternoon, so she didn't have to get started right away on the evening meal. Rather than lie down and let her thoughts run away with her, she picked up Elsie's book and took it to bed with her.

After reading the opening paragraph three times and still having no idea what it said, she put the book down and closed her eyes. "Please only send me good thoughts," she whispered to no one in general. The prayer felt futile: if God saw fit to kill her off, why would He help her get through it easily?

Helen pretended she was asking her mother's spirit for peaceful thoughts, who she had felt nearby lately. She asked, aloud, "Mammy, did yeh know I was there with yeh when yeh passed? Could yeh feel me there at yer bedside?

No verbal answer came but Helen felt her mother's presence, a flood of loving support, and finally the words, "There there, my wee lamb, I'm here."

Torn between despair and comfort—unsure whether her mother's presence was easily sensed as she inched closer to death or if it was her wistful imagination—Helen curled up under the quilt, drawing her knees to her chest, and sobbed with sorrow and frustration.

"Mammy?" Ella's wee voice came from the other bedroom. The squeaks of bedsprings were soon followed by the pitter patter of little feet on the wooden floor. Helen sighed and wiped her tears away just as Ella poked her head up to see her mother lying on the bed. "You cwying?"

"No darlin' … I'm not crying. Here," she said, offering a helping hand to Ella, "lie down with Mammy." Ella climbed onto the bed and curled up next to her.

"Shall we sing a song, my wee lamb?" Helen asked, and led Ella in a chorus of an old favorite, clapping as she sang:

Ally Bally, Ally Bally Bee,
Sittin' on yer mammy's knee.
Greetin' for a wee bawbee,
Tae buy mair Coulter's Candy.

Ella wasn't in the mood for a song so Helen dropped it after one verse. Ella jabbered away, pointing at a bird in a tree outside the window, laughing when it squawked at another bird that landed next to it.

"Yeh'll not remember me when yeh're grown," Helen whispered into her daughter's curls, "but I'll always be there. Just like my mammy is here with me now, I'll always be with you."

Helen longed for a way to impress herself into Ella's memory. Even though her own mother lived until she was fourteen, Helen couldn't remember her mam's face. She remembered her mam's hair color and the warm tenderness of her embrace, but the sound of her voice, the color of her eyes, the shape of her mouth and nose had faded from Helen's memory. Ella wouldn't remember even that much about her.

Buchan was four when their mother died and couldn't recall much at all, so she told him stories about her. Will, Jean and Willie would surely do the same for her but, after Helen died, who would keep Buchan's memory alive? As his second mother, it was her duty to display his Memorial Plaque and keep his posthumously awarded medals tucked away with other special memorabilia. After she was gone, would he be forgotten?

Ella was getting restless and squirmy so Helen rose and removed the child's nappy—she was mostly potty trained, but still wore a diaper to bed.

Helen seated her on the commode until she heard the trickle of liquid in the porcelain bowl. "All done?" Helen asked.

Ella smiled, spreading her hands wide, and replied, "Aw done!"

"That's my good girl," Helen said, giving her a kiss and taking her off the pot after giving her a wipe. "Yeh're getting so big! Let's get yeh into some clean britches."

They heard the front door open and Ella's eyes widened with excitement. "Oh!" she exclaimed, "Who's 'at?"

"I don't know, my wee lassie!" said Helen, "Is 'at our Jeanie?"

"Deanie!" Ella cried with joy and went pattering into the parlor, her bottom bare, with Helen trailing behind carrying Ella's clean knickers.

Jeanie hurried to put her parcels down in the kitchen, her eyes dark with concern as she asked, "Yeh're alone? I thought Aunt Elsie was here."

"Och, I sent her home," said Helen. "I was about to lie down but this wee monkey decided she was done napping."

"Well, go lie down!" said Jeanie. "I'll take care of the wee monkey." She took the pants from Helen and scooped Ella up into her arms. "Och, yeh have a naked bum! A cold wee bahookie! We cannot have that, can we?" She tickled Ella and the toddler giggled and squirmed to get down. "Not yet, yeh don't," said Jeanie, "let's get yer britches on and then yeh can run amok."

"Thanks, hen," said Helen, "I think I will go curl up with a book that Aunt Elsie dropped off."

"A new book?" Jeanie's ears perked up. "Can I read it when yeh're done?"

Helen laughed, "We'll see. Elsie says it's a bit scandalous, so I'll let yeh know after I'm done with it."

"Mother," Jeanie said, rolling her eyes, "I'm nineteen, old enough to be married myself so don't tell me I'm not old enough to read a bloody book."

"Aye, true enough," said Helen.

"Yeh want me to start supper?" Jeanie asked. "What did yeh have planned?"

"Mince and tatties," said Helen.

"Right," said Jeanie. She helped Ella climb into her big girl knickers and asked the wee girl, "Yeh want to help me peel some taters?"

"Aye!' yelled Ella, "Peel taters!"

"Don't give her a sharp knife," scolded Helen, on her way back to bed.

"I won't, Mother," Jeanie replied, heading to the kitchen with the child, "I know better than that. I'll give her a tattie and a spoon so's she can keep busy and feel grown."

Helen watched her daughters get busy in the kitchen before turning to her room. She crawled under the quilt, both grateful for Jeanie's help and dismayed that she needed it. She sighed and picked up Elsie's book and began reading, again: *Part 1—Mabel*

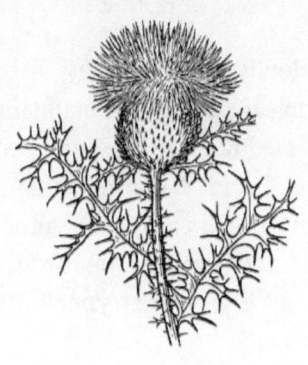

CHAPTER 17

July, 1923
Castle Gate, Utah

Last year, during the summer of 1922, the family found much to do in their new community, despite the strike. There were baseball games, ice cream socials, band concerts in the town square, backyard barbecues … the town hopped with enough commotion that there was little need to take the train to Helper or Price for entertainment, although the moving pictures in the bigger towns were shown in proper theaters, rather than in the multi-purpose room inside the Amusement Hall, seated on folding chairs.

This summer was even busier, without an active strike, but Helen's illness dulled the shine off the beautiful weather and festivities. Unless an event was at a nearby house, she was too fatigued or ill to attend. She chased her family out of the house to enjoy themselves, but at least one always stayed home in case she needed company, which was a delicate euphemism for saying Helen might need help getting to the commode. As of the Fourth of July, the biggest event of the season and the one that she most regretted missing, she was more or less a shut-in.

When Nellie was invited to a party in mid-July at the Jones family's home—to celebrate the birthday of their granddaughter—she had to be persuaded to go because she felt awful traipsing off while Helen felt so poorly.

Will walked her to the party. As adamant as he was about family loyalty and children taking care of their mother, he saw how hard it was for young

143

Nell to watch her mam slowly wasting away. It broke his heart to see his wife's namesake, wee Helen Jr., attempt to maintain a stiff upper lip.

Along the way, he cajoled her into having a good time. "There'll be lots of your friends there, lass," said Will, "and they've promised games and punch, and even ice cream! Yeh'll enjoy that, sure." As they approached the Jones' house, Will pointed at two girls at the front door and said, "That tall one's May Hardee, isn't it? She was at your birthday party, aye? I think Tommy Hilton's sweet on her."

Nellie perked up at the gossip. "Aye, and that's her little sister Saline. She's only twelve. Mrs. Jones is their granny, and it's their cousin's birthday. Did yeh know May and me are almost birthday twins? Our birthdays are only three days apart, except she's a year older than me, which means Tommy Hilton is far too old for her. He's even older than Wullie!"

"There, now, see?" said Will, "Yeh know somebody."

"Da, I'm not worried about that," she said. "I know everyone in town."

Will said, "Then go inside and have fun. Don't worry about Mam. She'll still be there when yeh get home. D'yeh want me to come get yeh after?"

"I'll walk home with my friends, thanks Da," she said and stood on her toes to kiss him on the cheek.

He wrapped her in a warm embrace and said, in her ear, "I love yeh, yeh know that, don't yeh?"

"I love you, too. See you soon," she said and turned to go into the house, leaving him on the walkway, watching her go.

Will waited until she was inside to turn back toward home. Torn between rushing to Helen's side and avoiding the inevitable, he walked slower than usual. After all, Jeanie was home with Helen. The thought of his beloved wife in the state she was in was enough to make a grown man cry. So, because it was still light out, he turned up the dirt road toward Pete and Jessie's house.

He climbed the front steps and opened the door, calling, "Hello ..." and stepped inside to see the family just getting up from the dinner table.

"Look girls, it's Uncle Wull!" said Pete, and his daughters ran to hug their uncle.

Will gave them both a quick squeeze and said, "Youse two wee lassies are getting so big! Soon yeh'll be looking for husbands."

"I'm only ten," Peg reminded him, "and she's only seven," she added, pointing at Annie.

"Aye, but together that makes seventeen," said Will.

"They'll be grown soon enough, Uncle Wull, no need to hurry them along," said Jessie. "Now, youse two, get back in here and help me clear the plates."

"Yes, Mam," the girls said in unison and returned to the kitchen.

"Will yeh have a drink?" Pete asked his brother.

"Is the Pope Catholic?" said Will.

Pete poured him a short glass of whisky and said, "Come on out back. It's a rare evening. The weather's just grand."

The brothers took their whisky outside where Pete led the way to a pair of homemade wooden benches installed far from the privy and near the vegetable garden that Jessie was so proud of. "How's Helen?" he asked, as they sat.

"She's not doing well, Pete. She gets weaker every day," said Will. "Och, I cannot go home yet. I had to get out of the house for a while so I made an excuse to walk Nellie to the Joneses." He sipped his whisky and said, "She's wasting away. She eats like a bird and only then because we'll not take 'no' for an answer. Jeanie makes her favorites and all she does is pick."

Pete looked down at his hands and said, "Aye, she's not looking good. I didn't want to say aught, but I was shocked when we stopped to see her on Sunday. But at least she's still up and about."

"Aye, she's not bedridden yet," Will said, hesitating before he spoke further, "Pete … don't ever repeat this to a soul … I'll deny I ever said it …" He looked at his brother for assurance. Pete nodded and Will continued, "I sometimes wish she'd die and be done with it. It's bad enough now and it's just gonna get worse. My poor wee Helen ... I can't bear it …"

"It's a trial, sure," said Pete. "It wouldn't be so bad if she'd made old bones, but she's still so young."

Will said, "Helen didn't want to come here, and I wouldn't listen. I sometimes wonder if she's dying from the homesickness."

"Och, away with yeh, Wull Garroch," said Jessie. They hadn't heard her come outside, so engrossed that they didn't hear the door hinges squeaking. She crossed the lawn with the whisky bottle in hand, and said, "Helen's happy enough here, so quit yer blethering. It's not your fault. It's God's will." She poured them both a refill and tsked her way back to the house.

"Pfft," scoffed Will, once Jessie was out of earshot. "'God's will,' my arse."

"Aye," agreed Pete. "Yeh cannot blame God, else all tragic deaths would be because He's a bastard."

"Aye, that's right," Will laughed. "He would be a bastard to will so much suffering." He paused a moment and added, "He is a right bastard though, isn't He?"

Pete looked up, his eyes searching the clouds. "No lightning yet but mind, there's a cloud looks like it's turning black, aiming at you."

Will grinned and said, "I'd best not push my luck." He downed his whisky and added, "I'm off away home before lightning strikes us."

Pete said, "I'm off away into the house before He misses you and hits me."

Will handed his glass to Pete and said, "If God's got it in for yeh, d'yeh think he cannot find yeh indoors? Thanks for the drink."

He cut across the yards to get to his own house. The sun was blocked behind the tall bluff to the west, but it was still early enough to be light. The shade cooled the valley considerably, so Helen would be more comfortable now.

He stood outside for a moment, steeling himself for the scene that surely awaited him inside: Helen would be propped up by several pillows on the davenport, trying to mend or knit to be productive, refusing to lie in bed until bedtime. "I'll sleep when I'm dead," she'd insist.

While her determination was admirable, her presence on the good furniture served to accentuate the dark circles under her eyes and the gauntness of her face. Until she became so ill, Helen rarely sat on the davenport, preferring to keep it "nice" for guests. If one of the children ever sat there for too long, she'd shoo them away and tell them to find something to do. To see her on the parlor sofa was a reminder that she wasn't well enough to sit at the dining table with her mending.

Tonight, though, Helen was asleep in the parlor when Will came inside so he closed the door behind him as silently as possible. He went past her to the kitchen where Jeanie sat with Ella on her lap, quietly reading her a story to keep her from making noise.

The toddler grinned at Will, reaching out to him, and said, "Da!"

Will scooped her up and said, softly, "How's my wee lass?" Ella put her arms around his neck and squeezed, and Will pretended to gasp, saying, "Och, yeh're choking me!"

Ella giggled and Will put her back on Jeanie's lap. "How's yer mam?" he asked, keeping his volume low. "Is she okay?"

"Well, as okay as she gets," said Jeanie, at the same low level. "She's just tired, no worse than usual."

"Where's yer brother?" he asked, wandering over to look out the kitchen window.

"Off with Tommy," said Jeanie. "He stayed until Mam fell asleep, then he went out. No point in staying here with naught to do. We can't play records or even sit on the sofa to read a book, so ..." She stopped short, realizing what she was saying and backpedaled, "... not that I mind if Mam wants to lie down there ..."

"It's okay, lass," said Will, "it's hard to know what to say or even what to think, isn't it?"

"Aye," Jeanie said, allowing Ella to turn the pages of the book, pretending to read, "I don't know how long I can stand it. Or how long *she* can stand it."

"Me and all," Will said. "Now hold yer wheesht. We don't want her to hear us talk like this."

Jeanie put a finger over her lips and nodded.

"Och, it's too early to go to bed," said Will, sitting to join Jeanie at the table. "At least for me. How about this wee monkey?" he asked, reaching over to ruffle Ella's blond curls.

Ella muttered, "I'm no' a monkey," and continued 'reading'.

"Aye, yeh are," Will replied and said to Jeanie, "Why don't yeh put her down for the night and we'll play some cards?"

Jeanie rose and said, "You get the cards. They're in the sideboard drawer. Can I trust yeh to not stack the deck?"

"Psht," Will scoffed, "of course yeh can't. Don't rush, so's I have time to stack 'em good."

Jeanie chuckled and left the room with Ella while Will dug the cards out of the drawer. Helen stirred and moaned, and Will froze. One thing worse than being in pain is to finally escape via sleep, only to be awakened. Almost as bad was to be the one who wakes the suffering person back into their misery.

Ella didn't want to go to bed, as evidenced by her loud cries. Will hurried to the bedroom door and said to Jeanie, "She's gonna wake yer mam. Let's take her out back and let her run 'til she's tired. We can play cards out there."

"Good idea," said Jeanie, following her father, with Ella in tow, out the back door to sit at the wooden picnic table Will and Willie had built last summer.

She put Ella down and said, "Go get yer ball," patting her on the bum and pointing at the rubber ball across the yard. "She's gonna get spoiled," Jeanie said, "when she learns crying hard enough gets her out of bed."

"These are special circumstances," he said, shuffling the cards and watching Ella run barefoot in the dirt. Even though she was a wee thing, she had learned that this grass was prickly and to not step on it. "Besides," he continued, "the poor wee lamb is gonna grow up without her mam. It can't do any harm to treat her with extra care, can it?"

"Aye," said Jeanie, "but I'll be raising her so don't you go spoiling her behind my back and undoing my hard work."

Will smiled and said, "Yes, ma'am." He sat quietly for a moment and then said, "I'm proud of yeh, lass. It's a shame this burden has become yers, but it's a common story. I know yeh'll be good to yer sisters." He stopped shuffling and laughed, "I don't recommend yeh try to be Willie's mam, though. He'll give yeh what for."

"Och!" she scoffed. "Unless you told him he had to listen to me and enforced it, I wouldn't want the job."

"He's practically a grown man," said Will, "almost eighteen. I barely want the job."

"D'yeh think ..." Jeanie hesitated, "... well ... I heard that when boys turn eighteen here they're supposed to go to Helper and prove they're a man by having a drink in every saloon down Main Street and, if they can make it to the end of the row sober enough, they ... um ... pay for a lady. D'yeh think Wullie would do that?"

Taken by surprise that his daughter knew about this men-only, local coming-of-age tradition, Will thought for a moment before responding. Jeanie was a bold girl but, even so, for her to mention a lady of the evening to her father was untoward. However, if she was bold enough to ask the question, he ought to respond in kind.

Finally, he decided to tell her the truth—yes, Willie might take on the challenge. Will knew secrets about his son that none of the females in the family knew, and one of those secrets was that it wouldn't be Willie's first time "paying for a lady."

Will sighed and confided in his future co-parent, "Aye, he might. That doesn't shock you, does it?"

"Nah," Jeanie replied, "Wullie's a dog, an absolute hound around the girls. I was wondering … his birthday's coming up in a few weeks and … like yeh said, he's turning eighteen. I wonder whether he'll do … that … while Mam is so sick. Or what if she's freshly dead? What d'yeh think he'll do?"

"I hadn't thought of that," Will admitted. "Honestly, hen, I don't know. But he's not such a dog that he'd do anything hateful. If he does it, it'll be to get his mind off … all this …" Will waved toward the house, "… so I wouldn't blame him and neither should you. Mind, I doubt he'll enjoy himself, so if he goes, leave him be."

"Well, I couldn't do it," Jeanie said, with an edge in her voice, "I could get good and blootered, sure, but I couldn't … you know … do that … other thing, with Mam the way she is."

"It's different for boys," said Will. "Surely yer mam and you have had a talk …"

"Oh, aye," said Jeanie, dismissively waving him off, "years ago when I asked her why she keeps getting pregnant if all her babies die."

Will fidgeted, not sure he wanted to know, but couldn't help asking, "And what did she say?"

"What you just said, it's different for girls and boys," Jeanie replied. "She said men and women have different priorities. A man's priority is to have a shag and a woman's priority is to survive it."

"Boy, the mosquitos are getting thick, aren't they?" Will said, slapping his forearm, pretending to kill one and said, "Let's go inside. I bet Ella will go down easier after some fresh air."

"So much for playing cards, eh? Yeh stacked the deck for nothing," she said. "I've got a good book. I'll lay down with her."

"Alright, hen," Will said, extricating his legs from beneath the picnic table. He had been sitting long enough to become stiff, so it wasn't easy. "I'll wait up for Nell and Wullie. I'll get yer mam off to bed, too, so you have the rest of the night off."

"Thanks, Da," she said, lifting Ella and brushing the yard dust off the toddler's feet with her free hand, then wiping her hand on her skirt. She carried Ella into the house, saying, "Let's go read, shall we?"

Jeanie took Ella to bed and Will returned to the kitchen table after pouring himself another measure of whisky. He lit a cigarette and sipped his drink, listening to his eldest child taking care of his youngest and the sounds his distressed wife made as she uncomfortably dozed on the good sofa.

He considered lifting Helen off the couch and carrying her to bed where she would be more at ease and able to stretch out. God knows she didn't weigh much these days and it would be an easy lift, but he didn't want to hurt her. Sometimes even bumping into her in bed at night caused her to cry out.

Their marriage bed had become a sick bed and he found himself mourning the loss of not just his wife but his lover. If he had known, the last time they were intimate, that it would be their last time … well, maybe it was best that neither of them had known, or the sorrow would have been unbearable.

As bad as he felt admitting it to himself, he envied Willie's upcoming dilemma. There wasn't much he'd rather do right now than drink himself stupid and spend the evening with a painted lady. Anything to keep his mind off of … all this. And that made him the bastard, not God.

CHAPTER 18

August, 1923
Castle Gate, Utah

By mid-August, Helen's condition had deteriorated so greatly that it was just a matter of time. Brothers Bill and John came with their wives to sit by her bedside after church on Sundays, holding her hand and, when she was awake, reminiscing of happier days. More often than not, though, Helen ducked in and out of consciousness and conversation was difficult. So, they simply sat with her and sometimes read to her, spending the final hours with their younger sister while they still could.

Jessie and Bertha took turns during the week. Whoever helped look after Helen would also help Jeanie make dinner—taking the extra home to their own households—in addition to the more difficult caregiving tasks of bathing Helen, dressings and cleanup during her lady's times until she stopped having them, getting her to the chamber pot when she was able, and changing and laundering the bed linens when she was not. Cancer was a bloody, shitty mess, no two ways about it.

Nellie's primary assignment was to look after wee Ella, Margie, Annie and Peggy and to take them out to play, keep the noise down and to distract her sister and cousins from the sounds coming from Helen's bedroom. Nellie welcomed the task: she didn't want to overhear her mother's suffering, either. The drowsy moans as Helen tried to sleep but couldn't, and the pain-filled shouts as she was turned in her bed, set Nellie's teeth on edge and she gritted them to keep from crying. She couldn't bear to look at Helen in this state, only making appearances often enough to show respect.

Willie wasn't much for going out with Tommy these days. He spent his evenings at home, often sitting next to his mother reading a book to pass the time while she tried to sleep, wiping the August sweat off her face and neck with a cool, wet cloth.

Will did his best to keep the family stable, sometimes overcompensating to the point of acting as if nothing was wrong. Stiff upper lip, and all. But he couldn't hide the worried wrinkling of his brow when noises from the bedroom erupted while the family sat down for their evening tea. He would get up himself from the table and go see what his wife needed. Most times, there was nothing he could offer beyond a soothing hand on her forehead, but occasionally he'd call out to Jeanie to assist with cleanup.

He had long since stopped sharing the bed with Helen. She needed room to toss and turn and the womenfolk gathered their currently unused winter quilts to make him a soft pallet on the floor, so he could sleep in the same room. This made for many sleepless nights and when Will couldn't take the lack of sleep any longer—out of fear of making deadly mistakes at work— Jeanie slept there instead, with Will on the davenport, his long legs dangling off the edge. The fact that he was sleeping on the good furniture and Helen couldn't object, indeed didn't even know, made it worse.

Three weeks into August, Geordie—a regular visitor during the week— came to see Helen and, as usual, he shooed the caregivers away. Geordie liked to sit with Helen, just the two of them.

Today she was livelier than usual. The weather was cool and a gentle breeze drifted through the window. She'd had no appetite recently and appeared almost skeletal, so Geordie was enthusiastic when she asked, "Would yeh get me a cuppa and a biccy?"

"Of course, hen," Geordie said and called out to Jeanie, "Jean, darlin' would yeh get yer mother a cuppa tea and maybe one of those nice shortbreads?"

"Aye, be right there," Jeanie replied from the other room.

"Yeh're looking well," said Geordie, turning back to his sister.

"I'm not so bad today," Helen said, "I feel as if I could sit up a bit. Would yeh help me?"

"Certainly," Geordie said. He hopped up from his chair and gathered some pillows to prop under Helen's head and shoulders. "How's that, hen?"

"That's fine," she replied, settling into a comfortable position. "I haven't felt this well in weeks."

"That's wonderful news!" Geordie cried, "I've been that worried about yeh. It's good to see yeh looking so chipper." He knew, though, from experience in the military hospital and from visiting Mary in her final days, that rallying like this meant the end was nearing.

"Aye, it's good to feel so chipper," Helen said. "D'yeh know, it's the strangest thing, but Buchan has been coming to visit me and so have Mammy and Da." She paused and continued, "I'll be wide awake, not dreaming, and they'll say they've come to take me home."

Geordie nodded and said, "Aye, I've seen that happen, during the war, with soldiers I was caring for."

"D'yeh think it's really them?" she asked.

"I don't know, pet," he said, "but I sat at many a soldier's bedside and watched them reach out for folks I couldn't see, but they were real as could be to the poor lads."

"It's kind of comforting," said Helen. "I'm not so afraid, knowing they're waiting to welcome me when I cross over."

"Aw, that's lovely, hen," said Geordie, as Jeanie entered carrying tea and cookies for her mam.

"Look at you, sittin' up!" Jeanie cried. "Here's yer tea and a nice biccy." Jeanie sat the cup and saucer, with two shortbreads, on the bedside table and helped prop Helen up even more before handing her the tea. "Careful," Jeanie said, "it's hot."

"Thanks, love," said Helen, "Yeh're an excellent nurse. Yeh've got a gift for it."

Tears sprang to Jeanie's eyes at the praise, and she blushed, saying, "Thank you, Mam. I only wish yeh didn't need me to be a nurse."

"Go on, hen," said Geordie, shooing his niece away.

Helen said to him, "Yeh've been so good to my wee'uns, like a second father. When are yeh gonna have a family of yer own?"

Geordie smiled slightly and said, "Now, hen, we both know that's not in the cards for me." They sat in companionable silence for a bit until Geordie said, "So yeh're being visited by ghosts, eh?"

"D'yeh believe they're real?" Helen asked, dipping a shortbread and biting into the soggy cookie.

"Oh, aye," he said.

She took a sip of tea and sighed, "Och, of all the things I miss, I miss a nice cuppa tea the most."

"Tell me about Mam and Da," he said. "What do they say when they visit yeh?"

"It's funny, they don't say much at all," said Helen. "Mostly they smile and glow with love. They look like they did back in Galston, when we were just wee."

Geordie grinned and said, "I don't remember a lot of glowin' and smilin' back then."

Helen chuckled, which triggered a coughing spasm. "Don't make me laugh," she said, lightly pounding her chest, smiling weakly.

"Sorry, hen, but it's good to see you laugh again," he said.

"Och, I know," she said, "it's good to feel like laughing again." She took another sip and bit into a shortbread. "Yeh know who's the gabbiest ghost? It's our wee Buchan."

"He always was a chatterbox, wasn't he?" said Geordie.

"Oh, aye," said Helen, gazing dreamily toward the wall in front of her. "He stands right there at the foot of my bed and talks, talks, talks." She handed her tea to Geordie and said, "I need to lie down again."

He put her teacup on the bureau and helped make Helen comfortable. "D'yeh want me to leave, or shall I sit here quietly with you?"

"Would you stay?" she asked, "Maybe read to me from my book? I haven't finished it and Elsie gave it to me ages ago." She pointed to the novel on the bedside table.

Geordie picked up the book and flipped it open to the page marked with a piece of yarn. He began reading and Helen sank further into the pillows as his voice droned and Buchan began to materialize before her, at the foot of her bed.

She smiled and weakly raised her arm, pointing for Geordie to look and see their wee brother standing there, grinning like he used to when they were young. But Geordie was immersed in his reading and didn't see Helen's raised arm before fatigue took over. She soon fell asleep to converse in her dreams with her beloved Buchan.

∅∅

Saturday, a few days later, the August temperature shot back up and the house was hot and stifling. All windows were open but, without any breeze, the curtains—which were closed to block the glaring sunlight—didn't stir.

Jeanie sat by Helen's bedside fanning her with a newspaper. Ella was napping, the men were at work and Nellie had been sent to fetch the doctor. Helen had a fever and her breathing was labored. Doctor McDermid had told them to come for him when, not if, her condition changed for the worse.

Helen was restless, drenched in sweat. "God, it's so hot," she moaned, "Inside me and out. I'm having fever dreams about being on fire."

Jeanie said, fanning a little harder, "Doctor McDermid should be here soon."

Helen closed her eyes and said, "Och, that cannot be good, if yeh've called for him. When will he be here?"

"Soon, Mam, soon," said Jeanie. She removed the damp cloth from Helen's forehead and rinsed it in the washbasin with cool, fresh water before putting it back on Helen's face.

"Jeanie, hen …" Helen looked her daughter square in the eye and said, matter-of-factly, "I'm really gonna die, aren't I?"

"Aye, Mam, yeh're gonna die," said Jeanie, matching her mother's straight-up tone.

"Yeh've been so good to me, lamb," said Helen. "And you'll be raising my wee'uns. I trust you to not let them forget their poor mam. I know I don't have to ask, but promise yeh'll take good care of 'em?"

Jeanie said. "Of course, I will."

Aye," said Helen, nodding weakly, "I'm proud of the woman yeh've become. Yeh've helped me give birth and now yeh're helping me die."

Jeanie teared up and laughed a little, "Yeh're not giving me much choice, are yeh Mam?"

"Aye," Helen smiled, "I guess I'm not. Sorry about that." She squeezed Jeanie's hand and said, "Then let's get it done, shall we? I'm tired and cannot take much more of this."

"Aye, Mammy," Jeanie said, stifling a sob, "If it was as easy as jumping out of yer skin, I'd give yeh a push."

"Uncle Buchan says he'll pull me out when it's time." Helen closed her eyes and said, "I think it's time," before she drifted off to fitful sleep.

Doctor McDermid and Nellie were at the doorway then. Jeanie heaved a sigh of relief and said, "Thank God yeh're here, Doctor. She's delirious with fever. She's seeing people that aren't there and she's dreaming that she's on fire."

The doctor removed the damp cloth to feel Helen's forehead with his palm. He then felt her face and neck, alternating the palm and back of his hand and said, "She's got a fever, all right. That's not just the heat of this scorching day." He handed Jeanie the cloth and said, "Cool that off, will you? It's like a hot compress."

"I just changed it," objected Jeanie.

"I'm sure you did," the doctor said gently, "but that's how hot she is. I know your mother has objected to morphine ..."

Jeanie interrupted, "She'll take it when the pain gets extra bad and she had some earlier ..."

"Yes," said Doctor McDermid, "but we're beyond dulling pain at this point. There's no treating this and she's going to get worse."

"I'll not stop yeh, she's the one who didn't want to take too much. She said it made her feel doolally," said Jeanie.

"It's a common complaint," Doctor McDermid said, "one that most people stop raising at this point. It's just a matter of time, now." Nellie gasped and left the room in a rush. "I'm sorry," he continued, "but there's no sugar coating this."

"Nell will be fine," said Jeanie. "She'll have to be, just like the rest of us."

"You're a brave girl," said the doctor as he administered the medication. He then handed over a supply large enough for a couple days and instructed her, "Give this to her whenever she needs it. Don't worry about how often. It won't be what kills her and, even if it did, it would be a blessed mercy."

Helen's pained breathing eased as the morphine took effect. Jeanie walked the doctor to the front door and was saying goodbye as Will and Willie were coming up the walk and Ella woke from her nap, calling for her mam. Jeanie turned to get the child before she woke Helen and left the men to speak.

"What is it, Doctor?" Will asked, surprised to see Claude McDermid here on a Saturday.

"Your wife has a fever, probably an infection, and there's no point in treating it other than alleviating her discomfort," he said. "I'd say she has a day or two, but no more than that."

Will nodded and patted Willie on the back. "Come on, son," he said, "let's go see your mother." Willie didn't say a word. He walked into the house, his head slightly hanging. "Thank you, Doctor," Will said, "You've been a comfort during this difficult time."

"I'm sorry I couldn't do more," Dr. McDermid said. "Call if you need anything. I left enough morphine so Helen's final hours should be pain-free."

Will shook the doctor's hand and went inside. Willie was in the kitchen pouring a small glass of whisky. Will didn't object—after all, Willie would be eighteen in less than a week—so he joined his son in a drink. "Brace yerself, wee man," he said, clinking his glass against Willie's, "here we go."

Jeanie came into the kitchen with Ella on her hip and poured a drink for herself. "She's asleep … well … drugged into a stupor," she said, "let's leave her be."

"Aye," said Will, gesturing to his oldest children to join him at the table, "let's drink to yer Mam, but no getting blootered. We need clear heads."

Nellie leaned against the doorjamb, watching them, and asked, "Can I have some?"

"How about a wee glass of port instead?" Will said. "Whisky's not a proper drink for a young lady. Jean's nineteen and taking on hard work, so she's allowed."

"Okay," said Nellie, and she poured the burgundy liquid into Helen's favorite cordial glass. She joined the others and sipped with them, in silence.

After they drained their glasses, Will said to his older children, "If youse two want another, I'll not stop yeh. There'll be no sleep in this house tonight otherwise. Consider it medicinal."

Jeanie poured seconds for herself and Willie but when she came to Will's glass, he put his hand over it and said, "No, lassie, I've had enough."

"Does anyone want to eat?" Jeanie asked. "It's stew and bread. Bertha brought it over."

"Thanks, Jean," said Willie, "I'll have a small bowl just to put something in my stomach."

"I'm not hungry," said Nellie. "Maybe later."

"Da?" Jeanie asked, rising to ladle a bowl for her brother and Ella, with a piece of bread apiece.

"Aye, hen, just a wee bowl and a small hunk of bread," said Will.

After eating in relative silence, Jeanie said, "Nell, why don't you take Ella to Aunt Jessie's and see if she can spend the night? Then we don't have to worry about her making noise and waking Mam."

"Can I stay, too?" Nellie asked.

"If it's okay with Jessie," said Will.

Relieved, Nellie picked up Ella and scurried out of the house. Just in time, too, because a crash came from the bedroom. Will arrived at the door first, Willie and Jeanie close behind him.

The room was only dimly lit by the day's last light, so it was hard to see Helen on the floor, on the far side of the room. She had tried to get up and fell against the washbasin stand. The ceramic pitcher had crashed to the floor and shattered, spilling water into a puddle. Will picked her up, laid her on the bed and checked for cuts, while Jeanie lit the lantern.

"No, Wull," Helen said groggily, pushing him away, "I need the commode ..."

"Now, hen," Will replied, his voice catching, "yeh're supposed to call for help. Especially when yeh're on the morphine. Yeh cannot get up on yer own."

"I ... I need ..." Helen stammered. She tried to sit up, but then leaned over the edge of the bed and vomited on the floor. "I'll clean that ... later ..." she said and then passed out again.

"Jesus," Will moaned, "it doesn't let up, does it? What does God have against her?"

"Hellooo ..." came Bertha's voice from the other room. Jeanie hurried to the bedside to clean the mess while Willie returned to the parlor to talk to their visitor.

"Is everything okay?" Bertha asked. "Only Tam said he saw Doctor McDermid here earlier and I just saw Nellie hurrying to Jessie's with Ella."

"Mam's on her last leg," Willie said, "Doc McDermid said she only has another day or two."

Bertha clapped her hands over her heart and cried, "Oh, no! Can I see her?"

"It's a mess in there," Willie warned, "Mam threw up and Jeanie's cleaning it."

"That poor girl has her work cut out for her, doesn't she?" Bertha said, rushing into the bedroom. "Jeanie, love," she said, upon witnessing the scene, "you've done enough. Let me take care of that."

Jeanie burst into sobs and dropped to her knees next to the vile, brown puddle. "How can she boak," Jeanie cried, "when she hasn't eaten in days?"

"Will, take her out of here." Bertha commanded, and he obeyed.

"Come on, hen, yeh're pure exhausted," he said, walking Jeanie from the room, his arm around her shoulder. He sat with her on the davenport and held her, patting her as she sobbed. "It's almost over," he said. "She'll be with the Lord soon."

"Peh! The Lord!" Jeanie scoffed into Will's shirt. "What sort of God would make anyone suffer like that?"

"I don't know, do I?" he said. "I've wondered the same thing myself." Jeanie sat back and Will said, "We need to let your uncles know, so they can see their sister for the last time."

"I can go to Uncle Geordie's now and tell him," Willie volunteered. "He can call Uncle Bill and Uncle John on the telephone."

"Aye," said Will, "off you trot. Bertha can tell Tam but stop on yer way and let Jessie and Pete know, without bringing Nell into it. She's upset enough as is."

Willie took his leave and Jeanie scooched further back onto the davenport, huddling into the corner of the armrest. She asked, "Da, what about Mam's funeral?"

"Yer mam chose the spot months ago where she wants to be buried, just across from Auntie Mary. I even reserved the plot next to hers so I can spend eternity alongside her."

Jeanie sat up and said, "Don't let's talk about you dying, too. I couldn't stand it."

Will chuckled, "I'm not going anywheres, anytime soon. Don't worry."

Bertha came in carrying a bundle of soiled rags and said, "Will, Helen's asking for you. She's not making much sense. I think she wants you to come and sit with her."

Will hurried into the bedroom and Bertha gestured to Jeanie to join her in the kitchen. "Come on, flower, let me get you a nice cup of tea and I'll rinse these out. Maybe we can play a game of rummy. What do you think?"

"I think yeh're an angel sent from heaven, that's what I think," said Jeanie as she joined her cousin's wife in the kitchen for a little distraction.

⚥

Helen's beloved family gathered Sunday afternoon for the deathbed vigil. The dining table resembled a holiday groaning board, with all the foods that neighbor women had dropped off so no one in the household needed to be bothered with meal preparation. The children were sent outside to play and Nellie was too distracted to watch them, so she was relieved when May Hardee volunteered to take the youngsters to the park.

The Littlejohn brothers sat at Helen's bedside as the womenfolk chatted quietly in the parlor, Nellie included. Will and Willie sat in the back yard, at the picnic table, smoking in silent companionship.

Helen was asleep, her breathing faint yet steady, as her brothers talked quietly. Geordie said, "Helen told me our Buchan is a regular visitor and that he'll help her cross over when it's time. She's been seeing dead relatives, beckoning her home."

Bill nodded and said, "When Mary was in her final days, she saw all sorts. If only the Lord would give our Helen peace and let that time come soon."

"Amen," said John.

"Here," Geordie said to John, "remember this year's Burns Supper at your house? Helen enjoyed hearing the old songs again. What say we give her a chorus or two?"

"That's a splendid idea," said Bill. "What should we sing?"

"I know, she loves this one …" Geordie said. He began singing, soon accompanied by his brothers once they caught the tune:

Ye banks and braes o' bonnie Doon,
How can ye bloom sae fresh and fair;
How can ye chant, ye little birds,
And I sae weary, fu' o' care!

The sounds of song brought the others to the room, and they sang along:

Thou'll break my heart, thou warbling bird,
That wantons thro' the flowering thorn:
Thou minds me o' departed joys,
Departed never to return.

Nellie interrupted with a moan, "Yeh're making her cry! Stop it!" She turned and ran from the room, weeping in earnest, as a lone tear trickled down the side of Helen's face. The sight brought the song to a halt as the others broke into sobs.

Geordie leaned forward to take Helen's withered hand, and said, "I'm sorry, hen." Tears streamed down his face and he kissed her hand once, twice, three times. Switching from the Americanized dialect he used when speaking to his brothers, he spoke in rich Scottish brogue, the way he always did with her. "Och, I'm gonnae miss yeh, lassie. I wish yeh didnae have to go sae soon. Tell Mammy and Daddy wee Geordie sends his love, will yeh?"

Jeanie, also overcome, joined Nellie in the parlor. The younger girl was curled up on the davenport, her head buried in her hands, her body wracked with sobs.

"Here," said Jeanie, sitting next to her sister and wiping Nellie's tears away with her thumb, "yeh're gonna have to shore yerself up. I'm just as torn up about Mammy as you, but Mammy wouldn't want us crying like this."

"Mammy doesn't know, does she?" Nellie wailed. "She'll never know because soon she'll be dead! I'll never get to talk to her again, she might as well be dead now."

Jeanie shushed her and gestured toward the bedroom in case they could be heard by Helen who, apparently, could still hear.

"Och, why doesn't she just do it already?" Nellie hissed, in a quieter voice, "Why is it taking so long? She's been dying forever!" She stopped crying abruptly and corrected herself. "I don't mean to be so wicked. I don't want her to die, I want her to stop … dying!"

"I know, hen, I know," Jeanie soothed.

Will came inside from the back yard with Willie behind him, overhearing his daughters crying. "Any change?" he asked.

"Naw," said Jeanie, "she's the same. We were singing to her, and Mam started crying at the old Burns songs."

Will's face fell and he said, "Just when yeh think she's no longer in there, that it's just her body ticking on, refusing to give up the ghost …" He went to the bedroom and nudged his way into the crowded chamber. "Would everyone leave us alone for a minute, please?"

All but Geordie streamed back into the parlor, some patting Will on the shoulder on their way out. Geordie sat clasping Helen's hand, raised to his own face, holding her palm to his cheek. Geordie said, "Youse were supposed to live happily ever after, here in America."

"Aye," said Will. "D'yeh think it would be wrong of me to ask everyone to go home? Yeh're welcome to stay, of course, but I think a houseful of people is making it worse for the children."

"No, of course not," said Geordie. "I'll take care of it. You sit here with Helen." He got up and paused at the door to say, "Thank you for letting me stay. I'm not ready to let go of her just yet."

161

"Of course," said Will, "yeh're her favorite brother."

"Well," Geordie smiled gently and said, "after wee Buchan ..."

"Aye," agreed Will, chuckling lightly, "after wee Buchan. Nobody can hold a candle to wee Buchan."

Geordie let everyone know it was time to say their final goodbyes and leave the Garroch family in peace. One at a time, they came to kiss Helen on the forehead and murmur their last words. Finally, the house was empty except for Will, Helen, their children and Helen's favorite brother. May Hardee had brought Ella home a short while ago, so it was a complete household.

As everyone gathered around the kitchen table, Jeanie ducked into Helen's room to check on her. Her bedding didn't need to be changed, thank goodness, but her lips were dry. Jeanie wet a cloth with clean water and trickled a few drops into Helen's mouth—just enough to alleviate the dryness, but not enough to cause her to cough—a skill Jeanie wished she had never needed to learn.

She sat on the edge of the bed and ran her hand across her mother's forehead, listening to her raspy breathing. She kissed Helen's papery cheek and went to join the others, pausing in the doorway to offer up yet another prayer that she would pass soon and cease this endless suffering.

"G'night, Mam. I love you," she whispered, and left the room.

ØȤ

Morning broke and Helen was still breathing, but now each breath came with a worrisome, rattling gurgle. Will reassured his children, "Doctor McDermid said this would happen. It means she's at the end of the road. It doesn't mean she's in any pain or discomfort."

"Did he say what we should do?" asked Jeanie.

"Just wait," Will said, "and keep quiet so she has a peaceful passing."

The house was so silent that only the ticking of the mantle clock and the occasional train could be heard alongside Helen's rasping breaths. They took turns sitting by her bedside, so she wouldn't be alone, while the others kept Ella pacified. It was Jeanie's turn when Nellie said to Will, in the parlor, "Da, can we play some music on the Victrola? I think Mammy would like that, as long as we play something more cheerful than they were singing yesterday."

"That might be nice to break this awful silence," Will said, "if we play it quietly. Just don't play anything with bagpipes, else we'll all be blubbing with the homesickness."

Jeanie listened from the bedroom as Will and Nellie chatted about which record to play. Ella toddled in and tugged on Jeanie's skirt asking for some lunch, so Jeanie put her finger over her lips and whispered, "Shhh, Mammy's sleeping."

Ella repeated the gesture and said, "Shhhh … I'm hungwy."

"Alright, lamb, I'll get yeh something to eat," said Jeanie. She rose from her chair and checked on Helen. There was no change—just the same endless, rhythmic rasping gurgle. She patted Helen's hand and said, "It won't be long, Mam. Uncle Buchan will be along soon." Jeanie turned and took Ella to the kitchen, unaware that Buchan was already there.

"Anyone else hungry?" she asked and received lackluster nods from the family. They had learned to eat when food was offered even if they had no appetite, which was most of the time anymore.

As Jeanie prepared a simple repast, Will held up a phonograph record and said, "Here, yer mam loves this song." He put it on the turntable, wound up the Victrola and placed the needle down on the record, which was scratchy with wear. The lilting orchestral melody of *Let Me Call You Sweetheart* filled the room.

"I think we need a new needle," said Willie.

"Could be," said Will, "but that record gets played a lot. Maybe that's what needs to be replaced."

"Either way," Willie said, "it could sound better."

"Wheesht," Nellie scolded, "we're playing it for Mam, not for you."

"Fine," Willie replied. "I'm just saying …"

"Yer tea's out," called Jeanie, and they joined her at the table.

They were still eating when the song ended and the needle, resting on the vinyl, made quiet little pops as it ran on the dead wax. "Get that, will yeh Nell?" asked Will and the girl rose from her chair to lift the needle.

Once again, the house was quiet, only the sound of the clock ticking. "Shall we play another?" Nellie asked.

As Will opened his mouth to respond, Jeanie raised her hand to silence everyone. "Listen," she said.

For several seconds, everyone remained still until Willie finally said, "I don't hear anything."

"That's what I mean," said Jeanie, and she rushed into the bedroom.

As what she was implying sunk in, the rest followed her and they saw, there on the bed, Helen's body bereft of spirit, finally gone to meet her Maker.

"Is she …" Nellie began.

"Not sure," said Will. "Wait a mo' …" Helen had fooled them before with painfully long pauses between breaths, so he was being prudent with any final declarations.

They stood around the bed watching for any signs of life, any lifting or falling of Helen's chest, listening for her to begin breathing again. In stunned silence, no one said a word.

Helen watched the scene from above, waving Buchan away as he urged her to continue to rise higher with him. "Wait," she said, "I'm not ready to leave yet."

"Are yeh mad?" he asked, "D'yeh really want to stay with that old bag of bones when we can fly?"

"Och, yeh're like Peter Pan!" Helen replied. "I want to make sure they're okay first."

Jeanie sat on the bed and pressed her fingertips lightly into the side of Helen's throat, feeling for a pulse. After a half a minute passed, she said, "I think she's finally out of her misery."

Will heaved a sigh and said, "Och, thank God, she's no longer suffering." He bowed his head and said, "Children, let us pray for your mother's passage into Heaven."

All but Ella bowed their heads and prayed. She toddled forward to climb up on the bed with her mam, but Jeanie caught her by the arm and hoisted Ella up onto her lap. "Mind," Jeanie whispered, her voice catching a bit, "Mammy's sleeping."

Ella put her finger to her lips and said, "Shhhh … she's seeping."

Nellie burst into sobs and Ella extended her arms to offer a comforting hug. "Don't cwy, you be okay," she said, reaching toward her teenaged sister. Nellie lifted Ella from Jeanie's lap, laughing a little, wiping the tears from her face.

"I be okay, Ella, I'll not cry," Nellie replied, sniffling and trying to smile. "Mammy's sleeping, so let's be quiet."

Ella put her finger to her lips again and nodded, joining her family in silence. Finally, Will cleared his throat to speak. "Wullie," he said, turning to his son, "would yeh mind fetching the doctor? He'll need to make an official pronouncement and fill out the papers."

"Of course," Willie said, and turned to go.

"May I go with him?" Nellie asked.

"Come on, hen," Willie said, not waiting for a response from their elders. "You can come with."

She gave Ella back to Jeanie and they set off to Doctor McDermid's office. Along the way, they passed a group of children playing at the park. Nearby, another group splashed and laughed at the river, cooling themselves on this hot August afternoon.

Nellie said, "It's strange, isn't it, to see people so carefree when our mam just died. I haven't been happy or carefree for as long as I can remember."

Willie smiled a little and said, "Well, you haven't been alive that long, so 'as long as you can remember' is only fourteen years."

"I feel like I'm a thousand," she sighed.

"How do you think I feel?" he asked. "In a few days, I'll be old enough to be drafted into the army."

Nellie's jaw dropped and she said, "Och, I forgot! Your birthday's on Friday. Now you'll always think of Mam whenever it's your birthday."

"It's not like she died on the same day," he said.

"No, but still ..." Nellie said, unable to drop it.

"'Still', nothing," Willie replied, as they approached the doctor's office. "That's something for children to be upset about. I'm a grown man and I've seen a few things ... things more important than boohooing if something bad happens on your birthday. Now let's go inside and see if the doctor's here."

"Fine," said Nellie, rolling her eyes, "I'm just saying, it would bother me."

"Well," he said, opening the door and ushering her inside, "it's a good thing it's not your birthday, isn't it?"

♉ ♉

Doctor McDermid's visit was brief. He expressed his condolences and asked the necessary questions to fill out the death certificate form, "Parents names and Helen's date of birth?"

"William and Jean Cochrane Littlejohn and," said Will, after scraping his memory for half a minute, "her birthdate was September 24, 1883."

Helen, who still hovered overhead watching the scene, told Buchan, "Typical man, getting it wrong." She hollered down into the room, in vain, "It's September 28, 1884, yeh numpty!"

165

Geordie arrived just as the doctor was leaving and said to Will, "I'll let Bill and John know, and spread the word to the community. I reckon we oughta run an obituary in the paper."

"Aye," Will replied, "I'll break the news to Pete and Tam's families. Tell everyone we'll have a funeral service tomorrow here at home, with a burial on Friday."

As condolences and floral arrangements began pouring in, though, Will learned that Helen was more popular in Castle Gate than he knew. When Geordie suggested holding an additional, public memorial service in town on Thursday, Will didn't argue. Even people who didn't know Helen well wanted to pay their respects to the superintendent's family.

Finally, Friday came, and Helen's kin faced the somber task of putting her in the ground. Although the walk to the cemetery was only about a mile, the Littlejohn brothers drove the Garroch families so they didn't have to walk in the August heat in their heavy black mourning clothes.

The motorcade rounded the bend into Willow Creek Canyon and turned into the dirt parking lot—with the office and entrance to Mine #2 on the left and the cemetery to the right—stirring up a cloud of dust in the dry, hot air. Topside workers at #2 removed their caps and nodded their condolences to the mourners, bowing their heads as the procession passed. A mile underground, beneath the cemetery, dozens of men labored in the cool tunnels below.

After the graveside service, family members tossed handfuls of dirt onto Helen's coffin before heading back to the Garroch home for tea and cake. Willie and Tommy walked back to the parking lot side by side, kicking up dust and transforming the color of their black shoes and trouser hems to rusty beige, with Nellie and May trailing behind just within earshot.

"I'll understand if you decide not to go," Tommy said to Willie, continuing a conversation from earlier in the day. "It's a hell of a thing, burying your mother on your eighteenth birthday, when you should be celebrating."

"Why, Tommy Hilton, what a thing to say!" May scolded.

Tommy and Willie stopped and whirled around, only now aware that their conversation was being overheard. Tommy—dismayed that his crush had taken offense—said, holding up his hands in defense, "I meant no disrespect, May. Mrs. Garroch was like a second mum to me and I'm sad, too. But a man's eighteenth is a landmark day. All I meant was it's a shame this happened on the same day."

"Hmph," said May, striding past the boys.

"It's okay, May," said Nellie, keeping pace alongside her, passing her brother and his friend. "Tommy's part of the family. I know he didn't mean anything by it. Mam treated him like another son."

"Thanks, Nell," said Tommy. "That's nice to hear."

"I'd like to know, though," continued Nellie, over her shoulder to the two young men who were now walking behind her and May, "what youse are talking about. Where aren't yeh going, Wullie?"

"Never you mind," Willie said. "Only some of the lads are busting my chops because we were supposed to go to Helper tonight."

Nellie turned to May and asked, "Did he just say 'never you mind' and then told me anyway?"

May arched an eyebrow and said, "Must be more to the story that he's not telling."

"Clever girl," Tommy said.

"Show some respect and stop flirting," Willie interrupted. "It's my mam's funeral." He gestured to Tommy to hurry his steps to pass the girls again and get away from his little sister, but Tommy only reluctantly did so, preferring to stay close to May.

"Anyway," said Tommy, catching up to Willie's hurried gait, "of course the lads will understand. No one's as heartless as that. They're just ribbing you. I don't know what I'd do in your shoes."

"I may go, just to get steaming drunk," Willie said. "It's been a long, hard year. I'm ready to blow off some steam and I think Mam would understand. Just don't expect me to buy any fanny. She wouldn't like that."

Tommy laughed and said, "Indeed she would not! You wouldn't be able to get it up anyway, sober or not, with her ghost watching you."

Willie scoffed lightly and said, "Amen to that."

They approached the parking lot and, as Tommy turned toward the car, Willie said, "Let's walk. I don't want to be around a lot of people right now." He removed his suit jacket and his tie, and led Tommy away toward the dirt path home, past the entrance to Mine #2, its office building, the fan-house, and the nearby bathhouse.

The two young men walked in silence through Willow Creek Canyon and around the bend back to the town of Castle Gate, where an empty house —with a spectacular view of the eponymous rock formation—waited for the family to begin their new lives, without Helen in them.

CHAPTER 19

December, 1923
Castle Gate, Utah

The fall months passed in a blur. Nellie went back to school, Will and Willie threw themselves into work, and wee Ella finally stopped asking where Mammy was. The only daily routine that changed much was Jeanie's. Keeping the house clean and everyone fed had already become her responsibility, but now she was no longer also a nurse and caretaker. It was a bittersweet relief: although her heart ached with missing her mother, Jeanie's workload lessened tremendously.

The house echoed with emptiness when it was just she and Ella home during the day, the silence only broken by the ticking of the mantle clock and the frequent wail of train whistles. Playing the Victrola to fill the silence only reminded Jeanie of Helen's illness and death. After all, Helen received the gift just last Christmas right before she learned of the cancer, and she died while her favorite record was playing, so the records contained musical memories tinged with sorrow.

The family slowly got used to this oddly empty life and their ability to cope grew a little every day. What would have been Helen's 39th birthday passed in September with somber remembrance, while Jeanie's and Will's birthdays in November—with Jeanie turning 20 and Will turning 42—were both just another day.

As those weeks passed, Will noticed he was less frequently invited to the homes of his former brothers-in-law, Bill and John. Neither were outwardly unfriendly, but even Bill and Elsie's wedding anniversary party came and went without an invitation.

When Pete mentioned this to Will, he could only reply, "Maybe I remind them of Helen's absence. Maybe they were inviting just Helen all along and I was a tagalong. I don't know."

Will's children were related by blood but he, Pete and Tam were now lacking that family connection to the men in charge. So, when Will learned of an upcoming opportunity to test with other men for a promotion to fire boss, he began studying in earnest.

A fire boss ensured there were no dangerous levels of gas in the mine tunnels, especially important as the men wore carbide lamps with an active flame on their caps. Methane was highly explosive and gathered in pockets near the ceiling. Carbon monoxide, an odorless and flammable gas, would kill a canary before men would notice it was poisoning them. Because he had worked in coal mines since he was young, and had training as a brattice man, Will was acutely aware of the importance of ventilation and clearing tunnels of gas pockets.

Will and over forty other Carbon County men took the train into Price on December 3 to test for promotions to foreman or fire boss, overseen by Bill Littlejohn. One of the questions on the application asked about citizenship. As Will had not yet filed for Naturalization, he took Bill aside and asked, "Might this block my chances, if I'm not a citizen yet?"

"Not for qualifying for a position, of course," said Bill, "but it might put your name further down the list for promotion, below men who the company knows are here to stay."

"If I go to the courthouse after the test and do it today," Will asked, "can I say on the application that I've applied?"

"As long as you promise to do it today," Bill said, "and don't tell anyone I know about this."

At the courthouse later, Will felt no hesitation while filling out the Declaration of Intention form, renouncing forever all allegiance and fidelity to the English King George, but he did choke up when he had to state that his wife was deceased. As he laid down his signature, declaring his intention to become a citizen of the United States, he felt a pang of disloyalty to bonnie Scotland. But his future lay here, in America, so he took a deep breath and put his name down in ink.

Getting off the train that afternoon in Castle Gate, Will spied Geordie coming out of the company store, so he hustled to catch up with him. "Ho, George," he called out.

Geordie turned and smiled when he saw who was calling him by the name no one used. "Well, if it isnae Big Wullie Garroch, as I live and breathe" Geordie said, stressing his brogue. "It's not quitting time yet and yeh're not dressed for work. Where are yeh coming from?"

"Just got off the train from Price," said Will. "I took the fire boss test today."

"Oh, aye? Best of luck to yeh," Geordie said.

"Cheers," Will said. "Are yeh off anywhere? Why not come back to ours and join us for yer tea? No doubt our Jeanie's made plenty."

"Don't mind if I do," said Geordie. "Jean's a fine cook, like her mam." As they walked north through town, he asked, "How are the wee'uns holding up?"

"Och, yeh know, same as always," Will said, "a little better every day but now and again it gets hard, when memories start rolling in and her absence rings so loud."

"Me and all," Geordie replied, nodding, "I have bad days like that, too. Helen was a sweet lass and I miss her so."

Will chuckled and said, "I don't know if 'sweet' is the word I'd use to describe our Helen."

"Aw, she could be when she wanted to," said Geordie with a grin, "but aye, I take yer point. Feisty and moody is more like it, but it's not kind to speak ill of the dead." He chuckled and, after a pause, said, "I'm glad I don't have to give her my news in person." He darted a glance around, as if looking for Helen's ghost, and finally said, "I'm thinking of moving to Detroit. Henry Ford's offering jobs and the walls of this here canyon are closing in on me. I feel like I'm drowning in tragedy, with a spooky sense of foreboding."

Will was dumbstruck for half a minute before he finally said, "Aw, Geordie, say it ain't so. Yeh're Helen's best brother, the only one who feels like kin."

"Cheers, Wull," Geordie said, "I love your family better than most but I've got the wanderlust, yeh know? The bloom is off the rose here. I'll come back to visit, sure, but it's time to move on."

"Aye, I sometimes feel the same," said Will. "I couldn't move away though, with Helen planted in the ground here. And, I registered for US citizenship today, after the fire boss test."

"Did yeh now?" Geordie grinned. "Congratulations! It's a grand feeling, being sworn in as a citizen. My application was fast-tracked after the war, as Uncle Sam's expression of gratitude for serving in his military."

"God willing," Will said, "we won't be having any more wars. Even so, I served King and Country down the mine. Helen would have been devastated to lose more than just Buchan to the Germans."

"Oh, aye," agreed Geordie. "Remember how she fussed when I enlisted? I still have the letter she wrote, scolding me."

"Aye," laughed Will, "she was furious and only settled down after you explained that they wouldn't take an old man like you into combat, and yeh'd serve in a military hospital."

"Well, that's not exactly how I'd put it," said Geordie, "but aye, that was the gist of it."

Will and Geordie arrived at the house and, when Will opened the front door, Jeanie's voice rang out from the kitchen, "Wipe yer feet outside! I'll not be havin' any snow tracked in!"

"Yes, ma'am," both men said, in unison.

"Uncle Geordie!" Jeanie cried with delight once she saw who was at the door. She wiped her hands on her apron and gave her uncle a hug. "What a pleasant surprise. Will yeh stay for yer tea?"

"Aye, lass, it's good to see you as well," said Geordie. "And, aye, yer father already invited me. I hope yeh've made enough for one more."

"Oh, aye," she said, heading back toward the kitchen. "I always make too much. It's only meat pies and tatties, and I'm baking a wee cake for puddin' after."

"I came on a good night," said Geordie, tossing his coat over the back of the davenport as Will hung his at the front door coatrack.

Nellie and Ella came from the kitchen next, wee Ella toddling excitedly toward her favorite uncle, squealing with delight as he lifted her high and swung her about.

"Yeh're just in time, Uncle Geordie," said Nellie. "I'm doing my homework and I'm stuck on long division. Jeanie's no help."

"Cheeky lass!" Jeanie objected. "It's not my fault I had to leave school after eighth grade."

Geordie shrugged and followed Nellie to the table where her homework was spread out, saying "I'm making no promises, lass."

"Will yeh have a drink?" Will asked Geordie as he followed them into the warm and cozy kitchen. At Geordie's nod, he poured a dram of whisky for each and joined them at the table.

Just then Willie came home from work and, at the sound of his entry at the front door, Will, Geordie and Jeanie all shouted, "Wipe yer feet!"

"Jings!" Willie called back, "it's a regular Greek chorus in there!" He joined them in the kitchen and, seeing the men imbibing, poured himself a drink before sitting at the table.

Will leaned back in his chair, sipping his whisky and watching his family gabbing around the table. He felt a pang of grief knowing how Helen would have loved this and that the reason Jean always made too much was because she couldn't, or wouldn't, get used to cooking for one less.

For a moment, he felt Helen's presence and smelled the scented soap she always used, Yardley's English Lavender. His breath caught and tears began rolling uninvited down his face, so he quickly grabbed his handkerchief from his pocket and pretended to sneeze so no one would notice. He wiped his eyes and blew his nose, and said, "Jeanie, hen, I think yeh've put too much pepper in them pies!"

Jeanie turned to Will quizzically and instantly recognized what that look on his face meant. "Aye, p'rhaps," she said. "P'rhaps I have." She poured herself a drink and sat at the table to join them, her cozy wee family, missing her mam her ownself.

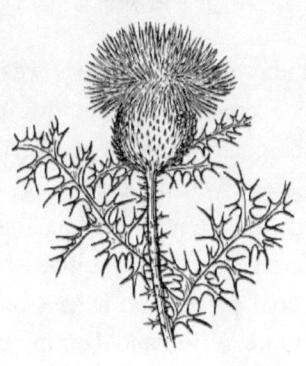

CHAPTER 20

Mid-February – March 7, 1924
Castle Gate, Utah

To Will's relief he was one of two men from Castle Gate who passed the fire boss test. In retrospect, it wasn't a surprise, considering his experience as a brattice man who was already trained to pay attention to air flow and quality, so the test was more about details, proving he knew them. Now it was a matter of waiting for an opening in one of the mines.

Work was slow, though, so no jobs opened up. In fact, men were being laid off and shifts were a precious commodity. With Will's connection to the Littlejohn family, and with a family to support, he worked more shifts than some single men with less pull or seniority. Those men were first to be cut from the list, and even Willie wasn't called in as often as others.

Meantime, Geordie's farewell party was a gala event, with no one in town wanting him to go. "Leave while yeh can still get a big sendoff," he said to Will and the kids, as they said their final goodbyes. Geordie's absence affected their lives almost as impactfully as when Helen passed. Helen and Geordie were like two peas missing from an otherwise full pod. The emptiness left by their departures, exacerbated by the grey winter skies and frigid temperatures, made for gloomy days, indeed.

Nellie had to take responsibility for her own happiness; there was no one else to do it. Without Helen as the glue holding them together—although Jeanie did her best—each family member was left to their own devices. So, Nellie planned a party for her fifteenth birthday, which was on March 13.

Even Ella's third birthday in late February was low-key. Jeanie baked a cake and crafted some ice cream out of snow, canned milk and vanilla extract. The cause for her celebration went over Ella's head, so presents weren't necessary, but she enjoyed the extra hugs and kisses and was a bit let down the next day when the attention had passed.

The first week of March was tough going. Mine #1 shut down in late February, due to falling coal prices and a lack of orders. With #1 closed, even more single workers like Willie and Tommy were laid off and some of the luckier married men with families to support joined the crew in #2.

Shift foreman Zeph Thomas met the new men at the entrance and offered a brief orientation their first day on shift. "Mine Number Two is the Utah Fuel Company's show mine," he told the men. "Like our other Castle Gate mines, electric lights line the main passageways. Point of interest, Number Two here was the first to use electric shot-firing, much safer than dynamite to blow the coal loose. Any day now we'll have electric cap lamps, too. The shipment just arrived to replace your carbide lanterns, but we can't distribute them until the batteries to power them also arrive."

The men exclaimed with excitement—electric cap lamps—how modern!

Zeph continued, "You'll be brought to the coal faces by mantrip, down a ten percent grade to the tunnels. The mine is miles long, the main passageway consisting of two tracks, one going down carrying men and supplies, and one coming out, with loaded coal cars."

He gestured ahead of them, into the entrance, "Once far enough in, the mantrip will either turn left down underground into the 'dips' or right, into the 'rises', up into this hill you see across the road."

Zeph went on, "As you'll see, off-shooting from both sides of the main passage are tunnels that run perpendicular to the main road and parallel to one another. Dips one through four are mined out, with some of the rooms eighteen feet wide and fourteen feet high. The new rooms you'll be carving out should end up just as large."

"You'll also notice," Zeph said, "that the sprinkler system installed to dampen down the coal dust goes all the way up the walls to a height of ten feet or so. Safety is paramount here."

"You've got your assignments," he finally said. "Be smart down there, and I'll see you all at the end of your shift."

As assigned, Will, Pete and Tam got off the mantrip at the stop between the sixth and seventh dip entries, with Tam being directed into the sixth left dip and Pete into the seventh right dip. Will was instructed to follow one of the foremen to be shown the brattice layout, before reporting to his assigned place at the far end of the sixth right dip.

Along the way, Will made plenty of mental notes. These ceilings were high and thick with coal that was still being shot down overnight. Plenty of toxic, explosive gases could get trapped up there in the cavities left behind by the fallen coal.

Their first day went quickly, as exciting as it was to work in a new place, with new things to learn, appreciating the fineness of the working conditions. Even the bathhouse was newer than the one in town and the water in the shower felt hotter. After the mantrip ride back into town, few of the men were in a hurry to get home on this warm and sunny afternoon so a group gathered in front of the Amusement Hall, swapping stories with the night watchman, T.L. Burridge.

"Say, T.L.," one of the men asked, "what's the news on the break-in at the Amusement Hall?"

"It must have been some of the local boys," T.L. began, but he was interrupted by someone asking, "Wait, what happened at the Amusement Hall?"

T.L. explained, "Last Saturday night someone climbed into a side window in the Confectionary … you know, they sell trinkets and sundries there … and stole about two hundred and fifty dollars' worth of jewelry."

"What makes you think it was local boys?" another man asked.

"Well, only one of our hometown boys would have even known there was any jewelry in there," he said. "Think about it. The big, company store would have looked better to a stranger. Plus, they knew exactly which window to bust into."

"That makes sense," said Tam.

"At least I didn't get blamed," T.L. continued. "I wasn't even working that night. But then, if I'd have been on shift, they wouldn't have even tried it because I can watch the Hall from the guard shack."

Charlie Huff approached along with other men just getting into town after their shift at the tipple, and asked the group, "You're all down in Number Two, are you?"

"Aye," said Tam, "some of us were out of Number One, before it was shut."

"I was supposed to be down there with you," Charlie said, "but I got fired a couple weeks back for pissing off the boss."

"Naw," replied Pete, "getting fired for pissing off a boss? Never heard of such a thing!" The men laughed and Pete asked Charlie, "What happened?"

"Well," Charlie explained, "you know I run the movie projector here on Monday nights. Problem is, my boss there is my boss at the mine, too. We argued over how to make the picture brighter. Next thing I know, he laid me off. He tried to pretend it's because work is short, but we both know the real reason."

"That's not right," said Will.

"It's okay, though," said Charlie. "I was making ends meet because I still had the job running the projector. But one day I ran into the superintendent ... that's your brother-in-law, isn't it, Will?"

Will nodded and Charlie continued, "So I asked him, 'Mr. Littlejohn, how long do I have to wait around without a job?' He asked why I wasn't working, so I told him. He said he'd get me another job, at the tipple. Boy, when my old boss saw I had a new job, he was spittin' mad!" Charlie laughed and his audience joined in, happy to see someone sticking it to the man.

Alma Hardee piped up then, saying, "Maybe you'll get my Welber a job at the flicker shows. Now that Number One is shut down, he wants me to put him on shift at Number Two, but I don't want my son working in the mines if he doesn't have to. I want him to get an education ..."

"Aye, I feel the same about our Wullie," said Will, "but sometimes life has other ideas about a man's future."

"Maybe so," said Alma, "and I'm not saying Welber was happy about it. Indeed, he was fit to be tied, but I'm the boss down in that mine, not just in my house, so what I say, goes."

Fay Thacker said to Charlie, "You may be better off here at the tipple. I had a funny feeling about Number Two after they shut down Number One and tried to send me over there. I got a job at Number Three, I felt so strongly about not going down to Number Two. Besides, we're working every day up there. Number Two is still just a couple days a week, isn't it?"

Jack Thorpe, one of the mine inspectors assigned to #2 said, "It's funny you had that strong feeling, Fay. My wife, Eva, had a bad dream a few weeks back and has been nagging at me to not go down there."

"What kind of dream did she have?" asked Will.

"Eva said she saw a ball in the sky that exploded into a bunch of beams of light," Jack said, "and those beams of light fell on some of the houses here in town. What am I supposed to do about a dream like that? It's not like an angel told her to make me stay home on a specific day, is it?"

At this spooky turn, the conversation petered out and the men left toward home. "What do yeh think?" Pete asked Will as they walked, knowing his older brother sometimes had the second sight. In fact, it was one of Will's premonitions that brought them here, to one of the safest mines in America.

"I dunno, do I?" Will said. "Since Helen passed, and I see and hear her so often, I cannot tell what's a warning and what's wishful thinking that I was with her again."

"Well," said Tam, "I'm not afraid of death, since the war, if it's quick. It's not the death I mind, it's the dying."

Pete shuddered and said, "That's plenty of that kind of talk. Just let us know, will yeh, if yeh get any premonitions?"

"Yeh'll be the first to know," said Will. He waved to his brother and his nephew and turned up the walk toward his little saltbox house in which his children waited for him, safe and warm.

CHAPTER 21

March 8, 1924
Castle Gate, Utah

The first week of March had been mild, almost like April weather, so the icy temperature on Saturday morning was a harsh reminder that it was still winter. Pete and Tam showed up, pre-dawn, at Will's door bundled in their warmest coats, gloves and scarves to walk to the tipple together. Before heading out, Will passed by his son's pallet, which was set up on the floor in front of the fire for warmth, and gave Willie a playful kick to wake him.

"Get up, you," said Will, "just because yeh don't have to go to work doesn't mean you can lay about."

"I wasn't going to," Willie objected, wiping the sleep from his eyes as he sat up. "The lads and I have a football match this morning."

"Och! Yeh'll be tossing a ball of ice, it's that cold out!" said Tam.

"Oh, no," moaned Willie, "it's been so warm! Why did it have to get cold again?"

"It's awright, wee man," teased Pete. "Go back to yer nice, warm beddy-bye while the grown men go earn a day's pay."

Willie shot his uncle a look and bit his tongue. "I'm getting up," he said, instead of exchanging barbs. He was too tired to verbally joust this morning.

"Have a good day," said Jeannie, bundled up in her heaviest sweater, handing her father his lunch pail. "See youse tonight."

"Thanks, hen," Will said and gestured toward Willie, "and don't let this'un go back to bed."

"I'm up!" Willie shouted, leaping to his feet. He followed the men to the door and closed it firmly behind them. "Good riddance," he muttered before heading into the kitchen, where the coal stove offered some warmth, for breakfast and a cuppa.

The men shivered as they walked, blowing hot breath into their scarves to warm their faces, heading uptown to catch the mantrip at the tipple to shuttle them to Mine #2. They walked fast, hunched against the cold with hands stuffed into their coat pockets, looking forward to wedging themselves into the railcar packed with other warm bodies.

The town butcher, Ben Thomas, climbed into the railcar with them at the last possible moment, about to start his first day working underground. The butcher shop was closed due to slack times, so—because Ben was also the well-loved Mormon bishop in Castle Gate—he was offered the favor of a shift in Mine #2 even though he had never worked below ground before.

"I don't know about this, boys," said Ben, settling in just as the car began moving, "if I didn't need the paycheck, I wouldn't be here. I was awake all night with misgivings to not go to work today. My wife begged me not to ignore what she saw as the Lord's warnings, but I told her it was nerves from never working in the mine before. That's probably what it is, right? It's awful deep and dark down there."

"Aye, in the tunnels it's dark, but only if yer lamp goes out," said Tam. "The main road has electric lights. And, aye, it's deep, but yeh'll forget about that once yeh're used to it."

"We'll take care of you," said another man. "The Lord wouldn't like it if we let anything happen to one of His bishops."

Before entering the mine they stopped at the bathhouse to change into work clothes and receive their assignments. While they changed, Henry Etzel could be heard from the other side of the room, hollering at the foreman, "That's a lousy spot! Assign me someplace else." When the foreman dismissively shook his head and moved on to the next man, Henry grabbed his lunch pail and stormed off, muttering under his breath.

On their way into the mine the men, laughing at Henry's foolishness, each hung one of their numbered, brass ID chips on a pegboard at the office before going below: when it came time to weigh the coal each man dug—identified by the matching brass chip on the coal car each sent back to the surface—their pay could be verified.

Next, the men were transported via mantrip deep underground. Like yesterday, Will took his place in room fifteen of the sixth right dip, while

Pete was again assigned to room six of the seventh right dip and Tam to room two of the sixth left dip.

Bishop Ben was assigned near Tommy Hilton's dad, John, who said, "Here, give me your cap." John lit a match and showed him how to light the attached carbide lantern, which was designed to not easily blow out with ordinary movement of the man wearing it.

"Is that safe," Ben asked, "an open flame like that?"

"That's why we have fire bosses," John explained, "to check for gas pockets, and why they sprinkle down the walls to dampen the coal dust before we start a shift."

John led Ben to his assigned spot in the seventh left dip, showed him how to attach his brass tag to his coal car and gave him a rudimentary lesson in using a pickaxe and shovel, teaching him the proper way to bend and lift, "Lift with your knees, not with your back, or you won't be able to move tomorrow."

"You're not going to be able to move tomorrow, either way," laughed a nearby miner, Ray Williams, gathering knowing chuckles from other men in the vicinity.

Ben said, "I appreciate it, John … or should I call you Tom? That's the name etched into your belt."

John smiled and said, "I couldn't find my own belt, so I had to wear my son's." He left Ben to his work, saying, "Ray is here if you need anything else."

Ray said, "Sure thing. It's not too hard on your brain, just murder on your back."

Meanwhile Will, Marty Kimball, and father and son duo Walt and Joe Kirby chatted amiably as they made their way to the furthest reaches of the sixth right dip.

"Yeh're about my lad's age," said Will.

"I'm twenty-one," Joe said. "I know Willie. I was supposed to be playing football with them today."

"Aye," Will said, laughing, "it's bitter cold out. Better off down here, earning a day's pay than freezin' yer clackers off."

Pete, in the seventh right dip, settled in to work with a couple of young men with Mediterranean accents. He said to Tom Pelly, the nearby machine-man with a strong Manchester accent, "At least I can understand you, even if yeh are English, but these two, what are they saying?"

Tom laughed and said, "Aw, they're areet, aren't you lads?"

180

Joe Cappelletti and Emmanuel Zagarakis, from Italy and Greece respectively, were used to the ribbing they got from the English-speaking miners, so they laughed it off and ignored the two old-timers.

"Besides," Tom said to Pete, gesturing toward his electric-powered Sullivan Short Wall mining machine, "once I start cutting into that coal face, you won't be able to hear yourself think, much less these two talking."

Up in room two of the sixth left dip, Tam was with Steve Andrakis and Kanaz Verges, waiting for fire boss Ed Cox to do a final check of the room. Coal had been shot down from the ceiling last night and Ed stood above them on the mound, double-checking the ceiling cavity for gas as there had been problems in this room in the past.

Meantime, the men made small talk with Ed Willis and Otto McDonald from nearby room one. Ed, whose job it was to lead the horse-drawn coal cars to and from the mine face, gossiped about his two wives and their most recent spat.

"Are yeh really married to two women?" Tam asked.

"Well," said Ed, a Negro in his late thirties, "I got married 'long about seven years ago, but we haven't lived together in a long time. I've been with my new woman a couple years now, but she's not my 'wife'. I just say that as a shortcut, you know. Makes her happy."

Otto laughed and said, "One wife's plenty for me, thanks. Millie and I were about to head back to our farm since the weather was getting so nice … well, up 'til this morning anyway. I got offered a shift so we put off going home for a few days."

Ed Cox crouched down atop the stack of coal and said, "Kanaz, let me see your cap lamp. My safety lamp blew out and I haven't got any matches on me."

Kanaz handed over his cap and Ed used the open flame to relight his safety lantern, which was designed to glow bright blue in the presence of flammable gases. Methane, which had collected in the ceiling cavity high above, had been inadvertently pulled downward as Ed crouched and, when the lantern fire touched the gas, it ignited and filled the cavity above with rolling flames.

Tam's military training kicked in when he saw the churning ball of fire fill the pocket in the ceiling. He pulled his cap down over his face and hit the dirt, face down, just as the flames expanded and shot through the sixth left dip tunnel. The ground shook with an explosion that took out the electricity that powered the lighting and machinery, and a massive rush of air blew out every cap lantern in the dips with a loud *fooomp*.

In the pitch-black silence that followed, experienced miners knew to not relight their lamps yet. The explosion had, no doubt, stirred up a widespread cloud of coal dust that was just as flammable as gas. As the initial shock wore off, the dark stillness was filled with shaky voices, in various languages, cussing and praying.

"Steady, boys …" one voice advised and, as he spoke, somewhere in the darkened mine one of the less experienced men lit a match.

This time, the resulting rockets of flame took out the rest of the mine, filling the tunnels with violent heat so intense that many of the coal walls were instantly coked and glazed. The force of the blast sent heavy machines, coal cars and horses flying. Rail tracks were twisted and the 800-pound steel gates at the mine entrance were shot across the canyon and embedded into the side of a hill half a mile away. Thick clouds of acrid, black smoke poured out of the gaping maw that remained of the entrance to Mine #2.

The blast blew out the power in the fan house just outside, disabling the fan that sucked bad air out of the mine. John Stagg was inside the fan house when the west wall was blown off and he ran to the office building, a hundred feet away, to escape the poisonous smoke and to call and alert the main office uptown.

Shift foreman Zeph Thomas was in the office, already making that call. The explosion had destroyed a wall there as well, along with the pegboard with the brass identification chips, obliterating that record of who was down below.

A mile away, inside Mine #3—where Fay Thacker was after his premonition about Mine #2—the workers felt the mountain shake as if coal within their own mine was being shot. Fay shouted at the assistant mine foreman, who was hurrying in his direction, "What are you doing, shooting down here without getting us out first?"

The foreman replied, his voice bordering on panic, "Number Two has exploded!"

The crew hurried to the surface, knowing that all hands would be called on deck, and many had completed rescue training. Once outside the entrance, they saw across the valley clear signs that the foreman was right. "Look at those clouds of smoke," Fay said, "only oxygen crews will be sent in."

Tommy and Willie had just begun their football game. Better an icy game than being underfoot with the women doing housework and hollering at them for being in the way. The boys felt the first explosion as it shook the earth like a rumble of thunder and stopped in their tracks, stalled in mid-play. "Was that what I think it was?" one of the boys asked.

The second blast followed his words, in response, and a shower of black, powdery coal dust rained down on them and the rest of the town as the air became noxious with a gassy burnt odor. The alarm siren at the tipple began shrieking and Tommy, who had trained on the rescue team, darted away to report for duty. Willie, who was too young for last summer's training as he wasn't yet eighteen, ran with him.

The boys pushed through a growing crowd in the town center of panicked wives and mothers, women screaming the names of their men who, just a short time ago, were lucky enough to pull a shift. Throngs of people filled the road, wailing and crying, stampeding to get down to Mine #2. At the south end of town, the road was obstructed by quick moving company employees attempting to keep spectators from clogging the rescue efforts.

"Trained emergency crews only!" they shouted but, try as they might, they couldn't block everyone. Tommy darted past, but Willie obeyed orders. The boys locked eyes for a moment—both of their fathers were down there. "Good luck," shouted Willie, "get 'em out of there."

"I will," called Tommy, and he ran off with other trained men and a scattering of hysterical women who had managed to push their way through.

Just then, what sounded like a third explosion shook the earth, leading the panicked women into a fresh chorus of wails. Willie turned toward home to check on his sisters. Surely, they must be just as terrified. He moved north, like a salmon swimming upstream.

May Hardee's older brother, Welber, drove by at a snail's pace, honking at the crowd blocking the road. Willie ran up and pounded on the car window so Welber stopped the car and rolled it down. Willie asked, his voice trembling, "What are you doing here? You were supposed to be playing ball with us, but we figured you talked your dad into letting you work."

"I was out late last night and slept in," Welber said, in a rush. "My dad and grandpa are down there."

"My dad, and my uncle and cousin, too," said Willie. "I'm heading home to check on my sisters."

Welber's eyes flashed with pain, "My sisters and mother are a mess. Mother shook me awake, hysterical. I was mad as the Dickens, at first ... I wanted to sleep in, you know, but then she told me what happened. Did anyone get out?"

"I don't know anything," said Willie. "I couldn't get close enough. They're blocking the road to stop the wives from getting through."

"My God," Welber said, his face ashen, "I would have been down there if Dad had let me. I was so mad at him, I damn near moved out."

Willie said, "I would have been down there, too, if it wasn't for layoffs."

Welber nodded and said, "I gotta go." He rolled up his window and edged the car forward, honking his horn again to part the crowd, just as a nearby woman shrieked, "Henry! Henry, you're alive!" Henry Etzel's wife pushed her way through the crowd and threw herself into her husband's arms, almost knocking him down.

"So I am!" Henry said, through a torrent of her kisses, "I'd have been down there if I hadn't argued with the boss ..."

Willie pushed north through the chaos, surrounded by voices shouting, "They'll be okay, they'll get out ..." with others screaming, "They're all dead! I just know it!" and "I saw it coming! I had a dream last night ..."

May Hardee ran past and he grabbed her arm to stop her. "May, I just saw Welber ..."

"I know," she said, breathless, "he's going to help. I told Mother I'd find some news. Do you know what happened?"

"I don't know anything," said Willie, "except that I have family down there and I have to check on my sisters."

May started sobbing, "My dad ... my grandpa ... and ..." her eyes wild, she asked, "What about Tommy? Why isn't he with you? He's not working a shift, is he?"

Willie said, "He's on the rescue team, so he went to join them."

"That's almost as bad!" May cried. "Look, Willie, I have to go. I need to find out what I can and report back to Mother."

"Of course," Willie said. "Good luck."

May ran south and Willie continued north, toward home, and soon saw coming toward him in a pack Jeanie, Jessie and Bertha, rushing forward when they saw him approach.

"Wullie! What do yeh know?" Jessie shrieked. "Are they okay? Did they get out?"

Willie said, weary of repeating it, "I don't know anything."

"Oh God, please let them be okay," prayed Bertha, her hands clasped over her heart.

"There's escapeways and plenty of air pockets," Willie said, shivering in the cold. "They're not letting anyone but rescue workers through. It's freezing out here … you might as well go home and wait for news."

"I'm not going home!" said Jessie. "Not with my Pete underground!"

"I'll head down to see what I can find out," said Willie. "I just wanted to make sure you were all informed. Aunt Jessie, there's nothing for you to do. They're blocking the road."

"Come on back home," Bertha said to Jessie, "we can't leave the girls with Nellie too long. They know something's wrong, and I don't want to leave my Margie alone."

"Aye, yeh're right," Jessie relented, "but you, laddie, you come home as soon as yeh know anything."

"I'll go with him as far as I can," said Jeanie, "and I'll come back with any news. Would you let Nell and Ella come home with youse?" Jessie and Bertha agreed and turned to hurry home.

Jeanie and Willie ran down the dirt road toward town, urgency propelling them, until they were slowed by the sheer enormity of the crowd clamoring for news at the company office. The road was jammed with cars filled with folks from neighboring towns, who had heard the news and came to gawk or offer help. At the depot, rescue crews from nearby towns poured out of train cars. They loaded their gear onto waiting flatbed trucks, climbing on the beds to be driven to the mine.

May was there and Jeanie pushed her way toward her. "May, what have yeh heard?" Jeanie asked.

"Nothing!" May cried. "They don't know anything yet!"

Willie tapped Jeanie on the shoulder and said, "I'm going to see if I can get past the roadblock." He wound his way through the crowd until he got to what was now an official barricade, with a rope in place.

Bill Littlejohn was there in his car, dressed in dungarees and a heavy, workingman's coat instead of his usual suit and tie, waiting in line to get through. Willie ran up to the driver's side window. "Uncle Bill!" he hollered loudly enough to be heard through the glass.

Bill shouted, "Get in!" and gestured toward the other side of the car.

Willie hurried around to the passenger side and climbed in. He had become numb to the cold outside until he felt the warmth and comfort of the inside of his uncle's luxurious automobile. Bill nudged his car forward, impatiently waiting his turn behind vehicles filled with rescue workers and other mine officials, each as important as the other. "Come on, come on …" he muttered.

"What do you know?" Willie asked.

"Not as much as I'd like," Bill said, "other than there's been a cave-in at the main entrance and the air is so toxic that crews can only go in wearing oxygen gear, if they can even get past the collapse."

"Did anyone make it out?" Willie asked.

"No, not yet," said Bill, "but maybe the men have found pockets of fresh air. The fan's blown out, and there's no power below, so there's no ventilation. If they can find their way to clean air pockets, maybe in one of the tunnels that's been bratticed off, they may be okay until we can clear the rubble."

"If anyone knows where to find an air pocket," Willie said, "it's Da. He's in charge of brattice, you know."

"Yes, that's one good thing, isn't it?" said Bill.

Finally, Bill's car was next in line and he was waved through. Even so, it was slow going with so many rescue vehicles. He parked next to the cemetery, as close to the mine entrance as he could get.

Smoke was billowing out of both the main entrance to their left and the escapeway opening at the far end of the cemetery, to their right. "God," said Willie, pulling his shirt collar up over his mouth and nose as a makeshift filter, "if it's this bad out here, imagine what it must be like down there."

"I know, lad, but I'll say it again," Bill reassured him, "there could be fresh-air pockets protected by brattice and your father knows where they are."

Zeph Thomas was at the blown-out office, directing and delegating rescue crews, when Bill and Willie arrived. "Bill," he said, "you made it."

"Of course, it just took forever," Bill said. "It's a mob scene back there."

Willie gazed, jaw agape, at the devastated entrance to Mine #2. What was formerly a solid structure—a clear-cut opening into the face of the hill with sturdy wooden framework and massive steel gates—was now a pile of rubble, a raw opening in the earth with deadly, black smoke seeping out of it.

"We have to get those men out," Zeph said. "At least one of the water pipes has burst and if we don't get it shut off the lower dips will fill, and those men will drown. The valve's only two hundred yards in, on this side of the cave-in. I've sent a crew in to shut it off." He paused and then said, his voice breaking, "Bill, I sent all those married men down there, men who have families to support ..."

"You weren't to know ..." Bill began.

"I would have been in there, too," Zeph said, "I was about to go on in with Jack Thorpe when I got a telephone call. It was the blacksmith, calling about fixing my son's bike. Jack was just telling me about a dream his wife had. She woke up screaming, 'Jack, you're going to burn!' He laughed it off, but I'll be damned if she didn't have a premonition."

"Zeph, I would have been in there as well," said Bill, his voice somber, "except I got in late last night from a Masonic Installation. I slept in this morning and didn't even hear the explosion. If I'd gotten up at my normal time I'd be in there, too, on the other side of that cave-in."

"Jack wasn't even coming in today," said Zeph. "We weren't going to be running a Saturday shift, and he had planned today off, but he told me that he went to the picture show last night with his wife and someone there told him the shift had been scheduled. If he hadn't gone to the flickers, he'd still be alive."

Their laments were interrupted by the shouts of men near the entrance and they turned to see the lifeline rope bouncing, as if someone inside was frantically jerking on it. The form of a man appeared through the smoke, but he didn't make it all the way out before his knees buckled and he collapsed. Bill and Zeph both grabbed their handkerchiefs to hold over their faces, took a deep breath, and ran in. They lifted the man, one under each arm, and dragged him out.

"Get him to fresh air!" Bill gasped, finally able to breathe once they reached safety.

"That's Tommy!" Willie cried and ran forward to help. He, Bill and Zeph dragged Tommy's limp body up to the nearby cemetery and propped him against the closest gravestone. Once they determined that he was breathing on his own, the older men stood and turned to go.

"Can we leave him with you?" Bill asked his nephew. "We need to get back."

"Of course," said Willie. Tommy was out cold. "Wake up, Tom, wake up," Willie said, slapping his friend's hand. Finally, Tommy's eyelids fluttered and he came to, coughing and retching.

"Willie!" he said. He looked around and saw the headstone he was propped against. He asked, "Am I dead?"

Willie said, relieved, "No, you're not dead. The air's cleaner up here, even if it is grisly, waking up in a graveyard." Willie's gaze wandered and rested upon Helen's grave, off to the edge of the cemetery.

Tommy sat up and said, "I told them that machine I was wearing wasn't working right but they said, 'It's only two hundred yards.' I had to do what I could, didn't I?"

Willie nodded and Tommy continued, "All I could think about was saving my dad, you know? I didn't get in very far. Boy, I just couldn't breathe. The gauge said I didn't have any oxygen. None! I was breathing straight carbon monoxide."

Tommy stopped to take a breath and went on, "So I jerked the lifeline. I knew I wouldn't make it back. I had to stay calm … if you lose your head and panic, you're done for. I walked as fast as I could and I could just see the light outside through the smoke. I was almost there but then the light started turning pink and blue." He laughed a bit and said, "It was turning colors! Finally, I had to break loose and run. Next thing I knew, I woke up here, of all places!"

He rose, unsteady on his feet, so Willie helped support him. "We better get back," Tommy said.

"Are you okay?" Willie asked.

"More okay than them down below," Tommy said. "That's my dad down there."

"Aye, me and all," Willie said, "I've been trying not to think about that." Now that Tommy brought it up, it was all Willie could think about. If only Da's second sight had prevented them from going to work … if only "good riddance" weren't the last words he directed toward his father …

He snapped out of his thoughts to see Tommy staggering ahead of him on the path, so he hurried to catch up. Up ahead, one of the foremen directed Tommy toward a military style tent, which had been erected for first aid, ordering him to get checked out before reporting back to his crew.

Willie approached Bill Littlejohn to volunteer in some way but waited because his uncle was in conversation with others in charge. Repairs of the electrical power, telephone lines and ventilation fan were of utmost urgency. Willie didn't want to interrupt, so he wandered to find someone looking for help.

The area was crawling with people setting up aid stations, along with groups of gawkers and wailing wives who made it through the roadblock. The spectators stayed out of the way, lest they get sent home for disrupting. It was easy to tell the American wives from the Mediterranean ones. The American women were more stoic and the Italian wives prayed and wept loudly, crying *"O dolor mia!"* as their kin held them back from darting into the mine.

Red Cross workers arrived with nurses and doctors, including Dr. McDermid, who were led to the first aid station. A concession tent, stocked with food and coffee, was set up nearby. The area looked like a military installation as everyone who had been training over the years reported for duty.

Two flatbed trucks pulled up to the bathhouse delivering the rescue crew from the nearby town of Winter Quarters and the forty-pound breathing apparatus they would soon be wearing on their backs. Willie helped them unload, following them—with their captain Stan Harvey—inside.

Willie couldn't help gazing at the morbid scene of clothing hanging on hooks, high above their heads. Those were the household duds that the trapped miners wore that morning before changing into their work clothes. He recognized his father's trousers by their patched hem.

The rescue crews also now changed out of their own clothes into complete work outfits supplied by the company. As soon as Stan's team was unloaded and dressed for their shift, they were ordered to report to the mine entrance. Willie, finally finding a place he could be useful, followed them out, helping to lug their gear.

On their way past a group of spectators, one of the wives called out, "Save my man!" Her words visibly shook the men, many clenching their fists and jaws with tension. This was not a drill.

Enough men were assembled to split the Winter Quarters team into two crews, with Stan Harvey in charge of the #1 crew. Stan and his team reported to John Petit, a former State Mine Inspector.

Mr. Petit said, "I need you to clear the opening. We've had a cave-in, and no one can get through."

"Yes, sir," Stan said, turning to his men. "Alright, boys, this is what you've trained for. Let's use our skills and our brains and be careful in there. We're here to rescue others, not need rescuing ourselves."

189

He led his men, wearing their bulky oxygen tanks on their backs—along with their goggles, nose clips and mouth pieces—deep into the opening where it was blocked three quarters of the way to the ceiling with dirt and rubble. The ceiling would need to be propped up to prevent another cave-in.

Team #1 used picks and shovels to clear out the cave-in, encumbered by their gear. They took measurements and passed them on to Team #2 outside, who stood at a safe distance from the smoke. Willie helped the second team as they sawed wooden beams down to size and passed them inside, to build a safe ceiling.

It was long, slow, arduous work and the clock was ticking. Noon came and went and still there was more debris to clear. By the time they had almost completed their task, Team #1's breathing apparatus was running out of charge, so it was time to swap out for another crew.

Stan passed on instructions to George Wilson, captain of the Standardville team, waiting nearby to take over, "We need you to install one final center post. We ran out of air before we could do it."

Mr. Petit continued the instructions, "Once you make that roof secure, go in a little further and let me know what you see."

George took his team inside and Stan returned his crew to the bathhouse so the next team could recharge the oxygen bottles. Willie followed along, helping the exhausted men carry the apparatus.

Their first shift complete with the mid-afternoon sun approaching the high bluff to the west, Stan and his fellows changed their clothes and wandered to the tent where coffee and sandwiches were being served. Outside the tent, Willie noticed a flurry of frantic activity near the newly repaired entrance, so he got Stan's attention and called him over.

Two of George Wilson's crew members were being helped to the bathhouse. They were in bad shape, but able to walk with assistance. George Wilson, though, was unconscious. He was carried, at a run, inside the first aid tent where Dr. McDermid and the medical team could work on resuscitating him.

Once the men who had carried George came back outside, Stan asked, "What happened?"

"I don't know, for sure," said one of the men, "but one of our guys got in trouble … I think he got some carbon monoxide, he and the other fella."

"Yeah," said another man, "he panicked and accidentally knocked George's nose-clip off, when George tried to help him. The two of them were in such a state that we didn't even notice George just laying there, out cold."

"He was still breathing when we got to him," said the first man, "but just barely, and he was a funny color."

The men continued but their voices faded as Willie's thoughts turned to frustration at how long this was taking. It was already three o'clock and the explosion happened just after eight that morning. Rescue workers had nearly died just trying to get into the mine. Meantime, almost two hundred men were still trapped inside, with no salvation in sight. If it was this bad up top, what was happening down below? Were there any air pockets like everyone was hoping? With the power out and the fan-house damaged by the blast, how would the toxic smoke get sucked out? How would air get circulated down there?

Two of Stan's men stood nearby, their conversation pulling Willie out of his depressive thoughts. One said, "George's brother, Jack, was almost killed in the Scofield mine explosion back in 1900. He was outside the mine entrance when it blew and it threw him and his horse all the way across the valley, just like them timbers and steel gates, yonder." The man pointed toward the far-away debris that today's explosion had sent flying.

"I did hear about that," said the other man. "He ended up with a metal plate in his head, didn't he?"

"Sure enough," said the first man, chuckling. "Those Wilson boys are made of hardy stock."

"Don't forget," another man piped in, "three of his other brothers died that day."

Just then, Tommy emerged from the first aid tent, a bit wobbly. He saw Willie and joined him, saying, "They want to send me home, but I think I'm going to stick around."

"Is that smart?" Willie asked. Tommy's face was ashen and his red, droopy eyes showed how fatigued he was.

"Smart or not, I'm still breathing and there's still men trapped down there," said Tommy.

As the boys spoke, a somber conversation among George's crew was taking place. The two lads listened in on the older men, as it became apparent that George Wilson had just died.

"Come on," Willie said. "I'll take you home. Come back after you get some rest."

Tommy agreed, "Just for a short while. I won't get any rest knowing there's work to do but I'm no good to anyone right now. Between you and me, I feel awful."

The boys hitched a ride back to town with Stan Harvey's crew and were dropped off at the hotel, where the men would be staying. Nearby, at the train depot, an entourage of men in suits and women with Red Cross armbands were disembarking, along with even more rescue crews.

As Willie, Tommy and Stan's crew climbed off the backs of the trucks —which then turned toward the train station to taxi the new arrivals to Mine #2—the crowd that now included newspaper reporters descended upon them, clamoring for updates. May and Jeanie were among them, and they rushed toward the boys.

"What's happening down there?" Jeanie begged. "Is Da alright? Did they get out? What about Uncle Pete? Tam? The rest of 'em?"

"Tommy, what happened to you?" May asked, alarmed. "You look awful!"

"Let's get away from the crowd," Willie suggested, and the four young people wandered a bit north of the mass of folks listening to Stan Harvey's men sharing their versions of the day's events so far.

"Nobody's out yet," Willie began, "but Uncle Bill thinks some of them might be able to find fresh air pockets, and Da will be best suited to lead them there."

Jeanie heaved a sigh of relief, but May asked, "What about the rest of them, the ones who aren't working near your dad? It's an awful big mine!"

Tommy said, "Our fathers know that mine like the backs of their hands. If anyone's going to lead anyone to safety, it's the Hardee and Hilton men."

"But how aren't they out yet?" asked Jeanie.

Willie and Tommy both hesitated, neither wanting to share how bad the scene looked. Finally, Willie said, "There's been a cave-in at the entrance and they're just about done digging it out."

"The rescue crews aren't even inside yet?!" Jeanie demanded.

"I'm sure they've made it in by now," said Willie.

"It's taking so long," moaned Jeanie.

"I need to get home and tell Mother," May said. "This is the first real news I've heard all day and Welber's not back yet to tell us anything. Tommy, are you heading home? I'll walk with you. You look like you could use a shoulder to lean on."

"Yeah, I need a little shuteye," Tommy said, fatigue finally setting in.

"Are you okay? What happened?" May asked, taking his arm for support as they walked off in the direction of their nearby, neighboring houses.

Willie and Jeanie turned toward home, the Castle Gate rocks looming ahead of them, and Willie said, "Tommy got a snootful of bad gas, underground. He spent half the day in the first aid tent. That's why he looks like that."

"Jings!" said Jeanie. "I'm that relieved yeh're both okay. Here's the news I've learned, here in town. That group of men getting off the train … did yeh see 'em?"

Willie nodded and she continued, "They're the high mucky mucks from up in Salt Lake City. They're bringing in crews from as far away as New Mexico, Arizona and Montana. Meantime, here in town, the women whose men didn't go to work today are helping those who did, taking care of babies and helping to cook meals and such. It's lovely to see folks pull together in times of crisis, intit?"

"I know what you mean. You should see it down there, Jean," Willie said. "Those rescue crews, they've been training for a disaster like this. They'll get the men out, don't you worry."

"Well," Jeanie said, "get it told to Aunt Jessie because here she comes." Jeanie pointed up the road where their aunt was bustling toward them, as fast as her middle-aged legs would carry her.

"Where've yeh been?" Jessie cried as she approached. "I've been watching out my window for yeh to come home. Are they safe?"

Willie said, sugar coating the news, unwilling to activate Aunt Jessie's histrionics, "Uncle Bill thinks they'll be okay. They've cleared out the entry where it was blocked."

"Och, thanks be to Jesus!" Jessie cried, throwing her hands in the air. "Bertha will be that relieved. The poor wee lassie is fit to be tied, her heart pounding so bad she had to lie down, worrying about her Tam." She turned her attention to Willie and asked, concern in her voice, "Are yeh hungry lad? Yeh've been down there all day."

"No thanks, Auntie," said Willie. "I had a sandwich at the site. They've got coffee and food for all the workers. I was just telling Jeanie, it's a sight to see, the way they have it all set up. Our men are in trustworthy hands."

"Aye, that's good to hear, laddie," Jessie said, taking Willie's arm and leading him home. "Now, you let me get yeh some tea and a nice biccy, get yeh all warmed up after being outside in the cold fer so long."

Jessie led her niece and nephew home, where the rest of the family impatiently waited for some good news ... good news that Willie couldn't quite deliver ... not truthfully, anyway.

ॐ

As the afternoon wore on, the stench in the air waned a bit but it still lingered. The sunlight began to fade and it got closer to quitting time, when women would normally be preparing for their men to return home for a hot meal.

Those who were lucky enough to have a husband or son who didn't work that day were especially loving to their menfolk that evening. For the others, a new kind of fear set in, the kind that the dark of night brings with it as the possibility of an empty bed becomes a probability.

The sun going down also meant the temperature dropped even further and it was just too cold to wander into town in a useless search for news. There was nothing to do but wait at home.

Finally, as the sky went completely dark, Bill Littlejohn's car pulled up in front of the house and Jeanie rushed to the door, welcoming him inside. She had just finished feeding Ella and she, Nellie and Willie all picked at their food. No one had an appetite except for the smallest of them, the only one who had no idea that Da may not be coming home.

"Come in, Uncle Bill," Jeanie said, ushering him toward the davenport to sit down. "May I take your coat?" she asked. "Get you a cuppa?"

"No, dear, thank you, I'm not staying," Bill said. "I was in town for a quick minute and wanted to give you an update while I was nearby. By the way," he said as he sat down, "I spoke with your Uncle Geordie today and he sends his love."

Jeanie smiled and asked, "Did yeh, aye? And how's he settling in?" She joined him on the davenport, lifting Ella onto her lap. Willie and Nell each grabbed a nearby chair, to join them.

"He's doing fine," Bill said. "He called when he heard the news of what happened here today ..."

Jeanie interrupted, her voice filled with concern, "How did he hear about something happening in our wee town? He's all the way in Michigan."

"Oh, well ... my dear, it's national news," Bill stammered. "He heard it on the radio. Anytime you have almost two hundred men trapped in a mine ..."

"So, they're all still trapped?" she asked.

"Yes, I'm sorry to say," he said, fidgeting with his collar as if it was too tight.

"I thought they had the entryway cleared," said Willie.

"Yes, they've cleared the cave-in, but the force of the blast pushed a number of coal cars uphill and now they're jammed up tight, blocking the way," Uncle Bill explained. "All that time, lost. The crews have concluded they have to go in via the escapeway, off the first left dip."

"Why didn't they do that earlier?" Jeanie asked.

"Sensible girl," Bill mused. "We've had crews working their way in there, as well, but it wasn't the primary focus of our efforts. Both entryways were blocked with gas and rubble, but now we know that the main entrance is impassable. And now, rescue efforts are on hold while they get the fan running again. This wasn't a priority because having the fan on might literally fan any open flames, but no real work can be done down there until fresh air is available inside. The oxygen-tank rescue gear can only go so far in and do so much when the air is so thick with toxins."

"What can I do?" Willie asked. "I felt like teats on a bull down there this morning."

Bill gave a wan smile and said, "Without training, my lad, there's not much you can do. You saw … anyone who's not on a crew is in the way. All the work from here on in is underground. You'd do best to help your womenfolk. Be the man of the house for all of them until we get the men back home."

Jeanie said, "Aye, yeh can run into town for news, so's I don't have to drag wee Ella out in the cold."

"I'm off away," Bill said. "Crews will be working 'round the clock, and I've got to get back … just came into town for some mine maps in the office …" He cleared his throat, realizing that he was rambling and, as he stood to go, he asked, "Would you children like to come stay with us for the night? Elsie would be happy to have you …"

Nellie shot her elder sister a hopeful glance, but Jeanie declined, bristling at being included in his blanket description of them all as children. "Thank you, no, Uncle," she said. "I don't know about the rest, but I'd like to be here when Da comes home."

"Me and all," said Willie.

"Yes," Nellie relented, "me, too."

"Well, call Elsie if you need anything," he said.

"We don't have a telephone, remember?" Nellie said.

"Yes, I'm sorry. I forgot," Bill replied. "My head is elsewhere, as you can well imagine." He turned to leave and said, "I'll check on you tomorrow. Take care."

Once it was just Will and Helen's four children in the house, their father's absence was even more pronounced. He should have been home by now. Even Ella sensed the fear, and she began crying, lifting her arms to Jeanie to be picked up, "Deanie, I want Da."

Jeanie hoisted her up to give her a hug and a kiss and said, "I know, my wee lamb. So do I. He'll be home soon, you'll see." Nellie's face began to crumple, and Jeanie sighed with frustration, "Oh no, not you and all!"

Nellie could no longer contain herself and she began to cry in earnest. She threw herself onto the davenport and wailed, "How do these things keep happening to us? First Mam, now Da! Even Uncle Geordie is gone. We're really orphans, now!"

"Hush, you," Jeanie snapped. "Don't say things like that when we don't know for sure. Da could come swanning in the door any time, and here's you, with him all dead and buried!"

Nellie thought for a moment then exclaimed, "With my birthday coming up! What if they bury him on my birthday, like they did Mam on yours, Wullie?"

"Now, that's enough!" Willie barked. "Stop being so damned selfish and thinking only of yourself!"

"No, listen! It's like we're cursed!" Nellie cried, refusing to be silenced. "We should have never come to America …" she howled. At Nellie's hysterics, Ella began crying again.

Jeanie, about to yell at her sister to shut up, stopped to consider what Nellie had just said. She patted Ella to quiet her and said instead, calmly, "Yeh know, Wullie, it is odd, intit, that Da brought us here because of a premonition he had about dying in the mine back home? And that these things keep happening near birthdays? Death and birth? Isn't that odd?"

Nellie nodded fervently but Willie rolled his eyes and scoffed, "I've had it with you women and your spooky ideas. I'm going out." He stomped toward the door and yanked his coat from its hook. "I'll be at Tommy's if you need me. I want to check on him, anyway."

Willie trudged toward town, his wool cap pulled down tightly over his ears, fists jammed into his pockets for warmth, ruminating over the conversation that he had pretended to dismiss but had actually gotten under his skin.

It was odd, wasn't it?

The moon was the tiniest sliver of a waxing crescent and the blackness of the road ahead gave him the fear, like a goose walking across his grave. The windows in the houses nearby were faintly lit by lantern light but that wasn't enough to illuminate his way into town on this dark night. It was a good thing he knew his way.

His thoughts wandered to the men down below submerged in even deeper, inkier blackness. There was nothing like the pure darkness in the mine tunnels. Without any source of light, a man literally couldn't see his hand in front of his face, no matter how long he gave his eyes to adjust.

At least Willie could see electric lights in town up ahead. At least the stars glittered above, the way they only can on a cold night with no clouds to block them and no moonlight to dampen them. He took in a deep breath of frosty air, even though it was tinged with toxicity, ashamed and grateful that he wasn't trapped more than a mile below ground in a blind tunnel with limited oxygen. Yes, the air stunk, here above ground, but how bad was it for them?

Willie pushed away the question trying to enter his head about what life would be like if his father was dead. He still wasn't over his mother's death. It was too soon to add to that grief. He sorely missed Helen every day, in a way he never recognized until she was gone. They were close in the sense that only mother and son can be, especially the only living son out of so many who didn't survive.

Yes, Jeanie made up for all the household duties, but it wasn't Mam's cooking or housekeeping that he missed. It was knowing that someone loved him in the way that only she could. He had never named that cavernous grief until this very moment when he … for the first time … honestly confronted the fact that Da may be gone forever, as well.

Just this morning he was playing football with his mates, grateful yet resentful that he wasn't called in for a shift. And just that morning he had wished good riddance on his kin, who were now below the earth, possibly dead or—bare minimum—in agonizing suspense, awaiting rescue. Not only was Willie not old enough to qualify for a shift, he wasn't trained enough to help save his family and friends. He was useless.

The thought took his breath away that he, useless Willie Garroch, may now be the man of the house, responsible for the financial and emotional support of his three sisters, just like Jeanie had to fill Helen's shoes. He had a new respect for her now. Jeanie had always been a bossy, second-in-command anyway, so no one batted an eye when she took over Mam's role. He wasn't ready. He'd never had to practice.

Nellie might be right. They may very well be orphans. And, at this moment, it did feel like they might be cursed.

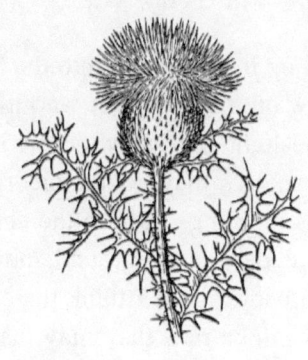

CHAPTER 22

March 9, 1924
Castle Gate, Utah

Willie woke at dawn Sunday morning on the davenport, after a fitful night. Jeanie was in the kitchen already, brewing a pot of tea and cooking up some porridge. She saw him stirring and said, "Mam would skelp yeh for sleeping on her good sofa."

"I know," Willie admitted, sitting up, "I missed her so much last night I thought sleeping here would bring her close, even if it was just to skelp me."

Jeanie chuckled sadly and said, "Aye, I thought about sleeping in their bed, for much the same reason. I couldn't stand their room lying empty, but I didn't just in case Da came home and wanted his bed." She got quiet for a moment then said, "I checked. He's not in there."

"God, Jean," he said, his voice breaking, "what'll we do if he doesn't come back?"

She angrily wiped away sudden tears and said, "We'll not have that kind of talk until we hear, one way or the other."

He nodded and joined her in the kitchen, pouring himself a cup of tea. "You're right," he said, "but wouldn't we have heard something by now if they were okay?"

"With no telephone? How?" she demanded.

In the morning stillness, the sound of a car stopping out front got their attention. Willie hurried to look out the window and said, "It's Uncle Bill."

"What's he doing here so early?" Jeanie asked, her eyes filled with trepidation.

Bill Littlejohn rushed up the walk and into the house, out of the cold, as Willie let him in. He blew on his hands for warmth and said, "I'm in town on an errand and saw the light in your window. I wanted to give you an update before I head back … they found George Harrison's and Jack Thorpe's bodies early this morning, close to the entrance where the cave-in occurred. Your men were deep underground, nowhere near the cave-in, where they may find breathable air. We think the explosion occurred above them and, since heat and smoke rise, they may manage to survive. George and Jack were in an area where there was some explosive violence."

"Oh, those poor men," Jeanie said, placing a hand over her heart.

"Yes, it's a tragedy. They were good men," said Bill, fatigue accentuating the lines on his face. "I wanted you to know we're making progress, so keep your hopes up. No news is good news. I'll be on my way and I'll send word when I get further information."

"Thanks, Uncle Bill," said Willie. "And please let me know what I can do. I hate feeling so useless."

"I will, if I think of anything, but moral support and running errands so the women don't have to take the children out in this bitter cold is important, too. You must be their backbone, their pillar of strength," Uncle Bill said and turned to go.

Bill climbed into his car and drove south on the mostly empty road through town, pondering the events of that morning. The first body, George Harrison's, was found just after 1:00 A.M. Bill didn't tell Willie and Jeanie, but Harrison's body was badly mutilated, his head crushed. He was in the machine shop just inside the entrance at the time of the explosion and was smashed into a cement wall.

Jack Thorpe was also found near the machine shop, as he had just walked into the mine—leaving Zeph Thomas to his telephone call with the blacksmith about his son's bike—when the explosion occurred. Jack was missing an arm and a leg, with part of his head caved in. Bill neglected to tell his niece and nephew that other bodies had been found, mangled, discolored and burned so badly they hadn't been identified yet.

A morgue tent had been set up near the entrance where the dead were carried, via stretcher, and examined in private for identification. If their faces were damaged beyond recognition, what was left of their clothing and pockets were searched for identifiable items. Doctor McDermid, of all the physicians working the scene, headed this gruesome assignment as he knew the men and could more easily name them as they came in, so their widows might be spared. Norm Harrison, George's brother, was only identifiable by an abnormality of one of his toes that the doctor recognized.

Bill dreaded, as he came to the roadblock, what would surely become an onslaught of similarly grisly news. This early in the morning, the roadblock wasn't yet crowded, although a growing congregation of people milled about the town center. It was too early for church and none of the buildings were unlocked yet, so folks were huddled near bonfires in steel barrels for warmth as they waited for news.

As he approached Mine #2, he saw that the crowd of openly crying spectators was larger than yesterday, as family members had found ways around the roadblock to stake out a position, hoping and praying that their husband, son, father or brother would be found alive.

Stan Harvey's crew was back on shift when Bill arrived and Stan caught him up on their progress. "We've found more bodies. Doc McDermid thinks one is Alma Hardee, but the body is missing its head, so he can't say for sure. One of Alma's relatives will need to identify the remains, most likely Mrs. Hardee, because this man is wearing a sock with red darning thread used to repair a tear in the black wool. A wife would know a thing like that."

Stan continued, "We've set up fresh-air stations inside along the main slope, now that the vent fan is fixed. Crews have been sent in with fire bosses, armed with safety lamps and canaries. We only have to use our oxygen in the offshoot tunnels. The main entrance is still blocked with a pile-up of coal cars and debris, so we're going in through the escapeway," he said, gesturing toward the secondary entrance on the other side of the cemetery, "now that it's been cleared."

Bill nodded and said, "Good work."

Stan led his men across the cemetery to the entrance of the escapeway where a receiving tent had been set up. Bodies were now delivered here on stretchers instead of the morgue tent at the main entrance, which was becoming too full to handle these extra procedures. This was where the bodies were initially examined for signs of life and, lacking that, any means of identification and then moved to the morgue from this receiving station.

Stan and his men entered the passage downward into the mine, where it connected to the first tunnel offshoot of the main road. At the intersection of the escapeway and the main haulage-way, Stan's crew turned left and traveled downhill. On both the left and right sides of the main, downward slope, the first four tunnels were mined out and bratticed off. The brattice was undisturbed, so no men had found their way behind them in search of clean air. Assignment maps showed that miners would be working at and below the fifth level.

At the third left entry, they found a rescue team from the town of Spring Canyon led by Dave Brown, along with Monroe Carlson's crew of men from Castle Gate Mine #3. Each man was equipped with water buckets to put out a small fire just inside the tunnel.

Dave said to Stan, "We've just about got this out, so go on down to the fifth left, where they're recovering some of the bodies."

"Bodies?" Stan asked. "No one alive?"

"Not so far," said Dave. "They've been bringing them out on stretchers, all stone dead."

Stan led his men further down until they arrived at the fifth left dip fresh-air base, where the team leader there told him, "My crew has found all but one of the men who were supposed to be in there, but we're low on oxygen so I'm sending everyone topside. See if you can find him."

As Stan's team installed their nose clips and mouthpieces, the other team leader continued, "We've got the telephone lines up again, so when you find a body, make a note of exactly where it was located and any pertinent facts. Call up and let them know what you found. Also, we're including these note slips with each body," he said, handing Stan a stack of blank papers. "Make sure each slip has the same information you called up so everything can be double checked."

Stan nodded and the team leader continued, "Check everything that might be a body, even rail ties and mounds of coal, because it's all covered with soot … everything's black, and there's standing water with soot floating on top so you can't even tell it's water. Damn near impossible to see anything. Good luck finding that last man."

Stan signaled for his crew to turn on their oxygen and follow him into the tunnel. From this point, there would be no talking, their mouths filled with breathing apparatus, communicating by gestures only. They progressed along the pitch-black track for a few hundred yards aided by their cap lanterns and Stan's three-cell flashlight until they found a horse-drawn mine car on its side, blown off the rail track, the dead horse still tethered to the car.

They reached the far end of the tunnel without finding the last body, so they turned around and headed back. Almost immediately Stan gestured that he saw the body, more visible from this new angle, lying in a ditch at the lower end of the entry where water had gathered. The body blocked the drainage, so the water level rose almost enough to cover it entirely. Between that and the soot floating on the surface, disguising the water beneath it, it's a wonder the body was found at all.

The Winter Quarters men took a moment to gather themselves. Finding a body was disturbingly different from just hearing that there would be bodies. Its face was unrecognizable so not a man among them could tell whether it was someone they knew.

Shaken, the crew silently loaded the body onto the canvas stretcher, a process made awkward by its sodden, dead weight, and found their way back to the base to make their notes and call in their findings. At that point, two men from the fresh-air crew took the body up and out of the mine.

Stan allowed his men a few minutes to rest and regroup, as he discussed their next moves with one of the nearby foremen.

"Alright, boys," Stan said when he returned to his crew, "we're heading down to the sixth left entry to set up a new fresh-air base and search for bodies in there. We'll be the first ones in, so no one has any idea what to expect. Steel yourselves."

Stan and his men strode down the sloping passage to the sixth left dip, where they set up an equipment base in the breathable air. Stan's team was joined by the rescue crew from the town of Clear Creek, led by Hal Norgaard, and Monroe Carlson's team from Castle Gate Mine #3. They divided their men, some staying at the fresh-air base to bear stretchers out of the mine, and others to don their oxygen equipment and go in search of bodies.

Stan and Hal led their men into the unexplored tunnel and immediately found their first bodies at the entryway to room one … one of the drivers was lying near his horse, which was tethered to a coal car.

Unable to speak with his mouthpiece in place, Hal gestured to Stan, pointing out the charring of wooden structures, like ceiling timbers and coal cars, as if to say, "Look how badly burned everything is."

Indeed, even the driver's clothing had been burned almost completely off, leaving only a few rags on the body, in addition to its leather belt and shoes. It was loaded onto the canvas stretcher and brought to the nearby fresh-air base, where one of the Castle Gate men said, "I know him. That's Ed Willis."

"How can you be so sure?" one of the Clear Creek men asked. "His face is discolored. That could be anyone."

"It's not discolored," said the Castle Gate man, "Ed's a Negro. One of the few of them on shift today, besides Archie Henderson and Prince Alexander."

"Aw, no," another Castle Gate man chimed in, "is Prince down here? He's one of the kindest people you'll ever meet. Used to be a pastor ... real well educated. During the great influenza epidemic in 1918, he risked his life taking care of entire families ... white families ... who were too sick to get out of bed. He ran himself ragged and no one ever asked him to. A lot of folks are alive today, thanks to him."

Hal, overhearing the nearby conversation, joined the men in fresh-air and interrupted to say, "That's not the only sad tale you'll hear today, boys. Make your notes, call him in and take him up top."

Back inside, Hal found Stan in room two, crouching next to a body on the left side of the room. When he saw Hal, Stan gestured and used hand signals to point out the body's position, as if to say, "See how he's face down?"

Hal nodded and Stan gestured for Hal to follow him out to where they could remove their mouthpieces to talk. As crewmen brought the body out to the fresh-air base with them, Stan said, "Look how he's holding his cap over his face. I think he saw a gas ignition and had enough time to react and throw himself face down."

The soot-covered body on the stretcher and its clothing were badly burned. Stan tried to move its arms down but could not. "He's got one helluva hold on his cap, doesn't he?" Stan was finally able to loosen the body's death grip and reveal his face, which was not burned at all.

"Oh my God," said one of the Castle Gate men, startled by the stark contrast between the charred body and the clean, intact face, "that's Tom Trow."

"Handsome Tam, they call him," said another. "Go figger ... his face is unspoiled even in death."

"Come on, men," Stan said, "we can't comment on every one of these poor bastards. There may be men still alive down here. Time's a wastin'."

Before going back inside, Stan said to Hal, "Let me show you something else in room two ... look up at the smoke. The entrance to the room isn't smoky, but as the floor pitches upward ... that's a six or seven percent grade there ... the smoke reaches the floor. I couldn't see the roof, it's so high up, but look for the mound of coal. I bet they shot it down just last night, or it would have been cleared away by now."

The two men proceeded into the hazy layers to explore. Stan pointed into the further reaches of the upward slope of room two, where layers of stratified smoke filled the air, and a large mound of coal waited to be shoveled away.

The sixth left dip tunnel wasn't as long as other tunnels so only twelve bodies were found over the course of the shift. Stan and Hal met up with foreman Monroe Carlson at the fresh-air base and Stan said, "There was a lot of heat in there but not much violence. That is, plenty of open flames but not a lot of percussion."

"You men go ahead and pack it in," said Monroe. "You've been at it for hours and you've worked a solid shift."

"I'll say," said Stan, "this kind of work is hard on a man's soul."

Back outside the mine, in the bright sunshine that belied the bitter cold, Stan searched for Bill Littlejohn among the crowd of rescue crews, medical aids and morgue workers. He found Bill in the partially destroyed office, distracted and troubled.

"Bad news, Mr. Littlejohn?" Stan asked.

"Well, yes," Bill sighed. "I know these men. I'm friends with many of them and related to some as well."

"Of course," said Stan. "Stupid question. I meant to ask is there any especially bad news."

Bill smiled wanly and said, "Not a stupid question. One of the men brought up today is related to my late sister's husband, and he and his brother are still down there. It's … hitting close to home and I can't get away to notify the family. I hate to think of how they'll learn the news."

"Can I help?" Stan asked.

"I don't see how," said Bill. "We're posting names of the deceased at the Post Office as they're identified, so they may have already seen the list by now. It feels like such an impersonal way to find out your loved one has died, but I can't put my own needs over the rest of the men. I'm needed here. It's out of my hands."

Stan nodded in sympathy and Bill continued, "They're finding bodies at such a pace that we've moved the morgue operation into town. We're taking them to the Knights of Pythias Hall where the doctor and his team are working to identify them so the bereaved families won't have to see the horrible condition of their men. Fortunately, though, our man isn't in such bad shape. His face wasn't damaged at all."

"I know the man you're talking about," said Stan. "He had his cap pulled down."

"Yes," said Bill, "that's the one. Tam came over from Scotland with my brother-in-law. He's related to the Garroch side of the family."

"Tam Garroch?" Stan asked. "That's not the name they called the man I'm thinking of."

"Well, it's pronounced Tom here in the States," said Bill. "And his last name is Trow."

"Right," said Stan. "Tom Trow. Come to think of it, they called him Handsome Tam."

"Yes, he was a bonnie lad ... I promised my niece and nephew ... those poor children ..." Bill paused before continuing, "...say, you know my nephew. He was with you during your shift yesterday, Willie Garroch. Any chance you can ... no, it's too much to ask, never mind. You've had a beast of a day yourself."

"I'll look for him when I get back into town," said Stan. "Willie's sister was uptown with him yesterday, so I know what she looks like, too. If I see either of them, I'll put in a soothing word."

"Good man," said Bill. "Thank you. Now get out of those wretched clothes and into a shower."

Stan looked down at his coveralls and saw they were gruesomely stained from hauling charred human remains. He stifled a shudder and said goodbye to Bill before heading to the bathhouse to shower and change, and then into town with his crew for a hot meal, some rest, and to share some consolation with Mr. Littlejohn's nephew and niece, if he could find them.

ഇൾ

Willie couldn't stand to be surrounded by crying females so he fled the house, saying he was going uptown to wait for news, where he was surrounded by even more crying females—and that's where he saw that the Knights of Pythias Hall was now being used as the morgue.

Every time the hearse-truck approached the KP Hall, company men stepped forward to create a barrier between the sobbing crowd and the stretchers loaded with covered bodies. An adjacent crowd waited at the post office where the list of identified dead was being continually updated.

Willie mustered the courage to climb the post office steps to check the list. The names weren't in alphabetical order. Instead, they were listed in the

206

order the bodies were found so he had to scan the names carefully … Ed Jones … Jim Karozis … John Huff ... Ed Willis ... Otto McDonald ...

Sure enough, there was one of the names he dreaded seeing: Thomas Trow. He groaned and blinked his eyes to clear them of tears, not wanting to believe what they saw. There was no denying it. Tam's name was there, in black and white. His cousin was dead.

There were still no Garrochs, to his relief. He knew plenty of the men who were listed, though, including Ed Jones, May Hardee's grandfather and, earlier in the list, her dad Alma. Poor May had two confirmed dead.

Over at the hotel, the transport trucks were dropping off another rescue crew and Willie saw Stan and his men wearily climbing the steps into the building. Stan stopped at the top and gazed across the crowd, as if looking for something or someone, then turned and entered the hotel. Willie briefly considered running over and pressing Stan for news but decided not to bother the man, who had surely just finished a brutal shift.

With the burden of bad news Willie turned and walked north, the Castle Gate rocks coming in to view ahead of him. This time, though, the magnificent bluffs gave him no comfort or joy. Instead, their towering presence made the valley feel more closed in than usual.

How was he going to tell Bertha? She adored Tam and Willie could not bear to cause her such pain, especially with her fluttery heart. He wasn't ready for that conversation. He needed time to regroup from his own grief. Tam may have been ten years older but they were still close as cousins.

Willie arrived at the house and ducked inside before Jessie or Bertha could see him from their windows, only to be greeted by the desperate cries of Nellie and Jeanie. Ella sat on the floor, playing with a ragdoll, blissfully unaware.

"What did yeh find out?" Jeanie demanded.

"Is Da okay?" Nellie asked.

"I don't know yet," Willie said. "He and Uncle Pete aren't on the list."

"What about Tam?" Jeanie cried. "Yeh didn't mention him. Is he on the list?"

Willie nodded, unable to spit out the words, and Jeanie gasped, "He's dead? Tam's dead?"

"Yes," Willie said, pointing at Nellie who was about to burst into tears, "and don't you start. This isn't about you."

Startled, she blinked back a howl and the waterworks and simply asked, "Are yeh sure about Tam?"

"His name's on the list," Willie said. "They've brought in almost forty bodies so far. I overheard the men are in such bad condition some of them can't be identified."

"Then how do we know Da's not one of them?" Jean asked.

"He wasn't working in the left dips, and that's all they've searched so far," he explained. He strode into the kitchen where Will kept his whisky and poured a drink. "Now leave me alone, will you?" he asked. "I have to think of a way to break it to poor Bertha."

"No," said Jeanie. "I'll tell her. This kind of news is better coming from a woman. First, I'll take a wee dram, myself, and I'll muster up the right words and the courage."

Willie sighed with relief and poured a generous glass for his older sister, grateful that she was taking charge. He had been an adult long enough that day.

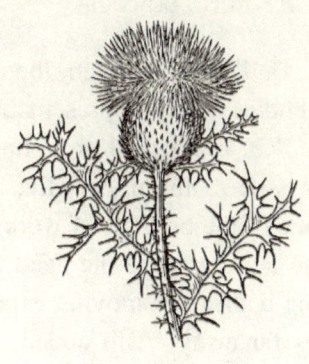

CHAPTER 23

March 9 (evening) - 12, 1924
Castle Gate, Utah

While Jeanie was breaking the news of Tam's death on Sunday evening to Bertha and Jessie, Governor Charles Mabey was arriving at the Castle Gate train station from Salt Lake City. He was met there by Bill Littlejohn, who was unable to hide his exhaustion, having been awake since Saturday morning, refusing to sleep while there were men still underground.

"Look, Littlejohn," said the governor, "it may be days before they're all found. I'm ordering you to go home and get some sleep. We've got a lot of work ahead, much of which only you can do, and I need you to be sharp. Let someone else fill your shoes, at least for tonight."

"You're right, sir," Bill acquiesced, "but first I'd like to make sure you're caught up. I want to be sure you know that Number Two was just inspected on February 13, and they found that the electric system, along with the ventilation and sprinkler system were all in good shape."

Bill also relayed that an order of 120 caskets would be brought in from Salt Lake City on the Monday morning train, with the remainder of the shipment later in the day. Also on Monday morning, grave digging would commence at cemeteries in Castle Gate, Helper and Price.

Bill told him, "Because so many are being recovered now, the bodies are being transported to the tipple via mantrip. We're taking them to the overflow morgue in a covered truck to prevent the public from seeing them. Then they're moved, under guard of American Legion members, to the KP Hall for preliminary identification and embalming before being casketed and carried to the Amusement Hall's largest room, the dance hall. That's where the families can view the bodies if they're presentable."

He told the governor, "On a practical note, housing and fuel costs for the families won't be an issue as the miners live in company houses and their coal is supplied as one of the benefits of working for Utah Fuel. We'll pay all owed wages to the families once the dead are positively identified, and we'll assist in shipping bodies and moving expenses of those who want to return to their families far away." Bill added, "Financial assistance to widows is a priority, with an estimated $5,000 per family in worker's compensation and burial costs covered up to $150."

Bill finally went home after taking the governor to the hotel, where a room was reserved for him. Otherwise, every available sleeping quarter in town was taken. Beds were occupied in shifts, cots were set up in the school and men were sleeping in cars, on tables, wherever they could find. The hotel kitchen was staffed by local women to keep the workers and distraught families fed all day and night, as needed. The hotel was feeding more than 600 people every 24 hours, with four cooks at the ranges and more than 15 young women waiting tables.

Monday morning, after the jarring panic of the weekend, the uptown area was quiet even though the crowds were still large, with most everyone too exhausted to speak in anything but hushed tones. The sounds that most often broke the stillness were the ever-present train whistles—which continued regardless of what this little town was going through—and the occasional outburst of grief as family members found their loved one's names listed in the post office lobby.

Tam's funeral was scheduled for Wednesday afternoon, March 12, in the Castle Gate cemetery. His, along with six others, would be the first funerals in town, with other men being laid to rest in Price, Helper, or transported to their hometowns. There were to be no full services, just a few words graveside, with a group memorial to be held once the search and rescue part of this nightmare was completed.

Will had reserved the plot next to Helen for himself last August. Bertha chose for Tam the nearest available grave a few yards from Helen's, along the western edge of the cemetery. The open site next to Tam was reserved for Pete, just in case.

Also Monday morning, Stan Harvey and his crew were back on shift. After the left dips had been explored, it was time to work their way up the other side of the slope, into the right dip entries. Work was postponed completely in one tunnel, where over a dozen bodies were inaccessible due to flooding that occurred before the main valve was shut off on Saturday. The water was almost ten feet deep, so crews had to fix the pumps—which had not been working since the explosion—before they could access the bodies.

While there was little evidence of violence in the upper left dips, that was not the case in the rest of the mine. The force of the second blast had torn rails from the track bed and thrown water pipes and power lines every which way. Great hunks of concrete were hurled incredible distances. And, although the bodies in the left dips were often gruesomely disfigured, those they found here were even worse due to the percussive explosion and length of time they had been waiting to be discovered.

Rescue crews worked around the clock, tirelessly, for days as the wreckage prevented quick excavation. On Wednesday, the day of Tam's funeral, Stan's team was working in the seventh right dip where a Sullivan Short Wall mining machine was found in a battered heap, having been hurled by the blast. The walls were discolored and cracked, and some of the pipes showed signs of melting.

Stan stopped for a moment to look for a reason why the conditions here, especially room six, would show signs of such high heat. The machine that had been used to cut the coal face was forty feet away, but the wall here in room six looked to be where it was blown from, as it showed signs of fresh cuts. The excess heat, then, was most probably caused by the stirring up of so much flammable coal dust by the machine.

In this tunnel, the bodies were in particularly bad condition, one of which was unidentifiable. While the men explored, Stan heard something hissing and whistling and—unable to speak with his mouthpiece in—he signaled for the men to check their gear. If anyone had a leaking oxygen tank, they would need to get to the fresh-air base, right away. After finding nothing wrong with any of the equipment, one of the men gestured Stan over to what initially looked like an empty mine car, but inside there was a body which was badly swollen and releasing gas through the mouth, causing the hissing.

All hope had been given up for finding survivors, so it was now a matter of locating all the men so they could be properly laid to rest beneath the earth, unlike their current entombment so far beneath the cemetery above. All needed to be definitively identified, no matter the condition of their remains, so their families were left with no doubts.

As the time for Tam's burial approached Wednesday afternoon, the weather was more unforgiving than in recent days. The icy temperature and gray sky now included a vicious wind that whistled through the canyons, cutting through clothing and going straight to the bone. On their way to the cemetery in the motorcade bringing the families of all seven miners to be buried, the Garrochs—in two separate cars, Jessie and Bertha with their children in one and Jeanie and her siblings in the other—asked their drivers to stop at the post office so they could check the list for Will and Pete's names.

Willie got out of the car into the blistering wind and hurried to the post office lobby, where he waited his turn behind others who were also desperate for news. Finally, he was at the front of the line and the list hung before him.

His eyes scanned the sheet of paper and stopped on the names of Jimmy and Dan Morrison, two young brothers who were related to Uncle Bill's first wife, Mary. Their father William was also on the list, found much earlier.

He read further ... George Tsouroupakis ... Levi Beck ... Emmanuel Zagarakis ... Joe Cappelletti ...

"Please, please, please ..." he prayed, hoping to not find what he was looking for but, sure enough, there was Peter Garroch after Joe Cappelletti and before Tom Pelly, the 104th body to be found.

His heart sank and he continued to read ... Walt Kirby ... Joseph Sargetakis ... Martin Kimball ... Joseph Kirby ... William Garroch Sr. ...

Both men were found, today. Da and Uncle Pete were dead. That was it. It was over. No more hope, no more waiting for news. That door had closed.

Willie stood for a moment, unable to move, not knowing whether to vomit or cry. Recalling the way Walt Baxter's son had reacted when he saw his father killed back in Coalburn, Willie bit his lower lip, hard, to distract himself from hysterics. He only allowed himself a brief lament that Will had thought Castle Gate would be the safe place. His father's usually unerring second sight had been wrong.

The woman behind him in line placed a gentle hand on his shoulder and said, "There, young man, we're all in the same boat. Would you kindly step to the side so I can see if my man's name is there, too?"

The touch of her hand brought him back to the post office lobby, so he begged her pardon and headed back to the car, wondering how to say it aloud. Da and Uncle Pete are dead. Their names are on the list. What's the best way to break the news?

As it turned out, it was unnecessary for him to say a word. His face said it all. As he approached, the women began crying immediately.

"My Pete? Is he there, on the list?" Jessie sobbed through the open car window.

"Aye," said Willie, "and Da, as well." He climbed into the other car, closing the door quickly behind him even though it was rude to do so, and sat beside Nellie. He was not in the mood for Aunt Jessie's theatrics. He was in pain, too, not that anyone would notice.

Jeanie, normally so stoic and strong, allowed herself to break down and cry a bit and Nellie, who was always on the verge of hysterics, dissolved into sobs. For once, Willie didn't admonish her and, instead, held his younger sister as she cried into his chest. While his sisters were thus distracted, Willie permitted a few tears to fall down his own cheeks. Wee Ella, dismayed by her siblings' behavior, began to cry, too.

"Deanie," she sobbed, "Where's Da?"

"Da's with Mammy now," Jeanie said, sniffling and wiping her eyes dry with her coat sleeve.

"Mammy's widda ainjoes?" Ella asked, repeating what she'd been told so often.

"Aye, my wee lamb, Mammy's with the angels," Jeanie said.

Ella's brow furrowed as she puzzled this out. "Da widda ainjoes, too?" she asked.

"Aye, clever lassie, Da's with the angels, too," said Jeanie, a brief proud smile playing across her face that her wee baby sister—the one she was now responsible for raising alone—was so bright.

As the car approached the cemetery, Jeanie pulled herself together and said to her siblings, "We'll have plenty of time to grieve for Da. Today is Tam's day and we need to be there for Bertha and Margie. Mind Bertha's dodgy heart."

Along with the procession of cars came two flatbed trucks carrying seven caskets, three of which were draped with American flags in honor of the three veterans of the Great War: Tam, Ernest Delaby and Alf Rice. All three were members of the American Legion and, even though there were to be no full-blown memorial services for individuals today, military tributes were to be offered. Four other men—Joe Ambrosia, Thomas Reese, David Evans and Orville Sanders—were also to be laid to rest that afternoon.

The cemetery looked like a bombed-out war zone with so many holes dug in, over one hundred graves in preparation for the bodies that were yet to come. As the mourners got out of their cars and approached the cemetery, the gravedigging work continued but a rescue crew on their way to the escapeway on the other side of the cemetery allowed the families to pass first, bowing their heads in respect. The coffins were each placed atop two planks that had been laid across their open graves, with care taken to tuck the edges of the three flags beneath the weight of the boxes, to prevent the dreadful wind from blowing them away.

Tam's burial was first. Two Episcopal ministers, one on either side of the flag-draped casket, commended Tam's body to the earth from whence it came, as the family stood around the perimeter. Reverend C.H. Johnson, of Price, began by reciting, "Everyone the Father gives to me will come to me; I will never turn away anyone who believes in me. He who raised Jesus Christ from the dead will also give new life to our mortal bodies through his indwelling Spirit. My heart, therefore, is glad, and my spirit rejoices; my body also shall rest in hope. You will show me the path of life; in your presence there is fullness of joy, and in your right hand are pleasures for evermore."

As he spoke, a cruel gust whipped through the canyon, whistling so loudly his words were drowned out. The flag was removed and ceremonially folded by the American Legion men, who fought the wind to do so. The coffin was lowered into the ground as Reverend W.F. Bulkely, of Provo, continued the commendation, "In sure and certain hope of the resurrection to eternal life through our Lord Jesus Christ, we commend to Almighty God our brother Thomas Trow, and we commit his body to the ground; earth to earth, ashes to ashes, dust to dust."

At this, Bertha let out a moan and her knees buckled. Jessie and Jeanie, on either side of her, held her up. Reverend Bulkely continued, "The Lord bless him and keep him, the Lord make his face to shine upon him and be gracious to him, the Lord lift up his countenance upon him and give him peace. Amen."

The mourners each threw a handful of earth onto the coffin as a three-rifle military salute rang out and Taps was sounded. The shell casings were collected and handed to Bertha, along with the folded flag. As if God took pity, the wind finally died and a gentle snow began to fall.

Six more times a similar process was followed, including two more military salutes, but the Garroch and Trow mourners did not stay. Not only was it too cold to linger, none were in any condition to offer support to their friends and neighbors who had also lost loved ones, with the fresh news about Will and Pete.

On their way back through town, Willie asked to be let out of the car in the town center. "I'll see if I can find out when the other funerals will be held," he explained. "I'll be home directly."

"It's deadly cold," Jeanie warned. "Be sure to bundle up and hurry home."

"I will," he agreed, not caring much about the weather. He cared more about not being in that house, with the tears and drama. With no idea where to go or who to ask, Willie wandered through the still thick crowd and found Tommy talking to one of the American Legion men who was guarding the morgue from widows trying to push their way inside.

"Willie!" Tommy said, nodding farewell to the legionnaire and joining his friend, "It's so long since I've seen you. I feel years older."

"Aye, me and all," said Willie. "I just found my da and uncle on the list. We just buried Tam."

"Aw, that's rough," said Tommy. "My dad's on the list, too. They thought he was me, at first, because he wore my belt, with my name etched on it. That's what one of them out of town doctors used to identify him, but my mum set 'em straight." Both boys snorted a humorless laugh, knowing how Mrs. Hilton would do exactly that. "He's being buried Friday."

"Where did you learn that?" Willie asked. "I don't know when they're burying my da."

"Check the Amusement Hall, where they're keeping all the casketed bodies," said Tommy. "The schedule's posted in there. Come on, I'll show you."

The boys were only allowed entry into the Amusement Hall after explaining why they were there. The number of people allowed inside at one time was kept low, due to lack of space. Closed caskets were lined up in rows, with narrow aisles between them for families and workers to move about.

There, on the schedule of burials, Willie found his father's set for Thursday, March 13, along with May Hardee's father and grandfather, Alma Hardee and Ed Jones.

"Did you know they still haven't found Alma's head?" Tommy asked Willie, keeping his voice quiet.

"No!" Willie replied, also in a low voice. "I didn't know it was missing."

"He was one of the first they found," Tommy said, glancing around to ensure they weren't overheard, "but they put off his burial because they were hoping to bury his head with him. I guess they've given up. They can't keep him above ground any longer." Tommy shook his head and said, "Poor May is fit to be tied. I can only imagine her mother …"

Both boys shuddered at the thought and Willie continued scanning the list. Pete was scheduled for Friday, March 14, along with his lodge brothers from the Independent Order of Odd Fellows, including Tommy's father, John Hilton.

Back outside, it was too cold to dawdle so they said their goodbyes. Willie pulled up his coat collar and began making his way home, pushing through the crowd, which now included another train load of new folks who had just arrived for the spate of funerals that would go on for days.

Weary of the never-ending stream of people and the perpetual state of anxiety, even the Castle Gate rocks ahead felt to him oppressive and looming, as if they were closing everyone in and binding them tightly in a groupthink of madness.

Before he got too far from the throng, he heard a familiar male voice calling his name, "Wullie! Wullie Garroch! Wait!"

He turned and peered into the crowd, unable to see the face of the caller through the people surrounding him, but Willie finally spied a hand rising above them, waving and flagging him down. He pushed his way through to find the man, whoever he was, and felt a rush of relief and joy when he saw that it was wee Uncle Geordie, who was too small to be seen over the heads of all the others.

"Jings!" Willie cried, "Uncle Geordie! What are you doing here?"

"What d'yeh think, yeh dafty?" Geordie said, as he pulled his nephew into a quick but hearty embrace. "Yer Uncle Bill didn't tell youse I was coming?"

Willie blinked in surprise. "No," he said. "We had no idea. We haven't seen Uncle Bill in days, but he's been busy with … you know … all this." He gestured at the mayhem surrounding them.

"That's alright," Geordie said, "I just hope Jeanie doesn't mind an unexpected house guest. The hotel is completely booked."

"Of course not!" said Willie. "We'll be happy to have you. Let me get your bag." He picked up his uncle's suitcase and they walked north together.

"Say," Uncle Geordie said, "how is it that I've lived in the States for so many years, yet I sound more like a Scotsman than you, a lad who's only been here a short while?"

Willie smiled wryly and said, "You don't have American cousins and friends teasing you for sounding like an immigrant. I just want to blend in."

"Och, lad, I can blend in when I want to," Geordie said, "but I'm a proud Scot through and through and if I can remind folks of that, I'll do so whenever I'm able. Remember the words of the Bard himself, 'a man's a man for all that.'"

"Aye, Rabbie Burns, I know," said Willie. "It's funny but, since you left, it feels like no one is keeping up the old traditions."

"Och! A travesty!" Geordie said. "I'll have a word with the old yins so the traditions don't die."

"The old yins have all died," said Willie, reminding Geordie of the reason for his visit. "I'm on my way home from Tam's funeral."

"Aye, I'm sorry I missed it. This was the soonest I could get here," Geordie replied, his voice respectfully lowkey. "How are you and yer sisters holding up?"

"Jeanie's her usual self," Willie replied, "holding the family together. Ella's too young to know what's going on. I'm worried about Nellie, though. We just learned that Da is dead and his funeral will be on her birthday, tomorrow. She made such a fuss about Mam's funeral being on my birthday."

"Aw, wee man, I'm so sorry," Geordie said. "Poor lass. We'll have to find a way to make her day special, somehow."

Willie nodded and said, "Either way, I know Jeanie will be happy to see you. We've all missed you."

"Aye, I miss everyone, too," Geordie said.

They arrived at the house and Willie let his uncle enter first. From one of the bedrooms, Jeanie's voice rang out, "Wipe yer feet!"

"Och, how I've missed my bossy wee niece!" Geordie exclaimed.

At the sound of his voice, Jeanie came rushing into the parlor from her parents' bedroom, arms filled with used bed linens. When she saw Geordie, she dropped the linens on the floor and ran straight into his arms, hugging him so hard she nearly knocked him over. "Uncle!" she cried, "Yeh're back!"

"Aye," he said, holding her tight, "I'm back."

Suddenly and quite unexpectedly, Jeanie began bawling in earnest, crying harder than Willie had ever seen. Jeanie rarely lost her composure but now, in the presence of one of the few truly loving adults she had left, she cried like a girl who had just lost both her parents and had the weight of the world on her shoulders. That weight brought her down to her knees, on the cold wooden floor, and Uncle Geordie joined her there, holding and rocking her until her tears began to subside.

"There, hen," he said, patting her, "you've got a heavy load. Let it out."

"Oh, Uncle," she said, once she caught her breath, "I'm that glad to see yeh. It's been so hard. Please say yeh're here to stay."

"Well," he said, helping her back up to her feet, "that's something I wanted to talk to youse about." He took off his coat and hung it on the hook by the door. "But let's say our hellos first. Isn't it customary to offer a wee dram to a guest in a Scottish household?"

"Och, of course!" Jeanie said, laughing and sniffling, relieved at the change of subject. "Where are my manners? Would yeh like a wee dram, Uncle Geordie?"

"I thought yeh'd never ask!" he cried, and the three of them headed into the kitchen, where they sat at the table and Jeanie poured them each a drink out of the nearly empty bottle.

"Where's yer wee sisters?" he asked, taking a sip.

"Nell's over at Bertha's, and Ella's in Mam and Da's room," Jeanie said. "I was changing the linens … they still smell like Da and I'm loath to wash him away ... Ella's in there jumping on the bed. It may as well be Wullie's room now … or, rather, the two of youse can share it, if yeh're staying."

"I'll stay for a few days," he said. "I'll get you through the funerals, but I must get back. I don't have the same kind of seniority I had here, and the Littlejohn name carries no weight in Detroit, so my job will not be held for long. If this wasn't national news, I wouldn't have gotten this much time off. But I was thinking that maybe youse can all come to live with me there. What d'yeh think? Come home with me?"

Willie and Jeanie looked at one another in surprise. "That never occurred to either of us," said Willie. "Right, Jean? Did you ever think about going to live in Michigan?"

"No, never," she said, "but I've never had reason to consider it before."

"I have a big enough house," Geordie said, "with two bedrooms and an attic that can be converted, and indoor plumbing and electricity. I even have a telephone and a radio. And, I think yer mam would like it if youse all came to stay with me."

"Och, I know she would," said Jeanie. "But we'll have to think about it. This is Mam and Da's final resting place and I don't like the idea of leaving them behind ..."

"Jean," Willie interrupted, "on that subject, Da's funeral is tomorrow, and Uncle Pete's is Friday."

Jeanie nodded, "Aye, thanks ..." she stopped for a moment then said, "Och! Nellie's birthday! Why couldn't they bury him on Friday? She'll never get over that ..."

"I thought of that, too," said Willie. "Uncle Geordie suggested we make it a special day for her."

Just then a giggle from the direction of Helen and Will's bedroom door caught their attention and they all turned to see Ella peeking around the threshold.

"Och! Who's that wee monkey?" Geordie cried. "Jeanie, hen, when did youse get a monkey?"

Ella came toddling into the room as fast as her little legs would carry her and into Geordie's outstretched arms, shouting, "I'm no' a monkey! I'm Ella!"

Geordie lifted her onto his lap and bounced her on his knee, "It's a wee talking monkey named Ella!"

"I'm no' a wee monkey!" she laughed, "I'm wee Ella! I'm a girl!"

"A wee girl monkey? Not a wee boy monkey?" he teased as he tickled her ribs.

"NO!" she shrieked with laughter, "I'm no' a monkey!" She squirmed down from his lap and darted out of his reach to Jeanie's side, giggling all the way.

"Och, yeh are a wee monkey," said Jeanie, lifting her little sister onto her lap and kissing the top of her head. "Yeh're my wee monkey."

Nellie came in the front door just then and stopped short when she saw their guest sitting in the kitchen. "Uncle Geordie!" she cried and ran in to hug him.

"Aw," he said, as he squeezed her in return, "I'm blessed to get such a warm welcome."

"What're yeh doing here?" Nellie asked, as she took off her coat and threw it over the back of a dining table chair before sitting down.

"I told yer Uncle Bill days ago that I'd be here," Geordie said, "to help youse get through this hard time. I suppose he hasn't had the time to come by to tell youse."

"It's that good to see yeh," said Nellie, her joy dissipating at the change of subject. "It has been a hard time. We just found out today that Da is dead, sure, and Uncle Pete, too. We buried Tam this afternoon and it was so sad. Poor Bertha …"

"Nell," Jeanie interrupted, "I may as well tell yeh now, Da's going to be buried … tomorrow."

Nellie fully understood Jeanie's meaning, that it would be on what should have been her special day, but she surprised everyone by remaining calm. "I expected as much," Nellie said, in a sad and quiet voice. "It doesn't matter. At least this way I'll always remember Da on my birthday."

"That's very mature of you," said Jeanie. "I'm quite proud."

"I had a long talk with Bertha this afternoon," Nellie said. "Did yeh know her da died when she was only eight? He was a blind violinist. Did yeh know that?"

"No, I didn't," Jeanie said.

"She reminded me that I had my da almost twice as long as she had hers," Nellie said. "It made me feel selfish to only think of myself and my silly birthday, when her wee Margie and Aunt Jessie's girls lost their das much younger. Margie's only six and Peggy and Annie are only ten and seven."

"Aye," said Jeanie, ruffling Ella's hair, "and this poor wee monkey is only three."

Ella giggled and said, "I'm no' a monkey!"

"Aye, yeh are," Jeanie said. She stood and seated Ella on her chair. "I better get some supper on the table or yeh'll be a wee starvin' monkey. I hope rumbledethumps is okay with you, Uncle Geordie. We've all been too preoccupied to make sure the larder is well stocked."

"When have I ever said 'no' to some good Scottish cooking?" Geordie asked. "Now, I noticed yeh're running low on whisky there. That bottle's almost empty. Have yeh got another stashed away, or do I need to make sure yer larder is well stocked with hooch?"

Jeanie said, as she gathered the leftover ingredients she needed for the evening meal, "We have one more unopened bottle. Wullie, will yeh fetch it? But now that you mention it, Uncle, I've been wondering what to do about that. Da always made those purchases and neither Wullie nor I know who to ask. If yeh'd set us up, that would be grand."

"What's a favorite uncle for?" he asked, uncorking the new bottle that Willie handed him and refilling their glasses. "Let's raise a toast to yer da. It's a sad occasion, sure, but I couldn't miss his funeral. After all, if I don't come to his …"

"… he won't come to mine!" all three said, in unison, and drank a toast to William Garroch Sr., who was there now only in spirit.

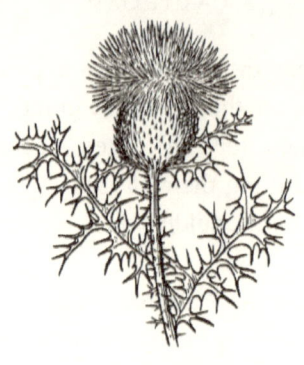

CHAPTER 24

**March 13-18, 1924
Castle Gate, Utah**

May Hardee and Nellie Garroch were both fifteen now, at least for three more days until May turned sixteen on Sunday. They held hands for moral support as they walked through the cemetery gate to say farewell to their kin to be buried on this day. May had days to get used to the idea of her father's and grandfather's deaths, as they had been found so early on. Nellie was still getting used to being an orphan, with the confirmation of Will's death less than twenty-four hours old.

Among the burial services Thursday, aside from Will, Alma Hardee and Ed Jones, the bodies of Prince Alexander and Ed Willis were also laid to rest, two of the three Negro miners who were killed in the disaster. Prince, the soft-spoken former pastor, was paid honor by many folks who braved the cold even if they weren't burying a friend or family member that day. Ed Willis' two "wives" walked arm-in-arm to his grave, having made peace during this time of grieving, although both women filed competing claims for his death benefits the day his body was found.

The services were much like those of the previous day with only a few words said to commend the bodies to the earth, in view of the group memorial service to be held later. Will was buried by Helen's side with a larger crowd than had been at the cemetery on Wednesday, as the temperature and the wind weren't nearly so brutal today.

The Hardee family was there with numerous relatives who had traveled from out of town to say farewell to Alma and Ed. Those who knew Will paid their graveside respects to their friend, as did the Littlejohn brothers to their late brother-in-law.

After the burial, Will and Helen's children went back to their house with Uncle Bill and Uncle Geordie, while Elsie and Uncle John went home with their families. Aunt Jessie and Bertha headed back to Jessie's house to mentally prepare for Pete's funeral on Friday. Jeanie served tea and cookies, plates of which had been delivered to the grieving families along with plenty of casserole dishes by neighbor women whose men weren't in the mine last Saturday.

Uncle Bill spoke first. "I don't like to bring this up so soon," he said, "but I'm here now and the conversation needs to be had. Your Uncle Geordie tells me that he has invited you children to live with him in Detroit. What are your thoughts?"

Jeanie began to speak but was interrupted by Uncle Bill, who held up his hand to silence her and indicate that he was asking the man of the house, Willie.

Willie sputtered for a moment, put on the spot like this. Jeanie had been the boss for so long—even before the deaths of both parents, she always outranked him—it never occurred to him that he would be expected to speak for the family.

Jeanie bit her lip and Willie recognized in her eyes the rage at being supplanted in favor of her younger sibling. He shot her a wide-eyed look, hoping to wordlessly convey his sympathy and shock, and sighed with relief when her expression softened a bit.

"Well," he began, "we haven't discussed it much. Uncle Geordie did make the offer but it never crossed our minds until then to leave Castle Gate. This is where our friends and family ... aside from you, Uncle Geordie ... live. It's the only place we know."

Nellie chimed in, not picking up on the unspoken message that the girls weren't invited to speak, "I want to stay here! My friends are all here, and my school ..."

"Aye," Jeanie said, taking advantage of Nellie's opening the door, "and this is where Mam and Da are laid to rest. I couldn't leave them behind."

"All good reasons to stay," said Uncle Bill, "and I agree that remaining here is the best thing rather than living with a ... bachelor ... uncle." Geordie glared at him, but Bill plowed on. "Can you make it on Willie's wages alone, without an adult in the house? Raising children is a big responsibility." He paused and continued, "Uncle John and Aunt Bethia have generously offered to take in your younger sisters. Personally, I think that's the answer."

Jeanie waited a few seconds before responding, her tone dangerously calm. "I've been raising these wee'uns and running this household since before Mam died. I can handle the responsibility ... especially if Wullie gets enough shifts and the company pays out compensation to the families." She said this last bit looking directly at Uncle Bill.

Uncle Geordie gave her a surreptitious wink and a brief nod of his head. He said, "Good girl. Yeh're always welcome to come live with me, if youse change yer minds, but good for you, for yer strength and courage."

Jeanie said, surprised, "Courage has naught to do with it. Yeh take what life hands yeh and yeh carry on. What choice do any of us have? We four got off easy, compared to Bertha and Jessie. At least our Wullie can bring in a wage. What are they to do? Find new husbands with over a hundred other widows competing for who's left, just to put bread on the table?"

Uncle Bill replied, "But wouldn't your sisters be more comfortable with John and Bethia, where money isn't a consideration? Wouldn't you like some relief from being an adult too soon? It isn't fair that someone so young shouldn't be free to court, to eventually get married and start her own family."

"Is that all yeh see for my future?" asked Jeanie. "Maybe I'd like to go to school and make something of myself!" She took a breath and evened her tone again. "I promised Mam I'd take care of her wee'uns and I keep my promises."

"Well, we won't force you into anything," said Uncle Bill, "if that's your decision. Let's wait and see what happens." He finished the last of his tea and stood to leave. "Geordie, how long are you staying?"

"I'm catching the early Sunday train," Geordie said, rising to walk his elder brother to the door.

Bill said quietly to Geordie, as he wrapped his scarf around his neck and stepped outside, "She just about called me all the bastards. She's a spitfire, that one."

"Aye, she is," Geordie replied with a touch of pride in his voice, "just like her mam." They said their goodbyes and Geordie returned to the kitchen table, where Jeanie was fit to be tied.

"Wait and see what happens?" she asked, fuming. "How much more could God fling at us? It's like Uncle Bill's waiting for me to fail! Is this house not spotless? Is there not always a nourishing meal on the table? Do I not give enough hugs to go around?"

Her brother and sisters didn't say a word, knowing better than to interrupt as she raged. She went on, "How does he dare come into my house and tell me what's what? Asking my wee brother for his opinion over mine because he's got a pecker in his pants?" Jaws dropped as she continued raving. "Mam and Da put me in charge, and I give my life for this family! Who the hell does Uncle Bill think he is?"

Geordie interrupted, "Nobody here doubts you. But take care what you say about yer uncle. Remember, little pitchers have big ears." He nodded in the direction of Nellie and Ella, who were watching Jeanie's tantrum with wide eyes and rapt attention.

"Aye, yeh're right," she said, simmering down a bit. "Only I didn't expect that question to ever be raised. Uncle Bill takes so little interest in our lives otherwise, it took me by surprise that he'd even care what happens to us."

"Of course, he cares," said Geordie, "but we should discuss this another time, after bedtime for wee monkeys." A master at distraction, he grinned at wee Ella and made like he was coming after her, his arms outstretched and fingers wriggling in tickling motion. She shrieked and ran, giggling, into the parlor where he followed her and lifted her high into the air, breaking the tense mood and changing the subject.

"Aye," said Jeanie. "Besides, it's somebody's birthday today so let's have something special just for Nell. How'd yeh like a fish supper?"

No one made fish and chips and mushy peas like Jeanie, so all agreed. She shooed everyone out of the kitchen and got busy putting together the special meal for her sister, on this horrible day when everyone could do with a pick-me-up. They had the rest of their lives to ponder their futures without parents. Today, Uncle Geordie was here and all was well, for now.

ෆ෭

Friday came, along with Pete's funeral. He and Tommy's father, John Hilton, were lodge brothers so their services were arranged with consecutive send-offs. Their surviving lodge brothers joined the mourners as did Geordie, who was old friends with Pete as far back as Scotland.

While Willie and Tommy stood graveside with the family after John Hilton's service, Willie noticed that Alma Hardee's grave was being exhumed, after having been filled just yesterday. He nudged Tommy and rolled his eyes in that direction to wordlessly ask if his friend knew what was going on.

"I'll tell you later," Tommy whispered, and Willie nodded in agreement. Their focus should be on the men they were mourning, not morbid gossip.

Poor Aunt Jessie was wailing, unable to contain her grief as Pete was laid to rest by Tam's side, only ceasing to cry once she and Bertha were on their way back toward the parking lot. Jessie sniffled and asked Bertha, "Do you remember that day in Helen's kitchen, when we first arrived, where we read each other's tea leaves?"

"I do," Bertha said, uncomfortable with the question. "Why do you ask?"

"D'yeh recall that I saw Tam receiving military honors and you shaking yer fist at God?" Jessie stopped walking and turned to Bertha to say, "That's just what happened the other day. I mean, aside from you literally shaking yer fist, but yeh may as well have."

"Aye, I do recall that," said Bertha. "It's haunted my dreams ever since."

"Then, I saw sickness and grief in Helen's tea leaves," said Jessie, "but we didn't know at the time it would be her who got sick. She thought it might be wee Ella, who was still so young and fragile."

Bertha nodded, "Oh aye. Where are you going with this?"

"Remember that nobody saw anything happening to Pete, other than him misbehaving?" Jessie asked. "What if that's not him down there in that coffin? What if they couldn't identify that body and just called it Pete because he's still missing and they had to give that unknown body a name? What if he ran off and left me and he's not really dead?"

"Aw, Jess," Bertha said, taking her arm, leading her forward again, "of course that's not what happened. Wouldn't there be an extra, unnamed man if that was someone else down there? Besides, Pete wouldn't leave you. You were his best girl."

Jessie teared up and said, "Aye, but I don't know which I'd rather, that he's dead or that he's still alive but run off. At least if he run off, he could come back," she said before bursting into fresh sobs. Bertha held and comforted her for a moment until Jessie pulled herself back together, saying, "We should go. I don't want to make a scene."

Jessie and Bertha caught up with Willie and Tommy in the cemetery parking lot as Tommy was filling Willie in on what was going on at Alma Hardee's grave.

"Stan's team was coming to the end of their search for bodies," Tommy said, "and there was one more man down there … Basil Gittins … he was working at the deep end of the mine, where it was flooded …"

"That's where they found the Morrison boys, days ago, isn't it?" Willie asked. "You know Jimmy Morrison was the youngest one killed? He was only sixteen."

"Yeah," Tommy said, "but Basil was further down, about as far as you can go. Anyway, Stan sent some men to follow the drain line back up the haulage-way to see if the suction hose was obstructed and they found that Alma's head had floated over and got pulled in by the suction and blocked the hose."

Willie's jaw dropped and Tommy kept talking. "So, they wrapped Alma's head up and took it to his house and knocked on the door. They asked for Mrs. Hardee and when she heard what they were trying to hand over to her, she lit into 'em and gave 'em what for, she was so upset. 'Why would you show me a thing like that?' she hollered at 'em. May's Uncle Alec took off outside to give them a pounding. I don't think he ever caught up with the poor bastards … they just weren't thinking, they were so shook up. Anyway, that's what's happening today, Alma's grave is getting dug up so they can bury his head with the rest of him."

"Jings!" said Willie.

Tommy was on a roll, "They also finally found Ed Cox … one of the fire bosses … on top of a pile of coal they shot down the night before. That's where they think the first explosion happened. Stan's crew thought that room was cleared but when they realized they hadn't matched Ed's name to any of the bodies, they went back and found him there. He was so black from coal dust that he blended right in with the pile he was on top of."

"That's where they found Tam, in that same room," Willie said. "They think he saw it happen because he had time to pull his cap down over his face and hit the dirt."

Bertha, who was standing nearby, gasped and clamped her hands over her mouth to stifle a cry.

Willie turned and saw that she and Jessie were there, listening to every word. "I'm so sorry, Bertha," he said, his voice filled with remorse, "you shouldn't be hearing this."

"Oh, my poor Tam," she said, her face contorting in horror and her voice shaky.

Willie put his arm around her, making every effort to not cry along with her, and walked her toward the car, saying, "I'm sorry. I didn't know you were there, but at least Tam was in better condition than most." She sobbed anew and Willie realized he was just digging the hole deeper, so he said, "Let's not talk about this anymore."

He opened the car door for her and helped her inside, followed by Margie and Jessie with her girls, all sobbing. With the last family funeral out of the way, it was time to go home.

♉♉

On Saturday afternoon, Jessie and Bertha gathered at Will and Helen's to discuss with Geordie what the orphans were to do. Geordie said to them, "I have no doubt that Jeanie and Wullie will do their best. But, while I agree that Bill's words were thoughtless, I can see his side, too."

Jeanie's mouth fell open with disbelief so Geordie raised his hand to silence any response and said, "Yer uncles live on the other side of the tracks and aren't a part of yer daily lives. I want to make sure, before I leave, that yer Garroch kin will keep an eye on youse. Otherwise, Nell and Ella may end up living with Uncle John."

He turned to the adult women and said, "I need to know whether yeh'll be able to help them. After all, yeh're both widows with small children and no wage earner. Yeh've troubles of yer own. Would youse go back to Scotland?" he asked.

Bertha said, "I was so sick on that ship I swore I'd never cross the ocean again. I'm homesick, of course, and I'd love for Margie to know her grandparents back home, but I don't know if I could bear the journey. Doctor McDermid says I have a leaky heart and should get enough rest and not put any extra strain on myself."

"Och, I'd go home," said Jessie. "My mam and da are gettin' old and my sisters are still there. But my Pete's buried here and I don't know if I could leave him behind."

Geordie asked, "I know money's an indelicate subject, but it cannot be ignored. Yer men made, what, about eighty cents an hour? And yer rent is ten dollars per month?" The women nodded.

"The company isn't gonna harass youse for rent, at least not right away," Geordie said, "but there will come a day when they'll want to collect. Do youse have any savings?"

All shook their heads, no. "Not much to speak of," Jessie said. "There's always something that took anything extra."

"It's my understanding," said Geordie, "that each family is gonna receive a five-thousand-dollar payout but it'll be portioned out over several years. Yeh'll probably get about sixty-five dollars a month."

Bertha said, "We could get jobs if we had to. Both Jessie and I worked in the woolen mills back home, so we know how to go out and earn a wage."

"Aye," said Geordie, "but there's no local woolen mills. Yeh'd have to move up to Provo or Salt Lake. Besides," he said to Bertha, "didn't the doctor tell yeh to rest?"

"We could take in boarders," said Jessie. "I wouldn't like having a stranger in my house, but if it puts food on the table … or maybe I will go back to Scotland after all."

As frustrated as Geordie was by the circular conversation with the indecisive widows, in contrast, Jeanie was in better shape to take on their uncertain future than the adult women to whom she was no longer related by blood. And, although he hated to leave them, his job in Detroit wouldn't wait forever and on Sunday morning, bright and early, Helen's children saw him off at the train station with promises to join him in Michigan if life in Castle Gate got too hard.

CHAPTER 25

Spring and Summer, 1924
Castle Gate, Utah

There were days when Jeanie wished she had taken Uncle Geordie up on his offer. Parenting her teenaged sister wasn't as easy as it sounded, back when the decision was made to stay. At the time, the three elder siblings agreed to work together and prove to the world that they were up to the task. And they did come together to keep Ella well fed and well loved. What Jeanie didn't expect was Nellie's gradual return to her adolescent tantrums.

Jeanie was under the mistaken impression … or hope … that Nellie had grown up overnight, realizing there's only so much money to go around and there was plenty of work to do, and no more Mam or Da to wheedle into letting her off easy on chores. Nellie bristled at so much manual labor … scouring laundry by hand over a washboard, peeling potatoes and making bread, getting down on hands and knees with a scrub brush to keep the floors and rugs clean. At least, though, Nellie finally understood why Jeanie always hollered at anyone entering the house to wipe their feet.

Uncle Bill kept Willie working, but there were only so many shifts to go around. Mine #2 was closed as investigations were held and repairs were made, so #1 was reopened. However, if orders for coal weren't coming in due to low summertime demand, all the nepotism in the world wouldn't change that.

Sometimes there wasn't enough money to cover the household expenses with only Willie's income. "At least we have that," Jeanie explained to

Nellie, when she complained, "Bertha and Jessie rely on charities for the widows. We'll be getting some help from the relief fund soon."

A nationwide fundraising effort ended up with the creation of the Castle Gate Relief Fund, in addition to workman's compensation which allowed for funeral expenses up to $150 and a death benefit of sixty percent of the typical weekly wage, not to exceed $16 per week, for a total of up to $5,000 over six years.

Public donations brought in over $132,000. After disqualifying boys over the age of sixteen and girls over eighteen—which left Willie and Jeanie out—there was a total of 417 individuals who qualified, throughout 143 families. More than half were children, and almost two dozen were expectant mothers.

The committee hired a social worker, a middle-aged, childless woman named Annie Palmer, who was passionate about helping the widows set their lives aright. She soon became a regular fixture in Castle Gate, visiting families and making extensive notes about their living conditions. The first order of business with Mrs. Palmer was to fill out an application with information about household expenses, debts, income and status of health.

Bertha objected, infuriated that nameless strangers on a faceless committee could order her to give over private information. She told Mrs. Palmer, "It's no one's business what I have or who I owe. If they won't help without knowing about my personal life, they can do as they please. The people that donated money gave out of the goodness of their hearts. It's the nosy committee, deciding from up high who deserves help."

Despite Bertha's refusal to cooperate the board decided to "return kindness" for Bertha's ill feelings and gave her the widow's benefit of $10 per month, the amount allowed for a household with one child. When Mrs. Palmer returned the next month with a check in her hand, Bertha apologized and filled out the forms.

Meantime, Bertha and Jessie went back and forth about whether to return to Scotland. Bertha wouldn't return without Jessie, not wanting to brave the ocean voyage on her own. The women traveled to Salt Lake City to ask the Industrial Commission to give them their full widow's benefits in one lump sum so they could go home and set up some sort of business together but their request was denied. This wasn't the way the law was set up, and no exceptions were to be made. Neither could survive on $64 per month, so jobs would need to be found. While they were in Salt Lake City, they explored the possibilities but decided that it wasn't a good fit. Next, they tried Provo, but none of the woolen mills were hiring at that time.

Jessie didn't mind filling out the forms—quite the opposite; sharing her personal information helped her deal with her deep sorrow—and she was awarded $13 per month for a household with two children. Pete's life insurance policy with the Odd Fellows Lodge only paid out $75, and her girls needed medical care. Peggy was nearly blind in one eye and needed glasses and Annie needed a tonsillectomy. Jessie needed extensive dental work and if the Relief Fund Committee would be willing to help, she wasn't too proud to ask.

Jeanie was fighting her own battle, that of not being taken seriously as an adult. She filled out the application hoping for relief fund assistance because, due to her gender and age, Uncle John was assigned as the legal guardian to Nellie and Ella, even while the girls remained living with Jeanie and Willie, and he was receiving and banking the company payout for them.

"I should have taken my Uncle Geordie up on his offer to live with him in Detroit," Jeanie said to Mrs. Palmer when pleading her case, both sitting on Helen's good davenport. "My uncles here don't trust me to do the right thing by my own sisters, the ones I promised my mam I'd take care of."

"Why don't you go to Detroit? Has your uncle rescinded the offer?" Mrs. Palmer asked.

Jeanie explained, "Uncle Geordie isn't married and my uncles here think he should have a wife before we live with him. I need Uncle John's permission to take my sisters ... my own sisters! ... and he won't consent. And I'll not leave them here without me."

"Well," said Mrs. Palmer, "I'm sure he's just being wise about the future of the family."

"Aye," said Jeanie, "I'm sure he *thinks* he's being wise, but he and Uncle Bill want the girls to live with him and that's not what our mam would've wanted. It'd kill her all over again if she knew her wee'uns were being split up."

"Are you and your brother not invited to come live with them?" Mrs. Palmer asked.

Jeanie said, "We don't qualify for the compensation ... we're too old ... so it would cost him to keep us, and he's already got a passel of wee'uns. Me and Wullie are on our own, and we're not receiving Nell and Ella's company payout. Uncle John says he's saving it for their education. I want them to get a good education, too, but we need help now! That's why I'm applying for the Relief Fund."

"Well," soothed Mrs. Palmer, "you're obviously a sensible little girl who wants the best for her sisters. I'll see what I can do."

Ten days later, the first check for $13 per month was delivered. Two weeks after that, though, Jeanie received an infuriating letter. She told Willie, that night after he returned home from the mine, "You'll not believe this but Uncle John, with Uncle Bill's approval, has asked for our relief fund checks to be sent to him so's he can oversee how it's spent."

"What?" Willie asked. "Why?"

"They don't think we're old enough and they're trying to prove it, the hard way," moaned Jeanie. Once again, they were left to rely on Willie's earnings.

Because life was so bleak at home and the pickings were so slim—and school was out for the summer—Nellie spent a great deal of time at Uncle John's and Aunt Bethia's house where there was plenty of food and fun with her cousins. Their house wasn't somber and wracked with grief. There, she could be an ordinary adolescent, even with the cloud over her head in the shape of the word *orphan*.

"Don't yeh see?" Jeanie asked Nellie on her way out the door to return to John and Bethia's, "They don't think I can take care of youse two, so they're squeezing us until we give in. Yeh're playing right into their hands."

"I don't care," Nellie wailed. "I hate it here! It's so sad and gloomy." She stormed out the door before Jeanie could cajole or berate her further.

The final straw came in August when Willie injured his hand. A one-handed miner can't work and, with no income, Jeanie had no choice but to let her sisters stay at Uncle John's house while she sought employment, among all the other women desperate to bring in a wage.

One day while Jeanie was in town checking the community notice board for job postings, one of the neighbor women said to her, "Isn't it kind of your aunt and uncle to help you children? You're so lucky, considering what so many other families are going through."

It was all Jeanie could do to bite back the opinion that their kindness wouldn't be necessary if he would only give over the compensation and relief funds that had been assigned to Will's children and allowed Jeanie to spend it as she saw fit. As Mrs. Palmer said, Jeanie was a "sensible little girl"—sensible, yes, but considered a little girl—infantilized despite being a mature twenty years old with significant experience running a household.

Soon their coffers ran dry and they were living on potatoes and cabbage, unwilling to ask the uncles for help. Jeanie wrote a letter to Mrs. Palmer, asking for assistance due to Willie's injury. After all, Jessie's emergencies and medical bills were being paid for. Perhaps a medical emergency of their own would allow them enough to get by until his hand was healed.

Jeanie walked to the post office to check for mail every day and she finally received a letter. When she saw by the return address that it was from Mrs. Palmer, she ripped the envelope open there on the post office steps, instead of waiting to get home. It said:

Dear Miss Garroch:

Your letter inquiring about the Castle Gate Relief Fund is received.

I remember you very well; and in reply to your question, will say that if there is need, of course you are entitled to some of the fund. In fact, I believe a small check has been sent to your uncle John, the guardian of the minor children.

Would you like to write and ask your uncle about it, or would you like for me to write him and tell him you have written me about your need? I shall be very glad to do so if you wish it.

When I go to Castle Gate again, I shall try to see you. In the meantime I hope your brother's hand will soon be well again, so that he can go to work.

Best wishes for the welfare of you all,
Annie Palmer

Jeanie's heart sank and she trudged home to show the letter to Willie.

"I can't ask him for help," Jeanie cried, after Willie read it. "Remember the strike back home, when Da was so angry at being cheated by the mine owners? He was so convinced it'd be better here, related to the company men. Well, so much for his second sight. We're getting cheated even worse, because it's our own kin!"

Willie shrugged, already beaten, and said, "Of course I agree on principle, but if I have to eat another potato, I'm gonna puke."

"But can yeh not see, he's squeezin' us?" she demanded. "I'll not go crawling to him, begging for help. He knows about yer hand. He coulda offered some of that money, but he didn't! He wants us to give up and let him have Nellie and Ella permanently, and I can't let that happen. I promised Mam."

"I hate it, too, Jean," said Willie, "but he's already got them. Nell likes it better over there and he's not going to let them come home, not without any food in the larder."

"Aye, and that's what gets my goat," Jeanie said. "They see us as the poor relations."

"I know, but we are the poor relations!" Willie argued. "Without Uncle Geordie, no one's on our side. They think our sisters are better off with our rich uncle, instead of here with us surviving on tatties and cabbage. And when it's said that way, it's hard to argue."

With the decision forced upon them, Jeanie grudgingly sent a telegram to Uncle Geordie asking if his offer still stood, but for just the two of them. He replied immediately, of course the offer was still good, and he'd pick them up at the station.

Their house was soon cleaned out of all personal belongings, some stored at Aunt Jessie's—things that were too bulky to take with them, like Helen's Victrola and her Brown Betty teapot—sentimental things that Jeanie would collect once she set up her own household. Furniture gifted by Elsie got divided between Bertha and Jessie. Everything else she and Willie owned got packed in two suitcases and Helen's steamer trunk.

Uncle Bill took them to the train station to say farewell. "I wish you the best," he said. "I know things didn't work out the way you had hoped but Uncle John will take good care of your sisters. I promise."

"I'll be back for them," Jeanie said, "as soon as I'm able."

"That's good," said Uncle Bill. "You find yourself a nice husband and set yourself up with a solid household and we'll revisit the question at that time."

"One last thing," Uncle Bill said as she and Willie prepared to board the train that was just pulling into the station. "Your mother had something that ought to stay with me, the head of the family … your Uncle Buchan's memorial plaque. I should have asked for it before now but in all the hubbub I forgot. If you'll tell me where you packed it away … with your other things at Aunt Jessie's house? I can get it from her."

Willie darted a glance at Jeanie's face. When she packed the plaque into the trunk to take it with them to Uncle Geordie's, she said to him in a voice filled with gravity, "This is all we have left of Uncle Buchan and of Mam to

235

remind us of who we used to be. God, how I wish we had never left Scotland." She then squared her jaw and tucked the plaque carefully away, deep in a drawer between soft items of clothing so it wouldn't get scratched.

Jeanie bit her lip. This was one sacrifice too far. She turned Helen's trunk upright on the wooden planks of the depot platform and opened it. She reached inside and pulled out the plaque, running her fingers for the last time over Uncle Buchan's name and felt a ripple across time, her fingertips connecting with the very same raised letters where Helen had run her fingertips so many, many times.

Without a word, Jeanie handed over the plaque to Uncle Bill, closed the trunk and gestured to the porter that it could be loaded. She stepped forward and boarded the train, without saying goodbye. Willie, nonplussed, shook his uncle's hand and boarded behind his sister.

The train soon started chugging north and Willie took one long, last look out the window at the Castle Gate rocks, through which their train would soon pass. As always, the sight took his breath away and he burned it into his memory so his awe and wonder would pass on to whichever future generations of his might come back and, like him, witness their majesty.

His time in Utah was done.

EPILOGUE

Final words from Helen
Castle Gate and the Great Beyond

Och, the pain doesn't end just because yeh're dead. Aye, I could follow
Buchan into the light, as he keeps trying to drag me across the veil. But I
cannot leave my wee'uns and my boys behind, suffering in such dire
circumstances. How could I? And, aye, I cannot help them without being
asked, so I hang about hoping they will. Meantime, it pure breaks my heart
to see my wee'uns split up and my boys, Wull, Pete and Tam, trapped down
below.

I don't mean trapped in that mine, or even in that cemetery. I mean
trapped in Hell … at least, that's where they think they are. I see, from up
here, that it's not any Devil roasting them in eternal flames of damnation.
It's in their own heads. They keep reliving their moments of death—the fire
and the heat, the shock and the terror—over in their minds and they cannot
get out. It's like a skip in a record, bouncing the needle back to replay the
same few seconds of music over and over and over until it drives you mad.

So many of the other poor miners who died alongside them are caught
up in it, too, thinking that's where they went when the explosion caught
them, unable to escape, trained that they're sinners and that's what they
deserve.

Not all of 'em, of course. Bishop Ben went straight into the arms of Jesus. I watched it happen. Jesus teased him, "I stood right there and told yeh not to go to work. But did yeh listen?"

Sadly, plenty of them others did get caught up in their own versions of it. I feel for them. I do. I'm enduring my own version, reliving the cancer. God, it took so long for it to end—the pain and the sickness … and the terror —I cannot let go of it, though, because to release my earthly suffering means going to the light. How can I do that and still watch over them?

Buchan tried to show me how beautiful it can be here, if yeh let yerself go through that tunnel. But I cannot follow Buchan while there's work to be done, in this place between the worlds.

He's the one who told me we cannot interfere unless we're invited. They have free will, just as we did, and it's not up to us to decide for them, even if they make mistakes. But who's gonna invite me, especially to help with this curse Buchan keeps going on about, when they don't even know about it? If I cannot tell them, how will they ever find out?

They have so much on their plates, they'll not have time to wonder. Bertha, she'll remarry and Jessie'll stop talking to her, mad as a viper she'll be that Bertha married so soon after Tam's death. She shouldn't be angry with Bertha. Tam didn't leave her with much to live on. Plus, there's her leaky heart. She needed a husband. Besides, Jessie'll eventually marry Bill Glover from Galston, after his wife dies, and go to West Virginia with him.

And I cannot be angry with John and Bill for taking my young wee'uns. Jeanie would want me to hate them forever because I asked her to promise to take care of her sisters but forces larger than us tore the family apart. It's that damned curse Buchan goes on about. It's bigger than all of us.

It breaks my heart to know what this'll do to my wee'uns and their wee'uns after them. I can see it, from here.

Wullie's gone so numb he'll abandon his own wee'uns because he cannot feel. In the end, he'll be abandoned by them. He'll not even know his grandwee'uns.

Poor wee Ella, not knowing her mam and da, will feel lost and alone. Her own wee'uns will have a broken mam.

Nellie, my Helen Jr., she'll end up married to that mafia gangster and on the run for her life, living her final days in fear.

And poor Jeanie, cheated by life, just like her da, will never go to nursing school ... and her son ... och, the heartbreak!

There'll soon be nobody left who remembers who we are or that we ever lived. Nobody will know there's dozens of men who died in that mine, trapped in a hell of their own making, who need help getting unstuck. My boys, they've been sucked into this curse Buchan says got passed to us by Granny Maxwell, who we never even heard of.

Buchan told me—when I argued with him about staying behind—that Granny Maxwell said to him, "Yer work isn't done, even if yer body is." He said she told him he could come back another time, in another body, and so can I, but I prefer to stay put, right here, for now.

I wondered why the Garrochs and other miners were the ones to flame out, not the Littlejohns. Why were they killed, and Bill and John spared? Buchan, who's had more time here than me to explore … as if time means anything here … said the curse doesn't only mean yeh'll die in fire. Yeh may watch others die that way, feeling yeh're to blame. Yer family may be torn apart. Yeh may have to endure sheer injustice. How it plays out for each of us is our own mystery. The men trapped with 'em have their own stories, their own versions of a curse or whatnot, keeping them in their own hell.

I cannot join Mammy and Da, all my grannies and grandas and poor wee babies up there in the brilliance. I'll stay here between the worlds, waiting for my boys to join me … join us … in the shining Great Beyond.

Without being invited, there's nothing I can do to release my boys from Hell. So, it's up to me to plant clues for my grandwee'uns to figure out. Buchan and me, we'll drop a trail of breadcrumbs for them to follow.

Maybe someday they'll find us and set us all free.

AFTERWORD

by Lisa Bonnice

Willie was my mom's dad. They were estranged and I only recall meeting him once, on a hot and sunny summer day in the Detroit suburbs when I was about five and he was about sixty.

He was a tall, bald stranger in a grey suit and tie, standing in my Uncle Bill's driveway. (Willie Garroch named his son William and my mom's middle name was Helen). We kids were called to get out of the pool to say hello to "Grandpa" and then the grownups went inside to talk.

I didn't know his origin story until after I had become a grandparent, myself. Mom never even told me that a mine disaster existed in our family history. She didn't talk about her dad unless I pressed her with questions and, even then, she would only express her resentment against him. Whatever happened between them caused a deep and seemingly incurable wound because she carried this grudge to her deathbed.

Because of this complete lack of information and dead-end inquiry, I only began exploring the Garroch/Littlejohn history after one of Tam's descendants messaged me on Ancestry.com in 2010, where I was busy exploring my father's Maltese roots. I had just discovered an unknown cousin from a branch of Dad's tree that had been behind a "brick wall" (genealogy lingo for dead end) and she was living mere blocks from my brother in Arizona, so I was content to let the Scots lie dormant.

Imagine my wonderment when I discovered this well-documented story of Castle Gate, Utah in the 1920s. There was a treasure trove of information and a tale that begged to be told.

Most of the names I used here were real people whose stories live on in old newspapers and historical archives. Utah is the genealogy capital of the

United States and Scottish records are excellent, too, so I was lucky this story happened in these places. The local Carbon County newspapers, typical of small towns, ran stories about birthday parties and social gatherings, like Burns Suppers, which were invaluable for learning about life in Castle Gate.

I had so many facts, I barely had to fictionalize any of this. Helen really did give birth ten documented times, with only four children living beyond infancy. Buchan really did live with Will and Helen before enlisting with the Royal Scots Fusiliers, only to be killed at the Battle of the Somme. He was injured during his first tour of duty in France and sent home to convalesce for nine months before being sent back to be shot and killed on October 12, 1916. Helen really did receive a "dead man's penny" with Buchan's name, and it hangs on my wall, in a place of honor.

Elsie was a dentist's widow—her first husband dying during the Spanish Flu epidemic—who married Bill Littlejohn the day after Thanksgiving 1921, right around the time the Garroch men arrived. Geordie did travel with Helen and the girls, and Bertha and Jessie did follow several months later, after the strike ended. The cast of the Broadway revue *La Chauve-Souris* was on board the Lapland, with Helen's family.

Geordie did put together that song list for his brother John's Burns' Supper. Nellie did go to a birthday party at May's grandparents' house while Helen was dying of cancer. Helen was buried on Willie's birthday (I don't know whether he bought himself some company that night or not). Will did apply for citizenship the same day he took the fire boss test.

The explosion and aftermath happened pretty much as told here. Willie and Tommy were playing football when the explosion happened. Tom Hilton, himself, told one of Ella's daughters this story years later while his wife, May Hardee Hilton, served homemade cookies.

Tommy did wake up in the cemetery after inhaling toxic fumes. Stan Harvey's crew did find Tam with his cap pulled down over his undamaged face. The miners' warning dreams and intuitive hunches, and those who had near misses—including Bill Littlejohn's oversleeping and Henry Etzel's argument with the boss—are all recorded.

Tam's funeral was the first one held and Bertha did cry out (according to the newspapers) as the vicious wind whipped through the canyon. Alma Hardee's body really was exhumed so his head could be buried with it. Not only is this officially documented, but the story of Alma's head is also local folklore.

Jeanie really did struggle to get financial help afterwards and lost custody of her sisters before she and Willie went to Detroit to start new lives (she did eventually get them back and raised them as her own, but that's a story for another day). Annie Palmer did call her a "sensible little girl" in her report, and even noted that the family lived in a well-furnished home that included a Victrola.

The personalities of the characters are as accurate as I could make them, working off memories of those I knew, stories I've heard about them, newspaper articles, genealogical records, and historical interviews.

I ran astrology reports for the Garroch and Littlejohn families, including personality and compatibility profiles, to guide me as to who they were and how they may have interacted with one another.

I used divination to ask them directly what happened next. Using Carrie Paris' gorgeous *Beloved Dead* oracle deck and our co-creation, the *Generations Oracle*, I was able to ask questions and get immediate responses. I began to recognize their presences as their personalities became known to me. I could tell who was "in the room" with me, watching over my shoulder and whispering in my ear as I worked.

Here's a fascinating example: one of the first things I did when I began this project was to run those astrology reports, using information I had at that time. I used the birthdate from Helen's death certificate because I hadn't yet discovered the Scotland's People website and I assumed the official, government certificate was accurate.

One day early on, I was stuck on a scene about Helen and, for the first time, I consulted her astrology profile to see how her personality might respond to the circumstance. As I read it, I kept 'hearing' these emphatic words: "This is wrong. This is wrong. This is wrong. This is *wrong*!!!"

By this time, I had learned about the official records site at ScotlandsPeople.gov.uk. I double checked there and found that the birthdate on Helen's death certificate was *wrong*. That date would have been given to Doctor McDermid by her next of kin, who were distraught and working from memory. The actual birth record information was recorded by her parents, who would know better than anyone. When I reran the astrological profile using the correct date, it changed Helen's personality. The first report was, indeed, *wrong*.

Occasionally, I created a fictional scene to weave in overall details, like when Uncle Geordie took Nellie on a mad dash to see Big Ben. They did take the train all the way from Scotland to Southampton, England, changing trains in London, and the fog really was remarkably thick, according to weather reports from that day. I don't know if Nellie actually got to see Big Ben when they were so close to it, but if I was her age and passing so close, I would have nagged the heck out of the adults to let me see it somehow. Maybe it's also because of my own frustration that the only time I've been to London, Big Ben was covered in scaffolding, for repairs. From what I know of Uncle Geordie, this is the kind of thing he would have done.

Another fictional weaving is when I blamed Walt Baxter's death for Will's initial reason to leave Coalburn. Their neighbor was indeed killed that way, on that date, with his son nearby. Helen would have been just learning about her pregnancy, and her history of infant deaths was tragically true. The shaft mines were notoriously dangerous, and the Castle Gate mines were industry gems.

The coal strike in 1921 did happen, and miners' wages were cruelly cut. Will's astrology report did suggest that he would have "second sight" and he has pushed his way through the veil to me via a medium friend (who had no idea who Big Wullie, as he called himself, even was), so I don't doubt he had some premonitions along the way. Whether Walt's death had anything to do with their decision to flit to the US, I don't know, but it was a handy way to weave together the plethora of facts that I did have.

To be fair to John and Bill Littlejohn, the telling of Jeanie's gradual loss of custody of her sisters may have seemed a bit harsh against them. According to the Annie Palmer file, Jeanie saw them as behaving unfairly. As an objective adult, I believe they were doing what they thought was best, but they could have handled it better. It was a different day and age, and the family patriarch would have seen this capable 20-year-old as a "sensible little girl." Perhaps they also felt disproportionately responsible, since they oversaw the mines and those kids were orphaned on their watch. There's no way of knowing.

Overall, this story is breathtakingly true. I had more facts than I could use. There is a great deal more history in the towns of Castle Gate, Helper and Price that I didn't write about, because this book is about my family's experience. Others whose families were also touched by the mine explosion have their own versions of the story to tell. This book is based on the facts that I found relating to my family, specifically, and I did my best to be fair and accurate.

As the saying goes, we don't really die until someone says our name for the last time. Most of our histories will die along with those who lived them, but not this one.

It took years of research and legwork, following the trail of breadcrumbs, as Helen put it in her Epilogue. The story unraveled until I finally had enough to put it down in words. I got to be very good friends with these people, and I miss them now that this phase of our work together is done.

Next up, Book 2, the origin of the Maxwell Curse

A Curse by Fire
(also a true story)

NAMES OF THOSE KILLED IN MINE #2 ON MARCH 8, 1924

Samuel Valentine Acord
Prince Alexander
Joe Ambrosia
Nick Ambrosia
David Anderson
John Anderson
Steve Andrakis
Nick Aquila
Kenneth Avery
Levi T. Beck
Cyrl Berg (Cirillo Bergamaschi)
Emil Berg (Emilio Bergamaschi)
William Berry
Dom Bertoglio
Mike Bertoglio
Joseph I. Bodily
Tony Botonakis
John Buzas
Gust Calivas
Mike Camperides
James Cappelletti
Mario Cappelletti
Joe Casselli
Bert Cirbairo
Edward B. Cox
Robert Crow
Mike Dacemos
Jim Dallas
Mike Damanakis
John R. Davis
Ernest Delaby
Harry Dodd
Robert Dodd
Pete Dunis
David R. Evans
Franklyn R. Evans
Frank Fieldsted
George Fieldsted
George W. Fullmer
George L. Fullmer

Tony Garegnani
Peter Garroch
William Garroch, Sr.
Louis Gialitakis
Steve Gianni
Andrew Gilbert
Basil Gittins
Brindley A. Gittins
Andrew Glenidas
Alma Hardee
George Harrison
Norman Harrison
Thomas Harrison
Ernest Head
Archie Henderson
John Hilton, Sr.
John Huff
William Huff
Joseph A. Ingram
Turl L. Ingram
Fukuzo Inouye
Samuel Rush Jacoby
Charles James
Bryan Johnson
Edwin L. Jones
Francis Jones
George Kanakakis
George Kappas
Demetrios Karozis
Mike Katsanevakis
Martin Kimball
Joseph Kirby
Walter Kirby
Zenta Koda
Andrew Komfosch
Steve Kondarakis
John Kontorinis
Jim Kopakis
Pantelis Koukourakis
John Kourgentakis

George Kulezakis
Kalantjis Kyriakos
Charles Lazaro
George E. Lee
Konstantinos Gust Logios
Gust Loukas
Tony Malax
Aetou Manoukarakis
John Marchetti
George K. Markakis
Mike Markakis
Ben Mascaro
Gust Mathioudakis
John McCluskey
Otto McDonald
Thomas Mihos
George Mitchell
Daniel Morrison
James Morrison
William Morrison, Sr.
James Murphy
T. Nakamura
Oscar F. Neil
Steve Nickolaris
Nick Paizis
John Palioudakis
Steve Palioudakis (Pallas)
Steve Pappas
Y. S. Park
Louis Patrick (Alois Petric)
Pete Pattello
Ben Pellegrino
Thomas Pelly, Sr.
Thomas Pelly, Jr.
Edwin Perkins
Neil Perkins
Tony Perpinakis
William Phelps
Frank Piccolo
William Pollock
James Preano
John G. Psaroudakis
Charles H. Quilter
Thomas L. Reese
Alfred Rice, Jr.
Walter Richards
Antonio Rizzuto

Orson H. Rollins
Theodore Rowe
Harry Sanders
Orville E. Sanders
Orville R. Sanders
Joseph Sargetakis
Sam Saris
Mell Seely
George Shurtleff
Clarence Simpson
Horace Simpson
John Slovenski, Jr.
George Sluga
Henry Eugene Smith
Oren Clifford Smith
Tony Mia Smith
Anthony Spendall
Stylianos Spyridakis
Leland C. Stapley
Eli Stavranakis
Theros Stavrianoudakis
Mike P. Steffanos
Ben Stevens
Geo Tagliabue
Tom Takeuchi
Joe Tellerico
Benjamin F. Thomas, Jr.
Jonathan M. Thomas
John Thorpe
Thomas Trow
George Tsouroupakis
Matthew Tyrer
Orson Ungricht
Kanaz Verges
Yasuzo Watanabe
Raymond A. Williams
Ed Willis
George Wilson
Adley Wood
K. W. You
James M. Young, Jr.
S. C. Yum
Emmanuel Zagarakis
Paul Zakariondakis
Mike Zanis

REFERENCES

Tragedy and Hate by Steve Sargetakis; Utah Historical Quarterly, Spring 1970, Volume 38, Number 2

Hecatomb at Castle Gate, Utah, March 8, 1924 by Philip F. Notarianni; Utah Historical Quarterly, Winter 1970, Volume 70, Number 1

Utah's Ellis Island: The Difficult "Americanization" of Carbon County by Philip F. Notarianni; Utah Historical Quarterly, Spring 1979, Volume 47, Number 2

Growing up Greek in Helper, Utah by Helen Z. Papanikolas; Utah Historical Quarterly, Summer 1980, Volume 48, Number 3

One Long Day That Went on Forever by Saline Hardee Fraser; Utah Historical Quarterly, Fall 1980, Volume 48, Number 4

Games of the Coal Camp Children by Marianne Fraser; Beehive History 07, 1981, Utah State Historical Society

The Emerging Social Worker and the Distribution of the Castle Gate Relief Fund by Michael Katsanevas, Jr.; Utah Historical Quarterly, Summer 1982, Volume 50, Number 3

A Struggle for Survival and Identity: Families in the Aftermath of the Castle Gate Mine Disaster by Janeen Arnold Costa; Utah Historical Quarterly, Summer 1988, Volume 56, Number 3

Women in the Mining Communities by Helen Z. Papanikolas; Carbon County: Eastern Utah's Industrial Island, Utah State Historical Society, 1981

The Next Time We Strike: Labor in Utah's Coal Fields 1900-1933 by Allan Kent Powell; Utah State University Press, 1985

History of Carbon County Ronald G. Watt; Utah State Historical Society, 1997

Coal in our Veins: A Personal Journey by Erin Ann Thomas; Utah State University Press, 2012

Meeting of the Rocky Mountain Coal Mining Institute by Will C. Higgins; Salt Lake Mining Review, June 30, 1916

Report on Castle Gate No. 2 Mine Explosion, Castle Gate, Utah, March 8, 1924 by B.W. Dyer, Chief Mine Inspector, John Crawford, State Coal Mine Inspector, and H.E. Munn, Coal Mining Engineer

The Castle Gate Mine Explosion: March 8, 1924 As I remember It in 1982 by Stanley C. Harvey

Interview with Tommy and May Hilton, May 24 and 30, 1974; Charles Redd Center for Western Studies, Labor Oral History Project, Brigham Young University

Interview with Annie Mills and Helen Houghton, May 24, 1974; Charles Redd Center for Western Studies, Labor Oral History Project, Brigham Young University

Interview with Fay Thacker, March 20, 1976; Charles Redd Center for Western Studies, Labor Oral History Project, Brigham Young University

Interview with John T. Houghton, March 25, 1976; Charles Redd Center for Western Studies, Labor Oral History Project, Brigham Young University

Interview with Charles Huff, April 10, 1976; Charles Redd Center for Western Studies, Labor Oral History Project, Brigham Young University

Interview with Naomi Phillips Parkin, April 16, 1976; Charles Redd Center for Western Studies, Labor Oral History Project, Brigham Young University

Diary of T. L. Burridge

Carbon County Historical Society Memorial Booklet, October 2014

Salt Lake Telegram articles, Salt Lake City, Utah March 8-18, 1924

Salt Lake Tribune articles, Salt Lake City, Utah March 8-18, 1924

The Sun newspaper articles, Price, Utah, March 8-18, 1924

Ogden Standard Examiner articles, Ogden, Utah, March 8-18, 1924

Deseret News, Salt Lake City, Utah, March 12, 1924

Gunnison Valley News, Gunnison, Colorado, March 13, 1924

Daily Herald, Provo, Utah, March 13, 1924

ACKNOWLEDGMENTS

I have a lot of people and resources to acknowledge. I pray I don't leave anyone out, and those I might forget to mention still live in my heart.

First, I want to thank the folks in Utah who helped me learn about Castle Gate, a geological landmark that's been partially destroyed and a town that no longer exists:

- Marjan and Marty Oakeson: Marjan (my third cousin, once removed) is a descendant of Thomas and Bertha Trow. Her husband Marty was the one who reached out to me many, many years ago on Ancestry.com, bringing this story to my attention;

- SueAnn Martell and Darrin Teply (Kitty and Bobcat) of the Eastern Utah Tourism and History Association. Both are founts of knowledge and SueAnn was always available when I had questions about life in the old town and mines, no matter what time I messaged her. Sadly, SueAnn passed away shortly before this book's publication, so she'll never see it in print, doggone it;

- Mike Martinez and John Fish—former residents of Castle Gate before the town was dismantled in 1974—who both gave me tours of where the town and landmarks used to be;

- Kathy Hamaker, of the Family History Center in Price, Utah, who maintains an online presence for Castle Gate at carbon-utgenweb.com. She helped me to track down my great-grandfather Will Garroch's Naturalization application, on which I touched the actual ink he laid down in December 1923;

- Jason Huntzinger and the Western Mining and Railroad Museum in Helper, Utah, who maintains an exquisite display of artifacts, including an original copy of the New York times from March 9, 1924, with a front-page story about the Castle Gate mine explosion, which I donated to the museum;

- Members of the Castle Gate Facebook group who shared their stories and their photos;

- All the reference librarians and records clerks in Salt Lake City, Helper and Price who helped me locate archived records, and attain copies and permissions to use them.

I want to thank the folks I met or corresponded with in the UK who helped me chase down my family's older history and learn about Scottish culture:

- Shirley Johnson and Morag Hislop;
- Sandra (long lost cousin) and Bobby Blackmore;
- Dave (long lost cousin) and Christine Hartley;
- The late Peter McLeish of the Coalburn Heritage Society;
- Heather Dunlop, of the Family History Collections at the Burns Monument Centre in Kilmarnock;
- Lindsay Freeland, author of *The Fallen of Lesmahagow Parish in the Great War 1914 – 1918;*
- Arlene Watson of the Lesmahagow Development Trust;
- The bartender at the Dreghorn Inn who gave me an old photo of "downtown" Dreghorn;
- The maintenance man at the Springhill Institute who let us inside to see where Will and Helen were married;
- Summerlee Museum of Scottish Industrial Life;
- The reference librarians and records clerks at the Mitchell Library in Glasgow who helped locate archived records and attain copies of same.

Other folks outside of those specific realms of research include:

- My daughters Kristina and Stacy, who traveled with me to Castle Gate on research trips;
- My husband Jeff and brother Mike, who traveled with me to Scotland (quite the sacrifice, I know);
- Gini England, elder daughter of Ella Garroch (Will and Helen's youngest child) and my mom's first cousin, who told me family stories I would have never heard otherwise; AND
- Sally Stanton, younger daughter of Ella Garroch, who shared with me the only photo I've ever seen of Helen, after many years of searching;
- Bill and Fran Garrock, my uncle (Willie's son) and aunt, who also traveled with me to Utah and knew some of the people in this story and helped define their characters;
- Rita and Roger Indrebo, who helped solve a fifty-year-old mystery and brought Buchan Littlejohn's Memorial Plaque back into the family.
- Robert Wilbanks, genealogist, who helped me discover the records of wee Annie Garroch's birth and death.

Other resources that were invaluable in the creation of this book are:

- Sandra Ingerman, who led me down the path of discovery of the curse and encouraged me along the way, and Barb Crow who was the first to point me in the direction I needed to look to find the curse;
- My family, friends, co-workers, and Shift Network audiences who tolerated my talking endlessly about this story and waited patiently while I took my time (in order to get it right!) writing it;
- The Shift Network for allowing and assisting me in exploring the vast subject of Ancestral Healing with experts all over the world, and all those experts I interviewed and had sessions with including but not limited to (in alphabetical order): Jane Burns, Desiree DeMars, Daniel Foor, Thomas Hübl, Shelley Kaehr, Natalia O'Sullivan, Christina Pratt, Victoria Wilson-Jones, Mark Wolynn;
- Carrie Paris, expert in ancestral divination and creator of the marvelous *Relative Tarot* and *Beloved Dead Oracle*, and co-creator with me of the *Generations Oracle*;
- Sharon DeBartolo Carmack, author of numerous books on genealogy including *You Can Write Your Family History*, and also the author of *Midlife Medium: A Genealogist's Quest to Converse with the Dead*. Sharon helped me to accept that, yes, those really are my dead ancestors communicating and helping me write this book.
- The Scotland's People website's excellent birth records (which include the time of birth) so accurate astrological personality profiles and compatibility charts could be run;
- Special thanks to the following for helping me learn to think in the gorgeously lyrical Scots dialect (even though that dialect was toned *waaay* down for the American audience): the casts of Scottish TV shows *Still Game* and *Burnistoun*; actors Peter Capaldi, Alan Cumming, Karen Gillan, Michelle Gomez and David Tennant (please note the preponderance of Doctor Who actors); comedians Kevin Bridges, Craig Ferguson, Janey Godley (Frank, get the door!) and, of course, Billy Connolly; and once again my friends Shirley Johnson and Morag Hislop;
- Curtis Michaels, my editor and dear friend;
- Clark Rogers, my old friend and publishing buddy who helped me get this across the finish line;
- Jessica Bell for her gorgeous cover design.

I want to thank all the real-life characters in this tale and others who lived in Castle Gate who told their stories to researchers or documented them in some way (see References).

I especially want to thank T.L. Burridge (a fellow child of a Maltese father) for his diary. In it, he wrote that he longed to be a writer and to be remembered for the stories he shared. When I read his words, I felt an instant kinship and promised to help make that wish come true, as much as I could, especially as he made a point of mentioning my family by name in his diary.

Finally, I want to thank my ancestors. I'm one of the living faces of those who came before me, and it is my honor to ensure they are not forgotten. They aren't just characters in a tragic saga. They were real people who lived and breathed ... and died in sometimes horrible ways. They wanted their stories told and the ancient curse lifted, and they made sure I got to work on these tasks. Thank you, Helen and Buchan (and all the others), for leaving such an unmistakable trail of breadcrumbs.

PHOTOS

Miners at the entrance of Castle Gate Mine #2, days before the explosion.
Photo courtesy of the Utah State Historical Society.

Funerals at the Castle Gate cemetery, and the nearby buildings for Mine #2.
Photo courtesy of the L. Tom Perry Special Collections, BYU Library,
Brigham Young University

The Castle Gate rock formation. Photo courtesy of the Utah State Historical Society.

Helen Littlejohn Garroch
circa 1899 (This photo
would have been taken
around the time she was 14.)

"Geordie" Littlejohn in his
US Army uniform,
circa 1918

Bill Littlejohn
(age unknown)

Jean Garroch & Sisters --- Castle Gate, Utah.

6-17-24. Visit By Mrs.Palmer. The father of these children was killed
in the explosion. Their mother had died from cancer six months before.
William Littlejohn of Castle Gate has been appointed guardian. William
the 18 year old brother works and gives money to Jean for the care of
the family. She stated that her uncle,the guardian does not let her use
any of the compensation money. The home was fairly well furnished,a victrola,but no piano. Ellen was on a visit with an aunt at Sunnyside.
The children had bought a monument for their parents at cost of $150
which is to be paid in installments. Jean is anxious to go to a bachelor
uncle in Detroit,who has asked them all to go there; but her guardian
will not consent to this. She felt a little bit resentful,but when told
that he was probably wise in what he was doing for her,she could see
that her uncle was looking to the future of the entire family.
Jean talked like a very sensible little girl,who wants to do what
is best for the family.

Above: From the files of social worker Annie Palmer, her notes about the Garroch household. There are minor mistakes, i.e., John Littlejohn was appointed guardian and "Ellen" is Helen, AKA Nellie. The aunt mentioned here is Bethia Littlejohn.

Below: the letter from Annie Palmer to Jeanie Garroch

Provo, Utah, August 30,1924.

Miss Jean Garroch,

Castle Gate, Utah.

Dear Miss Garroch:-

Your letter inquiring about the
Castle Gate Relief Fund,is received.

I remember you very well; and in reply to your question,
will say that if there is need,of course you are entitled to some
of the fund. In fact,I believe a small check has been sent to your
uncle John,the guardian of the minor children.

Would you like to write and ask your uncle about it,or would
you like for me to write him and tell him you have written me about
your need ? I shall be very glad to do so if you wish it.

When I go to Castle Gate again,I shall try to see you. In the
meantime,I hope your brother's hand will soon be well again,so
that he can go to work.

Best wishes for the welfare of you all,

Many more photos are available online at lisabonnice.com

A FEW WORDS FROM CARRIE PARIS

creator of *The Relative Tarot* and *Beloved Dead Oracle*

In *Castle Gate*, Lisa Bonnice masterfully weaves together the threads of history and spirituality, creating a captivating narrative that is both deeply personal and profoundly moving. Lisa's exploration of her family's history, set against the backdrop of the Castle Gate mine disaster, is a testament to her dedication to preserving the past and honoring the lives of those who came before.

What struck me most about this book is Lisa's unique approach to storytelling. Her use of the *Beloved Dead Oracle*, a creation of my own, adds a rich layer of spiritual connection to the narrative. Lisa's ability to channel the voices and wisdom of her ancestors through the oracle is nothing short of remarkable. It's as if the past and present are intricately intertwined, guiding her hand as she crafts this heartfelt tale.

Lisa's commitment to historical accuracy is evident throughout *Castle Gate*. Her extensive research and attention to detail breathe life into the characters and events, allowing readers to step back in time and experience the tragedy and triumph of her family's journey. She artfully blends fact with intuition, ensuring that the story remains authentic while also providing a cohesive and emotionally resonant narrative.

Moreover, Lisa's personal connection to the characters shines through in every page. Her deep affection for the people she writes about is palpable, and it's impossible not to be moved by the way she brings their stories to light. Lisa's exploration of her family's history is an act of love and remembrance, ensuring that their voices will continue to be heard for generations to come.

Castle Gate is more than just a book; it's a heartfelt tribute to the past, a spiritual journey, and a testament to the power of how storytelling can be a sacred act. I wholeheartedly endorse Lisa Bonnice's work, as it beautifully honors the beloved dead within her family's legacy in a truly unique and profound manner. This is a book that will stay with you long after you've turned the final page.

A FEW WORDS FROM DARRIN "BOBCAT" TEPLY

Surviving Co-Director of the *Eastern Utah Tourism & History Association*

I am honored to have been asked by Lisa Bonnice to write these words about her book, *Castle Gate*, in my recently deceased wife's place. What now seems like lifetimes ago, in researching this book Lisa contacted my wife (SueAnn "Miss Kitty" Martell-Teply) and me as co-directors of the *Eastern Utah Tourism & History Association* about the history of Castle Gate, the disasters there, and her relatives who were buried in the local cemetery. A few extensive tours, as well as photos, historical documents, and some electronic communications later we became fast friends.

Over the years we shared with Lisa the history of Castle Gate, its disaster, and Carbon County while driving her to various locations: the once thriving town-sites that were now nothing more than eroded foundations in the sand, exploited cemeteries collapsing into the coal mines below, twisting walks to the barricaded mine entrances, politically charged monuments, all of which were now resting amidst the rotting bits of mostly forgotten lives scattered in the overgrown sagebrush. We would research other bits and answer miscellaneous questions about what daily life was like a hundred years ago for the residents and ill-fated coal miners and families of Castle Gate.

Sometimes, we'd wonder where Lisa was going with her questions, other questions would be "aha!" moments for us. So, it is nice to be able to read her first book as it is all now put together in a linear form.

I often say that the dead and their ghosts choose some historian to tell their story and then push all the clues to them. We believe that this happened with Lisa, SueAnn, and me. Lisa's family at times "reached out" to dump information in our lap during our research and tours as one thread suddenly became many in a cascade of aged dominos falling on yellowing paper. Then we would find out that something similar happened to Lisa the same day, hundreds of miles away, that would push her research further along and back to us with our new information.

What you now hold in your hands truly is a rare "LITERARY UNICORN." It is an amazing, well researched and creative historical telling of the story of a family that came to America, became coal miners, struggled to survive, and got the short pointy end of the proverbial stick. What you hold is a piece of art, square-bound in a canvas of papers. It is a love-letter to Lisa's ancestors celebrating their contributions in a now almost forgotten time, in a mostly forgotten place, called Castle Gate.

READING GROUP QUESTIONS

1. How much do you know about your family's history? Have those who raised you shared the stories of those who came before them? If you're adopted, do you know anything about your birth family? If you have no information about your genetic family, are you actively searching, or do you plan to in the future?

2. If you've had genealogical DNA tests done, what have you learned? Were you surprised by the results?

3. Have you noticed patterns of illness or behaviors in your family that seem to be passed down through the generations? Do you know any history about how they came to be?

4. When you're able to step outside of your family's sphere of influence, you may notice certain expressions and eating habits that you didn't realize had a cultural origin. For example, the author grew up being warned about earning a *skelped bum*, without realizing until she was grown that this is a Scottish phrase, or that her mother (the daughter of Willie Garroch) tended to cook meals in the British fashion. What are your own family's folkways that you may have taken for granted?

5. The Castle Gate mine disaster happened in 1924. The Garroch family's living conditions were typical of that time, with no electricity or indoor plumbing. Now, 100 years later, we are thrown into a collective panic when there isn't enough toilet paper in the grocery store. What are your thoughts about the differences between life now and a century ago?

6. Think about the conditions that women experienced while traveling, with regard to dealing with a baby's needs (i.e. cloth diapers,

teething pain, bottles), personal hygiene and keeping up their ladylike appearance. Do we take modern conveniences for granted?

7. Miners were frequently killed on the job in individual accidents, in addition to disasters like the one in Castle Gate. Have you considered what life was like for the people who used to dig underground for our fuel, especially in the more rustic mines?

8. Jeanie Garroch was upset with her uncles for the decisions regarding the welfare of her younger sisters. The adults saw her as a "sensible little girl," even though she had solid life experience in taking care of an entire household. What would you have done with Ella and Nellie as one of the adults in Jeanie's life, considering it was 1924 and she was a 20-year-old unmarried female?

9. Numerous people in Castle Gate had premonitions about the pending explosion: each one mentioned in this book is documented. Some folks paid attention, some did not and others misinterpreted the messages they received. Would you have stayed home that day if you had a premonition like theirs?

10. According to Will and Helen's astrology charts, both would have had the "second sight." What were your ancestors' thoughts on divination and psychic phenomena, and what are yours? Do these abilities run in your family?

11. Both Helen and Buchan describe after-death experiences where they are greeted by loved ones on the other side. Have you or anyone you know had a Near Death Experience and/or communicated with the other side? Have you witnessed a dying person's deathbed visions of loved ones?

12. Do you believe in curses? If so, how do you explain this phenomenon? If not, how do you explain what others believe, in terms that make sense to you?

For extensive photos, links,
behind the scenes information
and discussion about

Castle Gate
and
The Maxwell Curse Trilogy

visit

lisabonnice.com

Did you enjoy *Castle Gate*?
Your review makes a difference.

www.ingramcontent.com/pod-product-compliance
Lightning Source LLC
Chambersburg PA
CBHW020913130726
47904CB00006BA/1909